Unforgettable
Summer

Unforgettable Summer

So Inn Love

Better Latte Than Never

CATHERINE CLARK

An Imprint of HarperCollinsPublishers

Library of Congress Control Number: 2013953794
ISBN 978-0-06-229525-5

Typography by Lissi Erwin
14 15 16 17 18   CG/RRDH   10 9 8 7 6 5 4 3 2 1

First Edition

Contents

So Inn Love

CHAPTER 1

"And you are?"

You've got to be kidding me.

I was the last person to arrive. I hate walking into a room that's already full of people—even if the room is the front lobby of a gorgeous seaside inn on the coast of Rhode Island, where I was lucky enough to be starting a great new summer job.

Being late wasn't the impression I wanted to make on my first day, especially since I'd barely gotten this job to begin with, and had found out only a week before that it was mine.

"Hi. I'm Elizabeth McKenzie," I said to the woman standing in front of me. She had short, reddish hair and a stocky, athletic build. She was wearing khaki pants and a white Tides

Inn polo shirt that looked as if it had been ironed. The short sleeves had actual creases. "But please, call me Liza," I said. "Sorry—am I late?"

"Just a minute or two. Miss Crossley." She held out her hand to shake mine, and gave me a quick once-over glance, as if she was deciding whether to approve of me or not. I was relieved that I'd removed that pink streak from my hair *before* I got here—she didn't seem the type to appreciate things like that. Her handshake was so strong, I nearly winced from her grip. "So you're the last-minute hire," Miss Crossley said.

She didn't sound all that happy with the decision, which was funny considering she was the Inn staff manager and she had to be *in* on hiring me, at some level. I wished she hadn't announced that I was "last minute" like that to the room. Everyone kind of looked up and focused their gaze on me, as if there might be something wrong, or suspect, about me.

As if I'd only made the security clearance by the skin of my teeth. As if I were only good enough when there was no other option.

Or at least that's what their faces told me. That I was being snobbed.

Yes, it's a verb. Especially useful around exclusive communities like this one. I actually hadn't known that much about it until three years ago when, because of my mother's job as a professor, we moved to a new town, where Snobs 'R Us was the name of one of the after-school clubs.

Just kidding. But moving right before sophomore year had been a little traumatic for me. Just when I was working my way up from being a lowly freshman, I had to start all over again, and the cliques at my new school didn't make it easy. It was like everyone had lived in the same town forever and I was the sole new person. That wasn't true, but that's how it felt until I made some friends. Now I was wondering if I'd just walked into the same situation here, at my perfect summer job.

One girl flashed me a sympathetic smile, so at least there was that. The room was filled with about forty people, taking up nearly every seat in the large, spacious lobby. It was starting to hit me that I was actually on the Tides Inn staff. I couldn't believe it. Everything had happened so fast, since I got the summons a week ago. My dream job, coming through. I might be late and I might be a little uncomfortable, but at the same time I knew I was lucky to be here.

I finally spotted an empty white wicker chair by the window, so I nodded to Miss Crossley and scooted past her to take a seat.

"Now, we'll do some introductions later on, once you've had a chance to get settled. But the Inn opens for summer season—the only season we have around here—in two days," she said. "That gives us two days to get completely perfect at everything we do. We don't accept less than perfection here at the Tides Inn. Our customers expect it, and we demand it. You've all been hired because of your extreme trustworthiness."

She made it sound as if we were about to go into battle, and we were the elite soldiers. The Green Berets—although I didn't think the Inn's color scheme was green. More like a blue-gray, the color of a whale you might see if you went out far enough in a sailboat. And instead of berets? We'd probably wear floppy bucket hats.

"Now," Miss Crossley went on, "some of you are new to me, some are old friends—" She stopped as the screen door creaked open and slammed shut with a bang.

A tall guy with brown hair, wearing long khaki shorts, flip-flops, and a navy T-shirt ripped at the neck, stepped into the lobby. He glanced behind him at the door, then turned back to Miss Crossley and smiled. He had the kind of smile that made you like him instantly.

"Someone's going to have to fix that before the guests get here," he said.

"Thanks for volunteering, Hayden. Nice you could make it," the manager said. She cleared her throat as she glanced at her watch.

So I wasn't the last one to arrive, after all. Victory! Or at least not total outright failure. I looked at him; his T-shirt said, "Mapleville Academy" on it, a place I'd only vaguely heard of but probably should know about. I thought it was one of those elite private schools in New England.

"Sorry, Peach. I got lost," he said.

"Peach?" several people repeated.

I'd only met Miss Crossley a minute ago, but I didn't get the impression that she was very "peachy" at all. Apple, maybe. Granny Smith Apple. Sour.

"In case the rest of you are wondering, Hayden's the only one allowed to call me that." Miss Crossley narrowed her gaze at Hayden. "And even then I'm not so sure, actually. And what do you mean, you got lost? You've been here the past two summers, plus I picked you up from the New York train yesterday. So where have you been?"

"I was trying to clean up the beach. I picked up some bottles and trash, then I was raking the sand—I lost track of time, I guess. Sorry."

"What, are you going for Employee of the Month already?" someone in the crowd called out.

"Hey, if the plaque fits . . . then put it on the wall," Hayden replied with a smile.

The guy sitting behind me groaned.

Miss Crossley didn't look impressed or amused, either. "Hayden, why don't you hurry up and take a seat so we can get started—or restarted, rather."

"Sure thing." He smiled at her.

"There's room here, Hayden." Two girls scooted over on a sofa to make a space for him.

"Now. As I was saying before I was so rudely interrupted . . ." Miss Crossley looked at Hayden and smiled. "It's great to have you all back this year. I know there are other summer jobs that might pay more, might be more exciting, or might be closer to home. We at the Inn—the Talbot family and I, and the rest of the adult employees—certainly appreciate the sacrifices you're making to be here. Living away from home—"

"That's a sacrifice?" the guy sitting behind me on the window seat joked. He was leaning forward onto the back of my chair, and he was sort of pulling my hair. I moved a little to tug it free from under his arm.

"More like a gift," a girl to my left added. I turned to her and smiled in agreement. It wasn't that living at home was so terrible, for any reason—just *old*.

"Well, it's not as if this is the Hilton," Miss Crossley said. "Actually the Inn is better than the Hilton, of course. But *your* living quarters—"

"More like Motel Six," a girl added.

"No, more like Motel Three," Hayden said, and everyone laughed.

Is it really that bad? I wondered. I mean, I figured that the dorm where all the employees stayed was nothing special, but I thought living on our own was cool enough. We didn't need it to be all that nice, considering we wouldn't be spending a whole lot of time in our rooms.

"Your accommodations are perfectly adequate," Miss Crossley said, the only one who didn't crack a smile. I wondered if she smiled much, period. Probably not. Too busy striving for perfection.

After an hour's worth of rules and regulations, Miss Crossley told us to take a break from orientation and go check out our rooms.

The boy sitting behind me stood and stretched his arms over his head, looking sleepy. "Orientation. Like it's college." He smiled at me. He had curly, sandy hair that he brushed back out of his face. "How much is there to know?"

"A lot, I guess." I didn't want to say anything bad, seeing as how I was the last person to be hired.

"She thinks so, anyway." He held out his hand. "Hey. I'm Josh."

"Liza," I said. "Nice to meet you."

"So you're new here?" he asked, and I nodded. "Me too. Don't worry, you didn't miss anything by being late," he said. Then he walked over to join and talk to some of the other guys.

I looked around the room at everyone gathered in small groups, talking and laughing and hugging. The way everyone was instantly talking to each other, it was obvious most of them knew each other already, from the summer before.

I glanced down at the information sheets Miss Crossley had handed us when the meeting broke up. "Room Assignments" was on top. I looked around the room at everyone, trying to guess who I might be rooming with, and who might become my good friends—with any luck they'd be the same people. The summer could either be great—which I was desperately hoping for and semicounting on—or terrible, depending.

I was skimming the list for my name when a petite girl with short dark-brown hair came up to me. She wore a red T-shirt and khaki capri pants. "Hi, I'm Claire. I think you're my roommate," she said.

"Hey!" I said with a smile. "I was just checking out the list and wondering how I'd figure out who you were. You'd think Miss Crossley would make a point of introducing us but . . . Are you psychic?"

"Well, since you came late, I got to hear your name, so I knew it was you," she said. "It wasn't my ESP—sorry."

"I knew there was a reason I came late. Everyone probably thought I was just lazy, or disorganized, but it was all a plan so you'd know who I was. Really."

"Sure. Obviously," Claire said. "I'm the opposite—I always get everywhere early. I even *try* to be late, but it never works out. You think that kind of thing is genetic?"

"I hope so, because that would give me a good excuse for being late," I said.

"Oh, come on. You weren't even the last person to show up. And I think the only person who noticed or cared—"

"Just happens to be our new boss," I put in.

Claire shrugged. "Yeah, so, she'll get over it. It might take her a few weeks, and you might have to be perfect in every other way, but it'll blow over."

"Yeah. Thanks. *That* puts my mind at ease." We both laughed. "Did you work here last summer, too?" I asked Claire. So far she seemed like a really nice person—we'd have no problem getting along. "Because it seems like everyone besides me has."

Claire shook her head. "Oh, I've never worked here before, either."

"Is it me? Or does it seem like kind of a club?" We stood

off to the side, watching the other girls squealing and hugging. They were all standing in a circle, and the only two people not in the circle were me and Claire. I felt totally frozen out, just like when I moved to my new school three years ago. I hoped college wasn't going to be anything like this, because I wasn't sure how many times I could go through it.

"I hate cliques. I got enough of this in high school, you know?" Claire said.

As she was talking, I saw a girl over her shoulder who looked very familiar to me. "Me too. Except . . . wait a second. I *know* her," I said. I hadn't noticed her when I came in, but I suddenly realized—it was Caroline Farlane! We both used to vacation in this town when we were kids. My grandparents rented a cottage just down the road, for two weeks every summer. This would be so cool! She kind of had an "in" already, and so could I, just because I knew her.

"Know who?" Claire asked.

Caroline used to be sort of a tomboy, but now she had shoulder-length straight blond hair, bleached and combed to perfection, and wore a flowered sun dress with high-heeled sandals. "Caroline?" I asked as I approached her. "Is that you?"

She turned toward me and gave me a confused look. "I'm sorry?" she said, fingering the strand of pearls around her neck.

"It's me," I said. "Elizabeth McKenzie."

"Oh, wow. Beth. I didn't even recognize you. Like, at all." She stared at my black tank, long khaki shorts, and black sandals.

"But didn't you hear me say my name when I came in?"

"I didn't see you come in. Zoe and I must have been talking," she said. "We had a ton to catch up on. That's Zoe, we're roommates." She pointed to a tall, pretty girl with similar features to her own.

You've heard of "the beautiful people," right? Well, that was Zoe. She was kind of stunning, actually, like she could model if she chose to.

"Anyway, you look . . . totally different." She implied that it was maybe not in a good way. "Is that a tattoo?" She pointed to a symbol on my arm.

"Not a permanent one. Just a last-night-at-home thing. My friends and I—we all did it."

"Hm. Interesting. Because they're banned, you know. If Miss Crossley sees that, you'll be in trouble."

"Noted," I said as I shifted to put my arm behind my back, in case our supervisor was approaching. "It's temporary. I can wash it off."

"Well, I'd suggest it," Caroline said in a snooty tone.

"Yeah, well, I've changed a little since we last saw each other,

I guess." I was probably about half a foot taller, for one thing. She was about twice as preppy. Our outfits couldn't have been more different, which was funny, because we used to be so alike. "And I go by Liza now. This is Claire, my roommate. What room are you in?" I asked, wondering if we'd be neighbors.

"Beth, your hair," she said, ignoring my question—and my nickname change. "Didn't it used to be blond?"

"Sort of," I said. "Anyway, how have you been? Wow. It's so cool that we're both working here. Who would have thought?"

"Actually, this is my *second* summer here," she said. Her voice wasn't necessarily cold, but it wasn't warm either.

"Oh." I nodded. What was I supposed to say—congratulations? She was expecting something, so I said, "So you liked it enough to come back?"

"Are you serious? This is the best place to work. Ever. How did you get in, anyway?" Caroline asked, as if this were the sort of nightclub where I'd be left standing outside, waiting in line forever.

I was going to tell her how hard it had been, and how I'd applied last year, too, and how my grandfather had pulled a few strings to get me in. But her attitude was bugging me, so I decided not to. "Oh, you know," I said. "It wasn't any big deal."

"Really."

"Really," I said. "So tell me what you've been up to. It's been a long time. I can't wait to catch up. You know what's weird, I haven't been inside here for a couple of years. Wow—I just thought of something. Remember when we got kicked off the tennis court here? Oh my God, that was funny."

"We did not."

"We did, too!" I said. "Remember those cute guys we met on the beach, and we were supposed to meet them here, and then—"

"Well, see you around, Beth," she interrupted me. Then she turned back to the group she'd been talking to when I first walked up, to Zoe and her other friends.

She's snobbing me, I thought. *Caroline, of all people, is snobbing me.* If she was part of the "in crowd," then maybe I didn't want to be. "It's *Liza*," I said to her back.

"Hey, Liza. And don't mind her, she's not that nice to anyone."

I turned and saw Hayden—the guy who'd arrived right after me—standing beside me. "Seriously?"

He nodded. "Caroline's not exactly the person you send out on the welcome wagon."

"Okay, but here's the thing. Have you ever *seen* a welcome wagon? Like, what's in it?"

"And who pulls it? Horses?" Claire added.

We all laughed, that kind of nervous laughter when you first meet someone.

"So you're Liza. And you are?" Hayden asked.

"Claire. We're new hires," she explained. "You know, apparently the only two new people here?"

"Oh, come on, you're not the *only* new ones," Hayden said. "That guy, Josh, over there . . . and that other guy, what's his name. There're at least five or six of you."

"Someone over there just called us newbies," Claire said. "I hate that phrase, or term, or whatever it is."

"I know," I said. "We can't help it if we didn't work here before."

"So, non-newbies," Hayden said. "Don't get a complex. Hayden Overton. Nice to meet you."

"Same here," I said. At least one person in the so-called in crowd was being nice to us. And as I'd learned from moving, that was really all it took. If one person accepted you or decided you were cool—then everyone would.

"You know what? You want to get out of here?" Hayden said.

"Aren't we supposed to go to the dorm?" Claire asked.

"The dorm can wait. *Believe* me," Hayden said. "Especially

since—" He stopped and looked at us for a second.

"Since what?" I wanted to know.

He shook his head. "Never mind. We've got half an hour before we need to meet up with Peach again. Come on, let's hit the water."

I looked at Claire. "I'm all for it. You?"

"Sure," Claire said. "Sounds good."

"You know what—I see someone I've got to say hi to. But I'll be right down, okay?" Hayden told us.

"He seems nice," Claire said as we walked outside onto the Inn's back porch, which stretched almost the entire length of the building. It had tables and chairs for guests, and standing on it, we looked straight out at the Atlantic Ocean.

"Very," I agreed. I stood on the steps for a few seconds, admiring the view. Then I stepped off onto the boardwalk and turned to look back up at the Inn. It was as gorgeous as I remembered. It was four stories tall, with white shutters and weather-beaten-looking blue-gray paint. Every room had two windows, and a few of them had small decks with big Adirondack chairs facing the ocean.

On the street side, there was a circular driveway, wide, welcoming steps, and a small open deck with wrought-iron tables and chairs under generous-size canvas umbrellas. The parking lot was set back a bit from the Inn, so small golf-cart shuttles were used to ferry guests and their belongings from their cars.

I loved the salty ocean smell that hit my nose as soon as I turned onto the road toward the beach. It was the same, every year, from the time I was a toddler until now.

The real reason I'd been late for the meeting was that on the way in, I'd stopped the car to get out and just breathe the salt air. It sounds dumb, I know, and I'd probably never admit it to anyone in the room—especially Miss Crossley, who was too no-nonsense for that sort of thing—but it's a ritual of mine.

It's not as if we lived *so* far from the ocean, but I still didn't get there very much, especially not during the school year. Every summer's first trip to Rhode Island made my nose so happy.

My boyfriend back home had been really upset—no, mad—when I told him I was going away for the summer. He didn't understand, but that was because he'd never been here, never seen how gorgeous it was. Anyway, we were only talking about ten weeks. That whole time he'd be busy working the graveyard shift at his uncle's boat factory, and we wouldn't have seen each other even if I was around, working at my dad's law office.

Anyway, it wasn't that kind of relationship. We went out when it was convenient, and we had a good time together—but I wouldn't die without him. I'd never had that kind of feeling for anyone. I didn't think I was the type of person to die for love, anyway. I wasn't into big drama.

"A private beach? This is incredible," Claire said as we stepped off the wooden boardwalk.

I slipped off my sandals before I jumped off into the warm sand. Since the Inn wasn't open for business yet, the beach was all ours. "I've never been on this part of the beach." I pointed to a public beach across the breakwater. "That's where we used to hang out. See how it's all crowded?"

Claire laughed. "You and Caroline hung out over there? Hard to believe."

"Why?"

"Oh, I don't know. You don't seem like . . . the same kind of people. To be friends, I mean."

"No. Not anymore, I guess."

I heard voices behind us and turned to see that everyone else had the same idea. They were all either walking—or sprinting—down to the ocean's edge like us, ditching their shoes and sticking their toes into the ocean.

"So where are you from?" Claire asked.

"I was born in Iowa. But now we live in Connecticut," I

said. "Outside Hartford. How about you?"

"Boston," Claire said.

"Cool," I said. "I've only been there once, but I thought it was great."

While we were talking, I was digging my toes into the sand, watching the water roll over my feet, which were sinking a little deeper with each wave and the undertow that followed. I loved that feeling; it was so relaxing.

Suddenly I felt someone's hands on my shoulders.

"Are you ready for your initiation, newbies?"

I turned around and saw Hayden standing behind me. He squeezed my shoulders. "Initiation?" I asked. What was he talking about? This didn't sound good. And here I'd thought he was being so nice to us. "What's that?"

"It's a rite of passage," a guy named Richard said as he swooped up Claire in his arms, with one quick motion.

"Hey! Miss Crossley never mentioned this," Claire said. "Put me down!" she protested.

"You're not actually going to—" I started to say, as I struggled against Hayden. "You're not serious. You think you can—"

"Yeah, I do." He picked me up by the waist, sideways, as if I were a suitcase under his arm, and dragged me closer to the water.

"Since when is there initiation around here?" Claire demanded.

"Since now!" And Richard lifted her in the air and tossed her into the surf.

Before I could laugh at her, I found myself being lifted over Hayden's head—and the next thing I knew I was underwater. It was freezing cold and bubbling up all around me as a wave tumbled over my head. My feet were standing on sand and crushed shells. I surfaced and slicked back my hair, the salt water stinging my eyes. Around me I could hear a few other people complaining, and Claire was yelling at Richard. All the new people were in the water, including Josh. As he waded out, he looked at me and Claire and said, "So it's us against them, huh?"

"I guess so." I glanced back at shore and saw Hayden watching me.

What he didn't know was that I didn't really care if I got tossed in—I was dying for my first swim in the ocean, anyway. So it didn't have to be in my clothes, but I didn't care. What a great feeling.

I looked at my arm and saw my temporary tattoo dissolving in the choppy salt water, colors streaming off my arm. I felt something tugging at me and found a long thick piece of seaweed—the kelp kind that reminds me of lasagna noodles—wrapped around my right leg.

Hayden was smiling at me as I strode out of the surf. "You actually *liked* that, didn't you?"

I pulled the seaweed off my leg and threw it at him as I walked past. "Doesn't everyone like swimming?" I asked him with a smile.

CHAPTER 2

"Why do I get the feeling this room is reserved for the new people?"

Claire and I stood in the doorway of Room 213.

"Thirteen equals unlucky," she said.

"Also unfurnished," I said.

Because our room was right next to the stairway, it had a strange, angled shape, like part of it had been chopped off.

"We get one dresser. Everyone else has two," Claire complained. "Our closet is the size of an old telephone booth."

I wandered around the room. It didn't take long. "And look at this chair. There's one arm missing, and stuffing's poking through."

Our room was at the end of the second-floor hall, near

the stairs, and had an L-shape, with our beds near the windows. There was a built-in wooden dresser, a tiny closet, one desk for us to share, and one semicomfortable chair with strange orange upholstery. The walls were bare and painted white, but at least there were pretty sage-green curtains on the windows.

I tried to open the windows, but they were jammed. I pounded on the sides to get them to budge. When I finally got them open, a fresh ocean breeze came into the room. I looked out the window. The dorm was set back behind the Inn, down a path, so the ocean view was blocked, but we did have a nice view of the Inn.

"Well, maybe it's small, but I still don't think it's that bad," I said, turning around.

I didn't plan on spending much time in the room anyway, when there was so much to see and do, being right on the ocean like we were. The room would be a place to crash at night, and that was about it.

"Wait until it gets hot in July," Claire said. "No air conditioning, and we're on the second floor. I bet this place gets as humid as anything."

"Yeah, but we'll always have that breeze off the water, right?" I pointed out.

Claire narrowed her eyes. "You like getting thrown into

the ocean, you like the smell of salt and fish, you don't care that we have the worst room, and you don't mind humidity. . . . You're one of those glass-half-full kind of people, aren't you?" she asked.

"Sometimes," I said. "It depends on my mood. I can be really dark when I want to." I smiled at her.

"Good. If you were going to be optimistic about everything, I'd go crazy," Claire said. "My mom is like that and it drives me nuts. She's always saying that thing about how when one door closes, another opens, or a window opens when a door gets slammed, or something." She laughed.

"Well, in this place, if a door gets slammed? I think we'll all hear it, whether or not the window's open," I said. From downstairs you could hear guys shouting to each other, while someone on our floor was blasting music.

The guys all lived on the first floor, and the girls on the second. I was still kind of surprised my parents finally let me go away to such an unsupervised place. Were they really aware of what I was getting into? A coed dorm? Did they not know, or did they know and not care? Were they just getting me prepared for what I'd encounter in college?

Maybe that was why they'd tried to talk me out of this plan at the beginning, even though my grandparents had supported it. They'd also tried to persuade me to go to an all-women's college. That hadn't worked, either.

"How did you end up here?" I asked Claire as I pulled a suitcase onto the bed. It sagged under the weight, which was pathetic considering it wasn't that heavy a bag. The bed felt suspiciously like a cot, the kind that might be issued by the Red Cross during an emergency. Did everyone in the dorm have thin mattresses, I wondered, or just us?

"I needed to get away for the summer," Claire said. She lifted a stack of perfectly folded T-shirts from her suitcase into the dresser. "I'll take the two bottom drawers, if you'll take the top two, okay?"

"Sure," I agreed. "You were saying . . . you needed to get away?" That was sort of intriguing, as an opening.

"Oh!" She laughed. "No big scandal—I didn't mean it to sound like that. I just couldn't stand another summer at home. Boredom. You know. Plus my older sister worked here a few summers ago and was always telling me how great it was," she said. "And *she* heard about it from her college roommate, who got her in. When I told her I wanted to apply, she said the most important advice she was going to give me was to beware of hookups."

"Beware of hookers? Really? Around *here*?" I tried to imagine a woman in a feather boa and short shorts, down by the boardwalk to the private beach.

"Hook*ups*," Claire repeated with a laugh.

I laughed, too. "Oh! Well, that's okay, I wasn't really planning any."

"Neither am I," Claire said.

I didn't want to completely rule out seeing someone over the summer, though. I was only human, and who knew what might happen between me and my probably ex, Mark? If we were really over, then I'd be free to date someone else. I didn't have a clue if I would, but I could. The beach would be the perfect romantic location, that was for sure.

"Anyway, my sister just said that this place can get really small, really fast, if you're not careful," Claire continued.

"Hm. Sort of like high school, then?" I asked with a smile.

"Yeah, exactly. God, I'm glad that's over," Claire said.

I nodded in agreement. I was glad to be moving on—and out—to college, too, but I didn't *hate* high school, not after I'd settled in and made new friends. The way I saw it, high school was a lot like a very trendy haircut. Fun while it lasted.

High school could get boring if you were complacent, if you did the same thing over and over. Same with hair. I preferred coloring mine, streaks of blue or sometimes pink, going platinum once or twice, and now, chestnut auburn brown, when I was naturally a blonde. (And no, I'm not going to beauty school. At least not until I flunk out of college.)

Claire unpacked several books, stacking them on the desk, making a bookshelf by using larger stacks at each end of the desk.

"Wow," I said. "Are all those for fun, or . . . ?"

"Reading ahead for freshman year at Columbia. Plus a few for fun." She pulled out a couple of paperback chick-lit novels and grinned. "Chaucer's okay, but . . ."

"Sometimes not so much," I added.

"Exactly."

"Miss Crossley made it sound like we'll be working all the time. Do you think we'll have time to read? And if we do, can I borrow *that* one? Not the Chaucer."

Outside our window, a bullhorn sounded. "Come on, everyone, time to tour the Tides!" Miss Crossley's voice boomed through a megaphone.

"She's so high energy it's painful. I meant to wash my hair after the salt swim, but, oh well." Claire sighed as she grabbed a ball cap from the desk and pulled it over her head.

"Good idea." I grabbed my Tigers Volley-ball cap.

When Claire and I walked outside, Miss Crossley met us with a look of disapproval. She was good at doing that. "Dress code rule number seventeen. No ball caps," she said.

There's a dress code? I thought. *Why did no one tell me?* "Oh. Sorry—" I started to apologize.

"No ball caps, except these." Miss Crossley opened a large plastic bag and handed us each an official Tides Inn cotton cap. They were different shades of sun-washed pastel, and the one I grabbed was a pale orange. I caught Hayden's eye as I pulled it over my head. He was already wearing a white one.

"How do you guys like your room?" Caroline asked.

"Fine. Thanks." I smiled at her. "It's very scenic."

"And spacious, don't forget spacious," Claire added.

"What's wrong with your room?" Miss Crossley asked as we assembled into a group outside the dorm.

"Oh, uh, nothing," I said. "It's fine."

"Good. So, moving on. Today we'll get the big overall picture," Miss Crossley went on. "You all need to understand the complete workings of the Inn. In case you're required to fill in for anyone, you should know a little about each other's jobs."

"Miss Crossley, do we really need to do this again? I mean, some of us were here last year, we know the drill," Zoe said. "How about if we split up and—"

"Zoe, you know as well as I do that a refresher course is never a bad idea," Miss Crossley interrupted.

Zoe didn't look as if she knew that at all. She turned to Caroline and rolled her eyes. The two of them definitely acted as if they were too good to be bothered.

"Now, you guys should know the rules. Day One, we stick together. That's our philosophy. Teamwork. Day Two, you focus on your particular area of responsibility."

"Day Three, we run away," Josh muttered, beside me. Since he was new, I wondered if he had an equally crappy room on the first floor, beneath us.

"Day Three, we hit the beach, right?" another person added.

"Only if your job is lifeguarding," Miss Crossley said sternly.

"No problem," Hayden said.

So that was why he'd been cleaning up the beach. It was his turf.

It figured that he was a lifeguard, I thought. He had the body for it. He'd lifted me like I weighed nothing, plus he had broad shoulders, plus he had the kind of rock-hard abs people refer to as a six pack . . .

Hey. I'm just reporting what I saw when he picked me up to toss me into the surf, okay? Strictly a journalistic effort.

"Listen up!" Miss Crossley said, interrupting my happy memory. "Here is the most important area of the entire Inn. The entrance. What guests see here influences their entire stay with us."

"So in other words, no hanging out by the entrance, smoking?" Hayden joked.

"No smoking anywhere on hotel grounds," Miss Crossley said. "Unless of course a guest requests that you step outside and offers you a cigar—"

"Then we *have* to smoke?" Claire interrupted.

"No, I was only joking. Though you should make sure he or she has a light!" Miss Crossley smiled.

"All right, Peach. Loosening up," Hayden said.

"Don't count on it," she replied sternly.

"Lighting cigars for people? My sister didn't mention the part about indentured servitude," Claire said quietly to me as we all moved into the Inn.

"I'm guessing there's a lot she left out," I whispered back.

Once inside, I checked out the reception and lobby area—when I'd come through earlier, I'd been in such a rush that it had all been a blur. There were sofas, big, comfy dark-brown leather ones, wicker ones for those in wet swimsuits, tables with issues of current magazines, and bookshelves from which guests could borrow any book they wanted. The reception desk was made of a rich, dark wood. Behind it were mailboxes for the rooms. An old-fashioned silver bell sat on the desk, beside the fountain pen guests would use to sign the

Inn's register. It was like something out of an old movie.

We used to come to the Inn's restaurant for lunch when my grandparents rented a small cottage down the road. Only once a summer, though, because it was too pricey, according to my grandmother, who, to be fair, could cook up a lobster and clam dinner herself that was equally good, if not better.

Still, I used to look at the teen servers and wish I could work here, especially a couple of years ago when I was desperate for a summer job. I always wanted to stay here, too, but my parents pointed out that not only was it too expensive, it would be silly considering my grandparents rented a cottage so close by.

Now I was going to be working here, at the front desk. Life was so weird sometimes. I was grateful to whoever had dropped out of the staff to make room for me. "Claire, did I tell you? This is where I'm going to be," I started to tell her.

"Actually, Elizabeth, I need to talk to you about that," Miss Crossley interrupted me.

Liza, I wanted to say, but didn't. "You do?"

"Yes. There have been some reassignments."

"There have?" I asked.

"Yes. Even though you were hired to help in the guest reception area, we've decided to go with someone with more experience," Miss Crossley explained. "Caroline pointed out that she has been here longer, and that it is a job she's wanted all along. So we reassigned you, based on seniority."

Or lack thereof, I thought as I checked out the area where I wouldn't be sitting, wouldn't be answering the phone, and wouldn't be greeting celebrities and other interesting people as they arrived.

Caroline looked at me and smiled. "It takes someone who knows the Inn inside and out. I'm *really* sorry, Beth," she said, in a voice so obviously phony that I knew she wasn't sorry at all. And if she knew the Inn so well, why hadn't she been the one who got the job in the first place?

"It's Liza," I reminded her. "And that's okay," I said, smiling at her. "I'm sure any job here is great, no matter what it is. So, what do you have for me then?" I asked Miss Crossley cheerfully. Stiff upper lip, glass half full, and all.

"Housekeeping," she said.

My heart sank. I was in trouble. They really hadn't read my application, had they? "Housekeeping" was ranked last on my list of desired positions. I was really terrible about cleaning my room at home. They should have asked my parents for references, because when it came to keeping a place neat and tidy? I had zero skills.

"Housekeeping," I repeated slowly. "Well, okay. I can keep house with the best of them," I lied.

"Happy to hear that," Miss Crossley said. "This is a team effort, and we need team players."

Okay, I thought. *But do I have to be on the clean team?*

I glanced at Caroline, who was smiling happily at her friend Zoe. Caroline had just gotten upgraded from housekeeping to front desk; of course she was happy. But I had a feeling that any idea I had that Caroline and I might still be able to be friends was as dead in the water as my front-desk job.

It's us against them, Josh had said. Was it really going to be that bad?

I was back in my room, tucking the sheets under my thin mattress, when Claire walked in carrying a couple of sodas. "You're not practicing, are you?" she asked.

I sank onto the bed with a sigh. "I know you don't want to hear this, as my roommate, but I'm not the neatest person. Having a job where I'm supposed to clean up after people is like . . . completely against type." Miss Crossley had given me a ten-minute seminar on "Ways to Remove Sand from a Carpet" that I'd already forgotten. Or blocked out. One of the two.

Claire handed me a soda. "You want to switch? I'll clean, you take kids sailing?"

"I don't know how to sail," I said. "Not well enough to teach it, anyway. I mean, if I were stranded on a desert island and sailing was the only way to get off, I suppose I'd figure it out, but . . ."

"I'll teach you," she offered.

"You're crazy. You're going to trade being outside on the water all day with inhaling harmful cleaning products?"

"You can always open the windows to let the fresh air in. You know, your famous ocean breeze," she reminded me.

I frowned at her. "Thanks."

"Besides, didn't she say they only use environmentally safe products that are organically made?" Claire asked.

"Okay, fine, whatever. Organic or not, it's still strong-smelling stuff to cover other, less pleasant stuff, isn't it?" I laid back on the bed and groaned.

Claire collapsed on her bed, laughing. "I'm not laughing *at* you. I'm laughing *with* you. Really."

There was a loud, booming knock on our door. I sat up and was surprised to see several guys crowded into our doorway: Tyler, Hayden, Richard, Daunte, and a few others whose names I hadn't yet memorized.

"So. You're the ones with Room Two-thirteen." Daunte nodded. "All right."

"'All right' what?" Claire asked.

"You should keep it down," Richard said. "There's a noise limit."

"There is?" I asked. Apparently there were lots of rules about this place I hadn't been clued in to yet. Was I missing all the handouts, or what?

"Yeah. If you want to be really loud, you have to come down to the beach with us," Tyler said. "We all go to Crandall's to kick off the summer."

"It's tradition. You have to come," Hayden said.

"Have to," Claire repeated, not sounding convinced. "Or . . . ?"

"You know what happened earlier?" Richard asked her. "Cold seawater, up your nose? More of that."

"Are you even supposed to be up here?" Claire asked. "I thought there were some fairly specific rules about 'fraternizing.' In other words, don't."

"Don't tell me you guys are follow-the-rules types," Hayden said.

"Not always," I said. "But on our first night? Kind of. Especially since we're new here, and people seem to love giving us a hard time about that."

"We'd never do that," Hayden said. "Us?"

"No, of course not," I said. "And we'd never throw seaweed at you."

He smiled at me.

Caroline pushed her way through the crowd. "If they don't want to come, don't make them," she said. "Maybe they just want to hang out here."

For some reason, that settled the matter for me. "Hang out here? In the dreaded Two-thirteen? I don't think so. Come on, Claire. Let's go."

"But—"

"It'll be fun," I said. "Grab a sweater."

"So this is Crandall's Point. Who or what is a Crandall?" Josh asked.

"It's the huge place up there, the one you can see from here." Caroline pointed to a gigantic, secluded house that looked almost as big as the Inn. "It belongs to the Crandall family and has for years. They made tons of money in the shipping business. You know, back when it was with actual ships. The eighteen hundreds."

She was acting like such a know-it-all that it really bothered me.

"Legend has it that Captain Crandall was out at sea, and he was several weeks late getting home. His wife used to pace back and forth on the widow's walk up there, looking for him and waiting, and she actually fell off—or jumped, some people say. He came home safely, but she was dead," I said.

"What? How did you know that?" Hayden looked at me, impressed.

"I used to come here with my grandparents. Way back when." *When Caroline wasn't so annoying.*

"I'll never look at the house the same way again," Richard said. "I had thought it was a bunch of old money, but now it's a lot creepier."

I thought of the time Caroline and I had met a Crandall cousin when we were taking a kayak class offered by the yacht club. Afterward we'd decided to go visit him, so we'd gone up to the Crandalls' house, rung the doorbell, and then ran away when we chickened out. I think a butler came to the door. I'm not sure, because my view had been blocked by the hedge I'd hid behind.

I wondered if Caroline remembered that, too.

"But they don't own this part, do they?" another new girl named Brooke asked.

"Own the sand and rocks?" Caroline scoffed. "No, I don't think so. I mean, they're not *that* rich."

"So how does the Inn get away with having a private beach, then? They must own it, too, right?" Josh asked.

"Some ancient law preserves their right to it, I think,"

Hayden said. "They don't own it, exactly, but no one else can use it. Go figure."

"So, can these Crandall people see us down here?" Claire asked.

"No. Well, if they can, they don't care we're here," Zoe said. "At least they've never said anything before."

"Having said that, I wouldn't run around naked or anything," Hayden suggested. "Just to play it safe."

"Oh, good, I'm glad you warned me, I was just about to do that." Claire rolled her eyes. "You know, you can take them out of high school, but can you take high school out of them?" she asked, and all of the girls laughed.

"Yes, but it's a painful procedure," Zoe said, and we laughed again.

Some of the other guys walked up carrying pieces of driftwood they'd collected. They dropped them into a fire ring made of stones and arranged them for lighting.

"Are we supposed to have fires here?" Claire asked as Richard struck a few matches and tried to get the fire going.

"We always do. It's fine," Hayden said.

"Fine, as in allowed? Or fine, as in you've never gotten caught?" Claire asked.

"We never got in trouble *last* summer," Caroline said.

"Obviously people can see us out here, so if it was a big problem, they'd tell us." Hayden shrugged. "We don't cause any trouble around town, so it's no problem."

"You know what? I still think I'm going to take off," Claire said to me in a soft tone.

"Are you seriously worried? They wouldn't fire us. The Inn opens tomorrow, they need us," I said.

"Who needs us?" Josh asked as he crouched in the sand beside me.

"Miss Crossley, the Talbot family, you know—everyone," I said.

"They do need us, but you should know—they're not afraid of canning employees," Zoe said. "Last summer they fired a couple of people."

"Oh yeah," Caroline said. "What was her name, the one with the tattoo . . . ?" She looked meaningfully at me, and I held up my arm to show her it had washed off. She ignored me.

"Terri," someone else added.

"Right. And what about that guy who partied with the guests after a wedding, and they found him sleeping on the front porch?" Caroline said. "Theo. Remember?"

"Miss Crossley went on a lecture for like a day and a half

about how wrong *that* was," Zoe told us.

"Okay. That's all I need to hear," Claire said, standing up and brushing the sand off the back of her shorts.

"Come on, relax. We're not doing anything illegal," Hayden said. "It's a bonfire. People build them on the beach all the time."

"Yeah, but . . . wasn't there something in our handouts about no beach parties?"

"What are all these handouts everyone keeps talking about? Why didn't I get them?" I asked.

"I don't know, but I have them all back at the room," Claire said.

"Miss Crossley would love to give you your own copies, too," Tyler said. "She can probably quote them from memory."

"Anyway, technically this isn't a beach party. It's a gathering," Daunte said. "Stick around."

Despite everyone's protests, Claire took off to go back to the dorm along with a few others, while the rest of us sat around the bonfire.

"Okay, so you guys have to give us the dirt. The skinny. The four one one," I said.

"What on earth are you talking about?" Caroline said. Why did everything she said to me end up sounding so disapproving? She sounded like a very uptight librarian at a very uptight library.

"You know, could you please give us the benefit of your venerable experience?" I turned to Caroline. "Is that better?"

A few of the guys laughed, including Hayden, and so did Zoe.

"Tell us what we need to know so we don't screw up," Josh said.

I nodded. "Nice translation. Thanks. Most of you guys have been here before, so tell us about it." I took a handful of sand and let it run through my fingers.

"Okay, well, here's what I would say." Zoe lifted a chunk of her long, straight dark-brown hair and flipped it over her shoulder. "You want to get on Mr. Talbot's good side, as soon as you can."

"Oh yeah. If you can do that, you're golden," Hayden put in.

"Is it hard?" I asked.

"And which Mr. Talbot?"

"Yeah, aren't there two of them? At least?"

"There's the younger one, who's not that young—he's like forty-five—and then there's the older one, who's seventy," Zoe said.

That was the one my grandfather knew. He called him "Bucko," but his name was actually William.

"The younger one goes by William, the older by Bill," another guy explained. "Not to us, though, of course."

"Isn't there a Mr. Talbot the third, too?" Josh asked.

"Yeah, Will, but he's only five," Hayden said. "So you don't need to worry, unless of course you end up having him in your playgroup one day. Who's got the little tykes group this summer?"

A couple of girls raised their hands.

"I hear he's kind of a brat. Is that true?" one of the girls asked.

"He's not bad. At least he wasn't last year."

"Anyway. How do we get the adult Talbots to like us?" I asked. I hoped I might have a head start, since my grandfather knew Mr. Talbot Senior. Still, it had taken me two years to get hired, despite that. Hopefully Mr. Talbot Senior hadn't soured on Grandpa, for some unknown reason. Hopefully Grandpa had been keeping up with his calls and Christmas cards and old-boy network stuff, like sharing jokes and cigars now and then. Virtually. Via e-mail.

"It's easy," Hayden said. "Just flatter them."

"Yeah, but not in a phony way," Zoe said. "They're really

nice guys, actually. Whatever happens, they're just trying to protect the Inn's image, so every once in a while, they flip out over something small," she explained.

"Like what?" I asked.

"You'll just have to find out on your own," Caroline said, in a somewhat ominous tone, as if I were bound to screw up. I got the impression that if I were drowning, she wouldn't throw me a life preserver. I don't even think she'd try. She'd probably turn and walk the other way.

What had I done? Was I forgetting some major slight on my part? Or was she remembering one that never happened?

I usually find a way to get along with almost everyone. The real person to worry about wasn't going to be a Talbot. It was *her*.

"Okay, so you asked us what you need to know about the Inn," Hayden said. "So tell us what we need to know about you." He looked right at me.

"Me?" I asked. "Don't start with me."

He laughed. "Why not?"

"I don't know. I'm not that interesting," I said. That wasn't it, but I just didn't feel like talking about myself to a bunch of people I didn't know. "I'd rather hear about stuff from you guys."

"'Not that interesting,'" Josh repeated. "Hm. You know,

the people who say stuff like that are always the *most* interesting."

"You know, that's true." Hayden smiled at me across the bonfire.

Why were they ganging up on me? "What can I tell you? I'm from a suburb outside Hartford, I'm cocaptain of the volleyball team, my birthday's March twelfth, which means I'm a Pisces. Oh and I also like piña coladas and walks in the rain," I said. "That's about it."

"Righhhht," Hayden said slowly.

"Okay, you're right, you really *aren't* interesting," Caroline declared.

"Fine, then." I turned to her. "Why don't *you* talk about yourself?" She probably liked to do that.

"We could be here for hours," Daunte joked.

"Stop it." Caroline laughed and tossed a handful of sand in his direction.

"Not cool. Not cool. I have contacts, remember?" Daunte rubbed at his eyes.

"You know, we could sit here all night trading astrological signs. But I think I'd rather go swimming. Anyone else?" I asked.

"Race you," Hayden said as he jumped to his feet.

"No fair—I don't know the way—"

"The ocean? It's right over there," Tyler said.

"I know, but—"

"Last one in is a rotten quahog!" Hayden yelled.

"Ew. Smelly," Caroline was commenting as I took off running for the water, stepping over rocks and stripping off my clothes as I did.

Don't worry, it wasn't *that* racy—I was wearing a bathing suit underneath.

I was tiptoeing into my room later that night when I knocked a book off the edge of the desk. It crashed to the floor and I saw Claire turn over in bed. "Sorry—I was trying not to wake you up so I didn't want to turn on the light," I said.

"It's okay. I heard you guys coming a mile away."

"Really?" I asked.

"Oh yeah. Remember not to say anything personal as you're walking up the path—you can hear everything," Claire said. "So how was it? Sounded like fun."

"It was great. A bunch of us went swimming, which was so cool, but kind of scary, too—I've hardly ever gone swimming at night in the ocean."

"It's dangerous," Claire mumbled into her pillow.

"Yeah, but Hayden was there, plus Lindsay, who lifeguards

at the pool, plus Sara, who teaches swimming," I told her. "So I figured I was safe, but you're right, it is kind of weird only using the light of the moon to see by. The water was calm, though. Anyway, half of us were swimming, the other half were watching out for us. It took me forever to find my clothes afterward—never leave your clothes on the beach when it's dark."

I kept babbling for a few more minutes before I realized Claire had gone back to sleep.

I quickly changed into my pajamas and climbed into bed. I guess I should have showered, because my skin was sticky with salt, but I didn't care. It would get old after a few weeks, but for now it was perfect, unlike the rock-hard cot I was lying on top of. Maybe I'd be more comfortable sleeping on the sandy beach, under the stars, I thought as I snuggled under the covers.

I thought of the way Hayden had looked at me as we both sprinted into the ocean, racing each other to be first to dive in. Afterward we'd all sat around the bonfire to warm up and dry off, and I'd caught him looking at me a few times across the fire.

So what? So you're kind of—or more than kind of—attracted to him, I thought as I tried to fall asleep. *You're not here to fall in love over the summer. That would only make everything really complicated.*

You're here to save money for college, and just have fun, I reminded myself.

But . . . wouldn't being in love *be* fun?

CHAPTER 3

Vacuuming. I hate vacuuming.

I ran the heavy industrial vacuum around the room, starting near the window and working my way backward to the bed. This was my fifth guest room so far, and I was cruising, nearly done with my block of rooms. I'd been lucky and nothing too challenging (or disgusting) had come up yet.

Although there was one challenge: The vacuum had superstrong sucking power and would sort of take off on its own if you didn't keep a tight grip on the handle. I could totally picture it taking off down the hall, cleaning everything in its path—and knocking down a few people, too. It seemed sort of possessed, like something you'd encounter in a horror novel. The fact that Mr. Knight, the "Clean Team" supervisor, had *named* all the vacuums, and this one was the "Hulk," worried me.

Mr. Knight had spent a few hours with us the day before, going over procedures, like how we could use special sticky tape to lift sand out of hard-to-clean places. He'd tested us by making rooms dirty and then having us clean them. He literally had white gloves he used to test our "surfaces," as he called them.

My test went something like this:

Mr. Knight: "And would you say that this is clean?"

Me: "Ye-es."

Him: "You call this clean."

Me: "Yes."

Him: "Really."

And then he showed me the white glove, which was not so white.

"So this is what they mean by commercial strength," I mumbled now as I kept vacuuming. I was being extra thorough, as instructed, so I pushed the vacuum underneath the bed and moved it around searching for "Inn bunnies," as Mr. Knight called them. Suddenly I heard a loud whirring sound. *Uh oh,* I thought, quickly shutting off the vacuum. Had it eaten the bedspread?

I pulled the Hulk toward me, but the wheels wouldn't

roll—they were jammed. And then I smelled something burning.

I quickly unplugged the vacuum and laid it on the floor. A black belt was wrapped around the roller on the bottom— and I didn't think it was part of the vacuum. I got down on my hands and knees and started to tug on the belt. Suddenly I saw a pair of feet in shiny black loafers standing beside the vacuum.

I looked up with a feeling of dread.

"What is going on here?" Mr. Knight demanded. "Have you broken the Hulk?"

"What? Come on, no one can bring down the Hulk," I joked.

"What have you done, Liza? It smells like you slipped a belt," he said.

"Something like that." Slipped one, devoured another. No steps forward, two steps back. I tugged at the belt that had gotten sucked into the vacuum, but no matter how hard I pulled, I couldn't get it free.

"Let me see that." Mr. Knight crouched beside me and examined the vacuum's rollers. "You've ruined it," he said sadly. "I think you've ruined it."

"Wait," I said. "Maybe if we both pull really hard—"

"No, this requires a professional. Leave it." He stood up

and brushed the dust off his knees. I reluctantly got to my feet, too. "I'll need to fix up the vacuum before we can get anything else done here. You're excused, for now."

"Excused?" I asked. That didn't sound good, at all.

"Free to go. Take a walk. I'll contact you later about making up the lost time," Mr. Knight said. "You can work a double shift tomorrow."

"Great. Sounds great," I said, faking a smile. *And after that, I'll do a triple shift, and then a quadruple shift . . .* But as much as I hated cleaning, I'd do anything he asked in order to stick around and make up for my mistake. "And I'm *really* sorry about the Hulk. And the belt."

"What belt?"

I turned around and saw a man in tennis whites, holding a couple of racquets, in the doorway.

Time to make my escape, I thought as I edged toward the doorway. "I'm sorry, sir. I didn't realize your belt was under the bed, and the vacuum didn't either until it was too late—"

"You ruined my *belt*? My Etienne Lavager belt? Do you know how much those cost?" the guest demanded.

"It may not be ruined," Mr. Knight said. "Just one moment." Finally he managed to unhook the belt from the vacuum roller, and it whipped through the air as it came free, snapping against the bedpost. When he held it up, there was a big crease in the middle and the edges were frayed.

Mr. Knight cleared his throat. "Of course, the Inn will reimburse you for the belt."

"You don't understand. That's the only belt I have *with* me."

Great. Now I was responsible for this guy's pants falling down, too.

"I'll need a replacement. Or twice the replacement value," the guest demanded.

"Certainly, sir, certainly." While Mr. Knight scrambled to make things right, I hurriedly ducked out into the hallway. I walked down the hall to the stairway at the end as quickly as I could. If this guy ever got his belt back, he'd probably try to strangle me with it.

So, Day One on the job had been a bit problematic. But in my defense? I'd told them not to put me in housekeeping! This sort of thing wouldn't happen at the front desk, I thought as I walked through the lobby, where Caroline was busy chatting with a couple of guests. I would be great at her job—and I wouldn't be at risk of getting fired. Though I couldn't exactly say this was all Caroline's fault, I wanted to, anyway.

I was almost out the door when I heard sandals skittering on the floor behind me. "Beth, where are you going?"

I turned around. Caroline was hurrying up to me. "Is everything *okay*? You look upset. Aren't you supposed to still be working?"

I looked at her for a second. I could tell her everything that had just happened. That was clearly what she wanted me to do, for some reason. We could laugh about it, or maybe I'd end up crying. But she was the last person I wanted to tell about my rocky start at the Inn. I had a feeling she'd enjoy it too much. "Everything's just fine," I said. "I finished early." Then I smiled, because that wasn't a lie—just a different take on things. "See you later!"

I grabbed my iPod and headed out for a walk along the winding oceanfront road. I took my time, admiring the beautiful large homes that faced the sea. I just tried to enjoy breathing in the salt air, while I calmed down by listening to loud music.

I could give up, go home, get back together with Mark. . . . I could do the same old thing I did last summer. But that wasn't me. I didn't quit things. Definitely not after one day. When I was second team on the volleyball team, I worked my way up to captain. When I bombed my SATs on the first take, I took them again and again.

After walking for a while, I came around a curve and saw fellow newbie Josh, walking from the other direction. He had

a small brown bag from the candy shop in one hand and a
can of energy drink in the other.

"You know it's a wealthy little town when the only shopping options are seafood, candy, and crafts," he said when we
got closer. He brushed his sandy-brown hair out of his eyes.

"Postcards everywhere. Food? Not so much," I said.
"Right?"

"Yeah, I was hoping for a burger and fries, but I guess you
have to have a car for that." He held up the small bag. "I've
got Smarties and Laffy Taffy, though."

I laughed. "Those should hold you over until dinner. So
how was the job this morning?"

"Brainless. I made a few mistakes, but nothing major."

"Hm. Wish I could say the same." I explained about the
housekeeping disaster, how I had mangled a belt and brought
down the Inn's most cherished vacuum. "They'll probably
ask me to leave, so I figured I should walk around and enjoy
the scenery before I go."

"Leave? You're not going to *leave*." Josh rolled his eyes.
"Mistakes happen, right? Like this morning, when I brought
the wrong order to the table where the younger Mr. Talbot
was sitting with this guy who turned out to be president of
the country club. They had a cow. But no, I'm not getting
fired. Actually they didn't even complain all that much, just

made a bunch of comments about squeaky wheels on opening day."

"Well, I must have been the squeakiest. Or maybe the smelliest. The vacuum practically started smoking."

"Doesn't it know that's harmful to its health?" Josh asked, and I laughed. "And you—you were exposed to secondhand vacuum smoke, so you can sue the hotel if they try to get rid of you. Anyway, where are you going? Postcards or candy?"

"Just for a walk. Visiting my old favorite places from when my family used to vacation here," I said. I debated whether to tell him where I was headed, but decided to keep it to myself, for now. I kind of felt like I needed some more time by myself.

"So, is it turning into one of those you-can't-go-home-again experiences?" Josh asked.

"Not yet. Anyway, see you around. Enjoy that candy."

Actually there was an off-the-main-road little coffee shop called Sally's Tea Room that I knew about. Maybe it was mean of me, but I didn't want to tell Josh and spoil it— not yet. I figured the place could be my escape, if it was still around—I hadn't been here the summer before, and I was hoping it hadn't vanished.

It was located inside an old, vacated bait shop, and the tiny sign by the door didn't give much away. Sally used to say she didn't want any tourists—just locals who got close enough to see that little NO MORE BAIT—JUST COFFEE sign.

I opened the door and went inside. Sally was still there, behind the counter, and the place was lively—all six tables were full. I said hello to her and ordered a large coffee. When I turned around from putting milk in my cup, I nearly dropped it on my feet.

Hayden was sitting at one of the tables. He wore deep orange-red lifeguard shorts and a white tee, and he was reading a book. "Hey, new girl," he said when he saw me.

"El—"

"Elizabeth. I know." He smiled. "Actually it's Liza. Have a seat." He pushed out the empty chair opposite him with his foot.

I smiled.

"You can call me Hayden," he said. "In case you forgot."

I hadn't.

"But not 'Hay' for short. It's a little too barn-friendly," he said.

"Besides, then people would say things like 'Hey, Hay,' which would be annoying," I pointed out.

"That's already happened. Way too many times." Hayden rolled his eyes. "So don't start, okay?"

I pointed to the paperback thriller he was reading. "I read that a couple weeks ago. It's good, don't you think?"

"Yeah, I kind of can't put it down. That's why I escaped here to read on my lunch break. Do you read a lot?"

"Tons," I said. "But not as much as Claire, I don't think—you should see how many books she brought."

"Good, I'll know where to go to borrow some then," Hayden said.

I smiled, thinking of the chick-lit novels Claire had unpacked. It was weird. A bunch of people *were* snobby, but Hayden didn't appear to be, which was cool considering he could be. He was the one who'd worked at the Inn three summers straight, and he seemed to sort of call the shots around the place.

"How did you know about this place?" he asked.

"My family used to vacation here, remember?" I said. "Why, did you think you discovered it?"

He laughed. "Kind of. This is my hideout. Not that I need to hide. I'm just saying, I come here to get away from the Inn. To read. Anyway, how's it going?"

"That depends." I took a sip of coffee. I knew I should be having herbal tea, to soothe my frazzled nerves, but that just isn't like me. Once I get totally frazzled, I tend to like to stay that way. Being mellow and laid-back is overrated, anyway. "Is getting talked to by the housekeeping supervisor on your first day a good thing?"

"Oh no. Tell me you're not working for Uptight Knight," Hayden said.

"Perfect nickname," I murmured. "And I don't know if I'm still working for him."

"Did you know he's in the family?" Hayden said.

"He is? You mean, in the Inn family?" I asked. "Is that redundant?"

He laughed. "Yeah, he's some Talbot cousin or other. He's not Mr. Talbot Junior's first cousin, I don't think, maybe he's one of those twice-removed-type deals."

I sighed. "Great. I think I'm about to be twice-removed, then." Was it too soon to call my grandfather and ask him to put in *another* good word for me?

"No, don't worry, nobody likes him," Hayden said.

"Good," I sighed.

"Not even Mr. Talbot Senior," Hayden added. "Supposedly he had to give him a job because he was in the family, so they stuck him with housekeeping."

I raised my eyebrow. "Is that where they put all the people they don't like?"

Hayden laughed. "No! Well, at least I don't think so. I don't know."

"Great. Thanks. So you're the lifeguard?" I asked.

"One of them," he said. "Plus I drive the Inn shuttle van,

usually in the evening, unless something different comes up. You know, we pick up guests at the train station. There's a train that gets in around seven—at least it's supposed to—from New York, and one from Boston that gets in slightly later."

"I love taking the train," I said.

"Oh yeah, me, too," Hayden said. "That's how I got here. See—" Hayden's cell phone rang, and he pushed his chair back from the table. "Sorry. I'll see you around, okay?" Then he went outside to take the call, which I have to say was kind of rude and kind of polite at the same time.

We were under strict orders never to use phones while we were on duty, not even to check our voice mail or e-mail. They were strictly for downtime, which meant I was planning to call my friends at home during my breaks and lunch hour. I took my phone out of my pocket and just as I did, it started to ring. I didn't recognize the number on my caller ID, but I picked up anyway.

"Hey, Liza? Miss Crossley was just here looking for you," Claire said.

I nearly choked on my coffee. "You're kidding."

"No. She wants to talk to you about something. I'm really sorry, but I gave her your number—I had to!"

"It's okay. Hey, how was sailing?"

"There were like ten kids for one boat. I'm just hanging out in our room for a couple of minutes recovering before my afternoon session." She paused. "In comparison to your job, not so bad, I guess. How was scrubbing toilets?"

I laughed. "That went okay, but then I trashed the vacuum cleaner." My phone started to beep, as another call came in. "I'll explain later—see you!"

"Is this Liza McKenzie?" Miss Crossley asked when I answered. "Where are you?"

"I'm on my lunch break." I supposed you could call it that. "In fact, I was just talking to Hayden. He's here on his break, too." I figured dropping his name couldn't hurt.

"Where is *here*, Liza? I need to talk to you now." Miss Crossley clearly was not impressed. "Could you meet me in my office in five minutes?"

"I don't think I can get there that fast. How about in fifteen?" I suggested, feeling very nervous. Had Mr. Knight gone to find her after he'd yelled at me? Was I going to be fired already?

Remember what Josh said, I told myself. They're not going to fire you. They won't. They can't. Not so close to the start of the season.

Of course, I'd been hired off the waiting list. Which meant there was probably *still* a waiting list.

"Ten minutes, Liza," Miss Crossley said.

I guessed that was her idea of compromising. "That's great!" I said.

How many times was I going to be phony and say that today? I was getting kind of unimpressed with myself.

I tossed my cup into the trash, waved good-bye to Sally, and hurried outside. To my surprise, Hayden was standing there. He was closing his phone with a snap, and about to climb on a bicycle. He looked around as I came out the door.

"Can I borrow that?" I asked, pointing to his bike. "Miss Crossley's kind of breathing down my neck—or cell phone anyway—she wants me there in ten minutes and I don't think I can run that fast."

"I have a better idea," Hayden said. "Why don't we both ride?"

"How are we going to do that?"

"Easy. I pedal, you sit on the handlebars."

"You sure that will work? I'm kind of tall," I said.

"Well, you could sit on the seat and I could stand and pedal," Hayden suggested.

I eyed the bike, which was a cruiser style with fat tires. "Where did you get this, anyway?" I asked.

"Oh, there's a shed out behind the Inn. It's got tons of old stuff like this. They used to be for nice bike rentals but they're really old."

"And anyone can use them?" I asked.

"Sure. You just need a key to the shed." He smiled and held up a small key. There was a semiarrogant tone that went with that, but I didn't mind. He had a bike—I needed one. "Climb on," he said.

I walked around to the front of the bike. "I haven't tried this since I was about six. I was a lot shorter then."

"And lighter, probably," Hayden said, adjusting his stance a little as we prepared to set off.

Was he trying to imply something? "Hey. If you want, I can pedal and you can ride." I looked over my shoulder at him as I balanced myself on the handlebars.

"I was kidding, okay? And you're only offering that because you just realized that if we crash, you'll go down first," Hayden said.

"I hadn't even gotten to thinking about crashing yet." As Hayden pushed off, I squealed and lifted my feet, and we started to wobble along the street. Fortunately there wasn't much traffic, which was good because we were weaving all over the place until Hayden straightened out the bike.

"You doing okay?" Hayden called up to me.

"This is great—" I started to say, honestly this time.

Then we hit a giant pothole.

The bike tilted to the right, jolting me off the handlebars. I landed on my feet, just as Hayden hopped off the bike, grabbing me by the waist to steady me. I looked over my shoulder at him. "I'm okay," I said.

"Sorry. I thought you were—uh—falling." He looked very embarrassed, which was kind of an odd look for him.

"No. I'm fine," I said.

Hayden leaned down to pick up the bike, while I refastened the elastic in my hair, which had come loose in all the excitement of the near-crash. "Maybe I should just walk," I said. "If I run, I could—"

"It was one pothole. Come on, get back on," Hayden said. "You know that old saying about having to get back on the bike."

"No," I said.

"Well, there is one." He grinned and patted the handlebars. "Come on, take two. And this time, when you see giant dips in the road? *Tell* me."

CHAPTER 4

Miss Crossley met me outside the
door to her office. "Iced tea?" she offered as we walked inside,
where she handed me a tall, icy glass, complete with lemon
wedge.

Somehow that made me even more uneasy and suspicious, even though she was having a glass as well, because she
was being so nice to me. *Too* nice. "Sure," I said. "Thanks."

"Elizabeth, here's the situation," she began abruptly.

I sipped my iced tea and tried to slow down my breathing.
Riding that bike with Hayden had gotten my heart rate up
to a slightly dangerous level. Then again, the fact my heart
was pounding probably wasn't the bike. It was the fact I had
only been here two days and was already getting my second

"talking to." It was like being sent to the principal's office, not that I would know much about that, except for a few dress-code violations.

Or maybe it was my encounter with Hayden that was making me feel out of breath. I couldn't explain what it was about him, but we clicked, as if I knew him already, only I didn't. Unless I was his cat, from a former life, reincarnated or something.

"Mr. Talbot Junior and I were talking at lunch," Miss Crossley went on. "We were evaluating our staffing levels, and we seem to have overlooked a few things."

Don't say my qualifications, I thought, *or lack thereof.* "You know, I'm really good at sports," I said. "Is there anything you need help with in that area? I could teach volleyball, or—"

But she wasn't even listening to me, not really. "We realized we have enough housekeepers, if we juggle things a bit. And we don't need you at the front desk, as we thought we did," Miss Crossley said.

"Right," I said slowly.

"And we're covered in the restaurant, we have enough servers around the clock," she said.

Last hired . . . first fired. I'd heard that phrase before. Was I about to find out what it meant?

They didn't have room for me. They didn't have a job.

And all because I was lousy at cleaning my room at home for my entire life. Why hadn't I paid attention when Mom yelled at me all those times?

"Is this just because I didn't get all the sand out of the carpet?" I asked. "Or is it because I sucked that guest's belt into the vacuum? Which completely and kind of ironically damaged the vacuum belt?"

"You did what?"

Oh. So she hadn't even heard about that. I coughed. "We got it out. No problem."

"As I was saying. Every once in a while we discover we're short somewhere," Miss Crossley went on. "So I've rethought your position here. You seem like the perfect person to give this new theory a try."

What new theory? "I do?"

"You have a lot of energy, and you're highly adaptable."

"I am?" This was kind of news to me. Hadn't my ex-boyfriend called me the most rigid, uncompromising, stubborn person he ever met?

But that was in a moment of anger, when I broke up with him because I wasn't ready to move things to the next level, and he was, and he wouldn't stop bugging me about it. Which is when my friends and I came up with our theory: You don't really *need* guys. Until you sort of just, you know, want one around. But if he's not good to you and won't listen to you? Forget him. You can do better.

"That's what your recommendations said, that you were a person who could handle anything. Therefore, as of right now, you're the official Tides Inn gofer!" Miss Crossley raised her glass of iced tea in the air, as if to clink against mine in a toast.

"Gopher? Is that like some kind of animal terminology?" I asked. "'Cause I prefer fox, if that's the situation."

Miss Crossley didn't look amused. She never did, around me. "No. It's a—a term. Gofer. Means you will *go for* whatever we need you to," she said.

"You say jump. I say off what?"

She laughed. *Finally*, I thought. I'd made her laugh. She didn't completely hate me, then. "Not exactly, but close. We'll assign you each day based on where we need help. We'll do it on a trial basis. If it doesn't work out . . ."

I thought of the beach, the Inn . . . all the friends and people at home I'd bragged to about this job. No way was I going home. "Oh, it'll work out. I'll be the best gofer ever. In fact, what can I do right now?"

"Well, we're a little shorthanded in the laundry room— got a little bogged down by beach towels," Miss Crossley said. "So if you could help out there, and then run them out to the beach cabana, and see what else needs picking up. And then—well, I'll have to see."

Did I mention I'm about as good at doing laundry as I am at cleaning mirrors? I almost said so, but stopped myself. "Laundry. No problem!" I said cheerfully.

But I couldn't help wondering: Was this job going to be the best thing that could have happened to me, or the worst? Being at Miss Crossley's beck and call could be a little stressful, but I'd rejoice at anything that got me out of vacuuming and cleaning bathrooms, so I wasn't about to complain.

"I think this will work best if we set you up with an exclusive Inn pager," she said. "Only the two of us will have the number. We should have it set up by tomorrow."

"Sounds perfect," I said. But all I could think was that moving from job to job was either going to be very cool, or very Cinderella-like—or some of both.

"What are you doing here, newbie?" Hayden asked when I walked onto the beach later that afternoon. He was standing at the ocean's edge, binoculars around his neck.

"Hi, old person," I said.

"Old person?" he repeated.

"Or is it oldie? If I'm going to be called new all the time, then you can be called old. Right? It only makes sense." I picked up a pink-streaked shell that caught my eye.

"Yeah. Okay. Anyway, what are you doing? Shouldn't you be keeping house, or whatever?"

"Didn't your pal Miss Crossley tell you? I'm the new go-to girl," I said.

He just stared at me. Actually he was looking me up and down a little, checking me out in my bikini, which I took as a positive thing. He didn't feel the need to look *away*, anyway.

"Hey." I snapped my fingers to get his attention back to my face. "Someone sends me to work on the beach, I dress for the beach. You know?"

I don't mean to sound vain, but I'm not sure his attention was totally on the water, or the people swimming in it. Fortunately for them, another lifeguard was stationed nearby, so there was backup if needed.

I gazed at the water for a moment and spotted a lone figure taking slow, deliberate strokes through the ocean. "Who's that swimming way out there?" I asked.

"Yeah, that's Mr. Anderson. He lives a ways down the beach and he swims a couple of miles every day," Hayden said. "Which would be impressive enough, but then he's at least eighty."

"Wow," I said.

"You're working here now?" Hayden asked. "On the beach?"

"I'm the Tides gofer," I explained. "I go wherever I'm needed." I saluted. "Sounds kind of militaristic, but that's Miss Crossley for you. *Does* she have a background in the military?"

Hayden still looked a little dazed.

"Excuse me. That's 'Peach' to you." I went over to unlock the heavy wooden locker in the dunes and started pulling out beach toys. Chelsea was collecting the kids in the Inn lobby and bringing them down—we were the two "Beach Time Players" for the afternoon, while parents played tennis, went golfing, or just lounged in solitude for a while.

When I turned around to bring a collection of plastic shovels and buckets down to the hard sand, I noticed Hayden was checking out something with his binoculars. *Me.*

I smiled and waved at him, and he quickly pulled them away from his face and turned to face the ocean again. I wasn't sure I wanted him to check me out while I was leaning into a footlocker, but oh well.

"So, uh, when did this new job start?" Hayden asked when I got back to him, pretending he hadn't just been examining me from afar.

"About two hours ago," I said. "Remember that meeting we hurried back for?"

He nodded. "My quads remember." He rubbed his legs as if they were hurting.

"Shut up," I said, pushing him.

"Uh oh. Here come the tykes. You'd better run. Ooh, look, there's Will the Third. Lucky you." He playfully popped me on the arm before heading back up the steps to his life-guard post.

Okay, so maybe there were going to be challenges to this new position. But if it meant I could hang out by the water—with Hayden nearby? I was all for it.

CHAPTER 5

"So how's the new job?" Josh asked me when Claire and I ran into him on our way over to the Inn for breakfast the next morning.

"It's okay," I said. "The best part is that I think I'll get to spend more time outdoors."

"Yeah. I wouldn't know about that," Josh said. He was working both as a server in the Inn restaurant and delivering room-service orders. "Although I did get an order yesterday from someone at the beach cabana, so I had to trek down there with a cooler full of beer and soda. It was very tempting to take it down to the beach and shake out a towel and just stay there."

"Except for the losing-your-job part," Claire said.

"Yeah, I started thinking about how much my textbooks are going to cost. And the guest gave me a huge tip when I got there, so it was worth it."

"It's so gorgeous here. I couldn't leave." I spread out my arms. "The view. The ocean. The salt air."

"You're obsessed with salt air," Claire said.

"I know. I tried to bottle it once, to bring home after our vacation, when I was a kid. Didn't work. So instead I keep buying candles that call themselves ocean breeze and they're so not," I said with a laugh.

"You know what you need to do? That semester-at-sea thing. That's made for you," Claire teased.

I laughed. "I totally should do that. I hear it's really expensive, though."

"Maybe you can get a work-study job. You know, on the ship," Claire said.

"Housekeeping," we said in unison, laughing.

"So what's today's gofer assignment?" Josh asked me.

"I have no idea. I have to wait until I get paged, or Miss Crossley finds me in person."

"That sounds like a real drag," he commented.

"Not always," I said, thinking of the afternoon I'd spent on the beach. Some assignments, like washing towels, were going to be chores. Others were not half bad, especially when they involved hanging out near Hayden. I wasn't completely sure how I felt about him, or whether I should even think about things like that, considering Mark and I weren't "officially" over for good, and considering I didn't even really know Hayden all that well yet.

But I did know that I liked spending time with him, and that I didn't mind looking at him.

Is that shallow of me? Well, okay then, I guess there's a shallow part of me. But honestly, it's 25 percent, at most.

No, really. It's the very top layer.

"Down to the Hull," Josh said as we walked in the side entrance of the Inn. We ate in the basement—literally—the employee kitchen and dining area, which was called the Hull. There was a lot of cute ship imagery around the Inn—well, at least some people thought it was cute.

"Otherwise known as servants' quarters," Claire said. "This is how it is in all the old English novels. The maids. In the scullery."

"Scullery? Isn't that on a ship?" I asked.

"And since when am I a maid?" Josh asked. "I'm like way too masculine for that."

"Uh huh." Claire laughed. "I think the scullery is where

they hid the people who did all the actual work," she said.

"Let's call this the Hullery then," I said as we walked into the kitchen.

It seemed as if we were the last people to arrive, which made sense considering breakfast was available from seven to eight, and it was nearly eight. Several other people were already sitting around the big, long tables.

"You know who checked in last night?" Caroline was announcing to the room.

"No, who?"

"C. Q. Wallace." She looked smug.

"And that is . . . ," Josh prompted as we picked up bowls, plates, and silverware.

"The famous author, of course," Caroline said. "His last book was in Oprah's book club and number one on Amazon for like a year."

"Still drawing a blank," Josh said.

Caroline let out a loud, exasperated sigh. "You must live under a rock then."

"You know what? I *do*," Josh said. "I'm not used to all this light, actually. My eyes, my eyes!" He shielded his face from the overhead fluorescents.

"Give me a break." Caroline groaned, as we all laughed.

I caught Hayden's eye across the room and smiled, then started to pour myself a bowl of cereal. The cooks sometimes made up chafing dishes of eggs and other hot breakfast treats, like pancakes or potatoes or French toast, for us, but our standard fare was cereal, toast, and fresh fruit. A continental breakfast, according to Miss Crossley.

"What's continental about this? That's one thing I've never understood," I said to Claire as I poured milk over my Frosted Flakes. "Does that mean European? Because I don't think Frosted Flakes are European."

"They must mean this continent then." Claire dropped a few slices of wheat bread into the toaster, while Josh grabbed an orange and a couple of bananas. I followed them to the end of a table to sit down, which just happened to be where Hayden was sitting.

"So how's it going?" Hayden asked.

"Fine. Except of course for the endless initiation tasks," I said.

The night before, we'd been conned into going out to the store for soda and snacks for the entire dorm, after we'd been told it was part of the deal of being newbies.

"Are there any more we should know about, so we can be prepared this time?" Claire asked.

"There's not really any *formal* initiation. You realize that, right?" Caroline asked. "Those guys were just making fun of you."

Was it me, or could she suddenly take the fun out of anything? When had she turned into such a killjoy? I was surprised Zoe wanted to be her roommate. Zoe seemed like she knew how to have fun. Maybe it was the fact I'd seen her boyfriend come to pick her up at the dorm on a motorcycle the night before. That tended to make a person seem daring and adventurous, even when she wore a helmet.

Caroline, on the other end of the spectrum, probably wouldn't even go near a moped or a scooter. It was strange, because she used to be the one who took risks before I did. How did we both change so much?

"Caroline's right. There's no formal anything around here," Hayden said. "But there are traditions, right?"

"Well, I didn't get tossed into the ocean last year when *I* was new," Caroline said primly.

"Oh. Then we'll have to make up for that. You free around nine tonight?" Hayden asked.

"Don't even think about it," Caroline said.

"Okay, but you realize your Tides Inn resume is going to be incomplete," Richard said.

"Like Harvard will care," she said.

"Ooh. Harvard. Impressed," I said sincerely.

She shrugged as if it was no big deal, but at the same time looked pretty pleased with herself. "My parents went there," she said.

"That's right! I remember," I said.

"What—you guys knew each other before now?" Hayden asked.

"Yeah. We both used to come here on vacation when we were ten, eleven," I said. I'd been here five summers in a row, from when I was ten to fifteen, and Caroline had been here three of those summers. "We had cottage rentals next door to each other," I explained. Which might have been the only reason we started hanging out, come to think of it. Proximity. Throughout history, the great friendship maker.

"We actually hung out all the time," I said, just to let Caroline know I hadn't forgotten, even if she had. I don't know why it mattered so much to me. I guess it's that I can't stand being snobbed by someone I already know. Like when you talk to a guy from school at a party, at length, about all kinds of personal stuff, and then you see him the next day and he's with his friends and acts like it never happened. Like he barely even knows your name. I hate that. When I'd first seen Caroline, in my first panicky moments, I'd had this hope that she might make it easier for me to blend in. Quite the opposite had happened. I was blending in just fine, but it was no thanks to her.

"So you guys go way back. That's very interesting," Hayden said.

"Well, we're not the only people here who know each other from before," Caroline said. "Zoe and Hayden are from the same town, and—"

"Not exactly the same town," Hayden explained. "Neighboring. We went to the same high school, that's all."

"Private day school," Caroline corrected him.

"Huh," I said. "Is that the famous Maple Leaf Academy?" I teased.

"Mapleville," Hayden said.

"Ah. Of course. Very interesting."

"Is it?" Hayden asked.

"Sure." I finished my bowl of cereal and walked over to set it in the sink.

"Did you know?" Hayden asked as he came up behind me.

"About you and Zoe?" I said.

He looked a little confused. "About me and Zoe what?"

"Going to the same private school," I said. "No, I didn't—"

"That's not what I meant." He set a plate and knife into the sink next to my bowl. "I was going to tell you that new people around here do all the dishes. Did anyone tell you yet?"

"Yeah, right," I scoffed.

"No, seriously," he insisted. "You fill up the dish racks over there, then carry them upstairs to the main kitchen—"

"Okay, so when do we get to be *not* the new people anymore?" I asked him. "Is there like a day of amnesty?"

"Yeah, this isn't a fraternity, you know," Claire added. "You can't keep hazing us forever."

"We're not doing anything that bad! Just teasing. Come on, lighten up," Hayden said to me.

"Yeah, well, it's not actually all that funny," I said, trying to keep a straight face. Because I wasn't mad, and I didn't care. They could ask us to do the dishes all they wanted, but it didn't mean we would.

"It's not funny?" Hayden asked, wrinkling his nose.

"No."

"Really."

"Really," I said. "It's getting old. Tired. Kind of sad."

We just looked at each other for a few seconds. His eyes were this deep, dark-blue steel gray, the kind that seem impossible to read.

"Liza. Liza? Liza!"

I think it took three tries before I actually heard my name being called, though it could have been more, because I wasn't paying attention to anything but Hayden for a minute.

Oh no, I thought as I turned around and saw Miss Crossley standing in the doorway. There were a couple of problems here. One, I was feeling this incredible pull toward Hayden, suspiciously like an undertow. I'd have to move from the spot where I was standing or I could be in trouble.

Problem Two, Miss Crossley was here looking for me. That might not be good.

"I was hoping I'd find you," she said. She snapped her fingers in front of my eyes. "But I'm a little concerned. Are you awake yet?"

"Sure—of course," I said.

"Well, you seem a little out of it."

"Just about to have my first cup of coffee. I'll be lively in no time," I promised. "Hyper, even." I shuffled over to the giant coffee urn and poured myself a cup to go. I had a feeling my breakfast was about to be over.

Miss Crossley nodded. "That's more like it. You're not staying up late, getting into trouble, are you?"

Not yet, I thought. "Of course not," I assured her.

"Well. Good morning, everyone." Miss Crossley surveyed the Hullery, nodding to different people.

"Hey, Peach," Hayden said.

"Hayden. You know how I feel about that," Miss Crossley said.

"Sorry, Miss Crossley. I'll knock it off, as requested." Hayden came over beside me and refilled his coffee cup.

"Now, Liza, I've reviewed our staffing for the day and I've figured out exactly where we need you," Miss Crossley said.

Why did I get a feeling of intense dread when she said that? *Please don't say housekeeping. Or laundry. Or something even yuckier.* It didn't help that across the kitchen, Caroline was sitting there with a smug smile on her face, like she couldn't wait to hear where I'd be stuck.

"I hope you packed an ample supply of sunscreen." Miss Crossley smiled at me. "We need you to pull some more beach duty. The tots group will be on the beach this morning, so we need extra hands for supervision. Be dressed and on the beach by nine."

"Okay, sounds great. Thanks!" I said, smiling at her— and at Caroline. If she thought I was suffering under this new arrangement, she was wrong.

"Now," Miss Crossley said. "Caroline, could you follow me back upstairs? I need to go over a few things with you regarding a very special guest."

"Oh, of *course.*" Caroline pushed back her chair.

I happily sipped my coffee. Now I had even more of a reason to be glad Caroline had the front-desk job instead of me. I got to be outside all day, while she had to be watched by Miss Crossley, and deal with "very special"—translation, very demanding—guests.

"The beach, huh? Interesting," Hayden commented. He sipped from his coffee cup. "You're new here, so do you know how to get to the beach?"

I could have swatted him, except that he was smiling at me in that impossible-to-resist way. "I'm pretty sure I know. You just follow the boardwalk, right?" I asked, returning his smile.

"Come on, Liza—let's go," Claire said, tugging at my arm. "I forgot my key and I need to get changed for sailing."

"Here." I started to hand my key to her, but she pushed my hand away.

"You have to get changed anyway," she said.

"Oh. Right. Okay. Well, see you in a while," I said to Hayden.

Claire and I walked up the steps and out the side entrance. "I didn't really forget my key," Claire confessed on our way back to the dorm. "But I had to ask—what's going on with you guys?"

"Who?"

"*Who?* Are you serious?" Claire cried. "You and Hayden, who else? You were oblivious to the world for a few seconds there, when Miss Crossley came in."

"Oh, that? It's nothing. I was just sleepy."

"I don't think it's nothing," Claire said. "I think it's something."

I laughed. "Have you ever seen that segment on David Letterman? 'Is this something, or is this nothing?'"

Claire didn't laugh. She looked so serious, though, that it almost made me crack up again. "Remember what my sister said. Beware of hookups. It could ruin your whole summer. And Hayden doesn't strike me as the kind of guy to just have *one* hookup per summer. That's all I'm saying."

"Don't worry. I'm not planning on getting involved with Hayden," I said.

Then again, who said you had to plan everything in life?

And how well did she know Hayden? Just because he was good-looking and sort of a flirt, that didn't mean he'd play the field. The beach, maybe. But not the field.

"I'm sorry," Claire said as we walked into our room. "I don't mean to tell you what to do."

"No, it's okay—we're friends. I don't mind the advice."

"You sure?"

"Yeah."

"Good. I know I'm ultraconservative about everything. You must think I'm totally boring," Claire said.

"Not at all!" I said. "We're just kind of different, that's all. But it's a good different. You're looking out for me, and I appreciate that." Then I set to deciding which swimsuit I wanted to wear.

When I got to the beach, I found out Chelsea and I would be working together again. We were supposed to have a large group of children, but apparently a few parents had changed their minds and canceled, because we only had three kids to look after. Which was a pretty sweet ratio, if you were a kid—and made it easy for us. They were brothers, ages five, seven, and eight, and assured us they were excellent swimmers.

"We believe you, we do," I said. "But we're going to hang around and swim with you, because we get hot, too, okay?"

"All right," the oldest one groaned.

I pulled off my sweatshirt and helped Chelsea haul out the toys. We set up the kids with an assortment of shovels, buckets, levelers—everything they needed to make the biggest sand castle ever, which they'd told me was their plan.

Chelsea ran back up to the Inn to get some breakfast because she'd overslept. I was standing on the wet sand beside the kids, keeping an eye out but not interfering, when I saw Hayden, out of the corner of my eye, climbing down from his lifeguard stand. This should be good, I thought.

"So. You found the beach," he said as he walked toward me.

"Found it just as I left it. Really sandy," I said.

He looked me up and down, appraising my second swim-suit of the summer. (I'd brought four, which sounds excessive, but isn't, especially when you buy them on sale.) This one was a smallish bikini, with a bright striped pattern.

"Did you bring enough sunscreen? I have some you could borrow," he offered.

"Shouldn't you be keeping your eye on the water?" I commented. "People might be drowning."

"I'm on a break," Hayden said.

"I guess they could be newbies, so let 'em drown, right?" I teased.

"Hey, I never said that. *Hey.*"

"No, but you implied it. But if someone drowns, no problem. The new people will perform CPR," I said.

"You know CPR?" he asked, looking impressed.

"And if there are jellyfish? The newbies will go swimming and get stung," I went on.

"Well, probably, because you won't notice you're

swimming with them until it's too late," Hayden said.

"So we're not just new, we're clueless now." I nodded. "Nice."

"Hey, I don't think that." He took my arm and started to pull me toward the water. "Of course as an *old* person, I'd know better than to stand so close to the water when it's still only sixty degrees, but . . ."

"Don't throw me in. *Don't!*" I cried, struggling to hold my ground. I dug my heels into the sand.

"Why not?" he said. "Give me one good reason—"

"Because I'll throw *you* in," I said. "And how would it look for the lifeguard to—hey!"

He'd grabbed my ankle and was about to lift me over his head.

"Quit it!" I said, dancing away from him.

You know how some people have chemistry? That was us. In like triplicate. To the nth degree.

I checked on the kids to make sure they were still okay—which they were. While I was talking to them, Hayden picked me up from behind.

"No fair!" I cried, pounding on his back with my fists as he spun around, twirling me with him. "Do not throw me in. Do you hear me? I'll come after you at night when you least expect it and—"

Over Hayden's shoulder I noticed Caroline had come to the end of the boardwalk, but she hadn't progressed any farther. Her sunglasses were lowered on the bridge of her nose as if she needed to get a better look at something. Or someone. Us?

What was she doing away from the reception desk, anyway? She never strayed from there—she considered herself too important to be replaced.

"And what?" Hayden asked. "Keep going."

"I think someone wants to borrow your binoculars," I said to Hayden. "Put me down, okay? This time I really mean it."

"What?" Hayden asked.

I went to point out where Caroline was standing, but she wasn't there anymore.

"Likely story. Caroline was out here?" Hayden scoffed. "I'm sure."

"She *was*," I insisted. "And here's proof." I pointed to the boardwalk, where Miss Crossley was now making an appearance. It was like a runway in a bad fashion show.

Except Miss Crossley wasn't turning back. She marched across the sand toward me, still in her shoes, a pair of shiny brown penny loafers, which she wore with plaid Bermuda shorts and a white oxford cloth shirt.

"Liza, are you paying attention to the children?" she asked.

"Of course I am," I said. I turned around to get Hayden to vouch for me, but he was already gone, disappeared up the steps to his lifeguard post. So much for backup.

"Where is Chelsea?" Miss Crossley demanded.

"She'll be right back. Honestly, Miss Crossley. I was watching three kids build a sand castle, at low tide. I've never let them out of my sight. Right, guys?"

The kids were too busy digging to respond.

I looked back at Miss Crossley and shrugged. "You know kids, they never—"

"Is that a pierced belly button?" she asked.

Wasn't it obvious? I could lie, and say I'd fallen on a staple or something, but what would be the point? "Yes?" I said tentatively.

"Hm. That's against dress code policy, Liza. No untraditional piercings."

I shook my head. "I'm sorry, Miss Crossley, but I never *got* all the stuff about dress code policy. I didn't know."

"Now you do. I'll be happy to give you any handouts you're missing. But Liza. Doesn't common *sense* tell you not to pierce your belly button?"

"I guess not," I said. "At least, not . . . *my* common sense," I murmured.

"You'll either need to cover it up or remove it," she said.

"I'll take it out," I promised.

"Good. And Liza? I'm watching you." She made this weird hand motion from her eyes to me, and back again, repeating it a few times. Not only was she sort of a taskmaster, she was nerdy, too.

No, Caroline's watching me, I thought as I crouched down to help the kids build their castle. *And I don't know why, but I'll find out.*

CHAPTER 6

"Kind of slow at the front desk this morning?" I asked Caroline once I made it up to the Inn on my lunch break. Brittany had come down to the beach to relieve first Chelsea, then me.

Caroline looked up from the women's magazine she'd been reading at her desk. "What's that?" She was wearing the Inn uniform all of us had—polo shirt, khaki shorts—but she had a fancy silk scarf tied around her neck, to dress it up, I guess.

"Oh, I just thought I saw you on the beach a while ago," I said. "Which was sort of odd, considering that your job is in here."

She flipped a page of the magazine with her nicely

manicured nails. "I was checking the tide. People kept asking me what the surf was like, if there were any good waves."

"Huh. Really," I commented.

"Yes," she said. "The phone was ringing off the hook with people asking."

"Really," I said again.

"You know, you should be wearing shorts and a T-shirt," she said. "Inn policy. No one's allowed in the lobby looking like that, least of all staff."

"It's a bikini top and a skirt. I'll get dressed in a sec," I promised, adjusting the big white beach towel tied around my waist, which at least covered my frowned-upon belly button ring. "This is an Inn towel, so doesn't that count for something?"

"You're in a bikini, so no, and it's not a skirt," she said. "In fact, if you wouldn't mind stepping away from the desk? I don't want a guest walking in to be offended."

I stared at her. "There's something offensive about me now?"

"No! Of course not. I just meant—you know, not everyone's comfortable around people who aren't dressed. That's all," she said.

"Uh huh." I wasn't buying it. I believe in being the tiniest bit blunt, when someone won't 'fess up. "Caroline, what gives?" I asked her.

"What are you talking about?"

"What do you have against me?" I asked.

"What? Nothing." She kept flipping through her magazine, not making eye contact with me.

"I mean, I haven't seen you in a long time. Did I do something to offend you, the last time we hung out? I hope you're not holding a grudge over something I did way back when," I said.

"Of course I'm not," she said. "I wouldn't be that petty."

I raised my eyebrows. *Really,* I thought. *Are you sure?*

She laughed. "Look, is this because I took the front-desk job away from you?"

"That's a whole separate issue, actually," I said. "But no. I'm glad I have my job, even if I don't know what it's going to be from day to day."

"I'd hate that," Caroline said.

Of course you would, I thought. *You're too inflexible to move around from place to place.*

Caroline also struck me as the kind of person who couldn't stand to get her hands dirty. She'd never want to build sand castles and jump over waves with the little kids. And she'd for sure never want to have to clean someone else's room.

Not that I wanted to do that, either.

"So why were you out on the beach a while ago as if you were spying on me? And why did Miss Crossley—who, from what I can tell, practically never leaves the building—come running out as soon as you went back inside?" I asked. "What did you tell her?"

"Nothing. She was on her way out when I was on my way in," Caroline said.

I thought about that for a second. It could be true, I supposed, but it was quite a coincidence. I decided I'd wasted enough of my lunch hour on this, and I was about to step away from the desk when she said, "Liza? It's just—you should know. Hayden and Zoe? They dated last summer. Like, very seriously."

"Oh." This was kind of big news to me, but kind of not. I'd seen the way Hayden and Zoe acted around each other, sort of awkward and maybe a little annoyed. Which I could see was the way exes acted, now that I knew about it. I briefly wondered who broke up with whom, and when. No doubt Caroline was dying to tell me, but I wouldn't give her the satisfaction of asking. Anyway, I could get the information straight from Hayden, if I really wanted to know. And I wasn't sure I did.

Caroline was watching me for some sort of stunned, or pained, reaction.

Instead I just shrugged. "Well, okay. What about that? I mean, why tell me?"

"I just thought you'd want to know. They were really close."

"Okay," I said.

"Really close," she repeated.

I figured she was trying to say, in her Caroline way, that they'd slept together. "I don't see how it really matters, but okay, now I know." I shrugged. "What other news you got?"

"What do you mean?" Caroline asked.

I leaned forward on the desk. "Tell me about Miss Crossley. Who did she date last summer?"

Caroline glared at me. "Ha ha. You think you're so funny."

"Come on, if you're spilling gossip, tell me everything. In fact, who did *you* date last summer? If I don't have the background on every single person here, I won't feel comfortable," I said. "I mean, this is the kind of stuff I was looking for that night at the bonfire. The dirt on everyone. But no one said anything."

The phone rang and Caroline grabbed it on the first ring, no doubt to avoid my question. "Thank you for calling the Tides Inn, my name is Caroline, how may I assist you?" she said in a sugary-sweet tone.

She had the perfect phony voice to be answering the phone. I would never have been able to match that, so she probably did deserve the front-desk job over me.

What was Caroline so worried about? Zoe was seeing

Brandon-with-a-motorcycle now, so it wasn't as if Caroline had to look out for her best friend's interests.

Does *Caroline* have a crush on Hayden? I wondered. Is that why she's being so rude to me, and why she wants me to stay away from him? Is that why she's spying on us?

If that were true, maybe she felt like she deserved him, since she'd known him longer.

Still, I couldn't picture her and Hayden together. He seemed too loud and adventurous and fun, and she seemed too rigid and, well, unfun.

But if she truly liked him, I could let her have him. I could wait until she got off the phone, and tell her not to worry, that Hayden was all hers and I'd keep my distance.

Except I didn't want to do that. So I walked out of the lobby onto the back porch, stretched my arms over my head, and took a deep, satisfying breath of the fresh salty air. I couldn't wait to get back onto the beach.

"Do you have to look so happy?"

I turned and saw a man sitting in one of the wicker chairs, near the edge of the porch. He had his feet up on the railing and a computer on his lap. He looked like he was in his forties, with slightly graying black hair, longish sideburns, and wore a loose linen shirt and jeans.

"I'm sorry?" I asked.

"You look too unbearably happy. And must you breathe so loudly? You even *breathe* happily," he commented.

"I just really enjoy the way the air smells here." Or, at least I *did*, I thought as I fanned the cigarette smoke away from my face. "What are those, clove cigarettes?" I asked.

"No, they're Turkish."

"Mm." Cool-sounding, but still cancer-causing, I was guessing.

I remembered Miss Crossley's instructions on our first day. *You don't have to smoke with the guests, but you do have to offer them a light.* Fortunately, this guy didn't need one.

"It's impossible to concentrate around here, with so much coming and going," he said. "And nobody told me this place would be full of children."

I was going to point out that he shouldn't sit on the entrance facing the beach, where everyone had to walk past, if he wanted privacy. But that seemed obvious—not to mention a little obnoxious. "I don't know, it's still kind of early in the season. I don't think there are *that* many kids. What are you trying to concentrate on?" I asked.

"Writing," he said.

"Oh. Oh!" I hadn't recognized him at first, but of course— it was the writer Caroline had mentioned at breakfast.

"And it's only June, and this is the sixth place I've stayed already this summer, and I haven't been able to write a word at any of them. Though that's not your fault. I mean, it is, but it isn't."

I laughed. "How is it my fault—like, at all?"

"It isn't. I was just grasping at straws. Speaking of straws, here we are now." He nodded at Daunte, who was carrying a tray toward us.

Daunte smiled at me on his way past, then set a tall glass on the table and had the guest sign the bill before heading back inside.

He grimaced as he drank it. "Horrible, awful stuff."

"What is it exactly?" I asked.

"Quintuple espresso, on ice, with a splash of grenadine and a lemon wedge."

The description alone was enough to turn my stomach. "And it's bad?" I asked. "Should I get you another one? Here—let me do that. I'll run to the kitchen," I offered.

"No, it's not the way it's made. I mean, it's supposed to taste ghastly. And it does, so I can't complain to the bartender."

"Barista," I said.

"Whatever," he said. "As long as it works, I don't care." He took another gulp and made a face. "Something has to work. Or else I'll have to pack, again, and move to yet another hotel for inspiration."

"How would moving help? I mean, how do you know this *isn't* the right place to write your next book? It could be the perfect spot, if you just give it a chance."

"Your optimism is tedious. But I'll take it." He looked over at me. "What's your name?"

"Liza."

He reached over to shake my hand. "C. Q. Wallace."

I wanted to ask what the C. Q. stood for, but I decided that would be rude. If a person chose to go by his initials, there must be a reason—probably that he didn't like his name. Anyway, I could get the information out of Caroline later. If she was still speaking to me.

"You work here?" he asked.

"No, I just offered to run to the kitchen for you because I'm such an optimist," I said.

He laughed and lifted his coffee cup. "Touché."

CHAPTER 7

That night I ran up to the shuttle van
just as Hayden was pulling away from the Inn. The van was
always parked right out front, on the circular drive, and I'd
caught him just before he left. I was panting and out of breath
as I knocked on the window to get his attention.

Hayden lowered the window and stared at me. "What are
you doing here?"

I waved my pager in the air, because I was temporarily
unable to speak.

He leaned out the window. "You need a new pager?" he
asked.

I shook my head. "Town. Have to . . . go to . . . town."

"Okay . . . Well, don't die on me. Get in."

I walked around and climbed up into the front seat of the van. Then I slicked my wet hair back from my face.

"Were you summoned out of the ocean?" Hayden asked.

I laughed. "Almost. I had just gotten out of the shower when Miss Crossley paged me."

"And what did she want? Did she say I needed company? An assistant, maybe, to carry all the luggage? 'Cause that would be nice."

"No!" I laughed. "I called and she said to come to her office, so I did and then she hands me this pen. And tells me I have to go to town with you and find more pens like this. And she tells me I have like thirty seconds before you leave for the train station. I tried to tell her I had a car here and I could drive, but she said this was official Inn business, so I should take the official Inn van—"

"No problem. There's a small office supply store near the train station," Hayden said.

"Oh. Okay," I panted. "Then it doesn't completely not make sense. You could have gone there, though, couldn't you? I mean, why didn't she ask you to just run in and get the pens?" I asked.

"I see. Trying to get out of work already." Hayden nodded. "You've only been a gofer for a couple days and you're already trying *not* to go for stuff?"

"No!" I said. Then I laughed. I seemed to do that a lot around him. Was he that funny, or was I that nervous? "Well, maybe."

"No, I know what it is. Miss C. probably didn't want me to leave the van, in case the train comes and nobody's there to meet the guests. Although that's completely ridiculous, because the train is almost never early. In fact, it's usually late by a few minutes." He pulled out onto the main road into town. I was busy combing my hair and squeezing the ends to wring out some of the extra water.

"Do you need a towel?" Hayden asked.

"No, that's okay. I can just dry my hair this way." I opened the window and let the warm evening air rush over me. The day had been one of the warmest yet, which was why I'd needed an extra swim, which was why I'd needed an extra shower. I'd even postponed dinner, preferring instead to spend the time in the water bodysurfing. Of course, now it was looking like I wouldn't eat at all, given that it was about a half hour trip to the train station, and by the time we got back it would be close to nine. But I could always sneak into the Hull and grab a bowl of cereal, at least.

"So. Pens," Hayden said. "Miss Crossley had a sudden urgent need for pens."

I shrugged. "I guess."

"Uh huh. She doesn't strike me as the kind of person who ever runs out of things," Hayden commented. "You know what I mean?"

What was he getting at? "What, you think I made this up? I didn't!" I said. "If I wanted to go with you, I would have just asked."

"Really."

"Really," I said. "Anyway, like I said, I have a car here. Last time I tried to start it, though, it wouldn't start. But let's say I did want to go to town. I'd drive that," I said.

"If it started," he said.

"Right." It was difficult to be indignant when you drove an old, slightly dented, slightly-to-very-unreliable car. And your hair was wet, and your hair made the back of your shirt wet, and you had thrown on jeans that were clinging to you because the night was so hot. And they weren't even your favorite jeans to begin with.

"So how many guests are we picking up?" I asked.

Hayden grabbed a slip of paper on the dashboard of the van. "Lyle, party of four."

"How does this work? Do they pay you? Do they tip you?" I asked.

"Tips are welcome and appreciated," Hayden said in a monotone voice.

I laughed.

"That's what it says in every other shuttle van or bus I've ever been in, but not this one," Hayden said. "But people seem to know, anyway. I carry their luggage, I tell them whatever they want to know about the Inn, the area, my college plans."

"You're like a tour guide," I said.

"Kind of. I guess," he said.

"You're the first impression they get of the Inn." I checked out his official Tides Inn polo shirt, khaki shorts, and Tides Inn ball cap. "You're dressed for the part. Shoot. I probably should be, too."

"No, that's okay. I'll just tell them you're some random girl I picked up on the way," Hayden said.

"Oh, thanks." I laughed. "That's how I dream of being known."

"And you obviously got caught in the rain. Not that there's been any rain," he said.

"Tell them you saw me swimming to town—no, drowning in the ocean—and you pulled over to offer me a ride."

"Good. That's good." He nodded. "Okay, so we've got our story straight."

"I'm surprised Miss C. didn't tell me I should be better dressed. She was a little frantic," I said. "Like, really stressed about these pens."

"Whenever she gets like that, it's usually because of a guest. So maybe those pens aren't for her, maybe they're for someone staying at the Inn," Hayden suggested.

I looked at the pen, twirling it back and forth in my palm. "You know what? You're right. I bet these are for that famous writer, C. Q. Wallace. You know, the guy Caroline mentioned? I actually met him and talked to him this afternoon."

"What's he like?" Hayden asked.

"What's that word that means someone's kind of rude . . . but funny? You know, someone who sits around and complains about everything," I said.

"What was he complaining about?"

"Writer's block."

"Wait a second. Didn't he have some huge best-selling book? Isn't that what Caroline said?"

"I guess. I don't know. Is there a bookstore in town where we could check out his books?"

"There is, but I doubt we'll have time tonight," Hayden said. "What with the emergency pens and all. Maybe another expedition, another night." He glanced over at me as he stopped at a red light.

What was he implying? Was he asking me out—sort of? I wondered. "Sure," I said slowly.

And then he just sat there and stared at me for a few

seconds, without saying anything. As if there was something about my face he was trying to memorize, in case he had to describe me or pick me out of a police lineup. I could feel this heat on my face, and it had nothing to do with the warm evening.

"Um, I think you can go now," I said, gesturing to the stoplight. "The light's green."

"Yeah, of course." Hayden coughed and turned his attention back to driving.

"Told you the train would be late."

I walked out of the small office supply store to find Hayden standing on the sidewalk, waiting for me, clutching an ice cream cone in each hand.

"Curmudgeon," I said.

"What?" Hayden laughed. "What did you just call me?"

"Not you. The guy who needs these pens." I held up the small brown bag that contained a dozen of the special pens. "I just thought of the word I was trying to think of before to describe him," I explained.

"Curmudgeon. Okay." Hayden held out one of the ice cream cones to me. "You like chocolate? Everyone likes chocolate, right? Which is what I was thinking. See, I was going to get a vanilla and a chocolate, to give you a choice, but then, if you chose chocolate, I'd be stuck with vanilla, which would suck."

"Always thinking of others, aren't you?" I asked.

"Hey, I can eat both of them," Hayden offered.

"What? No way." I took the waffle cone from him. "I'm starving—thanks. How did you know I missed dinner?"

"I didn't," Hayden said. "Anyway, it's not like you can't have dinner and ice cream."

"How much do I owe you?" I asked.

Hayden shook his head. "No problem."

"No, seriously," I said, taking a few dollars out of my pocket.

"Don't even." He pushed my hand away. "Save it for your next trip to the coffee shop."

"Okay. It's a deal. I'll treat next time we both happen to be there at the same time," I offered.

"We could always go together. To make things easier," Hayden pointed out.

He was doing that thing again, where it seemed like he might be asking me out, but I wasn't sure.

"Hm. Yeah, I guess we could. If we ever get the same break schedule again." That was seeming a little doubtful, since I wasn't going to know my breaks ahead of time. Of course, I could ask Hayden for his cell number, so I could call him whenever I did have time to meet at the coffee shop, but that seemed a little aggressive.

But I did have some questions I wanted to ask him. Since we were hanging out on a bench at the train station, eating our ice cream, now seemed as good a time as any.

"So, you and Zoe," I said. "You guys went out?"

"How'd you find out about that?" he asked.

"Caroline."

"Ah. And she told you because . . ."

I shrugged. "I have no idea. I didn't ask, if that's what you're implying."

"I wasn't."

"Okay, good. Well, she's quite the gossip, then."

"Yeah, and that's exactly why I was pissed when she got that front-desk job instead of you."

"You were?"

"She'll try to keep tabs on everyone, and she'll turn everything into a story that she just can't wait to tell everyone else. She's one of those . . . I don't know. My mom would call her a busybody."

"So. There's no story?" I asked.

"Sure, there's a story, but it's pretty short. We dated," Hayden said. "It was weird, because back home, we go to the same school—"

"The vaunted Maple Syrup Academy," I interjected.

"Maple*ville*. And we never even talked much there. Anyway, we went out for a while here, then it started to kind of be not that much fun anymore."

"Don't you hate it when that happens?"

"It happened to you?" Hayden asked.

"Sure. Once or twice, anyway," I said.

"So, are you—you know—seeing anyone right now? You have a boyfriend stashed at home?"

"Stashed? Like, where. Under the bed?" I joked. Then I realized that was kind of an unfortunate, misleading choice of words. "Not quite." I could tell him about Mark, but I wasn't sure I needed to, at least not yet. Anyway, we were on an official break, so Mark wasn't technically my boyfriend right now. He was my boyfriend-in-limbo.

"How about you?" I asked, turning the question back on Hayden.

"I don't have any boyfriends at home, if that's what you're asking," he said.

"I wasn't." Though I guess I could have, if I didn't know about him and Zoe.

"No girlfriends, either." He tossed the napkin into the trashcan.

Okay, so we'd established that we both were available.

Now what? Some people weren't seeing anyone, but that didn't necessarily mean they were available. Hayden could have sworn off dating, or he could be waiting for the perfect girl, or waiting until he got to college to have another girl-friend, or something like that. Because why start something now, when it was bound to implode in September? Then again, why not start something now—knowing it would be short-term?

Wow. There were two ways to approach this thing with Hayden. If it *was* a thing. If it had potential, the way I thought it did. The way he looked at me sometimes, I was pretty sure he felt the same way, that this could turn into something if we decided to go for it.

Lighten up, Liza, I thought to myself as I heard the train approaching from a distance. The guy bought you an ice cream cone. Nobody's saying this is destiny. It's about pens. I sort of wanted to ask him if he wanted to go to the beach later, when we got back to the Inn, but I thought it would be smartest to wait awhile and see where I stood with him before I got in any deeper.

That love undertow could pull you in and drag you out to sea if you weren't careful.

"If you could take the train anywhere, where would you go?" Hayden asked as we both walked up toward the opening doors, looking for the shuttle passengers. Hayden pulled a TIDES INN sign out of his back pocket and held it up, smiling at everyone who was disembarking.

"The train. Does that mean London's out?" I asked.

"Most definitely. Think a little closer to home." Hayden waved to one of the conductors. "Hey, how's it going?"

"Then somewhere west. How about Montana?" I said.

"You guys go to Montana?" Hayden called to the conductor.

CHAPTER 8

"Would you like that toasted?"

"Yes, with a smidgen of butter, and do you have any jam?"

"Packets right there, ma'am." I smiled as I dropped an English muffin into the toaster.

Miss Crossley hadn't even bothered to page me. She'd personally walked over to the dorm, pounded on my door to wake me up, then told me to be at the Inn by seven a.m. to work in the restaurant minicafé—more like a kiosk—for breakfast, because Julia had called in sick.

Never mind that I didn't know how to make decent coffee—Zoe was doing that. No, I was in charge of serving up muffins, bagels, and Danishes, and manning the cash register. Considering how much the guests paid to stay at the

Inn, I would have thought all their food was on the house, but apparently not. They were all too willing to fork over five dollars for a muffin and a cup of coffee. Then again, if they had enough money to stay at the Inn? Money probably wasn't an issue for them. And five dollars wasn't going to break them, the way it might break me, in the last few days before our first paychecks.

The little café was located on the left-hand side of the Inn, the opposite end from the restaurant. It was sort of out of the way, but I kept looking around, wondering if I'd catch a glimpse of Claire, who said she'd come visit me—before she rolled over and went back to sleep, that is—or Josh, or maybe Hayden.

Then again, if Hayden knew Zoe worked here, would he come by? Were they at the stage of avoiding each other, or was that long past?

"Do you usually work here?" I asked Zoe between customers. "I thought you worked in the restaurant."

"I do both," she said. "Three days a week I'm there, three days I'm here. Usually. Sometimes it's more time here and less there, or whatever."

"You don't make as much here, right? No tips," I commented.

"That's true, but you get a higher hourly wage, so it works out," she said.

"Oh, right, of course," I said as if I knew that already. But I hadn't thought about it. That made me wonder: What would my hourly wage be, since I worked at a different job nearly every hour? Did I get paid for doing things like running out on emergency pen errands? Or was that just considered fun?

I didn't need to be paid to hang out with Hayden, I could tell Miss Crossley. But if she wanted to do that, then fine by me. Depending on how I looked at it, either the money, or Hayden, was a bonus.

I thought about the way he'd looked at me a couple of times the night before, like when we were stopped in traffic, and how he was waiting for me outside the store, ice cream cone in hand.

"Excuse me, Miss."

I came back to the present and noticed a man was waving his hand in front of my face.

"Oh. Sorry, sir. What can we get you?" I asked him with a friendly smile.

He ordered a coffee and a bagel, which I got right to toasting.

"Space much?" Zoe asked me as she started preparing his

café latte. "Were you out late last night?"

"No," I said, but I felt an embarrassed blush on my cheeks. Being caught daydreaming about someone's ex-boyfriend, while she's standing right there . . . that's a little tacky, no?

"Well, I was," Zoe said under her breath. "Great party, over at a friend of Brandon's beach house."

"No kidding? Hey, how long have you guys been together?" I asked. If I could find that out, maybe I'd learn how long she and Hayden had been apart. I didn't know how that would help me, so maybe I was just being nosy.

"Oh, uh, since the end of last summer, I guess. And then sort of off and on, you know, because he lives here, and I don't. I was gone during the school year."

"Hey, guys." Josh walked up to the kiosk and leaned on the counter. "Some guy just called room service and ordered a quintuple iced espresso. Could you make that for me?" he asked.

"Sure," Zoe said. "No problem."

"I've never even *heard* of that many espresso shots. He wants me to bring fresh lemon wedges, too. And he wants it delivered to his room as soon as possible, as if that's new, I mean, who doesn't want things right away when they call room service. And he was completely grumpy about it, like I should know what he wanted before he even said it, and I should know who he is without him telling me."

I smiled. "I think I know who that is."

"Yeah. Me too. Room three-oh-one." Zoe took the order from Josh and started to make the drink. "He ordered the same thing yesterday."

"C. Q. Wallace," I said. "The writer."

Josh didn't look enthused.

"I hear he tips really well," Zoe added.

"And he's a writer?" Josh asked, sounding skeptical.

"A best-selling one, according to Caroline," I said. "She's supposedly read all his books." I caught myself before I said anything really nasty about Caroline; after all, I was working with her roommate today. "Anyway, he mentioned yesterday that he's having trouble with his newest book. Writer's block or something like that."

"Tell him I hope this works," Zoe said as she placed the iced drink on Josh's tray.

We were busy for the next five minutes, and then Josh reappeared.

"You won't believe this. He asked if I knew who someone named Eliza was," Josh said. "I told him this wasn't *My Fair Lady*, and your name wasn't Eliza, it was Liza, and yeah, I knew you." He took an envelope off his tray and handed it to me.

I unsealed the envelope, which was Tides Inn stationery, and pulled out a folded beige sheet of paper. When I opened it, a twenty-dollar bill fell out.

"You know, I'm the one who made his coffee," Zoe joked.

Thanks for the pens.
Now what am I going to use them for?
Well, there's always the crossword.
Uninspiringly and gratefully yours,
C.Q.W.

"Twenty bucks. Cool." I explained about the errand I'd gone on the evening before.

Zoe had been reading the note over my shoulder. "Just for buying some pens?"

"They weren't just pens. They're very special pens."

"What did you do, drive to Providence for him?" Zoe asked.

"No, I—" But I didn't get a chance to tell her, because suddenly there was a line. It was probably just as well, I decided as I reached into the pastry case. No point telling her about me and Hayden—since there *was* no "me and Hayden." Not yet, anyway.

* * *

"Hayden! You're not going to believe this." I started to climb up the lifeguard tower, but halfway up, I stopped.

Hayden was looking at me as if he didn't recognize me, so I paused for a second. Were his sunglasses too dark or something? Was he watching swimmers?

"Hayden?" I said.

"Yeah," he said in a monotone. He seemed embarrassed to be seen talking to me. He kept looking over my shoulder at something, or someone.

I looked down at my outfit and laughed. "Okay, so probably I could take off the apron now. I had to play coffee-shop girl this morning. Well, not coffee shop exactly, more like coffee kiosk."

"Right." Hayden didn't find me all that amusing, apparently. Was he in a bad mood, or what?

"Hey, is everything okay?" I asked.

"Sure." He shrugged.

"Really?"

"Yeah."

I didn't exactly believe him, but I didn't want to press the issue, either. If he wanted to talk, he would. "Okay, well, you're still not going to believe this. We've been rewarded." I held up the twenty-dollar bill. "And all for a dozen pens. I thought maybe we could split the reward and go for coffee at Sally's later. I owe you."

"What? No, you don't," he said.

"Yes, for the ice cream, remember?"

He might be remembering it, but he wasn't admitting it. "I can't really talk right now. I've got to watch the water."

"Right. Okay, I'll see you later."

That was weird. He hadn't asked where I was working that afternoon or whether I'd be coming to the beach. He hadn't actually seemed to care whether I even existed.

I didn't expect him to do cartwheels over a twenty-dollar tip, but as far as I was concerned, it was pretty cool. I thought we sort of bonded the night before—at least as friends, if nothing else. Now he was acting about as warm as, say, the ocean in February.

I threw my blue apron over my shoulder and headed down the beach on a walk. Sometimes you just couldn't figure out guys no matter how hard you tried.

"I can't believe you get to do this every day," I said. I gazed around the harbor at the various sailboats that were moored and a few bigger boats that were heading out to sea. There was a large saltwater pond, where Claire and I were sailing in one of the small Sunfish-type boats the Inn used with the kids.

"Sure, but it's not always fun," Claire said. "Remember that. I usually have a boat full of eight-year-olds who don't really know what they're doing, but they insist on doing everything."

"How many times have you tipped over?"

"None, so far. But that's only because I watch them so carefully. If I ever lose my concentration, forget about it. We'll be swimming. So what did you do this morning?"

I told her about working at the breakfast place, the tip from C. Q., and the conversation I'd had—or hadn't had—with Hayden earlier.

"The guy thinks he owns the Inn. Forget him," Claire said. "I mean, if you want to ruin your summer, then okay, go after him."

"I wasn't going after him," I said. "Really. I just—I don't get it when people act one way in public and another in private."

"It's called being two-faced. Come on. He can't be the first person you've met like that," she said.

"I don't know. Maybe he is," I said.

"You're lucky then. I can think of a dozen people in my homeroom like that."

I laughed. "Seriously?"

"Oh yeah. They'd be really sweet to you, if they needed

something. If not . . . well, forget it."

"Yeah, I guess I know people like that."

"So then the question is, what does Hayden need from you?"

"Other than my hot body and sparkling wit?" I joked. "Hm, let's think."

"I think he has to make out with all the new girls," Claire said.

"What?" I laughed for a second, but then stopped. It seemed kind of horribly possible. "Has he made a move on you?" I asked Claire.

"No, he's obviously starting with the easy conquests, like you, then working up to the more difficult ones, like me—"

"You are so about to go over for the first time," I threatened, laughing.

"You don't even know how to sail—"

"No, but I do know you need this!" I was about to take out the centerboard when my phone rang. I pulled my phone out of my shorts pocket, thinking that I probably shouldn't have brought my phone out on the sailboat. If we tipped over, good-bye phone.

"If that's Miss Crossley, tell her you're horribly busy," Claire said. "Tell her you're drowning."

"No, it's not her—she always uses the pager. I don't know

who it is," I said, flipping open my phone. "Hello?"

"Hey, Lize. Where are you?"

"Josh? No. Hayden?" I said. "That you?" It's always weird when someone calls you for the first time and you don't recognize their phone voice.

Claire looked up from the rudder she'd been adjusting.

"Yeah, it's me," Hayden said.

"How did you get this number?" I asked.

"What, is it off-limits? I got it from the employee list. Anyway, I was thinking maybe we could meet up and go for a bike ride later," Hayden said.

"A bike ride. On the handlebars again?" I smiled at the memory of Hayden and I tottering along the oceanside road, hurrying back to the Inn.

"Well, yeah, that'd be fun. But I don't know if we could go more than a mile without crashing," Hayden said.

"True," I agreed. "Good point."

"No, I have a bike for you, from the shed."

"So a bike ride." I glanced over at Claire and mouthed, *What should I do?*

She didn't say anything, but she didn't have to. I knew what she was thinking: Go slowly. Be careful. Don't do something stupid.

"Well, I'm kind of busy. Right now. Actually," I said,

"Claire and I are sailing. More like she's sailing, and I'm learning."

"I was talking about later this afternoon," he said. "Maybe after dinner—that'd be cool, right? We'd have more time, we could take off for a while."

"Oh. Well, I think I'm going to be busy then, too," I said.

"Really."

"Yeah. You won't believe what Miss Crossley has me doing." *Think fast, Liza. Think of some outlandish errand you're going to be on.*

"What?"

"It's for that writer. I have to, uh, do a bunch of errands for him. He wants to experience the authentic coastal . . . experience, so I'm actually driving him around the area, showing him the local hot spots. I guess he wants to experience the ultimate local seafood takeout or something."

"So where are you taking him?" Hayden asked.

"Uh, I'm not sure yet. But we're leaving around six. Maybe tomorrow—oops—sorry, the boat is tipping—whoa! Gotta go!" I hung up the phone after knocking it against the deck a few times, for maximum effect.

Claire was smiling at me when I looked at her. "Wow. That was some good improv. Your story kind of sucked, but I doubt he'll figure it out. Unless he checks the parking lot for your car . . ."

"So you and I will go for takeout," I said. "Big deal."

"Hey, great idea! No more scullery meals for us."

It felt kind of good, actually. If Hayden could blow me off, like he did earlier, then I could return the favor.

Maybe it only meant I was playing games with him, that I was playing hard to get.

But *shouldn't* I be hard to get?

Shouldn't everybody?

CHAPTER 9

Be careful what you wish for. It just might come true.

Those words kept echoing in my head. The night before, I'd tried to come up with some ridiculous task for Miss Crossley to send me on, and I'd invented a story.

Then she came up with something more heinous and involved than I ever could have imagined. I was stuck in her office, catching up on months of filing.

Filing. On one of the nicest days of the entire summer.

I'd started the night before and so far, had been working all morning on it. I couldn't imagine Miss Crossley, as organized as she was, getting this far behind on anything in her life. She tried to tell me it wasn't her fault, that the files actually belonged to the Talbots, but I wasn't sure I believed her. She could be one of those people who seems really put together . . . and then you ride in their car, and there's junk everywhere, like change on the floor, and old fast-food bags, and random notebook pages, and dried-up shriveled French fries.

Anyway, let's just say that *someone* hadn't kept up with the files over the winter. Or the summer before that. Or the entire decade before that.

I'd been crouched on the floor for a long time, so I stood up to stretch my arms over my head. Then I went to the window behind Miss Crossley's desk and looked out at the ocean.

There must have been a storm out at sea the night before—it had rained buckets here onshore—because the waves rolling in looked bigger than usual. I wondered if the swimming was dangerous—or just fun. I loved bodysurfing on days with big surf. Maybe Hayden had his hands full today. But I didn't want to think about him, necessarily. If I started to think of him that way, as someone I was interested in, I would end up ruining my summer. He obviously had some kind of issue, or at least he did yesterday at the beach. Maybe he was only moody, I thought. Of all the times he'd talked with me, he'd only been rude that one time. So maybe he deserved the chance to explain himself before I wrote him off completely.

"Excuse me, but what are you doing here?"

I turned from the window and saw Mr. "Uptight" Knight, my one-day housekeeping supervisor, standing in the doorway.

"I'm organizing and cleaning the office," I said.

Mr. Knight raised his eyebrows. "You are? *You?*"

"I'm very organized," I said.

"Yes, well, as long as there aren't any belts to be filed, I suppose you'll do a fine job."

Boy. You ruin someone's belt and some people never forgive you. It wasn't even *that* nice of a belt, even if it was designer, and even if it cost two hundred dollars, like the guest claimed. Personally I think he was just looking to make some easy money.

"Miss Crossley does know you're doing this, doesn't she?" he asked.

Was he joking? "Do you think I'm doing this on my own? For fun?" I replied.

"No, I'm just surprised." He straightened his tie. "She could have asked someone on my team."

I decided I should try to get on Mr. Knight's good side. Maybe he was on the outs, the least-favorite cousin, but he was still in the Talbot family. "Yes, but your, ah, clean team members are all busy doing something more important," I said. "Keeping the guests happy. This is a lower priority."

"And that's where you come in," Mr. Knight said.

"Uh . . . yes." Did he have to make me sound so awful? "I'm the Inn gofer. Like a temp. Wherever they need me, that's where I am. So this type of thing is the perfect project for me. Besides, I've been an office manager before."

"You have?"

I nodded as I slid some red hanging files into the cabinet. I didn't tell him that the office I supposedly managed was my mother's home office. And that I'd done it under duress, because I owed her some money, and that was the solution she came up with for me to pay it back. "Sure, I've been an office manager. I've done lots of this kind of stuff before—typing, filing, answering the phone—"

"Everything but vacuuming," Mr. Knight said.

"Yes, that's my motto, actually," I joked.

He looked at me as though I'd crossed some invisible line of good taste. Still too soon to joke about the demise of the Hulk, I guessed.

Freedom! Sun! Outdoors!

I didn't yell it out loud, but I could have as I ran back to the dorm to change into my swimsuit. Miss Crossley had told me I'd be free for a couple of hours, unless something she didn't anticipate came up. Which it probably would, so I was rushing—she had to give me a half hour anyway, because I was pretty sure that was the law. I left my pager on my dresser and then I practically sprinted from the dorm down to the beach.

I saw Hayden sitting atop his lifeguard chair and I really wanted to go talk to him, but I kept running. I sprinted into the ocean and dove under an incoming wave. I felt the cold water engulf me, the wave roiling the sand beneath me.

When I finally surfaced, I noticed something strange.

I seemed to be the only one in the ocean. As far as I could see, anyway. But then, it was almost lunchtime, and the place tended to clear out right around then—people headed in to take a break from the midday sun, or else they ate lunch and napped under big umbrellas.

I heard a loud shrieking whistle and looked back toward shore. Hayden was standing on the beach, his arms on his hips, a whistle to his lips. He blew the whistle again and waved his arms in the air.

Boy. He really wanted my attention. Maybe I wasn't wrong to think he was interested in me.

I swam back toward shore, catching one of the smaller waves and riding the crest of it to move along faster, since he looked a bit desperate. You know, some guys are like that, I thought. All you have to do is reject them once, and they decide they have to have you. Typical.

I stood up, leaned back to dunk my hair underwater, then strode out of the surf toward him. "Hey, what's—"

"Did you *not* see the caution flag?" he asked.

"What caution flag?"

"Right there." He pointed to a red, diagonal flag flapping in the breeze directly above his lifeguard stand. "It means no swimming."

"Oh. Whoops. I'm sorry." I looked up and down the beach. The water was definitely clear of people. They were all sitting under umbrellas, or lying in the sun, or playing Frisbee or volleyball. Definitely no swimming going on.

"Do you always break the rules?" Hayden asked.

"Ha!" I laughed. "No. Not *always*."

"Seriously," he said, with a frown to let me know he meant it.

"Seriously? Do I have to?"

"Have to what?"

"Be so serious. I've been stuck inside all morning, being *extremely* serious about cleaning and picking up and organizing and—after a while I just wanted to throw all the files out the window and watch them blow away in the wind."

Hayden looked at me as if I were going insane. And maybe I had gotten a little too much cabin fever. "What files?" he asked.

"Inn files. Since the year 1900. Miss Crossley couldn't find anything else for me to do, so she roped me into this huge straightening and tidying project." I groaned. "I started last night, actually."

"Hm. Funny. About last night. Weren't you taking that writer on a tour?"

"Oh, yeah. I was." Whoops. "After that, I mean."

"So, would that have been before or after I saw you and Claire shrieking and running into the dorm in the middle of that downpour around seven o'clock?" Hayden asked.

He was quite the detective, wasn't he? Why was I so stupid? "Why? Where were you?" I said.

"In my room. It's on the floor below yours, remember?"

I coughed. "Well, good thing we didn't go on that bike ride. I mean, really. We'd have gotten drenched."

Hayden folded his arms across his chest and stared at me. "Why did you make up an excuse not to go? I mean, if you don't want to hang with me, then don't, and just say that. It's not like I won't be able to *live* with that."

His tone was suddenly not so carefree and happy. He didn't even sound like the guy I kind of, sort of, knew.

Plus, I didn't like the implication that he could live after being rejected by me. Maybe it was true, but I liked to think of guys slowly falling apart after I turned them down.

"Me? It's not that I didn't want to hang out with you," I said. "Did I say that? No. Why would I?"

"I don't know. But admit it, you made up some convoluted story, instead of telling me you didn't want to hang out."

I thought about it for a second. I could lie, but what would be the point? "Maybe I did," I said.

"Okay, so I *was* right." He smiled, as if winning the argument was important.

"And you're excited that I did this? You're thrilled to be dissed?"

"Did I say that?" He laughed. "I just don't get it. Why did you do that?"

"Why did I? Because! You were so rude to me when I came out here to talk to you. I had twenty bucks to share with you. Plus the writer wrote this really cool note, and you could not have cared less. You didn't even talk to me."

"Maybe I had a lot on my mind."

"Sure," I said.

"What? You don't believe me?"

"I don't know. Should I?" I asked.

"Is it totally impossible that I would have a lot on my

mind? What, you think my life is easy or something?"

"Well . . . isn't it?" I asked.

"No," he said.

"Hm. Well, maybe you were, um, distracted. But if you were, it seems like it had a lot more to do with all the people hanging around."

"Exactly. All the people hanging around, in the ocean, swimming," he said. "You think I can just take my eyes off the water because you want me to?"

Well, didn't you, all those other times? I thought. *At least for a second or two?* "You didn't have to look at me—just talk to me," I said. "Anyway, aren't you doing that now?"

"No one's swimming now," he reminded me.

"Oh. Right." I realized with a shiver that I'd gotten really cold, standing there talking to him. The sun had gone behind a cloud, and my skin was covered with goosebumps. "Except that person over there." I pointed to an older man who was just beyond where the waves broke, doing a strong, sustained crawl motion.

"Oh, crap, that's Mr. Anderson," Hayden muttered, and he took off in a jog.

I grabbed my towel and wrapped it around my body, then I turned around and quickly made my way over the hot sand back to the boardwalk. The caution flag should have been up for that, I thought. Hot sand that will burn your feet—make it an orange flag, with red raging hot shooting flames painted on it.

And also maybe a caution flag for Hayden. Stay away. Trouble. They could show a guy in sunglasses with his nose covered in white zinc oxide, a big red X over his face.

CHAPTER 10

"Excuse me. Excuse me. Miss?"

Claire and I stopped halfway up the Inn porch steps. A couple was standing to our right. "Yes?" I asked.

"Would you be able to take a picture of me and my wife?" the man asked.

"Sure, no problem." I took the digital camera he offered and snapped several shots of the two of them, leaning against the banister. They looked like they might be wedding guests, all dressed up for the fancy evening ahead.

It was a Wedding Saturday—the first one I would experience at the Inn. The Inn was rented out for weddings almost every Saturday throughout the summer, and some Sundays, too. They were rumored to be very fun, because nearly everyone on staff worked at them.

So, instead of teaching sailing, Claire was going to be serving dinner plates, while I would circulate with trays of appetizers and champagne. It was an "all hands on deck" situation, as Miss Crossley phrased it.

In other words, the Inn catered the wedding and hired cheap help—namely, us—to pull it off.

The dining room had been completely transformed, with elegant tablecloth fabrics, fancy decorations, flowers draped on every surface possible, streamers hung from the ceiling, and a three-tier cake on a table in the center of the room. The room was quickly filling with guests filing in from outside, where the wedding had been performed on the grassy lawn overlooking the ocean.

I couldn't imagine a cooler place to have a wedding than here, right beside the ocean, in a classic place like this. Not that I was thinking wedding thoughts for myself, at least not for another ten years. Hopefully the Inn would still be in business then, and hopefully my to-be-determined-at-a-later-date (or *on* a later date) fiancé would agree that this was the place we wanted to marry. And if he didn't, I'd *make* him agree.

And that attitude, according to my mother, meant that I wasn't even close to being ready for marriage. Which was okay with me.

Claire and I went into the kitchen—I'd only been in the main kitchen a few times—and I was really impressed by what a massive operation the place was. I left Claire and headed to find the person in charge of appetizers. Miss Crossley was, naturally, in the center of everything, giving orders, filling trays, and sending people out to circulate with them, so I stepped up and got mine.

I made my way around the dining room and out on the porch, offering shrimp puffs. I went back to the kitchen and got a new tray, this one with tiny crab cakes. Then I was recruited to help fill water glasses, and then I was carrying trays of entrees out to the dining room and holding them while others served from them, and then I was summoned to carry pieces of cake to everyone after the bride and groom cut the wedding cake.

I was starting to wonder why everyone thought these wedding events were so much fun. I'd never worked so hard in my life. I felt like one of those Sherpas who works in the mountains, carrying everything. Okay, so maybe it wasn't *that* difficult, but still.

The first chance I had to catch my breath was when the bride and groom had their first dance. A lot of the staff were milling about in the kitchen. I started to walk outside, thinking I'd get a breath of fresh air on the porch, if it wasn't too crowded with wedding guests.

But before I got there, I saw C. Q. Wallace leaning against the open dining room doorway, looking in at the reception. "Weddings. What a waste of time," he said to me as I went past.

I stopped and looked at him. He was a curmudgeon, all right, through and through. "What did you say? What are you talking about?"

"Fifty percent of all marriages end in divorce, yet people still persist in having these expensive, elaborate weddings." He shook his head. "It's a gamble, if you ask me." He rubbed his glasses on the sleeve of his jacket, which he was wearing with a T-shirt, tattered jeans, and flip-flops.

"Are you married?" I asked.

He coughed. "No. Came close a few times, but thankfully, no. I was left at the altar once. Does that count?"

Bitter, party of one, I thought. "Right. Well, if you ask me, who wouldn't want to have a big party when they get married?" I asked.

"And I suppose you're going to tell me that this marriage is going to last, that they're fabulous together, yadda yadda yadda."

"No. I don't even know them," I said, glancing in at the bride and groom, who were dancing with the members of the wedding party.

"Oh." He laughed. "Well, sure, why would you?"

"But I'd say they picked a great place to get married, so they're off to a pretty good start," I said. I remembered something he'd told me when we first met. "Speaking of places. You're still here."

"Thanks for noticing."

I laughed. "No, I mean—you must be getting some writing done, or you would have left by now. So . . . are you?"

"Scads," he said, his voice heavy with sarcasm. "No, not scads—but some. I like how laid-back this place is, during the week. This weekend wedding stuff isn't exactly for me, so I'm heading up to my room for some peace and quiet." He started to walk away, but then he turned back toward me. "Listen. You're the Inn gofer, right? That's what Miss Crossley called you. Horrible name, not to mention it's a rodent, and you're a girl, but as the official Inn gofer—do you think you could score me a piece of wedding cake?"

"Sure." I smiled. "No problem. But wouldn't that kind of be saying you approve of the wedding?"

"No, it just says I like cake and I'm opportunistic," he

said. "I'd go in and get it myself, but I'm not really dressed for a wedding."

"It's okay—I've been wanting a piece myself. Be right back," I promised.

I walked into the dining room and grabbed two paper plates with generous-size pieces of cake—I had to take one with a blue rose frosting, because in my family getting one of the flowers on a cake is considered good luck. We usually fight over them at weddings and other events, which is kind of funny.

I was in the back hallway heading toward the stairs with the plates of cake when Hayden stepped out of the business center, in front of me, and blocked my path. "Cake for me? How thoughtful." Hayden took the plate in my left hand.

"Actually, that's for—"

"But let's dance first, I love this song." He took the other plate from me and set both of them on a chair by the window.

I hadn't even seen him working, but he was dressed in black and white like the rest of us. "Where have you been all day?" I asked.

"Valet parking," he said as he lifted my hands to his shoulders. He put his hands on my waist and pulled me close. "I was done for a while so I came in to check e-mail," he said.

"I thought this event was supposed to be all hands on deck, not all hands on Liza," I said, trying to fight how much I was enjoying being this close to him.

Hayden laughed. "Sorry. So what were we even arguing about?"

"You know what," I said. "You totally blew me off."

"Me? You're the one who made up some wacky story just to avoid seeing me," Hayden argued as we danced back and forth in the hallway.

"I'm sorry. That was dumb, but I was trying to get back at you," I said.

"You did. You retaliated, and now we're even."

"So let's start over," I said.

"Okay," Hayden agreed. "We'll start over." We danced in the hallway, barely moving to a slow song. I felt myself kind of getting lost in the moment. "What are we starting over?" he asked after another minute went by. He took a strand of hair that had fallen out of my ponytail and tucked it back behind my ear.

"I don't know," I said, a little breathless. "This?" And I closed my eyes and was about to kiss him when there was this loud ringing in my ears, like the bell that signaled the end of a boxing round. And like two boxers in a clutch, Hayden and I slowly separated.

Miss Crossley was holding the silver bell from the front desk in her palm. "You're needed at the front desk, Liza," she said briskly. "Caroline isn't feeling well and has retired for the evening."

"Too much champagne again?" Hayden joked.

"Hayden, I believe some wedding guests are in need of their car keys," she said.

"I'm on it," he said, and he literally sprinted away down the hall.

"Don't I need to be trained to work at the front desk?" I asked Miss Crossley as she led me through the lobby.

"We'll go over a few things," she promised. "It should be no problem for a person of average intelligence."

She could be so warm sometimes.

C. Q. Wallace stopped by the desk just as I took over. "Never got that piece of cake," he commented.

"No. Sorry. I got, um, redirected," I said.

"Well, gophers have a habit of losing their way. It's a trait of the species."

"Really?" I asked.

"No. The opposite, actually. They build elaborate tunnels. That's how they became known as pests. And they like to be alone, one per tunnel. Which doesn't bode well for your love life."

I felt my face start to turn red when he said that. Love life. Did I have one, or not? *What are we starting over?* Hayden had asked.

"Why do you know so much about gophers?" I asked.

"I'll do anything to procrastinate. I read entire books on weird subjects." He smiled. "So, any chance at all of getting some cake around here?"

"If I can't find any left-over wedding cake? We'll have a cake baked for you," I promised as I stood up.

Miss Crossley returned just in time to overhear me. She leaned over and whispered in my ear, "You're finally getting the hang of this."

CHAPTER 11

"We should have more days off,"

Josh said as we pulled back into the parking lot.

"Yeah, and more money to do things with on our days off," Claire added.

Miraculously my car had worked well that day, starting after only a few attempts, and it hadn't stranded us on the side of the road. We'd taken a trip to see Newport, and it was kind of funny to see my beaten-up, rusted, dented old car parked among the expensive BMWs and Mercedes.

"Can you believe some of those mansions?" Josh asked. "I mean, if you lived there, you wouldn't even ever see your family."

"No," Claire said, "just the butler, maid, and any other servants—"

"Who all come from the scullery," Josh added, and we all laughed as we climbed out of the car. "Like us."

Caroline was walking out of the dorm, and she stopped in the small parking lot. "Where have *you* been?" She looked at my car as if it might contaminate her air space.

"Newport. You know, slumming. The *new* people have to go to *New*port," Josh said to Caroline.

"Ha ha," she said. "Very funny."

Josh threw a bag over his shoulder. "I thought so."

"Me too," I added. "So, what did we miss around here?"

"Miss Crossley's been looking for you. All over the place," Caroline said.

I sighed. Couldn't that woman hire another gofer or something? I wasn't the only person who could fill in at the last minute, was I? Wait. Maybe I was. "But it's my day off. She told me I was off on Mondays, because it's the slowest day here."

"She needed you anyway." Caroline made it sound like a desperate situation. "Didn't you take your pager with you?"

"No. If I'm not working, then I'm not working. It

wouldn't do her any good to page me if I'm in Newport." I hadn't brought my cell phone, either, but that was because I'd forgotten it.

"If you say so. But I think you have some notes on your door. Don't say I didn't warn you." Caroline headed off down the path in the direction of the Inn.

"Ooh. Intriguing," Josh commented.

"Josh, notes from Miss Crossley aren't intriguing," I said. "They're annoying."

Claire and I headed upstairs to our room. We had a small bulletin board on our door, and there was a big yellow Post-it that said, "LIZA MCKENZIE," on it. As if there were other Lizas in this room that might be confused. I turned the note over and read Miss Crossley's note: "Ignore all earlier messages. Problem solved!" And there was a little smiley face drawn at the bottom.

"A smiley face? Since when is Miss Crossley a smiley-face type of person?" I asked Claire.

I plowed through the other notes from her. It was amazing how many times she'd come by in the six or seven hours we'd been gone.

The last note was in different handwriting that I didn't recognize, and jotted on an old envelope instead of a Post-it.

Where are you? We need to make a pen run tonight.
Meet me at the Shuttle at 6:30.
H

"I can't believe he changed his pen brand. How crazy is that?" Hayden asked.

We were walking on the beach. Our jeans were rolled up at the bottom and we walked barefoot on the hard sand just above where the waves washed ashore. It was a cool evening, and kind of breezy.

We'd taken guests with us to the train, and brought new ones back as well, so Hayden and I hadn't really had a chance to visit during the shuttle ride. For once, the train had been on time, so I'd sprinted to the office store and back.

"I guess writers will try anything when they're stuck," I said.

"How many nights has he been staying at the Inn already?"

"A week or two, at least."

"I'd use about *one* pen in that time. What does he do, use one per day?" Hayden asked.

"Yeah, he's tough on the pens. Wears 'em right out. By not writing with them. Go figure." I explained how Mr. Wallace had told me about his writer's block, which I guessed must have been disappearing, since he was sticking around and ordering more pens.

"I thought writers wrote on computers, anyway," Hayden said.

"He uses both, I guess. Hey, if he and Miss Crossley want to send me on these missions, and I get to hang with you, and get a tip from him? It's cool with me."

"Yeah, but what will we do when he checks out? I mean, what's going to be our excuse?" Hayden asked.

"Excuse?"

"To hang, like you said."

"Oh." I smiled nervously. "Maybe another slightly eccentric person with no car and an urgent need for office supplies will check in."

"Yeah, maybe," Hayden said. "Should we count on that, though?"

We walked side by side down the beach. Did we really need an excuse, I wondered, or could we just do this because we wanted to?

Hayden seemed to have slipped into a melancholy mood, so I took his arm and linked it through mine. "Everything okay?" I asked.

He shrugged. "Yeah."

"You sure?"

"No."

"Why? What's going on?"

"Just thinking about stuff. My family. I talked to my mom today. And, see, she and my dad . . . my parents are getting separated," Hayden said. "They just announced this like right before I was leaving for the summer."

"Oh, no. I'm sorry. That's hard."

"Yeah, it is. And my little sister—she's gone goth or something to protest."

"That's not the end of the world," I said.

"Yeah. But you don't know my sister. She was always really into girly girl stuff. Anyway, *she* called me today, begging me to come home for the summer because she hates both Mom and Dad," Hayden said. "Which I can't do, but I wish I could for her sake."

"Maybe she could come here to visit," I suggested.

"Maybe, but she wouldn't want to hang out with either my mom or dad long enough to drive here," Hayden said with a laugh. "She used to love it here. But now she hates the beach, the sun, anything not goth."

"It's a phase. Don't worry about it," I told him. "Hey, even I was goth once."

"You?"

"Sure. I wore all black, I wore dark lipstick, dyed my hair black . . ."

"And what happened?"

"I got bored. I kind of get bored quickly," I said. "Especially with hair. So when did you start vacationing here? What's your connection to this place?"

"Well, we used to come to the Inn when I was a little kid—like, very little."

"You were little once? No."

Hayden pushed me toward the surf, and my ankles got wet. "You're pretty tall yourself. How tall?"

"Five eight and a half," I said. "So tell me about your family some more. You have a little sister—any other siblings?"

"I have an older brother. He worked here for three summers, and that's how I got in," Hayden explained. "That's my connection. How about you?"

"This is kind of funny, but my grandfather knows Mr. Talbot Senior, from way back when. But even so, I got hired at the last minute," I explained. "And I tried to get hired last year, too."

"Don't take it personally. Everyone wants to come back, so there are only like five or six new slots a summer. And if you factor in all the people the Talbots know personally, or owe favors to . . . and then there are the people like me, whose siblings worked here, and unless *they* royally screwed up, then the Talbots reward them by giving a spot to their brother or sister."

"Yeah. Claire's sister worked here," I told him.

"So I'm guessing you don't have an older sister to get you in."

"Why? Did you want to meet her?" I teased him.

"*No*, I'm just trying to ask about your family," Hayden said.

"I'm an only child. I was one of those extremely difficult babies, so my parents decided to stop after me."

"No, come on. You're not *that* difficult."

"What? Shut up." I pushed him up the beach, and he stumbled on a couple of shells.

"Ow," he said, brushing a sharp piece off his foot. "Maybe you are." He looked up at the sky for a second, and I stopped walking to stand beside him. "We should probably turn around and go back," Hayden said.

"Probably," I said.

"It's getting late. We're lucky the moon is so bright tonight, or we wouldn't be able to see a thing."

I gazed at the moon, which wasn't exactly full, but was close. There was something really romantic about only seeing by the light of the moon, while letting the ocean's water roll over your feet.

"Feel like swimming?" Hayden asked.

"No, not tonight. It's kind of chilly for that," I said.

"Then let's sit down for a second and just listen to the water," he said.

"You like doing that, too? I used to drive my parents crazy by insisting on doing that. Plus I used to make them open all the car windows or else stop the car when we got within range of salt air, just so I could inhale it."

"But . . . weren't you coming toward the ocean?" Hayden sounded confused.

"Yes."

"So you'd be smelling the salt air for days, wouldn't you?" Hayden asked.

"Right. Sure, but that's nothing like the first *breaths* of it," I argued.

"Clearly you need to move."

"Clearly."

Hayden folded up his sweatshirt and made a pillow for both of us, and we lay back in the sand, next to each other.

"You should be a travel agent," Hayden said. "Or wait— no, you should be in advertising. You should write about this stuff."

"You think?" I asked.

It felt so natural to be with him like this, but at the same time it also felt wrong because I hadn't been completely hon-est. *You have to tell him about Mark,* I thought. But why did I have to? Mark was a nonissue. Though I could just see him saying, "You called me a 'nonissue'? Thanks a lot!"

"What do you want to do, you know, with your life?" Hayden asked.

"I'm not sure. Isn't that terrible? I should know. I'm going to college, you know?" I said. "What about you?"

"College sophomore."

"So, what's your major then?" I asked.

"I started in business. Hated it. Then I switched to chem-istry. Hated it. So I don't know." He laughed. "I guess I can fall back on lifeguarding, until I'm like twenty-five. After that it won't be cool anymore."

"Yeah, gray hair and lifeguards don't really match," I said.

"No?" Hayden turned over onto his side to face me. He started to play with my hair, and I stared up at the stars above us. I really, really wanted to turn toward him and kiss him, but now that I'd thought of Mark, I knew that I couldn't, not until I was honest with Hayden.

"Listen, there's something I have to tell you," I said.

"Uh oh. That sounds bad."

"No, it's not bad. It's just—remember when you asked if I was seeing someone? And I said, no, because I'm not. But I did have a boyfriend before I came here."

"Stashed under the bed, like I said."

I laughed. "No, more like working at a factory making boat parts. We're on a break for the summer. Probably longer, actually."

"Summer break, huh? I haven't heard of that. Well, did you guys agree that you can see other people?"

"The way we left it, we weren't all that . . . clear. Or mature." I laughed. "It was more like an argument. He said that if I came here I could forget about him for the summer. And I said fine, done, and I packed up and here I am. And we haven't spoken since. I mean, how could he be against anyone wanting to come here? It's like heaven here, you know?"

"You miss him?"

"Not yet. Not really at all, actually." Now that I thought about it, that was kind of strange. I guessed maybe we'd been ready to move on for a while, if I was willing to leave him for the summer and he was willing to let me go. "Anyway, it's pretty much over," I said. "But we haven't had that final conversation, so it's not over, over."

"I used to order my eggs like that. Over over," Hayden said.

I smiled. "Thanks for having a sense of humor about this." This conversation could have gone much, much worse,

I thought, considering I could have—and probably should have—shared this with him days ago.

Hayden held up his watch and pressed a button to light its face. 11:54. "It really is late—we should go."

We had a basic, but not all that enforced, curfew of midnight. We both got to our feet and jogged back the way we'd come, without talking much. When we got back to the Inn, Hayden turned to head that way instead of up the path to the dorm.

"You know what? I left some stuff at the Inn I need to grab," he said.

"I can wait for you," I offered.

"No, it's okay—you go ahead. I'll see you tomorrow," he said.

I let him go and didn't argue the point. I didn't want the night to end, but okay, maybe things were moving a little too quickly for both of us, especially considering I'd just sort of dropped a bombshell.

We didn't kiss good night, which was okay because I was still feeling weird about doing something with someone else without talking to Mark first.

"Where were you?" Claire asked when I walked into our room. She was sitting up in bed, reading one of the nonfun books she'd brought along. "You almost missed curfew."

"I was with Hayden," I said softly. I didn't want Zoe and especially Caroline next door to hear. I didn't want anyone else to figure out what was going on until I had at least figured it out for myself. I could picture Caroline with her ear pressed to the wall, just praying for some good gossip.

"What did you guys do? Or shouldn't I ask?" Claire said.

"Nothing. We went for a walk and we just talked about . . . everything," I said.

"Really. But it's past midnight," she said.

"I know. But I'm completely serious. Nothing happened."

"Remember, this place will get really small if you and Hayden . . . you know."

"I know," I said.

But the truth was, I could handle whatever came at me. I wasn't scared. Maybe I should have been, but I wasn't.

Or maybe some things were worth being scared to death about—and following through anyway.

CHAPTER 12

The next night, there was a party at

Crandall's Point. It was sort of impromptu in that no one told me and Claire about it. So, according to us, impromptu now meant "last minute, and you're not invited."

"The dorm is so quiet tonight. What's up with that?" Claire had asked me around 8:00.

"It's like everyone went somewhere, without us," I commented.

Then she vaguely remembered Josh saying something about a party. But why hadn't Hayden?

We headed out to Crandall's Point, and when we came over the crest of a sand dune, I saw two figures standing off to the side, behind everyone else. It looked like a guy and girl, so I was wondering who had hooked up—they were standing really close.

As we got nearer to them, I realized: It was Hayden. And Zoe. They were sort of huddled together against a big rock, as if they were shielding themselves from the wind. But there was no wind. Still, I felt a cold ripple down the back of my neck when I saw them. They had this look as if they were conspiring. They didn't even see us, so I slunk away feeling like I'd intruded on a private moment.

If Hayden and Zoe were still "close," as Caroline had so nicely phrased it, why hadn't he told me the night before, when I'd come clean about Mark? It wasn't like he hadn't had the perfect opportunity.

Did he not tell me about the party because he knew Zoe would be there? But that didn't make sense—they could be around each other tons, back at the Inn or the dorm. They didn't need a secret party to get together. Besides, she was seeing Brandon. Wasn't she?

Claire tugged at my arm to make me keep walking, because I was a little frozen in place, reluctant to proceed. "It's probably just one of those post-breakup talks you have to have," she suggested.

"What are those?" I asked.

Claire shrugged. "How would I know? I've never had one.

I've never dated anyone more than once."

"Once? What do you mean?"

"To a movie or a party or whatever." Claire grabbed a soda from a cooler and opened it. "Just never seemed worth it before now."

"Before now?"

"Before we go to college, I mean. Because you'll change so much. My sister said high school guys aren't worth it, anyway."

I looked at her for a few seconds. "I think you need to stop getting all your guy advice from your big sister. She sounds a little jaded."

Claire laughed. "You have a point."

"What took you guys so long?" Josh asked when we sat down beside him. "I was wondering where you were."

"You were?" Claire asked, sounding surprised.

"Well, yeah."

"We didn't know this was where everyone was," I said. *Because certain people didn't share information with certain other people. Because they are off having deep discussions with their supposedly ex-girlfriends.*

"Well, where else would we be?" Caroline said. "It's not like there are multiple hangouts to choose from."

"Sure there are," I said. "You just haven't thought of

them all. You're stuck in a rut."

Just then, I noticed Hayden walking over to the group. Zoe wasn't with him, which seemed strange. What had happened? He sat across the fire from us. I thought he might sit next to me, or at least maybe make a point of saying hi, but he didn't. I tried to catch his eye and wave at him, but it was like he was deliberately avoiding me. What had I done? Was this all about the Mark thing?

"Did Zoe take off?" Caroline asked him.

Leave it to her to find out the dirt, but this time I was grateful—she saved me from asking the question and looking desperate.

"Brandon picked her up," Hayden said. "Didn't you hear his Harley? We heard this loud exhaust roar out on the street, and she bolted."

Bolted because she was about to be caught with you? I wondered. *Or bolted, in general, because she's skittish, like a horse?*

Except she wasn't skittish, at all.

"The neighbors freaked. The Crandalls will be down momentarily to kick us all off their point," Hayden joked. "They're taking back their rocks."

"Is there a law against Harleys?" Josh asked.

"There should be," Caroline said with a frown.

"Don't you approve of Brandon?" Claire asked her.

"No, but I mean, it's not up to me." Caroline shrugged.

"And thank you, Caroline," Hayden said. "I'm sure Zoe appreciates you butting out of her life."

Caroline gave him a very huffy look. "I think she could do better, and so do her parents, but whatever."

I glanced across the bonfire ring at Hayden, but he didn't make eye contact. What was he doing, exactly? Were he and Zoe friends, or weren't they?

Everyone including Caroline knew that they went off to talk privately, and they didn't think that was weird. So everyone from last summer must know they still had some sort of connection *this* summer.

So what did that make me, for spending so much time with Hayden and thinking we might have a "thing"? A fool, right?

I was starting to wish we'd never found this supposed party. I definitely didn't feel like sticking around. "I'm going to take off," I said to Claire, who was laughing with Josh about something.

"Want me to go, too?" she asked, looking up at me as I got to my feet.

"No, you stay—I'm exhausted," I said. Which was one word for it. Some others were *confused, hurt, surprised, shocked,* and *baffled*. And I didn't even have a thesaurus with me.

I walked back the way I'd come, picking my way between rocks until I got to the flat sand, and then I moved faster. I almost felt like running, but if I did, and I got back to the dorm too soon, what would I do for the rest of the night? Or should I head to the Inn and look for a guest who needed someone to play backgammon with?

Yes, that was pathetic. But maybe I was pathetic, going after a guy who wasn't really interested if his former girlfriend was around and available. But she was with Brandon, wasn't she? It was really bothering me that I couldn't figure this all out, that the "inn crowd" seemed to know more than I did. The one person who might explain it to me was Caroline, but I couldn't ask her.

I was nearly back to the Inn when I heard footsteps slapping on the sand behind me.

He waited long enough, I thought as I turned around and saw Hayden.

"I have a surprise," he said.

Yeah. I think I already experienced that, I thought. "Really," I said.

"Come on, let's go to the top deck."

"We can't get up there," I said. *Never mind the fact that I don't know if I'm even talking to you.*

The deck was connected to the Inn's biggest and best

room, the honeymoon suite, and could only be used by guests who were staying there or for private parties. I'd never even seen it, not on our tour, because Miss Crossley said it was off-limits.

"The room's not rented tonight. I have a pass key," Hayden said.

I considered my options as we neared the Inn's front entrance. I liked the idea of an adventure with Hayden. I wouldn't mind seeing this famous deck. Plus, if we were going to argue, it would be very private up there—privacy wasn't something we'd have back at the dorm or out here on the porch.

"Okay, sure," I said.

We went inside and pressed the call button for the elevator. When it came, we stepped inside and looked awkwardly at each other. Unfortunately we were the only ones in there. Fortunately it was only four floors to the top. Hayden inserted a special electronic key card that made the elevator stop at the fourth floor. Once we stepped out, there was a hallway.

There were two doors when we got to the top: one for the honeymoon suite and one for the deck.

"You want to see the suite first?" Hayden asked.

"Not right now," I said. The last place I wanted to be with him was in a romantic room with a giant bed. I'd probably hit him over the head with a flower vase.

I walked outside and went around the edge of the deck, checking out the view. I could hear glasses clinking and people laughing on the front porch of the Inn. One male guest had a really loud, obnoxious laugh—an actual guffaw—and when I heard it, I glanced back over my shoulder at Hayden and we both laughed. I was grateful to the guy for laughing like that, because it broke the tension. Which wasn't to say there wasn't still tension, and a couple of things I wanted to clear up.

"So, when we were back at Crandall's Point?" I began.

"Yeah?" Hayden asked.

"The way you acted toward me, it was like we'd never hung out the night before—or ever," I said.

"What? No, it wasn't," Hayden protested.

"Yeah, it *was*."

"Look. If you want someone who's into PDA, that's not me."

"Well, I'm not into PDR," I said.

"PDR?" Hayden asked.

"Public displays of rejection," I said.

Hayden started to laugh. "That's really a term?"

"Sure," I said.

"It's just awkward, that's all," Hayden said. "People like to talk, and I don't like being talked about."

"What are you so afraid of?" I asked.

"Truthfully? I don't know. Let's talk about something else. I'm starting to sound paranoid."

"Okay." I took a deep breath. I was ready for whatever he had to tell me. "Can we talk about the Zoe thing?"

Hayden looked at me and raised an eyebrow.

"I'm not the jealous type. Really. Honestly I'm not. But tonight you guys were off having this totally . . . I don't know—"

"That? That was just family stuff. From home. I'll tell you about it sometime. But we're friends, that's all," Hayden said.

I wasn't sure whether I believed him yet.

"I mean, *you* know how it is, after you date someone. You're still a—a close friend, sort of. Aren't you and what's-his-name still friends?"

"I don't know. We haven't talked," I said. "So probably no. But okay, I take your point, I guess."

"So can we officially move on?" he asked.

I couldn't see why not, even if it felt a little strange. "Sure."

"Good." Hayden put his arms around my waist. "Isn't it great up here?"

"Yeah." I leaned back against him, enjoying the feeling of being close to him. We fit together perfectly. From the upstairs deck you could see everything around the Inn, the entire property, from the dorm to the tennis court to the sailing pond to the ocean beach.

"So how did you end up with a key?" I asked. "Wait, don't tell me. Miss Crossley gave it to you, like the key to the bike shed. You have your special privileges."

"No, actually I just sort of borrowed it for tonight, from the front desk."

"The front *desk*?" I pretended to gasp. "Was Caroline there?"

"She was fawning all over some California dude checking in," Hayden said. "She never even saw me."

I laughed. "You know what? I like this side of you."

"Which side is that?" Hayden let go of me and turned around, stopping to pose and flexing his biceps. "Front side, back side . . ."

I swatted him on the butt. "The daredevil side."

"Yeah. We'll have to be quiet though. If we get busted, we're in big trouble."

"Okay, so we'll quietly listen to the surf," I said.

"Very quietly."

"Definitely." I nodded. We stood there for a few minutes, me leaning back against him again, both of us watching the ocean. I closed my eyes for a while and just listened to the water, the rhythmic rolling sound of the waves.

Hayden gently took my shoulders and turned me so that I was facing him.

"Wasn't I being quiet enough?" I asked in a whisper.

"Too quiet." He traced my cheekbones with his fingers. "I thought maybe you fell asleep."

"No. Not exactly," I said as I looked into his eyes. "You have the coolest eyes. You know that? They're sort of blue, but then they're sort of gray—"

Hayden interrupted me by leaning down to kiss me. I wrapped my arms around his waist, and he pulled me in tight. We must have been kissing for a while, and I was totally lost in the moment. I completely forgot where I was.

Then the outside deck lights came on.

CHAPTER 13

We jumped apart. If that was Miss Crossley, or anyone on the Inn staff . . . We were so in trouble. We'd already been caught once by her, dancing when we were supposed to be working. If she found us up here? Even her favorite employee, Hayden, would be history.

"You said no one was staying here!" I whispered to him. "What are we going to do?"

I had a brief mental image of the two of us scaling the side of the Inn, like in a heist movie.

"Don't sweat it," Hayden said. "Come on, let's see who it is."

"This feels really, really weird," I said as we edged closer to the sliding glass door and peered into the honeymoon suite. Of all the rooms to *spy* on.

All of a sudden the door opened. Mr. Talbot Junior was standing there.

I opened my mouth to say something, but nothing came out. Not even air, because I'd stopped breathing.

"Hello, Mr. Talbot. Sir," Hayden said.

"Hayden, is that all you have to say? Hello?"

"It's . . . a nice night?" I added.

Mr. Talbot looked at me and his mouth turned into an even deeper frown. "And what is your name again?"

"Liza," I said. "Elizabeth McKenzie." I wished that it was Mr. Talbot Senior, who might actually recognize my name and give me a break.

"Elizabeth McKenzie," he repeated as if trying to memorize my name. "Well, Hayden and Elizabeth. What do you two think you're doing up here?" he asked. "Other than getting to know each other better." He coughed a few times. "Substantially better, I might add."

Hayden looked over at me, and if he wasn't turning red from embarrassment, then I certainly was.

"Still speechless? Well, imagine my surprise when I walked into the office to deposit some cash and receipts into the safe. There's a surveillance system in the office, and there's a camera trained on this deck when the room is vacant. Or have you forgotten?"

"I suppose, sir, that I did forget," Hayden said. "My apologies."

I should have known, too—I'd only just spent hours cleaning and organizing that office.

"So. What do you have to say for yourselves?" Mr. Talbot demanded.

That we're about to lose our jobs? I thought. *Good-bye, this has been a great place to work?*

"Mr. Talbot, I'm really sorry. I just wanted to show the place to Liza. It's my fault," Hayden said. "I take full responsibility."

"There are two people standing here, so in my opinion, you're both responsible. It's not as if you both don't know the rules." Mr. Talbot glared at me.

"I'm sorry. We definitely shouldn't have been up here," I said. "It's just—it's such a beautiful spot. We got carried away."

"It is beautiful," Mr. Talbot agreed. "And such a nice night." He took a deep breath and stretched his arms over his head. He seemed to be loosening up a little bit. "I wish I'd been up here, instead of in the office. Then you'd never have been able to get away with this."

I just stood there, smiling and feeling stupid. *Had* we gotten away with it? Or were we about to spend our last night at the Inn?

"I should have checked with you first, Mr. Talbot," Hayden said. "I mean, if I'd thought it through, I would have done that. It was an impulse decision."

"Hayden, I've learned over the years to trust you. And if you'll trust me for a second, let me give you a piece of advice." Mr. Talbot put his hands on the wall and leaned out over the deck. "And that is, never go with an impulsive decision. Never."

Hayden laughed. "I can see where you're right."

"Who said . . . fools rush in—"

"Where angels fear to tread," I said. "Alexander Pope."

Mr. Talbot looked at me with newfound respect. "Very impressive."

"My grandfather," I said. "He's always quoting that." And now I knew *why*. All those years he drove me nuts by saying that, he was trying to warn me for situations like this.

"Look, I realize you probably need to report this to Miss Crossley," Hayden said.

"Probably," Mr. Talbot agreed. "That would be the way we'd usually handle it."

"But if there's any way we could . . . I don't know. I know this is a lot to ask," Hayden said, "but if we could keep this between us, I'd really appreciate it."

Mr. Talbot didn't say anything for a minute or two. He was staring up at the sky. "Look, isn't that the Milky Way?"

"Actually, *that* is." I started to point out different constellations to him. That astronomy minicourse we'd done in school was really coming in handy. Mr. Talbot seemed to have forgotten all about the fact we were only seeing all these stars and constellations because we were standing somewhere we shouldn't be. "It's so amazing here," I commented. "You can see so much more here than back home."

"Light pollution. It's a problem," Mr. Talbot agreed. "That's why I love the Inn's location. That's why city people love to come here."

"You should mention that in the brochure," I said. "Talk about all the open sky and dark nights—"

"And romantic locations?" Mr. Talbot turned back to us. "Well. Hayden, I've been thinking about what you asked. It's asking a lot."

"I know that, sir—"

"But I'm inclined to agree with you. We don't need to share this." Mr. Talbot extended his palm and Hayden placed the key card into it. "Now, I should get back to the office, and you should get back to the dorm. And don't make any more stops on the way."

When we got back downstairs, Mr. Talbot headed for the office. Hayden and I looked at each other and I let out a big sigh.

"I think I'm going to go see if he, uh, needs any help," Hayden said.

"Sounds good," I said. For some reason I just wanted to get out of there.

We quickly went our separate ways without even saying anything else, like "good night," or "it was nice kissing you." I think we were both sort of in shock from everything that had just happened.

Then I ran back to the dorm and, of course, told Claire everything.

I mean, what are roommates for?

The next morning we were all eating breakfast when Miss Crossley walked into the Hull. Trailing her were all the employees from the restaurant upstairs, and everyone else currently on duty and in uniform.

"Are we having a meeting?" Brooke asked.

"I didn't know we were having a meeting," Caroline said.

Miss Crossley banged a knife against a glass to get

everyone's attention. Not that everyone hadn't stopped talking when she walked in, because she looked so serious and because the wait staff didn't often leave work to follow her around.

"I'll make this quick, everyone. We're letting someone go, and you need to hear it from me," Miss Crossley said.

CHAPTER 14

My last bite of wheat toast stuck in my throat. I gulped and attempted to swallow.

It was obvious what was about to happen. Once the effect of star-gazing wore off, Mr. Talbot had come to his senses and realized Hayden and I should be fired.

I tried to catch Hayden's eye, across the room, but he seemed to be deliberately avoiding me. That was probably a good idea, given the situation. Not that it would help, if Miss Crossley's mind was made up.

Suddenly I noticed that Miss Crossley didn't have her usual pressed-and-starched appearance. She looked a little overwhelmed as she rubbed the side of her face. "I've been up all night deliberating," she said. "It pains me to have to say this."

I chewed my thumbnail. The only person it could truly pain her to fire—would be Hayden. Her favorite, long-time employee. Me, she couldn't care less about, although in her eyes I'd already given her a little bit of trouble. And, as she'd promised that day on the beach, she was watching me extra carefully.

"Something happened last night," Miss Crossley went on.

I started to picture what it would be like to go home after only a few weeks here. How many people I'd run into, around town, and how stupid I'd feel explaining. "I got fired because I was making out with this guy." How lame was that? Why would I risk my job over someone I barely knew? I was an idiot. Pure and simple. This was a good reason *not* to fall in love. You did stupid things.

"An unauthorized Inn employee borrowed the van late last night, which is, bottom line, inexcusable."

I looked up at Miss Crossley. I felt like I'd just surfaced from being underwater. She was still talking, and she was saying that I wasn't fired. Hayden wasn't fired.

But Tyler was.

"Now, no harm was done. He didn't go on a joyride, or

get pulled over for speeding, or anything like that. And he was trying to help out a guest, by taking her to a convenience store on the other side of town. He was finishing his server shift around eleven o'clock, when she apparently settled her bar bill and asked for the trip. But it's just—it's bad judgment. He should have alerted someone on the night staff who was authorized to do that. Not taken it upon himself."

"How did he get the keys?" Hayden asked.

"He borrowed them from the desk drawer. She gave him a hundred-dollar tip, which is what I guess made him make a bad choice. Anyway, it's very sad. This was Tyler's second summer here and we hate to lose him, but we can't give him another chance." Miss Crossley shook her head. "Everyone, please remember. The rules exist for a reason. To protect you, and to protect the Inn and its guests. Now get back to work."

Claire and I just looked at each other. *Wow,* she finally mouthed.

"No kidding," I said.

"I thought you were gone for sure," she whispered.

"So did I." I took a sip of orange juice and my hand was shaking from nerves. I'd dodged that bullet. At least . . . I was pretty sure I had. Maybe Mr. Talbot hadn't seen Miss Crossley yet that morning. But he'd have to have been in on the decision to let Tyler go—so he must have kept our secret, as promised. Still, I didn't like the idea he had something to hold over our heads. If we made one more mistake . . . Hayden and I would be gone, too.

Sometimes there are things that you really don't see coming. You think one thing is going to go wrong, and you're completely relieved when it doesn't. So you relax. And then something else hits you.

I'd answered my cell phone while I was back in my room changing clothes for dinner. I figured it was a typical Mom call: Are you doing okay, are you eating right, are you staying out of trouble?

The answers would be yes, yes, and maybe.

But when I answered the phone, she paused for a second after saying hello, which isn't like her at all. She usually begins talking a mile a minute. That made me worry.

"Mom, what's up?" I asked.

"Honey, I'm afraid I have some bad news. Your grandfather—Grandpa McKenzie—"

"What?"

"He's had a heart attack. He's fine, really, but he's in the hospital under the doctors' care and everything's stabilizing now. We don't want you to worry, but we thought you should know—"

"Mom, I'm coming home," I declared.

"Honey, that's not necessary—"

"Yes, it is." I got kind of choked up trying to tell her that. I was about to start crying, but I didn't want to because then she'd worry about me, too, and she had enough to deal with already.

"Well, all right, but what about work?"

"They'll figure it out. Look, I'll get there as fast as I can." I glanced at my watch. It was after six already. "Which hospital, in case I make it in time for visiting hours?"

"County General."

"Mom, I'll have my cell on, so call me—give me an update—tell me stuff, okay?"

"You sure it's okay to leave?"

"It's okay, they'll understand. See you soon." I hung up the phone. Claire wasn't around, so I scribbled a note to her. Then I threw a few changes of clothes into a duffel and ran downstairs and outside to the parking lot.

I threw my bag into the backseat, then slipped the key in the ignition and turned it. Nothing. I tried again. No sound at all. A third time—and it sounded like an old person coughing. And then dying.

Of all the times to have a completely unreliable car. I couldn't stop swearing at it, but that didn't help. I got out and pounded the hood with my fists. Then I grabbed my bag and ran over to the Hullery. It was nearly dinnertime. There had to be someone who could help me, loan me a car—I could beg Miss Crossley if it came to that.

I raced inside and down the steps. I was hoping Claire and Josh would be there, but I didn't see them.

"Can anyone help me?" I said. Then I started to cry, and I hated crying in front of everyone, but I couldn't help myself. "My grandfather—he's had a—a heart attack. I need to get home and see him. My stupid car won't start—does anyone have a car I could borrow? I'm a really good driver, and . . . I'll pay you. Whatever you want."

"I don't have a car here," Richard said.

"Neither do I," Tara added. "I'm sorry, Liza."

Hayden jumped up from his chair. I hadn't even noticed him at the other end of the room. "I don't have a car here, but I can drive you to the train. It's at seven, remember? If we hurry, we can make it."

I vaguely registered the shocked looks on people's faces. I'd been so panicked that I hadn't even remembered there was a train.

"You can get pretty close to home, like New Haven, and get a connecting train, or else your parents or someone could pick you up somewhere along the line. Would that work?"

Hayden asked as he came over to me.

"Yeah—that's great. Let's go."

"Wait—I have to ask Miss Crossley, make sure it's okay to take the van," Hayden began. "After this morning—you know."

"You're an authorized driver. We'll call her on the way. I can't miss that train!" I ran up the steps, with Hayden following me.

"Are you and your grandfather close?" Hayden asked as we pulled out of the Inn parking lot. He'd just called Miss Crossley to let her know what was happening, so that was done, which was a relief.

"Kind of. Being an only child—I'm sort of their focus sometimes," I said.

"Is this the grandfather who knows Mr. Talbot Senior?"

I nodded. "Yeah."

"I'll tell him about it when I get back, then. He'd want to know," Hayden said.

"Yeah, I don't know if I would do that. Knowing my grandpa, he'll try to keep this a secret. He wants everyone to still think he's in excellent shape. Which he is, because he runs and swims and hikes. So this heart attack thing, it really doesn't make sense."

Hayden reached over and put his hand over mine. "If he's in great shape, that means he'll recover really quickly."

"Yeah?"

"Yeah. They'll figure out what caused it, maybe give him some medication—"

"What are you, a doctor now?"

"No, but I play one on TV."

I looked over at him and raised one eyebrow. I wasn't in the mood for jokes.

"Okay, so I've watched a lot of TV. And that's what always happens. Totally curable thing," Hayden said.

"Right."

"It's true," he insisted.

I stared out the window for the rest of the trip. I kept picturing my grandfather collapsing, or lying on the ground in pain. Where had he been when it happened? Was my grandmother there? I wondered. She was one of those tough-as-nails people, but even nails had their limits. I couldn't wait to get home and hug her—hug both of them—tightly.

Hayden and I got to the train station with about ten minutes to spare. I hurried to the ticket window and bought my ticket, then went back to the van for my duffel bag.

"You can take off if you want," I said to Hayden. He was

standing beside the van, leaning against it. "The train's on time for once."

"You're kidding. That never happens." He seemed a little disappointed, but maybe he was just stunned. "Well, that's great. You'll get home even faster."

I tried to smile, but I couldn't.

"Don't worry about anything. It's going to be okay. He'll be fine," Hayden said.

I nodded, unable to speak. The reality of what I might have to face at home was sinking in.

"I know you're worried, but your mom said he was okay now. He's in the hospital. They won't let anything happen to him."

I nodded again, and this time felt tears spill down my cheeks. They wouldn't stop coming.

"Liza, don't cry. Please don't cry."

Hayden leaned down and gently pressed his lips against my cheeks, softly kissing the tears. He gathered me in his arms and pulled me close. I rested my head on his chest, and he put his chin on top of my head.

I didn't move. I couldn't. I didn't want to.

And then I heard the train coming, and I grabbed my duffel and ran.

CHAPTER 15

My grandfather peered at me
through half-awake eyes. My aunt and uncle picked me up at
the train station, and I insisted on being taken to the hospital
right away. Visiting hours were over by the time we got there,
but the nurse said she would let us in anyway, for fifteen minutes.

"If you really want to get out of work, Liza, there are easier ways," my grandfather said.

I rushed to his side and wrapped my arms around his
shoulders. "Grandpa, are you okay?"

"I'm perfectly fine," he said. "How are you? And what are
you doing here?"

"Mom called—I had to see you. She said you'd be all

right, but I wanted to see for myself," I said.

My parents had decided to sit outside in the waiting room with my aunt and uncle, who'd brought them a late dinner from the outside world.

"They're keeping me here overnight for observation. Isn't that ridiculous? What will they learn by *observing* me?"

"That you're a stubborn old man who hasn't had a checkup in three years," my grandmother said. "That's what."

My grandfather ignored her. "So. How are things at the Inn?"

"Oh, fine," I said with a smile.

"Fine? That's all you're going to tell me about one of my favorite places in the world?"

"Well . . ." I hesitated. "I'm not really here to visit and chat, you know. I'm here to see how *you* are!"

"You've seen. I'm fine. Now tell me a story to take me away from all this." He swept out his arms, knocking a plastic water cup off the tray beside his bed.

My grandparents are the ones I confide in most. They don't tend to overreact the way my parents could. Platinum hair? Jet-black hair? Belly-button piercing? All fine. Or at least not freakworthy. My parents, on the other hand . . . They'd only agreed to let me go away for the summer after my grandparents persuaded them to.

Sometimes I know that what I'm telling my grandparents is going to go straight back to Mom and Dad, but there have been enough times when they *haven't* done that, so I still basically trust them.

Still, was I ready to tell them about Hayden?

"Don't we have more important things to talk about? Like how you are?" I asked my grandfather.

"That's boring. Give us something so we can live vicariously. I'm cooped up in this hospital room when I could be at the beach," Grandpa complained. "What does Bucko have you doing for work? Bill, I mean. Mr. William Talbot Senior, to you."

"Didn't Mom tell you? I'm the official Tides Inn gofer." I explained the various jobs I'd been called on to perform so far.

"Sounds interesting," my grandmother said. "And what about your social life? Friends?"

"Everyone's been nice," I said.

"And what about Mark?" my grandfather asked.

"Don't pry," Grandma said.

"Too late," Grandpa replied.

"Mark and I? We're on a break."

"What does that mean?" Grandma asked.

"It means . . . I probably have to go talk to him while I'm

home. I think I met someone who's . . ."

"Perfect for you?"

Was he? I thought about the way Hayden had held and kissed me that night while we waited for the train. "Yeah, maybe," I said.

"We'll be the judges of that. What's his story?" Grandpa asked.

I laughed. "You're so vague, Grandpa. I never know what you're getting at." I rolled my eyes at him.

"Spill," he said.

Thankfully the nurse came back into the room just then. "It's really time to go," she said to me.

"I'll spill tomorrow," I promised. "Right now you get back to sleep—I'll come by again in the morning."

I went to find Mark at his uncle's boat factory at 6:45 a.m. As I drove there in my mom's car, I tried not to think about the Inn, but I couldn't help wondering about everyone there and when they'd be getting up and what they'd be doing today. I'd been home for less than twelve hours, but it felt like the longest night in history. I really missed Claire and Hayden and Miss Crossley.

Just kidding on that last one.

I'd tried calling Hayden to tell him everything was okay,

but never reached him on his cell. I hadn't spoken to anyone back there yet.

Anyway, I figured catching Mark as he got off his work shift was a good idea. He couldn't avoid me, the way he could if I called ahead. Not that he would, necessarily. But I wasn't sure.

I was sitting on one of the picnic tables outside the factory when he emerged into the early-morning haze. He seemed a little out of it as he rubbed his eyes and focused.

"Yeah, it's me," I said, giving him an awkward little wave.

He said good-bye to his buddies and came over to me.

"Peace offering," I said as I held out a large cup of Dunkin' Donuts coffee to him.

"Thanks. I think."

"I brought doughnuts, too," I said, pointing to the bag on the table. "And a muffin, and a bagel, and—"

"What are you doing here, Liza?" He narrowed his eyes as he slid onto the bench seat across from me. "After all that, don't tell me you quit. Did you quit?"

I shook my head. "No. Not a quitter."

"Right," he said. "SATs. Volleyball. Et cetera."

"Right. So how's your summer been?" I sipped my coffee and reached for the bag to fortify myself with a honey-glazed.

"Are you kidding?" Mark asked.

"No, I'm interested." I tore off a piece of doughnut and put it into my mouth.

"Well. It's been fine. I guess. I work. I hang out. The usual." He took a blueberry muffin from the bag. Maybe I was here to tell him we were over over, but at least I'd brought his favorite flavor muffin. I wasn't completely horrible. "You?" he asked. "How's the summer?"

"Same as yours. Working, hanging out."

"Is it the dream job you said it was?"

"Yes. And no." Enough beating around the bush; this was getting ridiculous. "Mark? The reason I came home is that my grandfather had a heart attack."

"What? No!" Mark gasped.

"Oh, he's fine. That wasn't the big news."

Mark looked sort of like he wanted to hit me with the blueberry muffin.

"I have something to tell you," I said.

"Yeah, well. Me too," Mark said.

I was thinking his might not be a compliment, so I decided to forge ahead. "I kind of met someone," I blurted. "So—"

"Me too," Mark said, and this sort of sheepish smile crept up the corners of his mouth. Then we both laughed. "Some summer, huh?"

* * *

"Hey, Hayden. Though you told me not to say that. It's Liza. Just wanted to let you know everything's okay. I'll be back tonight—maybe you could pick me up? If you could call me, that'd be great. Okay, bye!"

This was like the tenth time since I'd been home that I'd called and Hayden's phone had gone to voice mail. I hadn't left a message every time—but they were starting to pile up. I could see that if he was already out on the beach, he wouldn't have his phone. But was he going to be working every second of the day?

If so, I'd have to get a message to him another way. As much as I hated to do it, I called the Inn's main number.

"Thank you for calling the Tides Inn, my name is Caroline, how may I assist you?"

"Hey, Caroline. It's Liza," I said.

"Liza who?" she asked.

"Liza McKenzie, who else?" She really killed me with this snobby attitude of hers. "Caroline, where is everyone?"

"What do you mean?"

"Could you tell Miss Crossley I'll be back tonight? I tried to reach her, but all I got was her voice mail," I explained.

"Oh, well, she's busy organizing the wedding for next weekend. It's Zoe's sister, did you know that?" Caroline asked.

"No. I had no idea," I said.

"It's going to be *so* much fun," she said.

"Great. Look, could you please ask Hayden to pick me up from the train, you know, on the normal shuttle run to the station?" I asked.

"Sure," she said. "I can do that."

"Thanks a lot," I said.

"How's your grandfather?" Caroline asked, seemingly out of the blue. She'd acted like she didn't care, until now.

"Fine, thanks," I said. "He's checking out of the hospital tomorrow, probably."

"Oh, good," she sighed. "He was always so nice to me. Remember how he used to buy us all that saltwater taffy? And the time he and your grandmother took us to Block Island? That was so much fun."

"Yeah, he's great," I said, surprised she remembered and surprised she was being so nice to me for a change. "Hey, thanks a lot, Caroline. I'll see you soon, okay?"

"Travel safely," she said. "Don't let any weirdoes sit next to you on the train."

I rolled my eyes. "Okay, Caroline."

As much as I'd loved seeing everyone at home, I couldn't wait to get back. I wanted to see the ocean. I wanted to see Hayden.

* * *

The train gradually slowed and pulled around the bend, up to the station. I was so anxious to get off of it that I was standing in the doorway with one of the conductors. "You know Hayden?" I asked. "The Tides Inn shuttle driver?"

"I'm sorry?" he said.

"Never mind." I grinned as I saw the van parked in the passenger pickup area. I couldn't wait to tell Hayden that I'd cleared things up with Mark, that we weren't on a temporary summer break anymore—it was permanent. That meant I was really, actually free to date Hayden.

I hopped off the last step onto the platform and walked toward the Tides van. Then I started to run, with a big smile on my face.

And then the driver's side door opened.

And Miss Crossley stepped out.

"Liza, about time you're back. We need you desperately. Hop in."

Funny, that's what I was hoping Hayden would say. *Liza, about time you're back. I need you desperately.*

I tried to hide my disappointment as I stepped up into the van. "I thought maybe Hayden would pick me up," I said. "Isn't he the official shuttle driver?"

"Yes, but he's busy manning the pool tonight because Lindsay had a family emergency, too, and everything's just chaos," Miss Crossley said. She put the van in gear and we pulled away from the station. "Glad everything turned out well at home. Now. About your schedule for the next few days."

I sank down a little in my seat, rolled down my window, and half-listened to her as I breathed in the not-quite-close-enough-to-the-ocean-yet salt air.

Maybe Hayden couldn't leave, like Miss Crossley said, I thought. Maybe it wasn't flat-out rejection.

But that didn't explain why he hadn't called me once while I was gone, or returned any of my calls.

What had I done?

Wasn't our good-bye as romantic as I'd thought it was?

Or had he just been taking pity on me because I was so upset?

CHAPTER 16

I found Hayden in his room later that night. His roommate, Richard, was there, which made things a little awkward. They were watching a DVD, which they didn't even pause when I walked in.

"Hey, you're back." Hayden glanced over at me. He was lying on his side, on his bed, and he didn't make a move to get up. I was expecting a big hug, not the cold shoulder. What was going on with him?

I went to sit next to him, pushing him over a little to make room. "Yeah, I got back on the train."

"So everything's okay?"

I nodded. "I called you to let you know." I didn't add "several times," because Richard was sitting there and I was feeling dumb enough already.

"My phone went swimming. Okay, so I went swimming, and it was in my back pocket," Hayden explained. "Anyway, it's history."

"Oh, really?" I said. That seemed like kind of a convenient excuse, but what could I do, disagree with him? I might tease him about it in private, but not in front of his roommate. "So then I asked Caroline to tell you I was coming back, and asked if you could pick me up."

"Oh, yeah? She didn't tell me," Hayden said.

I nodded. "I should have known. She was using her fake voice when I talked to her."

"Which fake voice? She has a few," Richard commented.

"Good point." I smiled at him. Then I looked back at Hayden. "My grandfather's doing really well. It was great to see him and spend some time talking."

"Good," Richard said. "I'm glad he's okay."

Was it me, or was Richard more interested in what had happened than Hayden? What was going on? "Hey," I said, jiggling his leg. "Are you okay?"

"Oh yeah." He shifted on the bed. "So did you see what's-his-name while you were home?"

Was that hurt in his voice? Jealousy? Or just plain annoyance? "I did see him. But not like you might be thinking. We split up, completely. For good," I said. I spoke softly in case there was any chance of privacy.

"Really." Hayden raised his eyebrows.

"Yes, really." *In fact,* I wanted to say, *I told him I might be seeing someone else. But from the way things look right now, I'd say that I got the wrong impression.*

"Oh yeah? Well, cool. Glad you worked things out." His voice betrayed no emotion at all—not relief, or excitement. Did he really not care at all, or was this just a show in front of his roommate?

"Okay, so . . . you guys enjoy the movie," I said as I got to my feet.

"You want to stick around?" Richard offered. "I could run down to the Hull, make us some popcorn or something."

I looked at Hayden for my cue. The way things were going a few days ago, I'd have thought: Yes, let's send Richard out on an errand. That'll give us time to be alone. But now? The one who needed to leave was *me.*

"No, that's okay. I have to unpack and things like that. See you, guys," I said as I walked to the door. I turned around as I closed it and made eye contact with Hayden, who was watching me leave. He made no move to get up. He didn't even smile at me.

What did I do? I wanted to scream.

But at the same time, I knew I hadn't done anything. I knew this was all about him.

Upstairs, I stopped in the hallway outside Room 203. The door was open, and inside, Caroline was sitting at her desk, writing in what looked like a journal.

"What are you writing?" I asked.

She slammed the black book closed with a thud. "Nothing."

"Relax, I wasn't going to *read* it." I couldn't imagine a more boring journal than Caroline's—unless of course she had a secret life. "I have a question to ask you."

"What's that?" She picked up a brush and started to nonchalantly brush her hair.

"Why didn't you give Hayden my message?" I asked.

"Message?" she repeated. She glanced at me in the mirror. "What message?"

"Don't play dumb. I called you from home—we spoke on the phone. I asked you to tell Hayden to come pick me up at the train. Next thing I know, Miss Crossley is there," I said.

"I don't know anything about that," Caroline said.

"You don't." Somehow I found that hard to believe.

"No. Honestly, Liza. I did give him the message. Miss Crossley must have decided she wanted to pick you up herself."

I stared at her for a minute, trying to remember what little tic she had for when she was lying. When we'd gotten into trouble as kids, she was the smooth talker, the one who got us out of things.

"But you know, maybe seeing less of Hayden isn't such a bad idea, if you think about it," she mused.

Did I really want Caroline's opinion on this? But somehow I couldn't resist asking, "Why's that?"

"Because. How well do you know Hayden—really?" she asked.

Better than I know you now, I thought. "Is there something I should know? Besides what you already told me?"

She shook her head. "No, never mind. Look, I'm just— you won't believe me, but I'm trying to look out for you," she said. "I don't think there's anything wrong in being a little cautious when it comes to . . . you know."

"What?" I asked.

She cleared her throat. "Getting . . . involved."

"You mean, being 'really really really close'?" I asked, using her euphemism.

"You know what? Forget it," she said. "Forget I said anything. Do whatever you want. Just don't come crying to me when it doesn't work out."

"Caroline? Don't worry. For one thing, we're not an item.

And for another, if anything did happen? The *last* person I'd come to for sympathy would be you." I walked out of her room without giving her a chance to reply, and into ours next door, slamming both doors behind me.

"Let me guess. You talked to Caroline?" Claire asked, looking up from her book.

"Did I mention I hate dorms?" I said. "There's no privacy anywhere—"

"You want me to leave? I can leave for a while," Claire said. "No problem. If you and Hayden want to talk or whatever—"

"No." I shook my head. "Hayden and I just talked. Or actually I talked, and he just sat there like a lump, as if he didn't even know me or care. I'm done talking to him," I said.

"Let's go out for ice cream." Claire slid her feet into a pair of sandals.

"Really? You think?"

"Let's find Josh and get out of here for a while." Claire pointed to the wall we shared with Caroline and Zoe.

"Good idea," I said. "I know just where we should go—Sally's."

"Who's Sally?" Claire asked.

"She runs a little coffee place. Come on."

* * *

"What are you doing here?" I looked up from the croquet wickets that I was placing in the lawn. "Children are drowning. And don't you have some zinc oxide to apply?"

"Ha. Very funny." Hayden dropped a long duffel that made a clattering wood sound. "I've been replaced."

I couldn't believe it. "What?"

"Yeah. I've been replaced. Go figure," he said. We were standing on the grassy lawn overlooking the ocean, and he pointed at the lifeguard stand, where another figure was perched.

"Like, permanently?" I asked. I could have yelled at myself for having even an ounce of empathy for him. He didn't deserve it. He didn't even deserve me talking to him.

"No, just for this morning," he said. "They hired someone new, from town, so they can have more of a pool to draw from, in case one of us—or me—gets sick and can't work, or if there's an emergency, like with Lindsay yesterday."

"A pool. Did they actually say that? A pool of lifeguards?" I laughed, despite the fact I felt more like killing him than joking around with him.

"Anyway, that's why I was in such a bad mood last night. Miss Crossley told me about some big event she wants me to help with. The Inn-lympics or something like that?"

"And you brought the mallets?" I asked. "Thanks. So

where are all the competitors?"

"Miss Crossley's in the lobby, going over the rules. Quite extensive, from what I gather," Hayden said. "I think she took the actual international Olympics handbook and just modified it a little."

"So. Should we practice?"

Hayden eyed the wickets I'd set up. "Sure."

The air smelled incredible that morning—like flowers and ocean and sunshine. Hayden and I were standing there in our sunglasses and Inn uniforms. We looked like something out of an Inn brochure. This could be such a nice scene.

"What color do you want to be?" Hayden asked.

"Red," I said. The color of anger.

"This is going to be wicket fun," Hayden said in a Boston accent.

It was funny, but I willed myself not to smile. I knocked the ball through the first wicket with one rocket shot.

"Wow. Wicket impressed," he commented.

"I can't believe you," I said as I walked over to it.

"What?" Hayden chose blue and followed behind me. His shot went farther.

"You're such a phony." I whacked the ball again when it was my turn.

"I am? Me?" He knocked through another wicket.

"Yeah. You pretend to be all nice to me, and sweet and romantic, and then when other people are around, it's like you don't even know me. Why?" I asked, sending his croquet ball flying off the grassy lawn and into the sand.

"What are you doing?" he asked. "And what are you talking about?"

We were approaching each other, croquet mallets in hand, and looking vaguely threatening, when Miss Crossley came running out of the Inn. "Liza, stop that!" she cried.

What did she think I was going to do? And why was she only yelling at me, and not both of us? Hayden looked equally murderous.

"We've had an emergency. Roberta's got her hands full because of an especially needy room," Miss Crossley said. "Especially needy" meant "completely trashed" in Tides Inn language. "We need you to help out. Rooms Three-eleven and Three-twelve still need cleaning, and a family's checking into both at noon, they requested early check-in. Could you be a team player and get those two rooms presentable ASAP?"

I'm definitely a team player, but on Uptight Knight's clean team? I wondered. "Are you sure this is okay with Mr. Knight?" I asked.

"Of course. Why wouldn't it be? Anyway, I call the shots around here," she said. "Follow me—Hayden, I'll be right back with the contestants!"

I glared at him as I thrust the red-striped mallet into his arms. "Have a good time."

About an hour later, I was cleaning when there was a knock on the door. I looked up from the coffee table I was dusting, expecting it to be either Roberta or Mr. Knight checking on me. I started dusting more vigorously and sprayed an extra layer of cleaner onto the table. Then I answered, "Yes?"

"Liza? I thought I'd find you here." Hayden stepped into the room.

"Brilliant," I muttered. As if he had figured out something difficult. Miss Crossley had only announced in front of him that I'd be in either Room 311 or 312.

"What's that?" Hayden asked.

"I'm busy," I said.

"This won't take long." He lifted the PRIVACY PLEASE sign off the doorknob and set it on the outside, then he closed the door.

"What are you doing?" I asked. "You can't do that." Of all the times for his infamous daredevil rule-breaking side to come out. "And shouldn't you be competing in the Inn-lympics?"

"I was a referee. A croquet referee. Have you ever heard of anything so lame?" He laughed.

"You can take over in housekeeping anytime," I said under my breath.

"Oh no. I'd never survive. Not neat enough. Let me do my Uptight Knight impersonation." He lifted up the corner of his shirt and ran it over the top of the dresser. "Aha! I have found a speck of dust."

I didn't find him all that amusing. Plus, I couldn't help wondering what he was up to, trapping me in a hotel room. Sure, we lived and worked here, but it was still kind of loaded.

"I can't believe they let you clean again," he said. "After the first time."

"I wasn't that bad," I said. "It was an accident. A runaway vacuum. It could happen to anyone."

He laughed, and I wondered why I was still trying to be funny, to make him laugh. He didn't deserve it.

"They're checking in soon, so I have to get this done."

"Come on. You can have some fun. So, I was wondering." He switched on the radio beside the bed, then he came over and took the cleaning stuff out of my hands. He ran his finger along my bare arm. "I know this isn't wedding music, but . . . you want to dance?"

I walked over to the radio and snapped it off. "You know, I was wondering something, too. What is your problem?"

"My problem?" he asked.

"With acknowledging me. With being in public together," I said.

He paced around the room for a second, walking over to the window and back again. "It's not you, it's me," he finally said.

I laughed. "What soap opera did you hear that on?" I scoffed. "And anyway—no kidding. It is you. We could be together. We could be *great* together, if you haven't noticed. But you've got some weird hang-up where you only want to think that some of the time," I said.

He finally sighed and sat down at the desk. "Okay, fine. You want an explanation. You know what it is? I hated how last year everyone knew about me and Zoe. I hated it. They all had their opinions, like they felt like they could discuss us. I didn't want that to happen again."

"Didn't want *what* to happen again?" I asked. "The girl-friend part or the gossip part?"

He swiveled back and forth in the chair. "The everyone-in-my-business part."

"I don't think that's it," I said. "I think you're, like, embarrassed of me, for some reason. I think you just don't want everyone to know about *me*."

Hayden shook his head. "That's not it. I just like to keep things private."

"Keep me private, you mean."

"Keep what happens between us private," he said. "That's why I put the sign on the door. Privacy please. Like if I could wear one of those around my neck."

"That could be arranged," I said. Very, very tightly.

"What do you want me to do?"

I was so angry, I couldn't even talk to him. "I don't know," I said. "But not what you've been doing."

"Look, if you want to find me, I'll be back at the beach later, from one to four," he said, and then he stood up and left the room.

Great. Now I couldn't even go to the beach.

CHAPTER 17

So I'd go to another beach, I decided once Miss Crossley released me for the day—or "for the time being," as she liked to say.

No problem.

I'd go to one in Newport. Or I'd catch the ferry to Block Island. Would that be far enough away?

Sure. But to get all those places, I had to drive and my car still wouldn't start. I was sitting in the scorching hot driver's seat, turning the ignition again and again, but nothing was happening.

Why did I have a feeling I'd be leaving my car at the Inn at the end of the summer, along with my hopes of a big romance? Not that Miss Crossley would let me abandon my car. She'd have it towed to the nearest junkyard. In fact, I was surprised she hadn't already done that—maybe she hadn't noticed it yet.

All of a sudden the passenger door opened, and Hayden stuck his head inside the car. "I didn't realize this loud screeching sound was your car. I thought it was a flock of seagulls that'd just spied a bag of potato chips."

I laughed, despite the fact I'd wanted to kill him the last time I saw him. "It does sound like that, doesn't it?"

"Let me try something," Hayden said.

"Hurry up, I think my legs are melting onto the seat," I said.

He closed the door, then pounded the hood a few times with the heel of his hand. "That didn't work, did it? So come on, go for a bike ride with me."

"It's going to start this time," I said as I turned the key in the ignition.

"No, it isn't. Your belts are shot, or one of them is, anyway." He peered in at me through my open window. He looked really good today, in a faded brown T-shirt and baggy green army shorts. "You're a belt killer. You know that? That's like twelve this summer."

"It's not *twelve*," I said as I got out of the car, the seat making a sticky sound. "Three or four, tops."

"That's not the point. The point is that biking to the beach is a lot more fun."

Fun with Hayden. Had I completely given up on that yet? "What kind of bike are we talking about?" I asked, narrowing my eyes.

"It's a mountain bike. Practically brand-new and totally nice," Hayden said. "I checked out all the bikes in the shed and it's probably the best one in there."

I was so tempted. It was about four thirty, and I really wanted to spend the rest of the day—and evening—away from the Inn. But the thing was, part of the reason I felt that way was because I needed to get away from Hayden. So how would spending my night off with him help?

"But I'm still mad at you," I told Hayden. "So I probably shouldn't."

"So ride behind me and spend the first hour yelling at me," Hayden said.

"You're going to wear headphones, aren't you?" I accused him.

"I'm considering it. How mad are you?" he asked.

"How far are we going?"

"I don't know. It's up to you. I was thinking we could ride somewhere, grab some takeout, maybe hit a different beach or something." He shrugged. "Whatever."

It totally went against common sense, kind of like getting a belly button pierced, as Miss Crossley saw it. I'd tried so hard to stand my ground with Hayden, to tell him what he was doing wrong. And part of me knew I shouldn't go anywhere with him until we had another "talk." But that wasn't the fun, adventurous part of me. Which was screaming, *What are you waiting for?*

"Whatever sounds great," I said. "Just let me grab my backpack."

"This is sort of creepy."

"I know, isn't it?" Hayden asked.

We were standing outside a large hotel about five miles up the coast from the Tides Inn. But instead of looking exclusive, it looked excluded—from guests, from renovations, from everything. The white paint was peeling, a few windows were broken, and the main entrance had a door that sagged.

"It's like a lesson, what could happen if the Tides ever closed," I said.

"If it ever closed, people would buy up the land in a second. I can't remember why the owners of this won't sell yet, but they refuse."

Hayden opened the door and we walked inside the old inn. "It only closed two summers ago. Mismanagement of funds or something like that," he explained. "Wouldn't it be amazing to buy this place?"

"And compete with the Tides? Peach would never forgive you," I told him.

"No, I suppose not. But wouldn't that be okay?" Hayden smiled. "No, actually I like Miss C. I mean, there's something cool about being that reliable, that consistent, all the time."

"Sure there is," I said. "I just haven't figured out what yet."

I heard a creaking sound and felt a shiver crawl up my spine. I'm not one to jump at the slightest noise or scare easily—usually. But something about this place was giving me the creeps.

"Don't worry about that sound. It only means the ghosts are out walking today," Hayden said.

"What ghosts?" I asked.

"Former guests. There was a double murder here back in the seventies," Hayden said. "People say that's what brought bad luck to the place."

I laughed nervously. "Maybe C. Q. Wallace should come here if he's still looking for material." I stepped closer to Hayden. "Do you think maybe we could go back outside?"

"Are you wimping out on me? That's not like you. Come on, let's check out the upstairs," Hayden urged.

"Did you ever read the book or see that movie *The Shining*, about that creepy deserted hotel in Colorado?" I asked. "Because this is reminding me of that."

"You're not the type of person to let this scare you. Are you? I mean, are you afraid of ghosts?" Hayden asked.

"No. Not really. But what if there are live people up here?" I asked as we ascended the creaky staircase.

"There won't be. The police come through here all the time," Hayden said with confidence.

I put my hand on his arm, trying to stop him. "Which is another reason we should go."

We both paused at the top of the stairs, and gazed into a room's open doorway. "Whoa," I exhaled. "If Uptight Knight saw this, he'd go berserk."

"More berserk," Hayden said.

"Berserkier," I added.

The room was stripped bare of furniture except for an old, rusted metal blanket rack, and a dust-covered desk that was missing a leg and listed to one side. A coffeemaker with mold growing inside sat on a desk, and the carpet smelled of something rotten.

"Okay, I think I need to take a shower just from looking at this place," I said.

"Yeah, me too. I haven't been here since last summer

when a whole bunch of us came over," Hayden said. "It's a lot more, uh . . ."

"Disgusting?" I suggested.

"How about a swim to get the dirt off?" Hayden brushed at his arms. "This hotel has a private beach just like the Tides, and at least that can't have gotten trashed."

"Let's go!" I said. We ran down the stairs, out the front door, and down the path to a small sandy beach.

"Where do we change?" I asked.

"Over there." Hayden pointed to a small beach hut connected to the hotel that looked like it could have been a cabana, once upon a time.

"No thanks," I said. "Not if it's anything like the inside of *that* place."

"Good point. Here, you change behind that dune." Hayden pointed to a grassy area that dipped down below the level of the rest of the property. I could probably conceal myself there, but still . . .

"I don't know. What if someone shows up?" I asked.

"Who's going to come here?"

"If you know about it, don't other people? And what if the police come by?" I asked.

"I'll stall them until you're decent," Hayden offered. He picked up my backpack from the sand and tossed it to me.

"Unless you'd rather swim in your clothes? Or without them?"

"Fat chance. I'll be back in a minute," I told him.

We raced each other to be first into the ocean. It was becoming a tradition with us—except this time, for once, I won.

I wasn't sure if that was a good thing as I came up gasping for air. I'd definitely chosen a cold spot to dive into.

"Did they lose their lease on decent temperature water, too?" I asked.

"The current must be slightly different here," Hayden said.

"You know, I always knew the Inn was exclusive, but I mean, are they *that* sheltered, from even the elements of nature?" We started to swim in the deeper water.

"You kind of have an attitude about the Inn and its guests. Do you think they're all spoiled?"

"Aren't they? I don't know. Maybe I'm just not cut out for customer service," I said.

We swam side by side for a few minutes, and I noticed Hayden kept glancing at the shore.

"Why do you keep looking at the hotel? Is someone there?" I stopped swimming and treaded water.

"No, don't worry so much. It's important to keep aligned with something onshore, so you don't mistakenly go too far out. If you ever get caught in a riptide, you've got to swim parallel to the beach until you get out of it."

"I've heard that," I said. "I think it happened to my grandmother once, and she swam out of it. But . . . are we *in* a riptide?"

"No. More like high tide." Hayden laughed.

"I have to say, it's pretty cool having my own personal lifeguard," I said as we swam back toward shore. I reached for the ocean bottom with my feet, finally touching sand. Hayden and I stood halfway in and halfway out of the water.

"Hold on, you're coming untied," he said.

Unglued was more like it. He was standing so close to me, his hands on my shoulder as he retied the stringy strap around my neck. I held my breath. The anticipation was killing me.

"How many swimsuits do you have, exactly?" Hayden asked. "I've counted three, so far."

"Four," I said.

"Oh. So I have something else to look forward to." He ran his fingers from my suit strap down my back.

"You could say that." I put my hands on his strong, tanned shoulders and felt the muscles of his upper arms.

Were we really doing this? I was so caught up in the moment that I barely had time to think. And yet I knew that I'd already decided I was ready to take this step with Hayden. But maybe I was assuming too much—maybe he wasn't ready.

"Do you think there is a PRIVACY PLEASE sign we could put on the beach?" Hayden asked.

"Why?" I asked. "Is anyone around that we need to worry about?"

"Just us. And maybe this will sound totally crazy, but that's what I want. Because . . . this is going to sound dumb, okay? But I feel like I can't get enough of you."

"It's not dumb. That's how I feel about you," I confessed.

We started to kiss, and then we started to shiver because the sun was setting, and a cold breeze was coming off the water.

"We should probably go," Hayden said.

I knew he was right, but I hated to admit that. "Probably," I said.

We walked out of the water, holding hands. "The sand's still warm, though," Hayden observed.

I glanced at him and smiled. I wasn't sure I should really do this. I should either leave now or be prepared for the consequences. Was I ready for this?

Yes.

"I have a beach blanket." I crouched by my backpack and

pulled it out. I unfolded the blanket and shook it out, placing it on the beach. As soon as I sat down, Hayden lay down beside me. I lay back on the blanket, too.

We looked at each other for a few seconds, as if we were both making sure we knew how serious this was getting.

Hayden propped himself up on his elbow. He pushed a strand of my wet hair behind my ear. "I had a really good time with you today."

I reached up and touched him gently on the lips. "Me, too."

He kissed my fingers and then didn't move for a second. He just kept looking into my eyes. "Liza?" he finally said.

I was starting to feel nervous about what he might say. *Please don't say we should take off. I don't want to leave now.* "Hayden?" I replied, a little breathless.

"I think . . . I think maybe I'm falling in love with you," he said.

"Really?"

"Really."

"Good," I said.

He laughed. "Why is that good? It's sort of torture if you ask me—"

"Because I'm falling in love with you, too," I admitted.

"Then we're even," he said.

"Even? What is this—a competition—" I started to say, but Hayden silenced me with a kiss.

To my right, in my backpack, I could hear a beeping sound. My pager was stuffed in the outside pocket.

I started to get up to check it, but then I stopped.

It wasn't about Grandpa, because they'd call my cell. So it was definitely work.

This time, Miss Crossley would have to wait.

I wasn't about to leave where I was right now.

CHAPTER 18

"That's the second time you haven't responded to a page."

Miss Crossley had paged me to her office first thing the next morning, to yell at me for not responding to her pages.

"The first time, I was in Newport and it was my day off," I said in self-defense. "And this time . . . well . . ." Did she really want to know what I was up to with Hayden? I definitely didn't want to tell her. Besides, I'd barely gotten used to admitting it to myself. "I didn't hear it," I said. "Honestly. It did not make a sound."

At least, not a sound that I wanted to hear. What is the sound of one pager buzzing? If a pager buzzes in a backpack and no one hears it . . . did it really buzz?

My stomach made a loud grumbling noise, and I realized I needed to grab some breakfast soon—very soon. Hayden and I had never gotten around to picking up that takeout meal, and by the time we got back to the Inn, the Hull was shut down for the night. We'd snuck into the dorm, it was so late.

"Well, if you say so. Perhaps you were out of range." She gave me a suspicious look.

I wasn't about to volunteer any information about how I'd spent the evening. "Out of range" wasn't a bad description, though. I thought about what Hayden had said: *I think I'm falling in love with you.*

"All right. Let's move on." Miss Crossley stacked a set of papers on her desk. "Today's assignment."

I loved the way she made it sound as if I were a secret agent. Secret agents didn't do dishes or clean toilets, though. At least, not the cool ones.

"C. Q. Wallace. You've become acquaintances, yes?" Miss Crossley asked.

I shrugged. "You could say that."

"You have a certain rapport. And he needs someone to help him with his manuscript," Miss Crossley said. "We've selected you because he already knows you, for one, and because it says in your application that you're a good typist."

I loved the thought of this assignment, but the beach was calling me. I wanted to be on the beach, with Hayden, not cooped up inside doing office work. I didn't care how many sand castles I had to help build, how many games of Wiffle ball I had to play. They could give me twenty kids to look after, just as long as I got to be near Hayden.

"But Miss Crossley. Is it really the Inn's place to help him with his book?" I asked.

Miss Crossley looked completely stunned, as if I had suggested stoning the author with rocks from the beach. "Yes, Liza, it's our place to help him, if it means he'll stay here longer. Do you know what long-term guests mean to this place? Survival, Liza."

I thought of the closed and shuttered hotel Hayden and I had visited the day before, which reminded me of why I hadn't answered her page. I felt a blush creep up my entire body, from my toes to my torso to my face to my scalp under my Tides Inn ball cap (where thankfully, it was concealed).

No matter what Miss Crossley said? Even if she docked my paycheck? I wouldn't regret ignoring that pager. I was still kind of in shock about it, though.

"So what would this involve?" I asked.

"I believe he has a handwritten rough draft he needs to

have typed. Something about carpal tunnel. You'll work side by side for today, and possibly more days in the future."

"So . . . no outdoor time? At all?" I asked. I felt like a dog stuck in a kennel.

"We'll see how it goes. You'd better go see him—he'll meet you in the lobby at ten," Miss Crossley said. "Oh, and Liza?" she asked as I stood up to leave. "That's the second time I've tried to page you and you haven't been around. Let's not have a third, all right?"

She didn't come right out and say that it was my last chance—that if I got a third strike, I'd be out—but I could tell that was what she meant. It wasn't fair, because I was the only employee who was on call all the time. But I sensed now wasn't the time to point that out to her. If she wanted me to be there for her—I'd be there.

"What's the book about?" I asked as I turned on the notebook computer C. Q. had brought downstairs to the back porch. He'd already plugged it into an outlet, so there was no hope of the battery running out and my job finishing early.

"It's about identity, love, American history, and . . . oh, you'll find out soon enough. It's a novel about a family that vacations at a large Rhode Island hotel."

"Kind of like *The Shining*?" I asked.

He frowned at me. "No. Great book, but no. This isn't a horror novel."

"So this large inn—is it based on this place?" I said.

"No. Resemblance to anything or anyone is strictly coincidental. Or whatever they print at the beginning of the book that means I can't be sued." He coughed and put out his cigarette. "Anyhow, it's not this place. It's a composite, of many hotels I've stayed at."

"In Rhode Island," I said. "Uh huh. Fine, whatever you say. Except you should probably change my *name*," I insisted as I typed in an exchange between the main character and an employee of the hotel. "And why did you make me short? I don't want to be short."

"It's fiction. Let it go," he advised.

"And speaking of names," I went on. If he could use mine, then I had a question about his. "What does C. Q. stand for?"

"Don't tell anyone. But nothing. I just liked the initials. My real name is Larry."

"Larry?" I wanted to giggle, but resisted.

"I know, Larry Wallace doesn't have quite the same cachet as a pair of pretentious initials."

"You're right. Larry Wallace sounds like someone who works at the car repair shop, or a phys ed teacher or something."

"My point exactly. What were my parents thinking?" He laughed. "They scarred me for life."

Caroline came out onto the back porch. She was watching us, but pretending *not* to watch us. "Checking the surf again?" I asked her.

"What?" she said in an innocent tone.

"Nothing." I kept typing.

"Wow. Liza, I didn't know you were a secretary," Caroline said.

"She's my creative assistant today," C. Q. said. "Now, could you get us some coffee?"

"I'm sorry?" Caroline looked highly offended.

"Don't be sorry. Just get us the coffee," C. Q. said.

I bit my lip to keep from smiling.

"I'll try to—to—find your, uh, server," she said.

"Or you could do it," C. Q. said.

"I can go do it," I offered, standing up. "If I'm your assistant, then—"

"No, you're not going for coffee, you're going for a landspeed record, typing this manuscript for me. Carry on. I take mine black," he said to Caroline. She made a tsking noise and walked away.

"*You* need to stay right here. The fewer distractions, the better." He stared at the beach for a second. "Oh, great. Here comes distraction number one."

What was he talking about? I looked up and saw Hayden walking toward the Inn. He must be on break. Just seeing him, I felt this magnetic pull.

"Keep your mind on your work."

"Sir, yes sir," I replied. "But anyway. Why do you say that?"

"I saw you two. I've seen you two."

"What?"

"Never mind," he said.

I glanced over at C. Q. (Larry), a new cigarette dangling from his lip, writing in a notebook. While I typed, maybe he could use up some more pens, I thought, or notebooks. Then Hayden and I would have the perfect excuse to escape together.

Maybe he could run out of his famous Turkish cigarettes. And maybe Hayden and I would have to go to Turkey—or at the very least Providence—to buy some more. If Miss Crossley wanted me to keep a long-term guest happy, I was willing to do my part. As long as Hayden went with me.

I had to work so late that night that by the time I got back to the dorm, it was nearly eleven. I'd missed the party at Crandall's Point—sitting on the porch and then after dark in the lobby typing, I'd heard everyone go rushing by. I'd missed everything. My back was killing me. But Mr. Wallace had his pages ready to send off, so tomorrow I'd have a break. I was more than ready to try something else.

I couldn't wait to see Hayden—being away from him for the entire day had been pure torture. Even though it was late, I decided to stop by his room to say hi before I turned in for the night.

I was about to knock on the door when I heard Hayden's voice. "I don't want to hurt her, but I have to tell her before tomorrow," he was saying.

Was he talking about me?

"So tell her," Richard said.

"I can't. She likes me now. She won't like me after I tell her," Hayden said.

I stepped back from the door. I was feeling really scared. I'd totally fallen for him. I'd slept with him. What did he have to tell me that was so horrible?

I definitely didn't feel like barging in right that second and finding out. Not without checking in with Claire first. I'd go upstairs—maybe he'd left me a note, saying he needed to talk. When he was ready, he'd come find me—probably he'd been waiting all night for me to show up.

I went up to our room. There was no note and no Claire.

Where could she be this late? I kicked off my sandals and sat on the edge of my bed, letting out a big, tense sigh. What was Hayden talking about? I took a deep breath and tried to collect myself.

You've got to go back downstairs right now, I told myself. You have to find out what this is about.

And I would—in just a few more minutes. I lay back on the bed, completely exhausted by the last forty-eight hours.

I never went back down to talk to Hayden. I fell asleep and slept so hard that the next day I slept right through breakfast, then got woken up by Miss Crossley pounding on the door, telling me to meet her at the Inn's main doors, at the shuttle pickup. I had vague hopes of seeing Hayden, but instead it was an Inn kids' trip to play miniature golf, race in go-karts, and hit in batting cages.

(They tried to do all that stuff without me, but I wouldn't let them. No way was I spending the entire day *observing*.)

Miss Crossley dropped us off at the amusement park at ten and came back for us at four. By the time she fetched us, almost all of us had sunburns and were completely exhausted from the intense heat and activity.

I had just enough time to rush to the dorm, shower, heavily apply aloe lotion, throw on my catering clothes, run back to the kitchen, and take my tray of champagne and sparkling water out to the dining room.

When I walked in, I looked around for the bride, knowing it was Zoe's sister, Anneke. I wanted to see how much she and Zoe looked alike. I couldn't find Anneke at first, because she and the groom were mingling, but I did spot them across the dining room.

I spotted Zoe next.

And then I saw Hayden.

There, sitting at the head table beside Zoe, was Hayden, wearing a dark-blue suit and looking extremely handsome.

What was he doing there? He didn't tell me he was going to the wedding.

They're old family friends, I tried to tell myself. They go way back.

Don't they?

Okay, so they were from the same town, so why wouldn't he be at her sister's wedding? It made sense. It was all extremely innocent and platonic.

Then I saw the wedding photographer stop at the table to take a photo, just as I was walking in that direction to say hi to both of them.

"Come on, everyone, say cheese. Kiss for the camera!" the photographer urged, and somebody in the crowd started to ring their glass with a knife, so the married couple would kiss.

Hayden put his arms around Zoe's shoulder, and then he pressed his lips against Zoe's cheek. She turned her head and he kissed her right on the mouth.

CHAPTER 19

The champagne glasses tumbled

off my tray and onto the floor.

Fortunately I was in the carpeted area at the time, so instead of shattering and drawing everyone's attention to me, they just sort of bounced and knocked into each other, splashing my shoes with champagne.

Unfortunately I let out a little shriek as it happened. So everyone looked at me anyway.

I caught Hayden looking over at me with a startled expression, and I glared right back at him. If I didn't strangle him now, it was only because there were about two hundred witnesses.

Was that why everything between us always had to be a

secret, because he was still trying to get back together with Zoe? Or had he been with her this whole time—while he was also with me?

Was I the stupidest girl on the planet—or in Rhode Island—or what? *Everyone knew,* I thought. *Everyone knew except me.*

Caroline knew—she tried to warn me to stay away from Hayden, in her own weird way. Richard knew—that was why he was so nice to me, because he pitied me. Maybe even Claire knew, and that was why she kept warning me against dating Hayden. Everyone else who'd ever hung out at Crandall's Point probably knew Hayden and Zoe still had a "thing." Or something. And they were all looking at me.

She likes me now, Hayden had said last night to his roommate. *She won't like me after I tell her.*

He was right. I wouldn't like him anymore, now that I knew he wanted to see two girls at the same time.

Uptight Knight was on me immediately. "Do you know how impossible it is to get the smell of alcohol out of carpet?"

I turned to him and raised my eyebrow. "We'll Febreze it."

Claire and Josh found me in the kitchen, where I was collecting myself by drinking iced tea mixed with lemonade and snacking on shrimp cocktail.

I must have downed five or six consecutive shrimp without really pausing, because the plate—which was supposed to go onto the tray and be served—was now empty.

"Where have you been?" Josh asked. "One whole table didn't get their champagne and we had to scramble for more glasses just in time for the big toast."

"Where have I *been*? Didn't you see me?" I asked.

They both shook their heads.

"You didn't see what happened? Well, that's two people out of two hundred. You must not have been in the dining room when it happened. I had a little accident. Dropped my tray. Screeched when I did it. Fortunately it was on carpet, but I got splashed."

"So you're in here recovering from spillage?" Claire asked.

"You could say that." I brushed a speck of lint off my black skirt, part of my official catering gear uniform. "You could also say that I'm recovering from seeing Hayden with Zoe. I mean, what *is* that?"

I wandered over to the kitchen doorway and looked out at the scene. Yup, Hayden and Zoe were still sitting next to each other. They didn't seem to be talking, at the moment, but that was because they were both eating.

"I noticed they were at the same table," Josh said.

"I guess their families are pals—you said they came from

the same town, right?" Claire asked. "So he must have gone to the wedding—you know, as a friend."

"That's what I tried to tell myself. But would a *friend* sit at the head table with the bride and groom and wedding party?" I asked.

"It's a pretty big table. So maybe," Claire said.

I glared at her. "Hey, I'm the optimist, not you. And would he kiss her on the mouth? Tell me—is it as bad as it looks?"

"It's not *good*," Claire said.

"I have an idea. Josh, dance with me," I said.

He groaned. "Please don't make me do that."

"One dance. It won't kill you."

"You don't know that. Have you heard the music?" Josh pretended to stick his finger down his throat.

I laughed. "Okay, so the music's kind of cheesy, but come on, just a quickie."

"Well, if *that's* what we're talking about—"

"We're not." I grabbed the sleeve of Josh's white button-down shirt and pulled him out of the kitchen, toward the dance floor, with Claire following close behind us.

"You'll owe me for this," Josh said as I put my hands on his shoulders, and he rested his hands on my waist.

"I know. I already do," I said.

We moved around the dance floor, staying in the middle

so that Miss Crossley wouldn't notice us. I tried to dance close enough to Hayden's table that he'd see us. Two could play that game. He wanted to have someone on the side? So did I.

Okay, not really, but I might be able to make it look that way.

"Take it easy," Josh said, as I leaned my cheek against his shoulder.

"Too close?" I asked.

"A little," he said.

I know Hayden saw us, because he and I exchanged yet another awkward glance.

Cut in anytime, I thought. *Cut in and show me—and everyone else—that we're together now, the way you said we were the other night.*

But he didn't budge. He sat there beside Zoe, taking part in the conversation at the table, without moving. I turned away; that was something I didn't need to see over and over.

The song came to an end, and I felt a tap on my shoulder.

I turned around, my heart beating faster.

"Excuse me, but aren't you employees?" a man in a black tuxedo asked. "Are you supposed to be dancing? I mean, this is my daughter's wedding, and if you're dancing, then what are we paying you for?"

I don't know, I thought, *but nobody's paying me nearly enough to put up with this.*

"Don't you have cake to hand out?" Zoe's father asked.

"Sorry, sir. We got caught up in the moment," I said. *The moment where I want to throttle your other daughter and her apparent date.* "It won't happen again."

"Got that right," Josh muttered as we headed off the dance floor.

I passed right by Miss Crossley, who was walking through the lobby in the opposite direction. "I'll be back, I promise," I told her, hoping that Zoe's dad wouldn't complain to her about me and Josh dancing. "I just need some fresh air."

"But—Liza—this is highly irregular—"

No kidding, I thought. "Ten minutes, okay? I really have to do this," I said.

She gave me a stunned look as I bolted out the back door. I ran past guests on the porch and nearly knocked down a woman walking back up from the beach.

Then I heard heels clattering on the boardwalk behind me. "Liza! Liza, wait up!" a female voice called.

I turned around and saw Caroline coming. She ran toward me, tossing her stilettos onto the sand, her fancy strapless dress (because she was a wedding guest, too) rippling in the wind. "Are you okay?"

I couldn't believe her nerve. "No. Not really," I said. "But you told me not to come crying to you. So I won't."

"I'm sorry," Caroline said. "I shouldn't have—"

"You know what, Caroline? You could have just told me. You had every opportunity in the world."

"Yeah, I guess I could—but I wasn't—I didn't really think they'd go through with it. They both wanted to call it off, but—"

"But what?"

"It was all arranged. A long time ago."

"So I was merely messing up their social calendar? You know what? Forget it. I don't want to know." I didn't want to listen to her, of all people, *explain* this to me.

I took off jogging down the beach, kicking the surf with my feet, wishing I'd come anywhere except the Inn for the summer.

CHAPTER 20

Hayden was sitting in the hallway

outside my door when I got back to the dorm, around two in the morning. His suit was rumpled, his tie untied.

I really, really wanted to talk to him. And I also really didn't ever want to see him again.

Was he waiting for me? Or was he just slumped there because he'd been in Zoe's room, which happened to be right next door to mine?

This dorm stuff sucked. It was like living in a fish bowl. And I was starting to feel like that one pathetic fish that's always at the edge of the bowl, staring straight ahead like it can't wait to escape.

If dorm life was what college was all about, then maybe I

should reconsider going away to college and stay home.

"Where have you been all night?" Hayden asked.

I was holding my sandals, and my legs and ankles were covered in sand that looked like a dusting of cinnamon and sugar. I'd tried to wash it off before I came inside, with the hose by the door, but sort of halfheartedly. If sand got all over the dorm, what did I care?

"I was walking on the beach," I told him. "Then I lay down to look at the stars and I guess I fell asleep."

"You slept on the beach," Hayden said.

"Yup."

"By yourself."

What was he implying? Did he really think I'd be out there with someone else? "Yup."

Hayden scrambled to his feet. "Do you know how dangerous that is?" He gave me this pleading look. "Promise me you won't do that again."

"It's not dangerous. I sleep with one eye open."

"Right," Hayden said.

"How long have you been waiting?" I asked. "Or did you just pass out here after the big wedding night?"

"I've been here since midnight," Hayden said. "Since Zoe and everyone else at the wedding crashed at the Inn. They rented the second and third floors, you know?"

"Fascinating." I opened the door to our room and walked inside.

I couldn't believe it. Claire wasn't home. Claire, who I'd been counting on to get me out of this. She was not in her bed.

Hayden, apparently seeing that she wasn't there, followed me into my room and closed the door behind him.

I walked over and opened it a crack. It wasn't that I was scared of him, or what would happen. I just didn't want him to think that he could have me all to himself. I was too mad to want to be alone with him. Let Caroline hear us argue, too. Maybe she could tell Zoe what happened.

"I didn't know how to tell you," Hayden began.

Oh God. Anything but that. What a horrible thing to say.

"My family was coming and I was all stressed out about that and I didn't know what to say."

"So you didn't tell me anything."

"Don't hate me," Hayden said. "I had to do it."

"Had to do what?"

"Had to be at the wedding today. It's—it's complicated."

"Not really," I said. "You and Zoe still being together is actually not all that complex."

"But we're *not* still together, you know that."

"Do I?" I asked.

"Yes."

"I thought I did, until today. Then everything started to look a lot different."

"You don't understand." Hayden paced back and forth between our beds, which was a pretty small space to use for pacing. "Our families—they expect us—they want us to be together."

"What?" I laughed. "Are you serious? This is the twenty-first century. Are you trying to tell me you guys have an arranged marriage or something like that? Because this isn't exactly the culture where that is the norm. So I don't think that's it. What's the problem, then? Am I not good enough for you? Because that's ridiculous."

"Of course you're good enough for me," Hayden said. "But our parents—they have these ideas. So I agreed to go to the wedding with Zoe, to make her parents happy, which makes my parents happy."

"I don't understand. But I do know that I can't—I don't— trust either of you. If you can't stand up to your parents—I mean, you're in college—and you're still letting them tell you what to do?"

"I don't have a choice. They expect things from me."

"And they don't expect . . . what? You to be with a completely scandalous girl from *Connecticut*? Ooh, scary. Do they restrict other states? What about Rhode Island, is that out?" I snapped my fingers. "I know. It's because I don't go to stupid Maple Syrup Acad—"

"I'm sorry, but I don't want to rock the boat right now. Too much is happening," Hayden said. "I was all worried about my mom and dad and whether they'd fight, and it took them like two seconds before they got into an argument, and then my sister, Grace, gets out of the car and she's wearing black lipstick and combat boots to a wedding—"

I started to feel sympathy for him, remembering our conversation on the beach about his family. But what was he saying? They'd been at the wedding—and he hadn't introduced me? All my sympathy was gone as I realized that. I'd never treat him like that!

"I want to be with you, Liza. You know that."

"I thought I did. But does anyone else? I mean in some ways, you're acting just like Caroline."

"What?"

"You're being a total snob! Whenever I try to bring up stuff we used to do together, she pretends it didn't happen, that it wasn't me she hung out with. And you do the same thing," I said. "Your parents aren't the only ones you're hiding from. You never want to be around me when *any* other people

are there. It's like we have no history. You always find some
reason to take off—"

"I do not. I don't know what you're talking about,"
Hayden said. "Everyone knows about us."

"If they do, it's not because of you!" I started to say, just
as the door popped open. Claire backed into the room, Josh
kissing her.

"Ex—excuse us," Josh said.

"Oh. Oh my God. I thought you guys would be, uh, out,"
Claire said. "Kissing and making up. Not in that order."

"We didn't exactly make up," I said.

"And we're not going to tonight," Hayden added.

"No. We're not," I said.

"Fine!" Hayden went out and slammed the door behind
him.

"What's he so mad about? You're the one who should be
mad," Josh said.

"Oh, I am," I said. "I'm furious." Then I sank onto my
uncomfortable, flat bed and curled up into a fetal position. "I
just *really* like him," I confessed.

"Like . . . in love?" Josh asked.

"I don't know. I guess I am, sort of. And I thought it
would be fun, but it isn't and I hate it."

Josh gave me a sympathetic smile, as if I had an illness that couldn't be cured. "Well, I'll let you guys talk. 'Night." He leaned over to rub my head, then he quickly kissed Claire before leaving.

"*Claire?*" I said the second the door closed. "All those things you told me about not—"

"I know, I know. But I couldn't help it," she said. "He's so cute and funny. I just want to be with him all the time—"

"Well, that's how I feel. No, that's how I felt," I corrected. Until tonight.

"Which is it?" Claire asked.

"Feel. Present tense. But with a lot of emphasis on *tense*. So when did you and Josh get together?"

"I actually have you to thank for that," Claire said. "When you asked him to dance this afternoon? I wanted to kill you. That's when I realized he couldn't dance with anyone but me. I mean, we'd gone out once, but you know me. I usually have my one-date limit."

"You were out so late tonight, I think that counts as three dates."

"But what about you and Hayden? What are you going to do?" Claire asked.

I shrugged. "I have no idea."

"You know what? In spite of everything, I don't think he's

a bad person. I really don't. I think he's confused, you know? And he made some bad choices."

"You're only saying that 'cause you're in love."

"I'm not in love," Claire said. "I'm in like. I'm having fun, for once."

"Okay, but you'll be spending so much time with Josh this summer, you'll probably never make it through all those serious books now," I teased her. "You realize that."

"Oh, well. Columbia will understand why I ditched the reading list," she said. "Right?"

CHAPTER 21

"But Miss Crossley—"

"You love the beach," she said.

I nodded. "I know. I do. I really do."

I wanted to say: And any other day, even tomorrow, it might be okay. But not this morning. Please, not this morning.

"I was just hoping . . . I really got into typing that book the other day. I kind of can't wait to see how it turns out. I was thinking maybe I could work with Mr. Wallace again."

Miss Crossley dusted her telephone while she talked. "That would be extremely difficult, seeing as how he checked out yesterday morning."

"No, he didn't," I said. "He couldn't have."

"What? Do you know something I don't?"

"He—he can't check out! He didn't even tell me he was leaving!" I protested.

Miss Crossley shifted in her office chair, looking a little uncomfortable. "Oh no. Do you and Mr. Wallace have some kind of personal, ah, relationship—"

"No, of course not. Nothing like that." I shook my head. "We were friends, that's all." And I had been hoping to lean on him today, like a crutch, I thought. He could tell me how love sucked, how high the divorce rate was, and what a load of garbage romance was, and I'd completely agree with him for once.

Forget about being optimistic. Optimism sucked.

"I liked working with him. It was kind of an apprentice thing," I explained.

"I see. Well, he did leave. I'm very sorry," Miss Crossley said. "So, can you be ready for the beach in about half an hour? Will Talbot is in need of a beach buddy."

I let out a deep breath, trying to release all the tension in my body.

It didn't work.

"Sure. Of course I can," I said. "I *love* the beach."

It's just that I'd love it a lot more if Hayden was assigned to another beach. Say, on Cape Cod. Just for a few days, just long enough for me to get my act together and fall back *out* of love with him.

I felt a hair color change coming on. Unfortunately I didn't think I had time to book an appointment at the Inn salon in the next ten minutes.

"Hey, you look great this morning," Hayden said when I showed up, trailing behind Will, who plowed straight ahead. He didn't even take off his sneakers before he sprinted into the water. He got his toes wet, then stopped, dropped to the sand, and started digging.

I glared at Hayden. "As opposed to other mornings?"

"What?" Hayden asked, looking confused. He apparently thought we'd made up; but since we hadn't talked since the night before, I didn't see how.

"Or as compared with Zoe," I said under my breath.

My attempt to be cool and pretend I wasn't hurt and that I was completely over him was failing. Badly.

"Is that the infamous fourth bathing suit?" Hayden asked.

I didn't answer him.

"Nice." He nodded as he stepped back to appraise me.

"Whatever," I said. "I think I'll focus on Will, thank you very much."

"Liza, swim with me!" Will yelled as he ran toward me.

"We're not swimming yet, but we can in a little bit," I said. I had it on good authority that Will had just eaten a late breakfast, so I wanted him to wait before we plunged into the ocean.

"No, now," he said.

"No, later," I said.

"You know what, buddy? Let's go on a shell hunt," Hayden offered.

I appreciated the gesture, but it was annoying as well. Did he think he needed to save me? I could handle Will on my own. "You're a lifeguard, not a nature lover," I said.

"I can't be both?" Hayden asked.

"Not when people are depending on you to save their life, no."

"There's nobody swimming," Hayden said.

"Maybe they heard you're the one on duty. Didn't feel like drifting out to sea while you searched for shells," I said.

He started to laugh. "Man, are you mad."

"Why wouldn't I be?" I replied.

Hayden was looking over my shoulder at something, or someone. "Caroline?" he said. I turned around.

"Your presence is requested in the dining room." She sounded as if she'd rather be anywhere else than talking to the two of us.

"What?" I asked.

"Yours, too," she told Hayden.

I was puzzled. "What's this all about?"

"I don't know what it's about, but Mr. Talbot wants to talk to you, over lunch," Caroline said in a bored tone.

"But ah—we're not dressed for the dining room," I protested. *And I don't want to go anywhere with Hayden!*

"Obviously. I can see that," Caroline said. "So, Hayden, you go get cleaned up and changed as soon as Lindsay gets here to take over for you. Liza—you can go now."

"Who's going to replace—"

"*I* am, all right?" Caroline said, exasperated.

I backed away slowly, watching her attempt to play with Will. He took two giant handfuls of sand and threw them at her. Poor Caroline, I thought. And then, poor Will.

And then I thought—poor *me*. This could only be a good-bye lunch, if it was me, Hayden, and Mr. Talbot. He knew about the time we'd been on the deck—and he must have some new information on us. How embarrassing.

I bumped into Hayden on my way out of the dorm. I'd changed into a khaki skirt and a flowered blouse. My hair was tied up in a loose bun, sort of, with lots of tendrils falling out.

I expected Hayden to say something about my appearance, but he didn't. He just glanced at me and kept walking toward the Inn, not looking at me. It was like the two of us were bracing for a firing squad.

When we got to the dining room, Guess Who was working as both server and host.

"Right this way, please," Zoe said.

I hadn't even seen her since the infamous wedding.

This was exactly why Claire warned me about no hookups. The place was closing in on all sides.

"This isn't some weird Dr. Phil intervention to make us all talk, is it?" I asked her.

"What?" Zoe looked at me as if I were crazy.

"Never mind," I said as she led us to the Inn's best corner table, by the biggest window, with a clear view of the ocean. An older gentleman was sitting there—it was Mr. Talbot *Senior.* And across the table from him was . . .

"Grandpa?" I said.

"Drove down this morning." He stood up and I gave him a hug. "Surprise!"

"Yes, it's surprising, all right," I commented. "It's so nice to see you! Is Grandma here, too?"

"Yes, but she's visiting an old friend—she'll be by this afternoon."

"I've arranged for you to have the afternoon off to spend with your grandparents," Mr. Talbot Senior said. "Miss Crossley's been notified."

"Wow. Thank you!" I said.

"You too, Hayden." Mr. Talbot nodded. "Enjoy the time off."

"Uh . . . thanks." Hayden opened his napkin and set it on his lap. I'm sure he was wondering, like I was, what the heck he was there for.

But then I vaguely remembered telling my grandfather about him, back when I was visiting him at the hospital. I sank down a little in my chair. I hoped my grandfather would be discreet, but then again, Hayden wouldn't be here now if I hadn't been indiscreet and blabbed about our possible relationship.

But you know what, I thought. If he was suffering and uncomfortable now, being here? That was too bad. He was the one who'd kissed *me* that night, before I left on the train to go home. He let me think we were in a relationship, and I'd only acted appropriately.

I wasn't the one being weird and hiding and going out with my former girlfriend just for appearance's sake. Not that I had a former girlfriend, but still.

"I understand you're feeling better, sir?" Hayden said to my grandfather.

"Oh, yes. Feeling just fine."

"Was something wrong?" Mr. Talbot asked.

"Just a touch of the flu, Bucko." My grandfather sipped his glass of lemonade. "Nothing serious."

"Grandpa," I said.

"It was a little warning from the old ticker, that's all," he explained. "A minor heart attack."

"I had one of those myself," Mr. Talbot said. "Maybe two or three."

I'm having one right now, I thought. *I don't know if I can sit here much longer.*

"So what have you two been up to?" my grandfather asked.

I shrugged. "Not much, really." Just sneaking away to closed beaches.

"Somehow I doubt that," he said. He turned to Hayden. "Are you treating her well?"

"Grandpa," I said through clenched teeth.

"You know, I'm always pleased when staff members become friends," Mr. Talbot said.

My grandfather chuckled. "Oh, Bucko, they're more than friends."

"Grandpa," I said again. If I gritted my teeth any more, sparks would fly off of them. *It's not like that—not anymore!* I wanted to scream. Why wasn't my grandmother there to rein him in?

"To young love." Grandpa raised his glass, just as Zoe came to the table to take our order.

"Excuse me," I said. "I'll be right back."

I pushed back my chair and practically sprinted for the women's room—except it wasn't that, it was a "ladies' lounge," with an elegant, antique sofa in an outer waiting room.

Once I was safely inside, I went to a sink and turned on the cold water, letting it run over my hands and wrists. I splashed my face and was searching for a towel to dry off when one was handed to me. I pressed it to my face, dried off, and looked up.

"We have to talk," Zoe said.

CHAPTER 22

"I ran into Claire this morning, in the hallway," Zoe went on. "Actually I think she was sitting out there waiting for me. I don't know how she found out what room I was in, but—"

"What are you talking about?" I asked.

"Here, in the Inn. You know I stayed with my sister last night—I mean, my whole family was here," she explained. She stepped up to the mirror and fixed her hair a little.

"Don't you need to get back to your tables?" I asked.

She shrugged. "Let them wait. The kitchen's running slow so far today, anyway." She leaned forward and touched up her lipstick. "So Claire told me about you and Hayden," she said casually.

This didn't seem like someone who was upset, but I wasn't completely sure.

"I had no idea you and Hayden were seriously involved. I'm really sorry you got the wrong impression last night. I'm still seeing Brandon, you know."

"That's what I thought," I said. "But then I see you and Hayden at the wedding . . . I mean, I saw you and Hayden together, and Brandon wasn't there . . . you have to admit that looked pretty bad."

"It was supposed to look good. To my parents," she said. "They love Hayden—or they love Hayden's family's money, anyway. When we broke up they were furious with me, all because Hayden's dad is some big-shot corporate guy and his family's so big and important in the community, and they thought it would be their 'in,' you know."

"Their 'in'?" I asked.

"They freak out about whether or not they're going to be accepted. We're sort of new in town. Anyway, I'm not seeing Hayden. My family doesn't approve of Brandon, that's all. We fought about it constantly. So I told them we were over, and I was back with Hayden."

"So is it like that on his end? Hayden's family wouldn't approve of me, either?"

Zoe shrugged. "What's there not to approve of?"

"I don't know. You tell me," I said.

"Well, we do come from kind of a snobby community, it's true. And our parents did want us to date, but that's not enough reason to actually stay together. Look, Claire said you guys argued, and I want to make it clear there was no reunion, or anything like that. We've been over since a year ago."

I wanted to believe Zoe, and for the most part I did, but a few things still didn't make sense. One, why did Hayden insist on being so secretive? And . . . "Then why did you kiss him?"

Zoe laughed. "I had a glass of champagne with my sister at the beginning of the reception—it went to my head. That's it. It didn't mean anything. Anyway, order the clam chowder and the lobster—it's the best stuff on the menu." Zoe opened the door and walked out of the ladies' room.

I fixed my hair for a second, then headed back to our table, where Hayden, Grandpa, and Mr. Talbot were all laughing about something. I opened my cloth napkin and smoothed it on my lap.

I couldn't believe Hayden hadn't taken the opportunity to bolt, without me there. But how could he? The owner of the Inn was dining with us. Neither one of us could leave.

"So," Grandpa said, turning to me. "What would you two like to do this afternoon?"

Hayden and I looked at each other across the table. I wondered if he was thinking what I was: *I'd like to get this lunch over with as soon as possible.*

Around 5:30 I was saying good-bye to my grandparents at the Inn's front entrance, by their car, when my grandmother said, "Is that little Carrie Farlane?"

I turned and saw Caroline walking up from the dorm. "Caroline, Grandma," I said. I tried to smile as I said it, so she wouldn't ask what was up.

"Caroline, how nice to see you!" my grandmother said as Caroline came closer.

"Hello, Mrs. McKenzie. Mr. McKenzie." She reached out her hand to shake theirs, but my grandparents insisted on hugging her. She looked embarrassed, but sort of happy, too.

"Wow. Look at the two of you, all grown up. I remember when you two ruled the roost," my grandfather said.

"We did what?" I asked.

"You were the dynamic duo. You were Lewis and she was Clark," my grandfather said.

I looked at Caroline and rolled my eyes. "Whatever, Grandpa."

"Enjoying your summer?" my grandmother asked Caroline.

"Definitely," Caroline said. "I mean, not everything is perfect, but—"

"You wouldn't want that," Grandpa interrupted as he walked around to the passenger side door. "Perfect is boring." He opened the door and slid into his seat, and I leaned in the open window and gave him a quick good-bye kiss on the cheek.

"We're on our way to meet friends, so we can't hang around. But it's so nice to see you, Caroline. Take care, Liza," my grandmother said as she got into the car. "Take care of each other, will you?" She waved out the window and called to us, "Have fun!"

I guessed I had never mentioned the fact that Caroline and I weren't exactly best pals anymore. We stood there waving at my grandparents, and I felt kind of awkward, as if we were kids again and they'd just dropped us off at the beach.

"How was lunch?" Caroline asked glumly as we watched them drive away.

"Okay. Weird, embarrassing. You know my grandfather, how he likes to joke around. So he joked about me and Hayden. Ha ha. So funny," I complained. I sat down on the wide steps. "I felt like it would never end."

"I don't know what you're so upset about," Caroline

replied. She sat a few steps above me. "One, Hayden really likes you. Two, you had lunch with Mr. Talbot. *Senior.*"

I decided to ignore the first part. "So?"

"So, I've been here two years and I've never had lunch with *any* of the Talbots," Caroline said.

"Oh. Well, it wasn't that fascinating," I said. "Confidentially and all."

"Still. It's not fair. You come here and in like two seconds you're part of the in crowd," Caroline complained.

"What? I am not," I said.

"Yes, you are," she said. She sounded really hurt about it, and I wondered if that was why she hadn't been glad to see me show up for the summer.

"Look. The only in crowd in my opinion is the one that you happen to be in. You know what I mean? It's your friends. It's something you create yourself," I said.

"Easy for you to say. It took me two months to make good friends last summer," Caroline said. "It was really hard. I mean, maybe if we both started here at the same time . . . it would have been easier, you know?"

"Yeah, it probably would have been. But you didn't make it easier on me when I showed up here," I reminded her.

"No. I guess not. I was so worried you were going to tell a bunch of embarrassing stories about me."

"Maybe I would have," I admitted. "If I knew any really *good* ones."

"Don't you?" Caroline asked.

"Not really. I mean, we were kids then," I said. "We did stupid things. It didn't matter—we had fun. Anyway, why do you care so much what everyone thinks?"

"Because! Don't you?" Caroline asked.

"Maybe at first," I admitted. "I definitely didn't like showing up and feeling like an outsider. But then, I knew my way around town, and I was working pretty hard so I didn't have time to worry about it, and I got to be friends with Claire, and Josh—"

"And Hayden—"

"And I kind of stopped worrying about it," I said. "But earlier, you were saying . . . Hayden really likes me?"

"Liza, you sound like when we were twelve," Caroline laughed. "You wondered all the time whether that boy at Sally's coffee shop liked you."

"Well, yeah, didn't *you*?"

"No," Caroline said in a haughty tone. "I *knew* he liked me."

"And you were going to ask him out—but then I was going to ask him out first—and then we saw him making out with that girl—"

We both burst out laughing.

"Oh my God, I was so crushed," Caroline said. "Totally devastated. I wrote about ten pages in my journal that night. Which reminds me, I have got to burn that thing." She smiled and stretched her legs out on the step. "So . . . how come we were so sure of everything back then?"

"Yeah, that's kind of funny. I don't know," I said.

There was a loud beeping sound and I pulled the pager out of my pocket. "Do you think Miss Crossley was standing up there in her office, waiting for my grandparents to drive off?" I asked Caroline.

"I wouldn't put it past her," Caroline said under her breath. We started to laugh, and then Caroline said, "*Don't* tell her I said that. Promise me."

"I wouldn't," I assured her. "See you later."

I realized I'd never really gotten an answer to my question, as to whether Caroline thought Hayden was still interested in me. But it didn't matter, really. At the moment I was just glad that we'd had at least one good conversation, and I wasn't totally crazy. We had been really good friends once. Maybe we wouldn't be again, but we didn't have to be enemies, either. I should thank my grandparents, probably.

I went up to Miss Crossley's office and poked my head into her office. "You rang?" I asked. "Do you need me?"

"Yes, uh, we—wait a second, Liza." She shuffled some papers on her desk. "We've just had word from Mr. Wallace. He's changed his mind and is heading back to the Inn, so I'd like you to go on the shuttle with Hayden to the train station. I think he'd appreciate if you welcomed him back," Miss Crossley said.

"But . . . can't Hayden do that by himself?" I asked.

"You're the one he has a connection with, since you worked as his assistant. It would be best if you went too. Meet Hayden by the shuttle at 6:30, all right?"

Miss Crossley? I've been really, really flexible. For days and weeks now. I've done everything you asked, I wanted to say. *But please don't make me do this, because I'm not ready to see Hayden and spend time alone with him yet.*

"Okay, fine," I said.

Fortunately we had guests to bring to the train, so Hayden and I didn't have to be alone—or talk—during the ride into town. We dropped them off, then waited for the train from Boston to arrive. I paced around the platform, trying to keep my distance, while Hayden leaned against the van looking bored.

Why did Miss Crossley do this to us? Couldn't one person easily handle this task?

When the train showed up, I didn't see C. Q. anywhere. I looked up and down the platform, watching every train door for a glimpse of him. But nobody appeared.

"Do you think he missed the train?" I asked as I walked back to Hayden. It was pulling away from the station. "Or maybe he fell asleep and missed the announcement for this stop?"

"What are you saying? He wasn't on the train?" Hayden asked.

Had he fallen asleep standing there? "Do you *see* him?" I asked.

"No, I guess not." Hayden tossed the set of keys into the air and caught them. "Oh, well. I'm not going to worry about it, I'm sure he'll call. Let's head back. Unless you want to grab an ice cream first?"

"Aren't you worried at all?" I asked as I climbed into the van through the sliding door.

Hayden turned around from the front seat, a puzzled expression on his face. "Aren't you going to sit up here?"

"No, I hadn't planned on it," I said.

"Well, it just feels weird, like I'm a taxi driver."

"Well. Aren't you?"

Hayden narrowed his eyes at me. "You know, your grandfather is a lot nicer than you are."

"Let's not get into discussing the topic of nice. You're the one who went on a date with someone else without even warning me."

"It wasn't a date," Hayden said as he started the van.

"Whatever. Let's get back to the Inn and tell Miss Crossley her favorite guest isn't checking back in." I scrunched down in my seat and tried to ignore the fact that even the tiniest glimpse of Hayden, from the backseat, was attractive.

"What are we doing here?"

Hayden parked the van outside the closed, dilapidated hotel. He got out of the van and walked around to open the sliding door. "I wanted to stop someplace private on the way back—somewhere we could be alone and talk."

"We could have been alone at the train station. We *were* alone. So why not then?" I asked.

"Just . . . come on. Walk on the beach with me," Hayden urged. He held out his hand.

This isn't fair, I thought as I got out of the shuttle, on my own. *Revisiting the scene of a crime of passion. Or just . . . the scene of passion.*

"This doesn't mean anything. That I'm willing to walk on the beach with you," I said.

"Okay, fine, it doesn't mean anything," Hayden said.

"You're just here for the sea air and exercise."

"Don't make fun of me," I said, but I was trying not to smile.

"I'd never," Hayden said.

We walked through the broken-down gate on the side of the hotel that led to the beach.

My eyes widened as I saw dozens of flowers strewn all over the sand. I wandered closer, stepping over a ring of white, pink, yellow, and red roses, mixed in with daisies and lilies. "How did these—where did you get all these?" I asked.

"One was a bouquet I stole from the front desk. Caroline turned her back."

"She should know not to do that when you're around," I said, and Hayden grinned.

"The rest I borrowed from the Inn's flower garden," Hayden said. "It was overflowing—I doubt anyone will notice. And before you say anything, it's not that I wouldn't buy flowers for you, but I really didn't have the opportunity—"

"No, it's okay. It's really nice," I told him.

I looked around and noticed a couple of the Inn's deluxe beach towels, folded and sitting atop a cooler.

"In case we feel like swimming. And I brought some mineral water and some shrimp cocktail because I heard you really like that," Hayden said.

And I was so about to get sucked in by the love undertow, which was quickly turning into a riptide. I dug my heels into the sand to stop myself.

"No, you're not doing this again," I said.

"What?" Hayden asked. "Doing what?"

"You have no problem being with me out—out here," I said. "If no one's around, then that's fine. You're wonderfully sweet and everything. But then in public, you have to either be single, or with Zoe, or—I don't know. But I'm not okay with the whole Privacy Please thing."

"So you're into the voyeur thing, then," Hayden said.

"Not funny," I said.

"Look, I came here because I wanted us to be alone. I want to spend time with you. Just you. I don't want people watching us, or commenting, or—"

"Or knowing about us," I said. "I don't know why, I really don't. But I've never been one to hide before. And I'm not going to be now."

"But don't you think it's kind of fun? Kind of, I don't know. Exciting. To have a secret?"

"I'm not happy being your secret," I said. "I thought I kind of made that clear, but apparently not."

"You're not being fair," Hayden said. "I'm trying to make

it up to you. What do you think, do you think all this stuff happened by accident? I arranged it all. I convinced Miss Crossley. You were on the beach with Will because of me, you went on the shuttle tonight because of me—"

"So what? That doesn't mean anything." It did, sort of, but I wasn't ready to give him credit for that. "Let's go," I said.

"Liza. Come on," he said.

This was killing me, but I had to do it. I walked over to the van and opened the passenger door. "Let's go."

CHAPTER 23

I walked out onto the Inn porch the next morning around eleven and stopped dead in my tracks. "Where did you come from?"

"Nantucket," C. Q. Wallace said. His feet were up on the railing, and he had a notebook in his lap.

"Really?" I laughed. "No—I mean . . . we went to pick you up last night, and you weren't there."

"You came to pick me up in Nantucket? How thoughtful."

"Yeah, well, I wanted to take a road trip," I joked. "No, we went to the train station to get you."

"Interesting. I wasn't coming on the train," he said.

"You never called to say that you were?" I asked.

He shook his head.

So Hayden had fabricated that whole scenario, like he said. And I was kind of impressed. He had persuaded Miss Crossley to let me go on an errand that even she knew wasn't real.

"I rented a car and drove down," C. Q. explained. "Got in this morning. And now that I have wheels, I'll be able to get my own pens from now on."

"Great," I murmured, wondering if I'd underestimated Hayden.

"Anyway. I assume Miss Crossley told you the drill? Can you type some of this stuff up for me?"

"She actually didn't tell me, but I'm not in the middle of anything else, so sure," I said. I figured Miss Crossley must be ill, since it was so late in the day and I hadn't yet been summoned. "But if you wrote it in Nantucket, how accurate can it be about this place?"

"Liza, it's a funny thing. But sometimes you need to leave a place in order to write about it. It's a matter of perspective." He handed me a pad of legal paper. "If you can type this new material up, I can e-mail it to my editor this afternoon and have her insert it into the manuscript."

"Okay," I said. "I guess." The whole process sounded weird and sort of unprofessional to me, but I guessed someone who wrote best sellers knew more than I did.

Dear Liza, I typed.

"Wait a second," I said. "Is this where my character gets really important to the plot?"

"Just type it," he said.

I stared at the piece of paper. It was familiar handwriting, but I didn't think it was his. "This doesn't look like your handwriting."

"I wrote it when I was driving."

"You write and drive? That is so wrong."

"Just type," he said again.

I'm sorry. I realize what you mean about secrets. And you're right I have been a phony. I need to fix that. Hayden.

"Is this all you have?" I asked. "Did you write this?"

"Please. I think I have a little more literary style than that, don't you?"

I smiled and gazed at the ocean. It was a beautiful day; the sun was sparkling on the water and a light breeze blew my hair back from my face. "Can you give me like five minutes?" I asked.

"I suppose," he sighed. "But seriously, after this, I do have something for you to type."

"I'll be right back." I sprinted down the boardwalk. As angry as I still was with Hayden, I wanted to see him and talk to him. He could apologize a few more times and explain what it was all about. Maybe I'd forgive him this time. I could see he really was trying now.

But when I got to the beach, Hayden was nowhere in sight. Lindsay was sitting on top of the lifeguard chair. I waved to her. "Is Hayden around?" I asked, forgetting my wounded pride for a second.

"He's gone for a few days," Lindsay said. "He went home."

"Home?" That seemed a little strange. I hoped nothing was wrong. "When is he coming back, do you know?"

"Saturday, I think," Lindsay said.

"Oh. Okay. Thanks!"

I walked back up to the Inn, wondering if there was a way to reach Hayden while he was home, or if I should bother. He'd made such a nice gesture the night before, and now this note . . .

But would it change anything?

"Got the tray?" Daunte teased me as I walked past him into the dining room on Saturday. We were hosting another wedding at the Inn.

"Yes, I have it," I said, rolling my eyes.

"You sure?"

"I'm sure." I shifted the tray of raspberry sorbet dishes in my arms. Every single one of my coworkers had been giving me a hard time about the way I'd dropped my tray the week before.

I flashed back to the last wedding. With any luck, this event wouldn't be nearly as disastrous, or as painful.

Then I saw Hayden get up onstage, next to the DJ. I didn't even know he'd come back yet. What was he doing? Was he going to sing? Was this a karaoke wedding?

"Excuse me, everyone. Could I have your attention please? I'd like to make a toast."

"Richard," I said, pulling his best friend aside. "He's not a guest at this wedding too, is he?"

"No, he doesn't know them at all." Richard smiled at me. "Don't worry, okay?"

What was Hayden doing? Now they were hiring the Inn to even take care of their toasts? What *wouldn't* these people spend money on?

"My name is Hayden, and normally I'd just park your cars, but today I have a special announcement. But if this takes too long or is too boring and you need your car, just raise your hand."

A few people in the audience laughed, while Hayden unfolded a crumpled piece of paper and cleared his throat. "Bear with me a second here. Okay." He looked at the crowd, but didn't seem to notice where I was standing. "I don't really know Maisie and Jacob, but, uh, I do know something about, uh, love," he said.

Just to be on the safe side, I set the tray of sorbet on the table closest to me.

"The thing about love is that you can't predict it," Hayden went on. "You can't plan it. It's like the weather."

Like the weather? I thought. *Doesn't the weather change really frequently? Some days love is warm, some days it's cold . . .* Where was he going with this? And why?

Claire came up beside me. "I don't know what he's doing, but I think it's going to be good," she whispered.

Josh stood behind her, his chin resting on her shoulder. "Or really, really awful," he said.

"Great," I muttered.

"Sorry, I can't read his—my handwriting." Hayden seemed to be squinting at the tiny piece of paper. "The person we love is the one we follow. The one who tells us how to be in the world, and lets us know whether we're doing the right thing or not. They're our bellwether," Hayden went on.

"Barometer!" someone in the crowd yelled out.

"Barometer," Hayden said, nodding. "That makes sense." He looked up at everyone. "You've got to check out the big barometer in the lobby, if you haven't already. Antique. Really cool." He took a deep breath and rubbed his neck, looking uncomfortable. "Anyway. True love can't be measured by a barometer, but if it could be . . ." He squinted at the paper again, then crumpled it into a ball and shoved it in his pocket. "Oh, what the heck. Liza? I'm sorry I've been such a jerk. I want everyone here—especially you—to know that . . . well, I really love you. Now just dance with me, okay?"

He handed the microphone back to the DJ and hopped off the stage. On his way over to me, as the music started, he took his key to the valet key cabinet and handed it to Miss Crossley. Before he could take another step, I rushed toward him, and he caught me in his arms.

I think maybe a couple of people were clapping. Maybe everybody was clapping. But I didn't hear them or the music, I was so happy.

We danced for a minute, and then I said, "Why isn't anyone else dancing? It's not *our* wedding. I feel like we're onstage. Everyone's watching us."

"See? I told you privacy wasn't all bad—"

"But it's okay," I said.

"Okay. Yeah, it is," Hayden said, smoothing my hair. "But still. You want to get out of here?" he whispered in my ear.

"Do I ever," I said. "But I've got this tray of melting sorbet—"

"Got it," Hayden said. He grabbed the tray off the table

where I'd left it and we quickly handed out dishes. Then we headed for the exit, and as we were walking out, C. Q. Wallace was lingering near the open doorway. "C. Q. helped me with the speech," Hayden explained.

"You mangled it, but oh well," C. Q. commented with a smile. "Now where's that wedding cake?" He moved past us into the dining room.

Hayden and I laughed and ran out onto the porch together, holding hands. I knew exactly where we were heading.

"You know, you could sell that piece of paper on eBay," I told him as I hopped off the boardwalk. I slipped off my shoes and left them in the sand. "Except that I'm not going to let you, because I'm going to save it."

"So how have you been?" Hayden asked as we walked toward the water.

"Fine. Bored. You?" I asked. "How was the visit at home?"

"We got some stuff sorted out. And I told them all about you."

"You didn't."

"I did. They'll be here next week to visit," Hayden said. "You can try to talk Grace out of her gothness."

"What? No way. I want her to like me," I said.

We stopped at the water's edge. We were both still wearing our catering uniforms. "So," Hayden said.

"So."

"Same as usual?" he asked.

"With a twist," I said. I reached up and put my arms around his neck, pulling him closer for a kiss.

Then, when he was really getting into it, I broke away and sprinted into the water.

"Hey! No fair!" He rushed in after me, diving under a big wave that was about to break. Hayden came up for air and dove again, this time tugging at my ankle. I held my breath and went underwater, too, and just as I did, my pager started to buzz. Underwater. Completely submerged. I pulled it out of my pocket to show Hayden, and he smiled, little air bubbles coming out of his mouth.

Miss Crossley wouldn't believe me even if I told her the truth about where I'd been when she paged me. So I wouldn't bother to tell her. Besides, it had to stop beeping soon. Right?

Better Latte
Than Never

Coffee Wench

It's my fifth day of summer vacation and I'm about to be killed by a Doberman.

This isn't the way I would have chosen to go. Having my legs gnawed off, just because I have to skate to work at Gas 'n Git. No one else is out here at 5:30 in the morning; no one will find me until after 6:00. I'll bleed to death from multiple puncture wounds. I'll come down with rabies and froth at the mouth, like a human cappuccino machine.

The dog charges out of his yard, high jumping the fence, when he sees me coming down the street. Then he races behind me, trying to nip at my heels. I don't know why he'd want to do that, unless he's not fond of his teeth. These heels are dangerously large; there are wheels attached to them.

Where is this dog's owner? Where are the dog police?

I try to decide whether I should brake and scare him with the loud noise of my screeching worn-out rubber heel, or whether I should speed skate to the end of the block, but that's probably impossible because there are so many large cracks in the sidewalk that I'd end up flat on my face. All I know is that this dog wants to kill me. Or just maim me, maybe. This is the third day in a row he's pursued me like I'm breakfast.

I can't skate down the other side of the street, because there's no sidewalk over there. I'd take another route, but there are no other routes—unless I go about five miles out of my way, which I'm not doing at 5:30 a.m. I probably shouldn't even be out here this early by myself, but it's the only way I can get to work and I have to work mornings because this is the only shift I can get at the only job I can get.

The phrase *running out of options* comes to mind.

The phrase *pepper spray* also comes to mind.

There must be a town ordinance against this. Even *Lindville* has standards for keeping dogs from killing innocent girls on in-line skates.

Suddenly the Doberman loses interest in me and runs back toward his yard, jumping back over the fence.

I adjust my courier bag and helmet and focus on the street

again. Another day, another near death by Doberman. This is the type of summer I've always dreamed of.

Later that morning, I'm standing behind the counter at Espress-Oh-Yes when the world's worst coffee breath walks in.

I've only been working here for three days and already I recognize him, a guy in a pinstriped suit who is as jittery as a hummingbird. He is tense, he drives a silver Lexus and parks next to the side door in a No Parking area, and he orders the Premium Morning Blend, Tanker size, at about 6:50 a.m. Then he comes back later, intermittently, throughout the day, the way headaches do sometimes.

I work at a mini coffee shop that's inside a gas station, so all of the sizes are linked to the automotive world: Coupe, Sedan, SUV, Tanker. The coffee machines are shaped like gas tanks. They have pumps and little black rubber hoses that dispense hot beverages instead of flammable liquids. I wear an apron that has a black-and-white checkered-flag pattern, and a red plastic name tag that's shaped like a sports car.

It's just one more reminder that I'm not allowed to drive. My parents confiscated my license a few months ago, because I had two accidents and totaled the station wagon that they gave me when they bought a new sedan for my father's realty business. I'm spending my summer paying them back for all the auto body work over the past year. My parents say they don't trust me, and their insurance rates are through the roof, and would be even higher if they kept me on the policy. "You've become too much of a liability," my father told me as he stashed my license somewhere in his desk.

Let me tell you. There's nothing more annoying than working at a coffee shop inside a gas station—and not being able to drive. Especially when you want to drive far, far away from here.

I pour the guy's coffee and shuffle him down to the cash register, inhaling deeply and then holding my breath, which is hard to do when you're supposed to greet the customer and tell him how much he owes. Good thing I have a lot of practice at holding my breath, because our town smells pretty bad sometimes, due to having some extremely large cattle feedlots nearby. We actually have an "odor hotline" here in Lindville, and some days the phone has to be ringing off the hook. The combination of manure and slaughterhouse aromas makes this a very fragrant place to live.

"One forty-nine," I say, then I stop breathing again, close off all intake valves: nose, mouth, even skin. Close the pores! Like it's a ship or a sub going down. Batten down the hatches. Whatever *batten* means. It sounds like a mistake I'd make on a vocabulary test; the past tense of *to bat*.

"What do you think of the nice bright sunshine this morning!" Coffee Breath says.

"Mm," I say as I hand him his change and he drops two quarters in the tip cup. "It's, um, nice. And bright." Exactly. *Do not inhale, do not inhale*, I tell myself.

"You know what? I think we're in for a long, hot summer. I guess we'll be switching to iced coffee pretty soon, right?" He laughs as he puts the top on his Tanker.

Either iced coffee or an oxygen mask, I think. His laughing expels a lot of breath, proving once again that he drinks coffee at home before he comes here. I take a huge step back and nearly trip on the black rubber floor mat.

"Take care, see you later!" he calls as he heads for the door.

"Thanks, good-bye!" I breathe deeply. Finally. Oxygen. I drink a shot of cold water to try to clear out the porous cells in my throat. It's a curse to have such a heightened sense of smell, it really is.

We have this jar next to the cash register and it's piled high with fruit candies and mints, just for people like him. But he won't take one, will he? He just drives off to wherever he goes every day, where he can torture more people with his breath.

Fortunately, there's a lull and I sort of collapse against the wall as I wait for the next customer. I need time to recover.

I wish the truck driver who wears strong cologne and always has minty-fresh breath would come in.

"So what horrible thing did you do to end up here?" the boy behind the cash register asks me as I push back my hair and retie my Espress-Oh-Yes apron. He rings up car washes and bottled soda, reads music magazines from the store newsstand, and turns up the store radio really loud whenever a U2 song comes on—if our manager's gone, that is. He's usually so busy reading or writing in a notebook that he doesn't talk to me. He's lucky because he doesn't have to wear the checkered-flag apron—just a red polo shirt with the Gas 'n Git logo.

"What are you talking about? I didn't do anything," I say.

I think he's trying to look like Bono, but he just isn't that good-looking. I'm sorry, but it's true. He's wearing blue-tinted plastic glasses like Bono's and has longish brown hair brushed back like Bono's. But he's got a crooked nose and I think he's trying to grow a mustache. I'm not sure, though—it could just be lint. Doesn't he realize that Bono is mustache free? Or is he going for the stubble look? Anyway, the Gas 'n Git polo shirt seriously interferes with this attempted rock-star look.

"Come on," he says, and I can swear I hear a slight, fake Irish accent in his voice. "Give me a break. You've got to have a story. People don't end up working here without a story."

He's right. I do have a story. But I'm wondering, if that's true, then what is *his* story? I've never seen him around town, until I got this job. He seems too old for high school, but only by about a year. So where did he come from? What's *he* doing here?

"Well, if you're not going to share the details, then could you at least explain your name tag? Are there typos? Because I don't think I'm reading it right," he says.

"It's Fleming."

"Fleming?" He can't quite comprehend it. Most people can't. "Is that your first name or your last name?"

"First," I say. I don't bother to explain that it's my middle name—that I was named for Peggy Fleming, the American figure skater who dazzled the world wearing chartreuse and won a gold medal in the 1968 Winter Olympics. Peggy Fleming inspired my father to get into ice skating, so he named me after her. And then he was on a roll with the concept and decided to give my brother and sisters figure skaters' names, too: Torvill and Dean, the almost-five-year-old twins, and then there's my little sister Dorothy Hamill Farrell, who's three. My mother is pregnant again, and who knows what name they'll choose this time.

Some people think these skaters' names are really cute— like my parents and grandparents—but I don't. It's really hard to walk around with an Olympic champion's name. People tend to expect things of you, and if you don't deliver . . .

Also, nobody else my age has the name *Peggy*.

No offense, Peggy Fleming. My dad, Phil Farrell, creator of the not-so-famous Farrell Flip, still worships you, and I think you're incredible, too. And no offense to all the other Peggys, or Peggies, of the world. I just don't *feel* like a Peggy.

I also don't look anything like Peggy Fleming. We're complete opposites. She has beautiful long brown hair and blue eyes. She's petite and graceful. She's a gorgeous, artistic skater, and a very knowledgeable and entertaining commentator.

Me? I have long, wavy sandy blond hair, green eyes, freckles, I'm five foot eight, and I haven't ice skated well—or much at all—since the eighth grade. Enough said.

"Fleming. Interesting," the guy says. "Anyone ever call you phlegmball?"

"No," I say. "But thanks for asking."

He frowns at me. "Do you go to Franklin?"

"No," I say.

"Oh. So you go to Edison?" he asks.

"Yes," I say.

He stares at me for a minute and is starting to look irritated. "You know, you're incredibly talkative. People really love that in a coffee wench. I bet you'll score lots of tips.

Oh, yeah. You'll be rich in no time."

I don't answer him.

"Well, thanks for asking, Fleming. My name's Denny," he says. "But my best friends call me Perkins."

I smile. "Really?"

"I was just kidding," he says as he takes a customer's credit card.

I decide to ignore his joke, even though it is sort of funny. "Where do *you* go to school?" I ask.

"I'm between schools," he says.

This sounds interesting. I've heard of being between jobs, and between boyfriends. But between schools? Is he taking a year off? Or was he kicked out? "Well, where *did* you go to school?" I ask.

"I'm a proud graduate of New Horizons Day Care," Denny says. "After that it all went downhill and turned into a bland mix of study halls and very scarring marching-band experiences." He shudders, making a face.

"You? Marching band? I can't picture it," I say.

"Neither could I. Quit the Franklin Mustangs' finest after freshman year," he says. "Started focusing on real bands. Now I write music. Well, not music exactly—songs. Lyrics. And some poetry." He pushes a strand of hair behind his ear.

The gas station poet, I think. Great. Does he write epics

about unleaded? "So . . . are you ever going back to school?" I ask.

"I took the last year off, after graduating. I'm supposed to start college this fall," Denny says, "but I don't know if I'll go."

"Really? Why not?" I ask.

"Do I *need* classes?" Denny shrugs. "I don't know. I think I'm doing okay on my own."

"Working here is okay?" I ask. In what universe? I'm about to ask him where he's going to college when the place gets really busy again.

I'm starting to get into the rhythm of the espresso machine when Mr. Stinson, owner of Western Wear Bonanza in the mall, comes in. Despite the heat, he's wearing corduroy pants and a beige wool cardigan sweater with wood buttons that look like Brazil nuts. It's like he's never really left England. Mr. Stinson has terrible vision, even with his giant tortoise-shell glasses on. Maybe he won't see that it's me, I think. Maybe the obnoxious apron will distract him.

I keep my head down. "What would you like this morning?" I mumble.

"Yes, hello, I'd like . . ." Mr. Stinson is about to order when he realizes that it's me standing behind the Muffins of the Month. "You," he says, glowering at me.

"Hello, Mr. Stinson," I say politely. "How are you?"

"What is the likes of you doing here?" he asks.

It's a long story, I think. *And you know part of it.* "What can I get you?" I ask, still trying to be friendly.

"Well, now, let's see. How about if we start off with a check to pay for the damage you did to my store window? And then perhaps you could return the belt you stole, and the leather bag . . . well, the list goes on, doesn't it?"

"I didn't steal anything," I say. "I bought all those things with my employee discount—"

"Which I never should have extended to you. It was a privilege, not a right. Do you understand the difference, young lady? And then there's the small matter of a smashed window."

"Um . . . I thought your insurance covered that," I say.

"There's a little *item* in insurance called a *deductible*. I don't know if they bother to teach you that word in dreadful American high schools, but the word is *deductible*."

I want to fire wooden stir sticks at Mr. Stinson. Do I know the word *deductible*? It's why I'm working here—it's why I'm standing here asking for his coffee order.

But Mr. Stinson and I have had this argument a few times before, so I decide to move on. "So. Would you like some tea this morning?" I ask.

"Do you know, you absolutely ruined my Christmas season." Mr. Stinson's bushy eyebrows are twitching in time to the song on the radio. "You left me high and dry. You—oh, never mind, my blood pressure's high enough without this— without coffee—without seeing *you*. In the future, I'll find somewhere else to purchase my petrol." He shakes his head and grabs a bottle of juice, heading for Denny's register, not even dealing with me.

As if I'm going to be so hurt that he won't fill his tank with our gas—excuse me—*petrol*.

After he leaves, Denny turns to me with a sort of smirk on his face. "So. That's how you ended up here."

"What?" I say.

"*You're* the one who sent the bronc-riding Santa Claus mannequin flying into his store window," Denny says. "I saw that in the newspaper."

Not much happens here, yet I've been in two *Lindville Gazette* headlines so far, and I'm only sixteen.

Denny nods. "Impressive. But what was the bit about the stolen leather items?"

"I didn't steal anything," I tell him.

"Come on, Fleming. Face facts. You're a shoplifter with a leather fetish. Just admit it. You know, because once you own up to it, you can get help."

"I didn't shoplift, and I'm not into leather!" I protest.

"Then what was he talking about?"

"It's a long story."

"Uh-huh. That's what they all say." Denny is trying to build what looks like a log cabin out of rolls of peppermint Mentos.

"Who says that?" I mutter.

"Hey, this place is a *haven* for former offenders, don't worry," Denny says. "Kelly? Hacked into computers. Rick? Embezzled money from a bank. And our manager, the fair Jamie? Guilty of identity theft. She screwed up, though, and chose a really bad identity."

"You're joking, right?" I say. "You *are* joking."

Denny's house of Mentos collapses and a couple roll off the counter to the floor. "Only a little," he says as he picks them up and puts them back into the display rack.

"What about you? What's your offense?" I ask. *Besides that thing you call a mustache and the fact you're putting floor-lint-covered candy back on the rack.*

"I have done nothing," Denny says. "I'm just here to counterbalance the rest of you people. But let's just say we'll be counting the coffee beans from now on, okay? And I for one will be keeping a closer eye on my wallet, not to mention my cash drawer."

I glare at his black leather wallet, which is hanging on a metal chain from his pocket. Denny rides a motorcycle and thinks that gives him dispensation to wear certain kinds of clothes and accessories.

"Don't worry," I tell him. "I'm not interested in your wallet. Believe me."

"That's what they all say." Denny swings his wallet around like a lariat. He grins as he walks toward me. The metal chain catches on a drawer handle and nearly rips the belt loop off his jeans.

"This is all your fault," he says, trying to unjam the metal chain. "You're one of those bad-luck kind of people, aren't you?"

"Oh, yeah. I'm cursed or something," I say.

Actually, that isn't far from the truth.

How Am I Driving?

I get off of work at noon. It's only six hours, but it seems like the longest shift ever, maybe because it starts at 6:00 a.m. I've been smelling and serving coffee all morning, and I'm thinking I may never drink coffee again. Which is all right; I've never liked it that much—I mostly just drink it at IHOP because of the refillable pitcher. And a certain waiter.

"There comes a time when everyone has to make sacrifices," my dad said when we talked about me taking the Espress-Oh-Yes job. "And you have reached that time, P. F."

Other sacrifices in my life: I look after my siblings a couple of mornings a week, the days I'm not working at Gas 'n Git, while my mom's at the radio station and my dad's figure skating. That's just the scheduled summer baby-sitting. That doesn't count the other times I know I'll be called on to help. And I have to turn over almost all of the money I'm making to my parents because I owe them for the car repairs.

I'm taking the bus to French class, starting today, because of that certain IHOP waiter and because I can graduate early if I get ahead on my credits. I want to travel for a while before going away to college. I'd love to go to France and actually *use* my French, but since I probably won't be able to afford it, I'll start out just cruising around the States, checking out places I've been before and places I haven't. My parents and I used to travel a lot, before we settled here. I was a world traveler, or at least a U.S. traveler, until I turned six. It's very sad to contemplate that my life was more exciting as a toddler than it is now. I try not to think about it. I try to focus on getting out of debt and hitting the road.

Of course, for that I'll need a car. Which is also why I'm *here*, this summer, not working as a camp counselor like my best friend, Suzanne. It's all about paying my parents back.

I look up at the bus-stop sign, which has our town's motto on it: LINDVILLE IS KINDVILLE—BE A GOOD NEIGHBOR! DON'T LITTER. There should be a garbage can next to the sign, but there isn't. That figures.

At school we have different versions of the town slogan

carved into the desks and written on lockers, including: Lind-ville is Kind-a-lame-ville, Lindville is Stinkville, and Lindville Sucks.

All I know is that it will be a happy day when I see that "Lindville is Kindville" sign in my rearview mirror.

Because it will mean two things: one, I am actually driv-ing a car again, and two, I am leaving Lindville for greener pastures. Which won't be difficult to find, because we mostly just have brown pastures here.

At 12:06 I see the Lindvillager, precisely on schedule, com-ing down the street. Lindville's not big enough to have actual bus-size buses—we have the short kind, the type that you ride on at an airport when you catch a car-rental shuttle.

The town had a contest to come up with a cute name for the bus system when they started it a few years ago. "Lindvil-lager" is the best they could do. The bus has fake wood trim, like it's an old-fashioned station wagon. Unfortunately, the paintings of the cute little village on the side got obscured by giant ads for radio stations and restaurants, and just recently those got removed and replaced by a huge ad for July's big annual event, the Lindville Rodeo Roundup Days—as if we could forget they're coming in July.

The pseudo-bus pulls up in front of me with a screech.

When the door opens, I see it's Kamikaze Bus Driver again. This guy has this route nearly every day, which worries me.

He has no sense of speed limits. He constantly cuts in front of cars. He merges without even glancing in his side mirror. He takes off when a passenger's foot is barely off the bottom step. He's a Driver's Ed *Don't*. You know those "How Am I Driving?" stickers they put on trucks? Now I know why they don't put them on Lindville's buses.

If my parents knew this was the person driving me around town, they would give me back my license and a car so fast it would make even Kamikaze Bus Driver's head spin. Only I'm not sure if it could spin, because he has so much gray hair on his face and neck and such a long beard that it might choke him. He wears a peace-sign button on his lapel every day, and occasionally adds another sixties memento to his outfit via wristband or headband. The back of his uniform shirt constantly has this wet trail of sweat down the middle of it, which, unfortunately, is something you notice when you sit behind a person.

There's this sign over his head that says, YOUR DRIVER: _____. PROFESSIONAL & COURTEOUS. Kamikaze Bus Driver won't fill in his name, because if we don't know his name, we can't complain about things, like how two days ago he raced across a railroad crossing to beat an oncoming freight train, right as the bar was lowering.

But the *really* sad part is, that's probably the most exciting thing that's happened to me so far this summer.

I have hope, though. For some strange reason, I have hope.

I take a seat behind an elderly woman with a laundry bag, and in front of a guy with brown hair and a mustache, tight Wrangler jeans, and a T-shirt that says, FORGET THE WHALES, SAVE THE COWBOYS!

I always sort of wonder how other people end up on the bus. Not that it's a bad thing; just a curious thing around here, because most people seem to have their 2.7 cars per household, no matter what shape they or the cars are in. People just *drive*, and if they can't, they get someone else to drive them. I think there are more gas stations per capita here than in any other town or city in the country. Hence the fact that I can get employed at Gas 'n Git. People need gas; gas stations need warm bodies to run them.

Me? I'm on the bus because a week after I got my license in November, I crashed while turning into the Happy Hamburger parking lot. Happy Hamburger is the most popular lunch place for our school. You would think we wouldn't want to eat burgers, since we drive past so many cattle in feedlots every day, but no, it's like there's something in the air that makes you want beef, because you don't want to let the town down or something. We have to make sure the meat business thrives, because that's where our parents' jobs are, and if it dies, we all die with it.

Anyway, that day freezing rain was falling and the streets were icy and I turned left while accelerating, which I found out later you're not supposed to do, and the car started to skid. I couldn't remember which direction to steer, whether to brake or not, so the car just kept sliding sideways. First we knocked over the giant brown plastic steer out front. Then we skidded right up to the Happy Hamburger and fishtailed right into the building.

Everyone from school was inside, either in line or eating. Everyone *saw* us. It was so embarrassing.

But then this amazing thing happened. Steve Gropher, who I didn't even know then, came running outside to see if I was okay. Well, technically he could have been coming to check on Suzanne and her ex-boyfriend Rick, who were in the car with me at the time, but he ran right over to *me*. He was there in about two seconds and he said he'd seen it happening because he looked up from the ketchup pump dispenser just in time.

I wasn't hurt, but I was in shock, and I kept saying, "Oh, God, I can't believe I just did that. Did I just do that? I can't believe I just did that," over and over, while he sat there next to me and someone called an ambulance and a tow truck and my parents. We were all fine—just some cuts and bruises—but everyone thought I was bleeding profusely because Steve had been clutching those little paper cups of ketchup when he ran outside and they'd gotten crushed in his hand and spilled all over both of us when he hugged me and tried to calm me down.

I didn't know Steve then, because he had only moved to Lindville that fall. All I knew about him was that he was a junior like me, he was a waiter at IHOP, and that he was very good-looking. So that was my happy accident, if there is such a thing.

As far as my vehicular career goes, things went downhill after that. Of course, my parents wanted me to get a job so I could pay them back for the one-thousand-dollar deductible they had to spend to get the car fixed up. All the good jobs were taken, but I got this Christmas-season job working for Mr. Stinson at Western Wear Bonanza. He was trying to drum up business, so he rented this mechanical bull called "Rudy the Red-Nosed Rein-Steer." If people could stay on the bull for fifteen seconds, then they got to choose a "Bonanza Bonus," which was a cheesy free gift, like a bumper sticker or a bandana.

It turned out that no one could stay on the bull very

long. There are plenty of real, authentic, hardworking cowboys around here who could have stayed on for hours, and had enough left afterward to kick Mr. Stinson all the way to the food court. But most of them don't shop at the Sunset Mall, so instead we got a lot of suburban customers with no skill.

I was working the night shift one Saturday when Suzanne and some other friends from school came by. We were joking around, and I thought it would be funny if I put the store's Santa Claus mannequin on the bull and let Santa ride for a while.

It *was* funny. Very, very funny.

Until I turned the speed on the mechanical bull up too high, and Santa went flying off the rein-steer and into the left-side front window of the store. The glass cracked and Santa landed facedown on Mr. Stinson's "A Proper English Christmas" display, wrecking the plum pudding.

Needless to say, Mr. Stinson fired me. "You are a retailer's nightmare," he said. "Have you no concept of responsibility? Move on, Miss Farrell, move *on*. I never want to see you again. Not even as a customer. You are a bad seed," Mr. Stinson said. "A very, very bad seed."

Needless to say, Mr. Stinson is a little over the top. I didn't like working for him and I was actually okay with losing the job.

A couple of weeks later, I went to work for Bob's Pizza. They didn't care about my retail history, but they maybe should have checked into my driving record. I'm not sure I need to really go into it. Let's just say that it involved a desperate attempt to match the competition and deliver pizza in thirty minutes or less.

I totaled the car that had just been repaired. My father gave me some lecture about making the same mistake twice. My parents donated the banged-up station wagon to charity. And now I take the bus.

So, I guess you could say that I don't do well with steering—or steers. Part of the reason I took the job inside Gas 'n Git is that I thought it might bring me good karma, spending time around gas pumps and helping people in cars. If there's a fuel god, I'll pray to him or her. It can't hurt.

The Lindvillager pulls up in front of the school. As I start to get off the bus, Kamikaze Bus Driver puts his hand on my arm. "Excuse me, miss," he says. His voice sounds like tires on a gravel road. In the rain.

"Um, hi," I say, pulling my arm away from him.

"Next time you work at the gas station—tomorrow?" he asks in a gruff voice, his words emerging from the curly beard in a muffle. He doesn't take off his octagon-shaped sunglasses.

"No, not until next Monday."

"Okay, then. Monday. Bring me a large coffee." He shoves a couple of dollars at me.

The last thing this man needs is more caffeine, I think. But okay, whatever he says. My life can't get weird enough. Now I'm taking coffee orders from insane bus drivers.

I have to get out of this town.

En français, s'il vous plaît

On the blackboard there's a sentence: *C'est le premier jour de la plus de votre vie.*

"Today is the first day of the rest of your life." Or something like that. *En français.*

Actually I think it's the first day of Intermediate Semi-Accelerated-Because-It's-Summer French. Monday, Wednesday, Thursday, 12:30–2:00.

I take a seat, and right away a girl who was walking across the school lawn beside me takes a seat next to me. We exchange awkward smiles. She has perfectly straight, long reddish hair and is wearing a purple tank top with a washed-out silver crown on it. I don't know her, and I'm guessing she goes to Franklin. This is a combination summer school at Edison High, for students from all over the region. The teacher from Franklin, Monsieur LeFleur, is supposed to be excellent. Everyone raves about him, about how he makes crepes and teaches the geography of France with travel videos.

I glance up at the clock. It's 12:30. Where's Steve Gropher?

To take French—or any foreign language—in Lindville in the summer seems very bizarre. This feels about as far away from France as you can get. We're sitting in a hot classroom with the windows open, it's ninety degrees outside, and the hot wind is blowing smells from the rendering plant into the room. If you've never smelled a rendering plant, it's sort of like spoiled, canned cat food that's been left out in the sun to bake. Not that I've ever had a cat, but that's what other people say.

This kind of situation isn't exactly covered in phrase books. *Comment est-ce qu'on dit?*: "It smells like death today"?

I glance at the clock again. Now it's 12:35. Where's Steve? And where's Monsieur LeFleur?

A woman enters the classroom a few minutes later and quickly takes roll. This doesn't make sense, unless Monsieur LeFleur is running late, or unless he is too brilliant to take roll and has someone else do it for him—a French secretary. Except that she doesn't sound or look French. She's wearing an American-flag T-shirt with a styleless khaki skirt and blue sandals.

I look around the classroom as I hear names called. Steve said he was going to take French this summer, too. I could have sworn he said he'd be in this class. We talked about it a couple of times. But he's a no-show. He's not even on the class list. I can't believe he blew it off. I recognize a few other people in the room from Edison, but I only know them vaguely.

"Good news, class," the woman says after finishing roll. "Your teacher, Monsieur LeFleur, is ill today."

People around me start high-fiving each other, and then the woman says, "Therefore, you will be doing quiet reading of your textbook for one hour, and then I will give you a quiz."

"So what was the *good* news?" the red-haired girl next to me asks. "Did I miss something?"

The woman frowns at her. "The good news is that you might have gotten out earlier than usual if you hadn't just been so rude." She clears her throat and looks at her list. "Your name is, again? *En français, s'il vous plaît.*"

"How can I say my name in French?" the girl asks.

"You know what I mean," the woman says. "Introduce yourself, *en français.*"

"*Jeu mappel* Charlotte Duncan," the girl says in a flat

accent as she cracks her gum.

"Charlotte. No gum chewing in French class."

"Don't French people chew gum?" Charlotte asks.

A few people laugh and the woman clears her throat. "The point is that you will be working on pronunciation in this class. *You* will be working on it especially hard. Gum and candy interfere with this important step. But never mind, for now—begin reading. I am sure that Monsieur LeFleur will be here for your next class. He has not had a sick day in eight years."

I crack open my textbook, and Charlotte leans over toward my desk. "How do you say 'bad air day' *en français*?"

"*Je m'appelle Lindville*," I say, and we laugh. It sort of makes up for Steve not being here. Sort of.

Rooty Tooty, What a Cutie

"So what are you up to now?"

Charlotte asks me as we're dismissed from class. Even though I just met her, for some reason I confide in Charlotte and tell her I want to go to IHOP after class. I tell her that it isn't because it's international and it isn't because it's a house and it isn't because of the pancakes, though they are an excellent side benefit. I explain there's this waiter I know, who I kind of want to see, who was supposed to be in French with us. I don't know why I'm telling her all of this. Pouring my heart out isn't something I usually do. But she's just so easy to talk to that before I know what I'm doing, I've confessed my need for an IHOP fix.

"The waiter's a friend of yours?" she asks.

"Sort of," I say.

"You like him." She nods knowingly. "Let's go."

I'm so glad she's going with me. Going alone seems sort of pathetic, although I was willing to do it.

IHOP is very close to Edison High, which means it's a huge school hangout. It's only a ten-minute walk, but no one ever actually *walks* there. It's just not done. Unless you're me, and you can't drive, and you have a desperate need to get to IHOP. Then you walk. It's a horrible walk, but it's my favorite one.

Charlotte and I make small talk as we wait for a light to change so we can sprint across the street. There isn't a crosswalk and there's never a light for pedestrians. That's just the way it is here.

We walk past prairie dogs in a vacant lot on the side of the road, perched atop dirt mounds, chirping to each other. They've taken over fields like this all over town, and they keep building new colonies and growing in number, despite the fact that they're constantly getting run over when they try to cross the road to other, more vacant lots.

It's windy and a few small tumbleweeds blow across the breakdown lane ahead of us as we hike through the brown dirt on the side of the road. So much dust is in the air that my eyes keep watering. The good thing about the wind is that it's now blowing hard in an easterly direction, and the feedlot odors are blowing out of Lindville and into the next town. We export our bad air. Sort of the way World's Worst Coffee Breath exports his bad air into Gas 'n Git.

I glance up at the billboard hovering over us. There's a painting of a giant black bull, with the initials IZ branded into his flank, facing down a couple of grinning rodeo clowns. DON'T MISS INSANE ZANE! LINDVILLE RODEO ROUNDUP DAYS—JULY 10–JULY 20. LASSO YOUR TICKETS TODAY! it says in loopy, brown rope-style script.

When we first moved here, back when I was six, I thought this was so cool. I couldn't wait to go. I watched the big parade, I cruised the petting zoo, I begged my parents to take me on rides every day, I ate a pork chop on a stick, I had a riding lesson and got my picture taken with a cowboy. I loved everything about Rodeo Roundup Days.

Now, it just seems sort of worn out and maybe a little sad. The parade with longhorn cattle, town officials waving to the crowd from pickup truck beds, and marching bands wilting in their heavy uniforms in the summer heat. The bucking bronco contests and the side show of "Amazing Farm Animals." The carnival rides with the jaded, inattentive operators who chew tobacco and spit the juice on the hot pavement— and occasionally hit my shoe, like one did last summer.

"You know what? I think that Village Inn pancakes are

better than IHOP's," Charlotte says as she kicks an empty beer can out of her way. "I think actually that maybe they're exactly the *same*, but at Village Inn maybe you're expecting less, so you're not disappointed, whereas a place that brags about pancakes—well, you know, they have a higher standard to live up to. And living up to standards is like . . ."

"The worst," I say. Does she know what it's like to have a former competitive figure skater for a dad? And a meteorologist mom who can predict the temperature every day to within one degree?

"Exactly," Charlotte says as she dodges a flying taco wrapper being whipped along by the wind. My mom would know precisely how strong the wind is, but I'll just say "very strong."

At IHOP, there's a young, blond hostess I don't recognize, who tries to seat us by the bathroom. We insist on a booth by the window. Steve's tables are usually in this area, but as soon as we sit down, I notice that he's across the restaurant, working on the other side of the hostess station. I try not to take this as a sign of things to come.

Seeing Steve, I completely forget about everything else that happened today. Good, bad, indifferent—it doesn't matter. Rooty tooty, what a cutie. He's about six feet tall, which is important when you're five foot eight like me. He has short, spiky blond hair and blue eyes, and a scar on his cheek that he got from jumping off a house roof in fourth grade and landing on a tree. He has another scar, on his knee, from where a car hit him when he was riding a bike.

Maybe I like him so much because we're both so accident prone. And he doesn't like his name, either—he even stole my idea and used his middle name, wearing a "Josh" name tag at IHOP for a few months.

Steve can beat almost anyone at pool, and there was a rumor going around school that he was in a 12-step program for a gambling addiction. Don't ask me why that's cool, but it is. Steve's lived in a few different cities, the way I used to, the way I wish I still could sometimes, except then he wouldn't be in any of those places, so what would be the point? He has a dozen plans for getting out of Lindville when he graduates. He works as many hours as he can here, even on Saturday nights, because he's saving all his money to go on this cross-country trip, which he's going to do the day after graduation.

Whenever we hang out, we always talk about the places we'd rather be, or want to visit, or live in, and we always sort of talk about it like it's something we could do together, if we weren't stuck in Lindville celebrating the sports event or holiday *du jour*. Like the way we talked about both taking French so we could go AWOL on the spring class trip to Montreal.

Instead of Steve, someone named Roger who I've also never seen here before takes our order. Roger wears large square glasses and looks about forty years old.

"That's not the guy. Is it?" Charlotte asks once he's gone. "Please tell me that's not the guy."

"No, that's not him!" I start laughing, forgetting Charlotte doesn't know me yet and I have to explain. So I do. I tell her about how I met Steve, how we kissed a few times, how I keep hoping we'll go out.

I don't tell her the stupid things. Like how, because Steve was a new guy in town, I decided that must mean he was The One. I don't tell her how, the first time Steve and I kissed, on New Year's Eve, he whispered in my ear, "I can't believe I just did that. Did I just do that? I can't believe I just did that," teasing me about how we first met and how freaked out I was. I don't tell Charlotte how happy that made me, because it was the best thing that had happened to me in so long, and that I thought my new year was off to this incredible start. I don't tell her that the next time I saw Steve, at school, he acted like it had never happened. Because I could handle being the New-Year's-fling girl. Sort of.

We kissed again on February 15. He was a day late for being my Valentine. We were working on this heinous group history project for school, and decided it would be more fun to ditch the group and make out instead.

The last time we kissed was when he rescued me at a St. Patrick's Day party. This guy who was either carried away by the love of the Irish—I do have green eyes and a few freckles—or the cups of green beer would not leave me alone. I don't even know who he was—someone's cousin, from another town. He kept trying to put his arms around me, and then he actually pulled me onto the sofa and I sort of screamed. Steve told the guy to get lost, and then he and I hung out on the porch for a while, and one thing led to the usual. He even ditched his friends at the party to walk me home, which seemed huge to me. No guy had ever walked me home before.

I don't know if his friends got mad at him, or what. But it's like ever since then, there's been this tension between us. Or at least, *I* feel tension, because he's acting like we're only friends and that's it, as if nothing ever happened, as if we haven't kissed and had these really intense conversations. I don't *get* it.

I have hope, though. We're due for another fling. It's been almost three months. We're overdue. If we were a library book, there would be a huge fine due on us.

I look across the restaurant at Steve, who's carrying a tray of beverages to a table of two middle-aged guys in overalls and baseball caps. Why does he have to wait on them and not me?

"French. Give me a break," Charlotte says, flipping through our textbook, glancing at the photographs. "I am not into summer school at all. You know? I'm only taking this class because I've gotta get the credit so I can graduate next year, because I'm behind in credits." She explains how she and her little sister and her mom have moved four times in the past five years due to job transfers.

"That sounds kind of hard," I say, although I'm a little envious, too.

Charlotte takes a sip of her water. "Yeah. It is. It's like— you just get to know people, and then you leave. But I get to meet tons of people, so . . ." She shrugs. "How about you? How long have you been here?"

"Forever." I tell her how we traveled around constantly when I was young because my father was competing and then performing as a professional figure skater. Then we settled down in Lindville when I was six. My dad got a job as a realtor, my mother became a radio meteorologist, they decided to have the big family they'd always wanted, and we haven't been anywhere fun in years.

"So wait a second," she says. "Your dad—he's like Brian Boitano or something?"

"Not quite. No gold medals," I say. "But he's good."

"Wow. That is so cool. I'd love to see him sometime. So hold on. Do you skate?" she asks.

"Not really," I say. "I mean, I used to, but then I quit."

"How come? God, I totally admire anyone who can do anything athletic," she says as Roger comes over and sets a syrup carousel on our table with absolutely zero flair.

"Your order will be right up," he tells us before vanishing into the kitchen.

I glance over at Steve. I have to go talk to him. This is the first time I've seen him since summer vacation started.

"So you're taking French. What else? Are you working?" Charlotte asks me.

I nod. "At the coffee place Espress-Oh-Yes—you know where the Gas 'n Git station is, on Highway eighty-seven? Inside there."

"Hey, that's cool," Charlotte says.

"Not really," I tell her. "I have to be there before six in the morning, and I have this coworker who thinks he's Bono."

"Oh, yeah? Well, I work at Shady Prairies," she says.

"You're kidding," I say. Shady Prairies is a huge, new retirement apartment complex on the east side of town. When they put it in five years ago, they took down a lot of old trees to make room for pools and a golf course. If there's any shade left, I'd be surprised. "What do you do there?" I ask.

"I work in the dining room—serving. It's sort of fun, actually—they have two seatings for dinner, at four-thirty and six, and then we're out of there by eight. The people are nice—most of them, anyway. They always want to know what I'm doing with my life. If I have direction. Then they tell me about these trips they took like fifty years ago, and how I've gotta get out and see the world before it's too late." She pauses and cracks her green-colored bubble gum. "Which is true."

I look over at Steve bringing a tray of food to a table. As I watch him, I make circles on the table with the blueberry syrup dispenser, but it keeps getting stuck to spilled syrup on the table.

"Oh." Charlotte looks up at Roger as he sets her plate in front of her. "Thanks."

I thank him, too, as Charlotte covers her pancakes with all four kinds of syrup and a packet of mixed-fruit jelly. She puts a dollop of ketchup on the side of her plate, as if she's thinking of dipping later.

I stare past her at Steve, who's joking around with a table of police officers. He really has a rapport with the regulars here.

Charlotte taps her fork against my plate to get my

attention. "So, that's him?" She gestures behind her with her fork.

I nod. "Sorry. Was that way too obvious?"

"He's cute. Go say hi," Charlotte urges me. "Ask him why he's not suffering through French with us."

"Really? Should I do that?" I ask. "I don't know, though. Do you think I should? I mean, my pancakes are going to get cold."

"Like you're going to eat them if you don't go say hi. What do you have to lose, anyway? Go for it," she says.

Charlotte's attitude is so different from Suzanne's. Suzanne is usually telling me to hang back and wait for him to make a move. That hasn't exactly been working too well.

I set my napkin on the table and brush off my khakis. I wish they weren't so crinkled, but hey, it's been a long time since 5:00 a.m., when I got dressed. As I walk across the half-empty restaurant, I try to think of something witty to say, something that will impress him. First I see Steve perching on the end of a booth bench. I wonder who he's talking to—probably some more of his regular mid-afternoon customers. I can't see because of the wall partition separating that section.

Then I get closer and I see who he's sitting with. He has his arm around this beautiful girl who has an IHOP uniform on and I realize it's the new blond hostess and they're kissing.

He's not taking French class with me. He's Frenching some other girl.

I stand there for a second, doing my prairie-dog-in-headlights look, unable to move. I stare at her name tag: JACQUI. I wonder what kind of name that is, what kind of spelling that is. Meanwhile, JACQUI and Steve don't even notice I'm standing there.

And while before, I just *thought* this was shaping up to be the worst summer of my entire life? Now I know it's true.

"Hey, so what did he say?" Charlotte asks when I go back to our booth.

"I don't know," I say, sitting down with a squeak of vinyl. "I mean, nothing. He was with this girl. The hostess."

"What do you mean, he was with her?"

"They're making out," I tell Charlotte.

"What? No way." She sounds indignant. Charlotte cranes her neck to see them. She can't, so she stands up and half walks over to them, taking a few extra napkins off a service cart to give her trip purpose. "That girl looks like she's made out of plastic," she says when she comes back. "Did you see that nose job? And her hair color is *definitely* not natural."

I try to smile, because I appreciate what Charlotte's doing. But it doesn't really matter who the girl is. It just matters that Steve wants to kiss her and not me.

Weather on the Nines

At 6:45 a.m. I wander into the kitchen and my little sister Torvill is clamoring, "You're up, you're up, you're up!" She says things in threes now—it's her phase *du jour*, or rather, *du summer*.

It's the first day this week that I don't have to be at Gas 'n Git by 6:00. Dad just woke me on his way out, and Torvill, Dean, and Dorothy want their breakfasts. Mom is at the radio station to do her morning forecasts. I've got to watch the kids for the next four hours, until Dad gets home. Three mornings a week—and whenever else he can find time—he drives to an arena that is open year-round for serious figure skaters. He has a Russian coach named Ludmila, and he's trying to get up to speed so he can go on some Masters of Skating tour.

"Come on, you guys," I say, "don't you want to go back to bed? I think it's raining. Isn't it raining?"

I glance at Dorothy, who is sitting in the middle of the kitchen floor, making a perfect, tall stack of plastic containers, in descending size. She'll be an engineer. She's brilliant and scientific that way.

Torvill runs over to the window. "It's sunny, it's sunny, it's sunny!"

"Then why do I hear water?" I ask.

"We were running water in the sink," Dean says. "Dad said to wash our hands."

I look at the kitchen sink, which is about to overflow. I rush over and turn it off, then pull the drain stopper free.

"Yogurt, yogurt, yogurt!" Torvill sings.

I rub my eyes as I look at her. Is it my imagination, or is her pink Barbie sleepwear suddenly a size too small for her?

Dean starts kicking the refrigerator. He wants to be a kickboxer, and thinks he should practice on every household item and anyone who's standing nearby.

I move Dean aside and get out the milk, yogurt, cereal, and fruit snacks. There's a note from Mom on the counter: "Peggy—Pears in Fridge, Please Use Up."

Like I want some aging, moldy pears for breakfast. They're not good enough for anyone else to use up, but they're okay for me? Or does she mean I should foist them on to the kids? It's unclear, like most of her early-morning notes. I want French toast, not pears. I want Eggs Benedict brought to me in bed, on a tray. In a fancy hotel. In a large city.

But no. I've got moldy pears and kids throwing cereal at me. And it's another fragrant Lindville morning.

We never should have traveled so much when I was young, because it makes me want more things than Lindville has. When I was born, my father was still competing as an amateur. But after he came in 4th at Nationals and then 8th and then 16th, he realized he was in a very bad trend, which could only eventually lead to 32nd, 64th and 128th. Not that they let that many skaters compete at Nationals, but you get the gist.

He had this move he created, called the Farrell Flip, where he held his hands a certain way on his hips when he did a flip jump. But it never really caught on the way the Salchow and the Axel did. He was never successful enough to end up on a cereal box, is what it boils down to.

So he decided to give up his Olympic dream and join an ice show. Starting from when I was two, we were on the road all the time, going from city to city, which might sound hard, but it was great. I met lots of people with really extreme makeup back then. I was only a toddler, so it couldn't have influenced me that much, but who knows? Maybe that's why I have such an aversion to eye shadow, and why I love staying in hotels and visiting new places. And why I hate being stuck in one place year after year.

When Dad got tired of skating in sweltering costumes, sometimes playing to big crowds, sometimes playing to empty rinks, occasionally crashing into the boards when he couldn't see out of his eyeholes, it was time for me to start school. We moved here because they both found jobs and we're close to my grandparents. But Dad still dreams of hearing Dick Button, former Olympic champion and a skating commentator for many years, talk about his marvelous power and spark and grace on the ice. I'm not sure Dick Button ever said anything about Dad. I think it's something he may have fantasized about, the way he decided certain skating judges conspired to keep him out of international competition.

Torvill insists on three pieces of toast, while Dean only eats things that are grape. All they want to talk about is their fifth birthday party, which is still an entire month away. It's right at the end of Rodeo Days, and Dean wants to have the party at the rodeo, with both a magician and a bucking bronco ride; Torvill wants to have a clown, pony rides, and a pizza party at Smiley's Pizza. They won't stop arguing, but at least

Dean isn't kicking anything.

Dorothy sits quietly, ignoring them, and makes a giant stack of Cheerios that could win a record for tallest cereal tower ever. She eats the Cheerios that don't make it onto the tower.

The pears will have to wait.

I'd rather take the kids to IHOP, but I tried that once, a few months ago; it not only didn't work, it was the most stressful forty-five minutes of my entire life, especially when the roving balloon artist was making a rabbit and Dean reached up and popped the balloon with his fork.

Fortunately, Steve wasn't there to observe my hair with blueberry syrup and bacon toppings.

Steve. IHOP. Suddenly I remember what I've been trying to forget: Steve and that hostess. I push the thought away again. I can't think about that now. I'm pretending it didn't happen.

I toast myself a bagel, sit down at the table with the kids, and take the rubber band off the *Lindville Gazette*. Every article on the front page somehow relates to the upcoming Rodeo Roundup Days. The only front-page story *not* about the rodeo is about a gas-station robbery.

I don't want my parents reading that. They'll make me quit my job, and then I'll have no way of leaving the house, no way of repaying them, and I'll end up trapped here forever. I fold that section over and toss it into the recycle bin.

I open the next section. It's sports and obituaries. Softball games people have won, and cancer battles they have lost. In between are scattered giant ads for cars and trucks and, of course, Rodeo Roundup Days tickets.

"Come on, guys—it's almost time," I say, at 7:25.

Torvill hits the mute button on the TV and I flip on the radio perched on top of the refrigerator. It's preset to 1230 AM, KLDV, which has "traffic and weather on the nines." This is sort of absurd, because there isn't that much traffic here, and the weather does not change often. But KLDV has to do it, because the station is part of some big conglomerate radio network and that's one of their trademarks.

There's a little jingle, a very boppy and upbeat song that Dad helped to write, introducing KLDV's "Link to Mother Nature." It has this line that seems really dumb to me: "She has her ear to the ground, and her eye on the sky!" I always picture Mom lying on dew-covered grass with her head pressed against it, her clothes getting soaked as she gazes up at the sky, squinting because the sun is in her eyes.

She's live in the studio on weekday mornings, and then they tape her forecast and play it throughout the day until the night guy comes in. She occasionally does remotes, too. Sometimes I'll catch my mom describing what it's like outside by using her hands and making big, sweeping motions—the way she used to when she was a TV meteorologist.

"Good morning, KLDV listeners, and a special good morning to Dorothy, Torvill, and Dean," my mother says quickly, in her ultra-smooth radio voice, which is slightly perkier and also slightly huskier than her normal one—a weird combination that works.

"Mom, Mom, Mom!" Torvill screams.

"Shush," Dean tells her.

Dorothy dismantles her Cheerio tower and starts forming a cereal circle. "Sunny," she declares, announcing her own forecast. "Mostly sunny."

Mom only went back to work after the station told her she could say hi to her kids on at least *one* of the nines. They finally settled on 7:29, so every weekday morning I'm home with them I have to make sure we tune in. I told my mother not to say my name anymore, because it was embarrassing, but it feels kind of strange not to be on the list, like I'm not part of the family anymore.

"This is Christie Farrell, your link to Mother Nature, and here's today's weather outlook! Your morning temperature is sixty-eight degrees, up from an overnight low of sixty-two.

But this coolness won't last long. We have an area of high pressure that's creating this gorgeous, hot sunny weather. Get ready for another scorcher. Today's high should be right around ninety. If you can find your way to a body of water— a pool, a lake, a river—jump in! If you're working outdoors, make sure you drink *plenty* of water to avoid dehydration. As always, there's a slight possibility of thunderstorms this afternoon, so keep an eye on the sky to be safe."

Everyone is so busy keeping an eye on the sky. Who's watching where they're going?

The telephone rings a minute later, so I go into my father's office to answer it. It's sort of like a skating museum, with bookshelves covered with pictures of Dad and trophies and medals he's won. There are a couple small trophies of mine on a top shelf, which I tried to convince Dad to put in the closet.

"Hello?" I say, grabbing the phone.

"Oh, hi, Peggy, it's Mom. I was just calling to make sure you were up."

"Mom, of course I'm up," I say. What's even worse than being expected to do so much is not being trusted to do it.

"Oh, good. Did you get a chance to tune in?"

"Of course we did," I say. "I never forget to do that."

"Well, did you eat the pears?"

"No, Mom," I say.

"Because they're ripe," she adds.

As she goes on and on about the fruit varieties in our crisper, I spin the globe next to my father's desk. I close my eyes and stick out my finger to stop the globe and see where I should head on my first worldwide trip.

"Peggy, are you listening?" Mom asks just as I open my eyes and see I've landed on Greenland.

"I'll check out the pears," I tell her as I spin the globe again.

Peggy, Peggy, Peggy

At 12:15 I am sitting on the front steps, watching the kids play, occasionally flipping through my French book, wondering how to say "Sorry I am so late" in French. Neither Mom nor Dad has called yet, and both are late. It has to be about ninety degrees outside. I take a deep breath and wish I hadn't. Today is definitely an 8 on the Lindville Aromatic Index: Stay inside and close the windows if you can. Light a candle.

I keep trying to convince the kids we should go inside where there's air-conditioning and better-smelling air, but they won't. Dean is practicing kickboxing against the garage door. Torvill is swinging on the swing set, and Dorothy is constructing castles in the sandbox that actually resemble

European castles. Every time she finishes one, Dean comes over and kicks it down. Then Dorothy quietly, solidly, patiently rebuilds. She doesn't even cry. She never cries.

My father honks the horn as he finally pulls into the driveway. He gets out of the car and is wearing shiny black nylon warm-ups that fit like tights, and a red T-shirt with a cutoff bottom and arms. He has red-white-and-blue sweat-bands around his wrists and forehead. His dark brown hair is standing up, styled by sweat—where he still *has* hair, that is. He has clogs on his feet, and his warm-up pants are three inches too short.

He looks like a refugee from a Broadway dance production. The guy who probably didn't get a callback.

Torvill, Dean, and Dorothy run to Dad and cling to his legs. I stand up and grab my backpack.

"So how was your workout?" I ask. My dad, the three kids, and I are all piled into his car. He's dropping me off at school, since he got home too late for me to skate there or take the bus. He's driving really fast, but I decide not to mention this. Driving instruction from me doesn't go over well with my parents.

"It wasn't great," he says. "My triple Salchow still isn't there, and I was seriously traveling on my spins. I just could not focus today." He is gracefully turning the wheel with one hand while he sips from a giant commuter mug of hot green tea in the other. He does everything semi-gracefully. It's his gift.

Still, my father is the most macho male figure skater I've ever seen. He never wore sequins when he competed. He wore only black, white, and various shades of gray, and—when he wanted to make a statement—a hat or a cap, like the one he wore for his Mary Poppins program, when he skated to "Chim Chim Cher-ee." Even when he was in the ice show, which had a lot of very embarrassing costumes, he got to be the tough guy—he'd play a policeman, or a dinosaur, or the Beast.

I admire my father tremendously for his athletic ability. When I watch old tapes of him, I can't quite believe this is the same guy. He volunteers at the town rink all winter, coaching little kids, getting people to donate their old skates, and organizing mini-shows. I took lessons from him, too, of course. We used to spend *hours* together while he tried to make me into a great skater.

The plan was sort of working, until one junior regional competition where I missed all my jumps and was on my rear end more than my skates. I don't like to think about it much. All I know is that I grew three inches in one year and suddenly nothing worked anymore. My dad took me to a sports psychologist for weeks afterward to try to help me deal with my "mental block," but it didn't work. It was like I had taken over someone else's body when I turned twelve, and I didn't have instructions on how to use it.

Let's just say that I don't spin well anymore.

"What's new with you?" Dad asks.

"Summer school. French class. Lots of homework," I say. "Gas station job. All very exciting."

"Don't worry, P. F.," my dad says. He likes to call me P. F. because those are his initials, too. "Things will pick up." He glances over at me and smiles. "Why don't you come down to the rink with me tomorrow? I could use a tough critic."

"I'm a tough critic?" I ask.

"Brutal," he says. "Remember when you said my back flip was the generic version of Scott Hamilton's? How everything I did was pewter-medal quality? Or wait. It could have been aluminum quality."

"Sorry about that. I was just mad because I couldn't do anything right that day myself. Remember?"

"I remember," my father says. "But you know, it has been a while since you tried, and you have been in-line skating a lot, so it could be time for *your* comeback, too."

"Right. Right, Dad. Sure," I say. "Any second now it's *all* going to fall into place."

"Don't laugh—that's how it happens," he says, signaling a turn. "So when can you come to the rink with me?"

"I don't know. Maybe in a couple of days—I have to see what my work schedule is for next week."

"I think you're too busy this summer. You should be relaxing, hanging out," Dad says.

This from the man who told me I had to take the job at Gas 'n Git because I had to pay him and Mom back, who asked me to take over breakfast duty so he could go skate this morning, who is now speeding into the Edison High parking lot to drop me off for French class and I have only *une minute* to spare.

"Well, whenever you can make it," Dad says, and smiles at me.

I lean over and kiss his cheek before I get out of the car. Even though my dad can be annoying, I think he's the one person on earth who still has faith in me—even after everything. "Bye, guys!" I say to my sibs. "See you this afternoon."

"Peggy, Peggy, Peggy!" Torvill chants.

My name does not sound better when it's chanted in threes.

I see Charlotte racing across the parking lot toward me. I stop and wait for her, figuring it's better to be late together.

I'll make up a story about the bus breaking down or some-thing. *L'autobus était très tard.* Hopefully, Monsieur LeFleur, or a reasonable facsimile, will be too busy teaching to notice my bad grammar.

FEN

I'm sitting on the roof of Mrs. Duncan's car and I don't see Steve anywhere. Charlotte's lying on the hood, staring up past the towering streetlights at the night sky.

Charlotte's mother lets her borrow the car one night a month, and tonight is her lucky night. Instead of driving somewhere, though, we're parked at the Lot, and we're studying French. Or we're supposed to be.

This already feels like a routine for us, even though I've only known Charlotte a couple of days. She's just so easy to talk to, and since her friend Ashley is gone for the summer, too, we've instantly become best friends.

I like the new routine, except for the Steve-not-showing-up

part. He's usually here with Mike Kyle, but I haven't seen Mike's Camaro yet tonight. Mike is one of Steve's best friends, but I don't know him that well. I just know they do everything together, but for some reason he won't talk to me—I'm not worthy enough. I don't really care what he thinks, except that if I knew him it might make it easier for me to hang out with Steve.

I have to be home by 10:00, so I'm running out of time here.

I've been waiting for Steve to show up since 8:00. Not that I know he's coming, for sure, but everyone ends up here on weekend nights whether they want to or not. I'm wondering if the IHOP girl was just a temporary fling, the way I guess *I* was. Maybe they only kiss at work. Maybe it's the allure of the blue vinyl booth. In any case, if Steve shows up by himself, I'm going to talk to him. It's been decided. By Charlotte.

I'm not sure how this particular parking lot ended up being the Lot. I guess in part because, since Discount Mania closed, the warehouse-size building has been vacant and there are no merchants to complain about us.

Another reason is that the Lot's a good turnaround spot for when people are cruising on Twelfth Street. The Lindville police have tried everything to stop the cruising on weekends, but nothing works. Every once in a while we all just have to

drive up and down the same ten blocks, sitting and standing in the backs of pickups, or standing with our heads out
of sunroofs, screaming at the top of our lungs. Usually it's
a sporting event kind of thing—we won, or we might win,
or we should have won—but sometimes it just comes out
of nowhere, this accumulation of a need to scream. Maybe
because we're stuck in Lindville and we can't get out.

Charlotte's wearing a pair of faded jeans and a tiny pink
T-shirt that says Brooklyn on it. Her hair fans over the car's
hood and drifts in the breeze. "We have to be the only people
here tonight even thinking of studying. Who studies in June?
And on Friday night? Nobody."

"You're right," I say.

"So is he here yet?" she asks.

"No," I say. "You know what? Maybe we should quit talking about my love life and talk about yours instead."

"Well, back in Springfield I was seeing this guy Austin
kind of seriously. But then we moved," Charlotte says. "He
wanted to do the long-distance thing, but I said no way. So
I thought I'd wait a little while and see if anyone here was
worth going through all that again. Seriously depressing."

"And? Anyone yet?" I ask.

"Yeah. There's this guy at Shady Prairies."

"Isn't he a little *old* for you?" I ask.

"No!" Charlotte shrieks, and we both start laughing really hard. "He's not a resident. He *works* there," she says. "His name's Ray—he's seventeen. We hang out after work sometimes. He's got really nice arms."

"Arms." I nod. "Well, okay."

"Hey, you go crazy over a guy who makes pancakes, so I don't want to hear about it," Charlotte says.

"He doesn't *make* pancakes. He *serves* pancakes," I correct her, and we laugh. "And he has nice arms, too."

"Yeah. So he's not here yet?" Charlotte asks again.

I survey the Lot. "Nope."

"He must have gotten stuck at work. Like in some syrup," Charlotte jokes. She sits up and steadies herself by grabbing the driver's-side mirror. Then she hops off the hood and straightens her T-shirt. "So should we walk around?"

"Definitely," I say as I scoot to the edge. My short denim shorts nearly get caught on the radio antenna as I slide to the ground. I don't know why I'm wearing shorts, because it really cools down at night here and I'm starting to shiver. Walking beside Charlotte, who's about four or five inches shorter than me, I feel very conspicuous. Suzanne is slightly taller than me—she plays volleyball and basketball—and I'm more used to walking around with someone my height.

"I doubt there's anyone here we even want to see,"

Charlotte says, "you know? I mean, who is even here?"

"I don't know," I say. It's different in the summer, because some people are away for the season; some are home. The thing we all have in common is that almost everyone seems bored.

Some people are running around, playing with a glow-in-the-dark Frisbee. Some are playing music out of their cars. Some people are smoking and some people are dancing and some are drinking.

"There's a FEN," I say as we check out a guy sitting on the tailgate of his pickup.

"A what?" Charlotte asks.

I laugh. "Sorry. FEN is the code word Suzanne and I came up with for new good-looking guys we haven't seen before. It stands for 'Further Evaluation Necessary.' We need to know more about them before we can proceed," I explain.

"FEN. I like it. Well, don't worry. We'll find out about him. We'll definitely evaluate as necessary," Charlotte says. "You know . . . maybe a physical evaluation."

We laugh, and while Charlotte stops to talk to a friend, I suddenly see Mike Kyle's Camaro, and Mike getting out and leaning against it. I walk toward him. Would it be rude for me to ask him to step aside so I can see if Steve's in the car?

Mike stares at me for a second.

"Hi," I say, feeling stupid because I'm by myself, and no one walks around the Lot by themselves. Also, Mike and I have talked all of three times before, and that was only because he was forced to acknowledge me because Steve was talking to me.

"Hey," he says. "What's up?"

"Not much. Really." I peer past him, wondering if Steve's back there somewhere in the clump of people getting out on the other side of the car.

"You're here this summer?" he asks with sort of a nice smile.

It seems sort of obvious, but I nod. "Yeah."

"I thought you went to camp," he says.

"Me? No. That was Suzanne," I say. Are we that inter-changeable?

"Oh."

He's a sparkling conversationalist. But he looks good in a black T-shirt. That is something.

"Hey, Fleming," a girl with short black hair says, coming over to us. She was in my Current Events class last year, but I can't remember her name. "Savior" seems like a good name right now. She has about seven small earrings in one ear and one giant earring that looks like a metal bolt in the other.

"Hey," I say, smiling. I step away from Mike and closer to

her. "How are you? How's your summer going?"

"It sucks," she says, as she peels a layer of polish off her thumbnail. "I'm working at my mom's salon. I sweep up hair."

"Well, I pour coffee at the Gas 'n Git," I say.

"Dead, disgusting hair," she says. "Sometimes dandruff."

"Okay, you win," I say, laughing.

A guy near Mike moves, and I notice Steve and the IHOP girl, Jacqui, leaning against the back of the car. They're standing so close that I can't even see air space between them. And they're kissing. Suddenly my good mood vanishes.

"So, Fleming, if you want to come by the salon, I can give you a free cut maybe—I'm learning," the girl says.

"Hey, uh, thanks," I mutter. "And if you ever want free coffee—you know where to find me." I quickly run off and find Charlotte and tell her we'd better get going or I'll miss my curfew.

"You look weird, Fleming. Your eyes are too bright or something. What just happened?" she asks.

"There's Steve—and that IHOP hostess again," I say, discreetly pointing in their direction. "And for some reason they have to kiss repeatedly in public."

Charlotte narrows her eyes at them. "Pig. But don't worry, you'll get him back."

"I can't get him *back*," I say.

"What are you talking about?" Charlotte says. "God, you're a hundred times prettier than she is."

I blush, hoping that's somehow true. "No. I mean, I can't get him back because I never had him in the first place," I admit. It was one thing when he wasn't seeing me, but he wasn't seeing anyone else, either. Then I could come up with theories about how he was a free spirit. Now he's happily chained to someone else.

"Oh. Well, that sucks." Charlotte pops her gum. "Forget him, okay? We've got FENs all over the place here."

"We've only seen one," I point out.

"Come on! Where there's one, there's more," Charlotte says. She puts her arm around my shoulders. "Let's get out of here. We're done studying. Right?"

"Considering that we never really started? Yeah," I say with a smile.

"We can do it on Sunday," Charlotte declares. "It's not like we have anything else to do on Sunday."

I think I'm supposed to go to a childbirth class with my pregnant mother on Sunday. Case in point.

"Anyway, if I don't get the car back on time, my mom won't let me have it next month," Charlotte says as we amble back toward her car.

As we start to pull out of the Lot, Mike and Steve come up

beside us and pass us, peeling out onto Twelfth with squealing tires. I can't see if that Jacqui girl is with them. Maybe they ditched her, I think hopefully. Maybe Steve's realized that she's plastic, that he's made a terrible, horrible mistake. I can dream, for at least the next few seconds anyway, until we catch up to them at the next stoplight and I see her blond head in the rear window.

Your Love Is Like Roadkill

Saturday morning, Dad is busy getting three For Sale homes ready for their open houses—which means he makes sure the places have been vacuumed and decluttered, and he buys large floral arrangements. Dad's into flowers. I think he misses having them thrown onto the ice for him.

Mom has to do a radio remote from Gabe's Auto World. "I promise, Peggy, this is the *last* one," she said last night, which is what she said after the previous one. "I keep telling Bill, but he keeps saying they can't get by without me." And they can't, because Mom is great at remotes where she has to pitch products and run contests and interview shoppers. She has this gift. She can talk to anyone and never has dead air time.

I take Dorothy, Torvill, and Dean to the neighborhood playground, two blocks away. Because I'm the tallest person there, I end up holding all the neighborhood kids up to the overhead bar, which has a pulley that lets them slide to the other end. The kids scream my name and climb on me. They call me "Peggy the Gentle Giant." They don't get tired of doing this, but my arms get tired after fifteen minutes. Mrs. Klipp, from across the street, comes over to ask me how my summer's going, as if it's not obvious.

Mom gets home before Dad. She comes into the house, gets the kids started on lunch, and then turns to me. "So you're going to be here tonight, right?"

I'm in the middle of eating a banana so I have to swallow before I can ask, "Um, what?"

"You're going to be home tonight—to watch the kids?" she asks.

"Excuse me?" I say. "I am?"

"We're having dinner out with Laurie and Brandon, remember?" she says.

I shake my head.

"I left you a note," she says. She rifles through a stack of library books on the counter and a small piece of pink paper flutters to the floor. "Didn't you see this?" she asks as she struggles to bend down and pick it up.

"No," I say. "Nobody could have seen that."

"Oh, well." Mom hauls herself back up by the oven door handle. "We wanted to go out tonight, and I just thought—well, I didn't think you had any plans. So I figured you could watch the kids while we're out. We might be home kind of late—around midnight."

I can't say anything because I'm actually sort of stunned. Let me get this straight: I was here all morning watching the kids, and now they want me to be here all night, too? What if I had plans? What if I wanted to go out on Saturday night like most normal sixteen-year-olds?

I want to tell her that I can't, that I have plans, that it's going to be absolutely impossible. But it isn't. And besides, Mom has dark circles under her eyes where her makeup has sort of caked, and she looks exhausted. I'm not sure how going out with friends will help, but maybe it's what she needs. "I guess I could do it," I say.

"I knew you could! Did you hear that, guys? Peggy's going to hang out with you tonight," Mom says as she doles out sugar cookies. She doesn't even say "thanks" or "that's nice." She just says, "How about renting a movie?"

"Little Mermaid! Little Mermaid!" Torvill says.

"We don't have to rent that; we own it," Mom says, interrupting her before the third "Little Mermaid."

Do we ever, I think as I head up to my room, close the door behind me, and savor my few minutes of solitude. I turn up the radio and lie down on my bed, completely exhausted. I stare at the giant poster of New York City beside my bed, which is next to the poster of Boston, which is next to San Francisco. The other side of my room has framed prints of Provence, Rome, and London. The ceiling is a world map covered with neon-bright stickers to mark the places I want to go. Occasionally the stickers dry out and fall on me when I'm asleep and I wake up with DEFINITELY! or DUBLIN on my face.

I close my eyes and try to picture that it's a Saturday somewhere else. I'm shopping on Fifth Avenue. I'm standing by the ocean—no, I'm surfing in it. I have tickets for the ballet. I'm visiting ancient ruins or Buckingham Palace.

I'm not staying home in Lindville watching kids' videos I've seen a hundred times before.

Around three o'clock I skate to Gas 'n Git.

Denny is there, writing in his notebook between gas transactions, and wants to know what I'm doing. "You're here on your day off. *Why?*" He puts down his pen and looks up from his notebook.

"To pick up my check. And I'm getting presents for a friend." I want to send Suzanne a care package.

"You mean *gitting*, don't you?" Denny asks. "Please use the trademarked phrase while in the store. Jamie's here today, you know—better not do anything un-employee-like."

I shrug. "Okay. So how's it going?"

"Everyone's grumpy because the pay-at-the-pump receipt printers aren't working, and apparently it's a tragedy." Denny rolls his eyes.

"Devastating," I agree.

"Jamie's trying to fix them. She's on the phone with Gas 'n Git Central. In the meantime, no one has to prepay, but everyone still comes in here in a bad mood," Denny says. There's a little crackle on his gas-pump monitor, and Denny clicks the speaker and says, "You're okay on seven . . . Kevin." He looks out the front window and waves at a guy who's filling up. "See, I know him, and that rhymes, so it's sort of cool."

"Sort of," I say.

"Hey—while you're here, you mind listening to some lyrics? I'm sort of stuck," Denny admits.

"Um. Okay," I say. I can see how he would be stuck, if *seven* and *Kevin* are what he's working with. I'm actually very curious to hear what Denny writes about. His motorcycle, I'm guessing—and his accessories. Or about the cruelty of wanting a mustache and not being able to grow one.

Denny clears his throat. "This town has no soul, it's a hollow shell with nothing to fill it," he begins to sing. It sounds suspiciously like a familiar U2 song, but with different lyrics. "But with you by my side—no, wait, that wasn't it." He peers at the words on the page. "But you won't give in. You won't give in. And your life has gone . . ."

"Country?" I say.

He frowns at me. "No. Your life has gone—"

"To the dogs," I suggest.

"Shut up," he says. "Your life has gone around the bend, and your love is like a . . . well, I wanted to put in something about the road. Your love is like a stop sign?" he asks.

"Speed bump," I suggest. "Or how about roadkill? Your love is like roadkill."

"You're really awful at this," Denny says. "Come on, just actually try to help me, okay? How about . . . Your love makes me yield. I can't yield to your love. No—I can't *stop* for your love."

"But you can at least slow down and let me jump out of the car," I say. "Right?"

Denny frowns at me.

"What—I was serious," I say, thinking of Kamikaze Bus Driver, how this song could be his theme.

"Okay, then. Next song." Denny tears the sheet of paper

out and crumples it into a ball and then flips to a fresh page in his notebook.

"Your love is a crumpled page," I say.

Denny taps his pen against the counter. Then he looks at me. "That's not bad."

"And I can't throw it away," I add.

"Okay, *that* is bad."

"Fleming!" Jamie says. Our boss walks out of the back office and dumps a stack of receipt-paper rolls on the counter. "How are you? What a coincidence that you dropped by. I need to talk to you."

"Coincidence?" Denny scoffs. "Not exactly. Our paychecks are ready."

Me, I'm worried that she needs to talk to me. She's not going to fire me. Is she?

"I have a problem, and I was wondering if you could help out," Jamie goes on. "I've lost my Saturday-night coffee person."

"Thank *God,*" Denny says as he swipes a customer's credit card. "That guy was—"

Jamie clears her throat loudly and we move away from the counter a bit. "Anyway, I was wondering if it would be at all possible for you to pick up the shift."

"You mean . . . permanently?" I ask. Can my summer get

worse? I have to work on Saturday nights now?

"Yes. We could trade it for your Friday day shift, because I have someone who can cover that," Jamie says. "So what do you think? The shift is from three to eleven, and you'd be working with Denny."

I stare at the freezer and contemplate my options. Working with Denny isn't bad, because he's a known quantity. And I can either work here or risk being stuck at home. And I know that Steve has worked Saturday nights forever, so I wouldn't be missing anything there. And I do have to keep this job. "I'll do it, but I can't start tonight," I say.

"That's fine. That's perfect. You're a *life*saver," Jamie tells me. Then she goes over to replenish the coffee tanks.

I wander around, shopping, while Denny rings up gas sales. As soon as Jamie goes back to the office, Denny rushes over and shuts off the coffee machines. He dumps more coffee into the filters, then presses the "Resume" buttons.

"What are you doing?" I ask.

"She makes the worst coffee. God. Undrinkable. She doesn't use enough, and it comes out tasting like dirty water," Denny says.

"So why do we sell Jamie's Java Blend?" I ask. "And why is she here making coffee when she doesn't usually?"

"Rick didn't show up for like the hundredth time, so she

fired him. So, you taking the Saturday-night shift?"

"Yeah," I say.

"Cool. So you're here to buy stuff. Why aren't you shopping at the mall?" he asks.

"Employee discount. Plus, it's too far away," I say. "Plus, there aren't any good stores there."

"True. Very true. I *long* for a decent store in this town," Denny says.

"You could write a song about that," I say.

Denny smiles. "Right." He comes out from behind the counter and follows me around the store.

There are only three aisles of food and auto supplies. I grab a rain bonnet and two packets of ibuprofen. I get a plastic coffee mug with the Espress-Oh-Yes logo for Suzanne, and then head for the candy aisle. I stack chocolate bars and bags of fruit-flavored candies in my arms.

"So what is all this for?" Denny asks.

"It's a care package," I tell him. "My friend's a camp counselor, and you know how camp food sucks."

Denny shakes his head. "Not really. I've never gone to camp. I'm not exactly a camp-type person."

"What kind of person is that?" I ask.

"You know. The kind of person who likes living in a cabin with a bunch of other people and hiking and sitting around a campfire. Roasting marshmallows. Singing. All together." Denny shudders.

"You sing," I say. "You like singing. You write songs."

"They do *skits*, okay? I don't think I need to say any more." Denny rushes over to ring up another gas sale.

A few minutes later I carry my stash of gifts to the counter and drop them in front of him. "Ring away."

He starts scanning the items and asks, "What are you doing tonight?"

I really hope he isn't trying to ask me out. I know he isn't—that he wouldn't. But the question always makes me think that, anyway. "Hanging out with my sibs," I say. "Technically you could call it baby-sitting, except I'm their big sister."

"Baby-sitting. On Saturday night," Denny says.

"Yes."

"You are *exciting*," he says. "Do you know that?"

He's acting like this was *my* idea. "At least I won't be working *here*. Yet."

"And at least I'm not at camp. Give your friend my sympathy, okay? Here." He grabs a few packs of spearmint gum, pays for them, and tosses them into the plastic bag. "She'll need these. They don't let you brush your teeth much when you're at camp. You have to go down to the river or whatever."

"Thanks," I say, surprised by his generosity.

"No problem. Rvoyr," Denny says.

I stare at him for a second until I realize what he's saying. "Yeah. *Au revoir* to you, too."

On my way home, an eighteen-wheeler veers into the bike lane and nearly dusts me.

This town has no soul. And nobody yields to your love. Nobody yields, period.

Maternity Moments

I am sitting on the floor of the Lindville Medical Center's Lamaze Lounge. I am the only female in the room with a flat stomach. My mother is fifteen minutes late for our first childbirth class. The other people sitting in our circle are mothers, and fathers, and unborn babies. People are looking at me and wondering why I'm not "showing" yet, why I don't *have* a partner, why I'm in this class when I am so obviously not pregnant. "People!" I want to say. "It's not me!" I cannot believe Mom isn't here yet. I can't believe she's doing this to me. This is so embarrassing.

I'm only here because Mom wants us to "bond" by having me there for her next—and she claims her last—baby delivery. I don't know how I feel about it. Most of the time I'm either scared or disgusted, but every now and then I'm sort of flattered. Only . . . what if the next baby comes out kicking like Dean?

The Lamaze Lounge is on the fifth floor of the hospital, just past the nursery. I'd think just being here for the first time could make you need some deep-breathing techniques. Just to walk past the maternity ward and hear some of the screams coming out of those rooms. What really gets to me about being in hospitals is the smell, a disgusting mixture of chemical cleansers, disinfectants, hot cafeteria food . . . and things you don't want to think about.

If Mom doesn't show up, maybe I'll check into the ear, nose, and throat ward, see what they can do about my heightened sense of smell. Maybe they could use plastic surgery to rebuild my nose, take out all the sensors while simultaneously making it perfect and cute, like plastic hostess-girl Jacqui's.

I've never been to the hospital for myself, but I've been here on the fifth floor twice before. Torvill and Dean took a while to arrive, so Dad and I camped out here together in uncomfortable orange chairs. Dorothy was born more quickly, and I stayed home with the twins and my grandparents.

We're in this class basically for me. Mom knows everything already. She knows the doctors, the nurses, the procedures, the gift-shop hours, and even the best vending machines.

"Peggy! I thought we were meeting at home," Mom says as she rushes into the lounge. She looks like she just got off a bike. She's wearing black Lycra shorts, a yellow jersey, and her hair is wet with sweat. She looks like she is fresh off the Tour de Lindville.

"Mom, you left me a note telling me to meet you here," I say. I look around at everyone in the room. See? I want to say to the rest of the class. It's *her* we're here for. Not me. You can save your lectures on teen sex. Believe me. I have nothing going on, so they'd be wasted on me.

"I did? Really? Wow. Is it me, or am I going straight from having babies to having memory loss? It's like one minute you're having maternity moments . . . you know, where you can't get out of a chair . . . to senior moments, where you can't remember where the chair *is*." She sits down carefully on the carpeted floor, her round belly stretching the yellow nylon top, her belly button showing through the fabric.

She's just so clueless when it comes to maternity clothes that it's almost cute. Almost. She just starts wearing Dad's clothes and lots of XLs. When she was pregnant with Torvill and Dean, she bought some XXLs. Friends always try to give her their old maternity clothes, but she won't take them, unless they're maternity sportswear.

My mother is a very good athlete, which is probably

why she can handle her pregnancies so well. She's really into cycling, but she kind of takes the bike shorts a little too far, in my opinion. Early in your ninth month, maybe you shouldn't be wearing maternity bike shorts, even if they make them.

"Welcome, class, welcome!" The teacher, Monica, is bright and sparkly and also pregnant, but not nearly as far along. "I'm so glad you're all here to begin this wonderful journey with me." She looks at me and smiles, with a semi-confused look on her face.

I want to tell her: Nobody could feel more confused about me being here than I am.

"As you probably know, this class will teach you various methods of preparing for the joyful experience of giving birth to your child," Monica continues. "You'll learn valuable relaxation and visualization techniques, do breathing exercises—and of course we'll practice some ways to make you more comfortable during your labor."

"Like anyone can be comfortable during labor," Mom says under her breath to me.

I start to giggle, and Monica suddenly fixes her gaze on us, like we're the problem students that need to be reined in early to set an example for the rest of the class. "So, why don't we start by introducing ourselves?" she says, her smile a little less wide. "Perhaps *you* could start." She gestures to Mom.

"I'd be glad to," Mom says in her super-cool radio voice. "I'm Christie Farrell, and—"

"Christie Farrell—from KLDV?" a woman across the room asks eagerly. My mother nods. "Oh, my gosh, I listen to your forecasts *every* morning."

"Well, thank you very much," my mother says with a polite smile.

"You're usually right. Except about that snowstorm back in March," the woman says.

"Yes. Well, the moisture indicators simply weren't there, what can I tell you?" Mom's smile fades as the woman describes how she was stranded without a coat or a windbreaker and how awful it was. Mom hates having her forecasts criticized. She's a perfectionist, like Dad—she'd do her forecasts over if she could. She has this framed Mark Twain quote over her desk: "Everybody talks about the weather, but nobody does anything about it." Then she has a neon-pink Post-It stuck onto the glass that says, "But I'll keep trying."

Monica clears her throat and says, "I'm sorry, could we get back to the introductions? Please?" She holds out her hand toward my mother. "Christie, if you could continue?"

"Yes. Well, this is Peggy," my mother says, still disregarding that I'd rather be called Fleming. "She's going to be my birth coach this time. I thought it would be fun for us to do this together. I've been here before, of course, but this is all new to Peggy."

Monica studies us for a second. "You know, I'm so glad you're here. This can be a *very* bonding experience for a step-mother and daughter."

"Yes, well, I'm her mother. Not her stepmother." Mom smiles awkwardly. "Just to sort of clarify. I know we don't look much alike right now, but that's because I've got this baby here and I haven't been able to get my hair highlighted. But you can see she got my height, and we've both got lots of freckles. You see, what happened was, my husband and I had Peggy when we were quite young, and so then we decided to wait a while before we had more children. So we waited, and now we have three little ones at home, and we've definitely got our work cut out for us with another baby coming, don't we, Peggy?"

Work cut out for me, *you mean*, I'm thinking. They love Mom at KLDV, because she can talk and talk and talk and easily fill dead air and easily fill in for sick DJs and easily do a remote from a car dealer or a new store or even the rodeo. But when I'm with her? I wish she wouldn't.

"Before we start today, can I ask anyone else if they get really bothered by all this high pressure?" Mom goes on. "I feel like it's so dry that my body on purpose starts retaining more water than it needs to. I mean, I could just use a nice, heavy rain for a couple of days."

Oh, my God. I'm dying here. Why does she have to do this? Why does she have to talk about water retention and weather? I ignore her voice and count to ten. When I stop counting, she's still talking.

"Excuse me, Christie? We'd better get going with the rest of our introductions," Monica says, still smiling. She moves on to the next couple, who can barely talk. They're just staring at us like we rolled in from a traveling carnival, like we're in the Rodeo Roundup Days Stranger than Fiction stage show.

Mom reaches over and squeezes my knee. "You look sick. Are you feeling all right?" she asks softly. "It's so hot in here, isn't it? I feel a little faint myself." She leans back against me and stretches out her legs.

Deep breathing techniques can't come soon enough for both of us.

Everyone Looked Dead

"Hey, it's Tonya Harding. What's up?" Denny is in a cheery mood when I show up for work on Monday at 5:45 a.m.

I glare at him. I can't believe he's calling me "Tonya." I've just been almost chomped on by the Doberman, who got so close that his slobber rained on my leg when he barked at me. I grab my checkered apron from the closet in back and put it on over my red-striped T-shirt and black capris. Not a good outfit, because the apron is so long I look like I'm not wearing pants, but I was too sleepy to think about it when I got dressed at 5:00. I go behind the counter and start prepping the machines, brewing coffee, organizing sweetener packets, restocking the cups, filling the Thermos containers with milk and half-and-half.

"Hey," Denny says when there's a break in the action. "Did you hear what happened at the Conoco on Twelfth yesterday?"

"No, what?" I ask.

"They got held up last night," Denny says. "It was even on TV because I guess that's the fourth robbery around here in the last two weeks. They had a reporter there and everything. The lighting is really terrible at that Conoco. Everyone looked dead. I mean, if we get robbed, we've got to think about where we should stand when they interview us."

I'm not thinking about being photogenic. I'm still stuck on the words *dead* and *robbery*. "Did anything bad happen?" I ask. "Did anyone get hurt?"

"Nah. They hadn't safed the money yet, so they lost several hundred bucks. But don't worry," Denny says. "I got the guy's description. They said he's between five-six and six feet tall, and he wears sunglasses and a baseball cap as a disguise."

"*That* really narrows it down," I say.

"Hey—it's something to go on," Denny says. "Also, he has brown hair and a mustache."

"Again. We're talking about half the population of Lindville," I say. The other half either don't want a mustache, or includes guys, like Denny, who obviously want one but can't grow one. His has gone from lint to fuzz, but seems to have paused there.

Denny shrugs. "The guy supposedly has this fixation with scratch tickets. At least that's what he pretends to buy. Then, while the clerk reaches down to tear them off for him, the guy pulls out a handgun and asks for all the cash in the register."

"A *gun*? Really?" I don't want to imagine a thief walking in here. I decide that I'm never filling in for anyone on the gas side of Gas 'n Git. I'll only serve coffee. I won't go near scratch tickets. "So, do you think he'll ever come here?" I ask nervously.

"One can only hope," Denny says.

"Hope?"

"Don't you want to be on TV?" Denny asks.

"That depends. Will I be alive or dead?" I ask.

Then again, I have such bad luck that I probably work at the only place that won't be robbed. Nothing that exciting will ever happen here.

About five minutes later, a guy in a baseball cap and sunglasses comes in and tells Denny he wants one "Six-Bun Salute" ticket and one "Prospector's Gold Nugget." Denny looks over at me and grins before reaching under the glass to get the tickets.

He's the kind of person who really would enjoy being

robbed. He could set the scene to music, something by U2, of course.

The customer asks for cigarettes, pays, and leaves.

"Yeah, well. Maybe next time," Denny says with a loud sigh.

I feel sort of fidgety and start restocking the mint and candy dish. Then I take paper cups and fill them with mints, too, and stagger them along the counter so there's no way people can miss them. World's Worst Coffee Breath is on his way, and I will get to him sooner or later.

I don't know how this wall of mints will save me from a man with a handgun, though. I'll pretend it's a fort, and duck.

I feel very stupid as I get onto the Lindvillager at noon and hand Kamikaze Driver his cup of coffee. I hold the cup out to him and feel everyone on the bus staring at me, maybe a little jealously. This could establish a dangerous precedent. Soon I'll be carrying trays of coffee to the bus. I'll be the world's first bus attendant.

"You didn't say whether you wanted cream and sugar." I give Kamikaze a handful of sugar, sweetener, and nondairy creamer packets, which he stuffs into various compartments and cup holders in the dashboard.

"Cream, next time. The real stuff," he grumbles.

"Okay, but I don't take the bus every day," I say. "Usually Mondays, Wednesdays, and Thursdays, but—"

"I know your schedule," he says.

The way he says it makes me think of a TV movie. *He Knew Her Schedule: The Peggy Fleming Farrell Story.* Since when is a bus driver keeping tabs on me? And why? Just because he needs coffee? So why not bring a Thermos in the morning, like a normal person?

Then for some reason he keeps looking at me, not closing the door. He's waiting for something. "Fare, please," he says.

I drop my quarters into the box.

Then he holds out his hand.

"I just paid," I say. "See the green light?"

"Change, please," he insists.

I sigh and take out some change from my pocket. I can't believe he wants change back from his coffee purchase. I delivered it onto a *bus*. This guy has no idea what I went through, carrying a hot paper cup up a steep slope.

I am about to say something when he shuffles the money around in his hand and then gives me back a quarter. "Thank you," he says. "Next time there will be more in it for you."

"I'm so grateful," I say.

Kamikaze sips his coffee, then charges back into traffic

before I can even take a seat. I reach out for a seat back to hold on to, but the bus swerves and I fall onto the end of a seat that's already taken, right into the lap of none other than Mike Kyle.

I'm shocked. Mike's never been on this bus before. This runs against the laws of nature. I'm just so stunned that I can't help blurting, "What are you doing here?" completely impolitely. Then I realize I'm still sitting on his lap. There's a really awkward moment where I have to untangle my bag from where it's wrapped around Mike's knee. "I mean, *sorry*," I say as I get up and move to the seat behind him.

"No problem, don't worry about it," Mike says. He sort of smiles. His face has that lean and chiseled look, like he could pose for something, but I'm not sure what. Maybe a calendar of hot high-school guys who don't go to class all that often.

"Sorry," I say again, putting my bag on the floor in front of me. "It's just . . . his driving. It's hard to stay uninjured."

"Yeah. So what was that? You brought him coffee? Like, personal delivery?" Mike asks. "Is he your dad or something?"

"No!" I say firmly. "We're not related. He asked me to do it, and I have to take this bus three days a week, so . . ."

"He's kind of scary, so you do it. I get it. You know, he almost just took out a guy on a moped back there." Mike gestures to the back window.

"You're kidding," I say. "No one rides mopeds here. That's like something out of my French book."

"Your what book?"

"French? Summer school?" I shake my head. "Never mind."

"Yeah, okay." He turns back around and looks out the window for a minute.

I stare at the back of his head, at his dark brown hair. He's good-looking, but in an unconventional way. I never really noticed before, because when he's around, Steve's around.

Mike turns back to me and asks, "So what are you doing this summer? I thought you went to work at some camp."

"No, that was my friend Suzanne," I tell him. Again. "I'm working at Gas 'n Git, and, well . . ." I decide not to go into the birth-coaching, debt-paying, baby-sitting glamour of it all. "That's pretty much it."

"Oh. Well, that's cool."

This is bizarre. Mike Kyle is actually making conversation with me. He's barely ever acknowledged my existence before. He always sort of looked at me vacantly, as if either he or I weren't there. Is it because we're both stuck on a bus with a crazy driver? People definitely bonded in that *Speed* movie.

I think maybe I should keep the conversation going. If I can talk to Mike, maybe I can get closer to Steve. This has never been my m.o., but obviously my previous M.O. wasn't working all that well and I clearly need to make adjustments.

Kamikaze honks the horn at something, pulls over at another stop, and then spins the wheel. We're back in action, as another rider lurches into her seat.

"So. How come you're riding the bus?" I ask. "Is your Camaro in the shop?" I lean forward and rest my elbows on the back of his seat.

"Ha. Good one. My Camaro." His lips get this pinched, skin-too-tight look, like being alive and breathing suddenly hurts.

"Oh. Sorry," I say quietly.

"It was my dad's. He took it back. He got really mad at me because Gropher and I were racing it Saturday night, out in the fields."

"Saturday night? You mean . . . after I saw you?" I ask.

He nods. "Yeah. My dad said I didn't respect the car or something. Just because I ran over some cornstalks."

"Cornstalks?" I ask, my eyes widening. "What happened? How did he find out about it?"

"There was corn in the driveway. I mean, not actual *corn* corn, because it's too early for that, but there were stalks. He was furious. He cleaned out the car and he's selling it now. He gave me this lecture. It completely sucks. I can't do anything for the rest of the summer, basically." Mike rolls his eyes. "I have to take this bus or ride my bike everywhere. It's the pits."

"I know," I say. "I'm in the same boat. I mean, um, bus." I laugh nervously. There's a very awkward moment of silence, where I wait for him to say more, and wait for me to come up with something else to say. I decide to plunge right into what I really want to know. "So what are you and Steve going to do now?" I ask. Besides hang out with IHOP hostesses? "I mean, it's kind of a long summer if you don't have a car. Trust me."

"Yeah. I know. I guess I'll have to get a better job," Mike says. "Earn enough money to buy my own car."

"What about Steve? Why doesn't he buy a car?" I ask.

"I *know*." Mike slaps the seat back of the older passenger in front of him, startling him. "God, he makes me mad. He's holding on to all his money so he can buy a van or a truck next year and drive all over the country. Some stupid plan like that."

I smile. Some stupid plan that I want to be *in* on. Although the van concept is a little disturbing. I remember my aunt and uncle's conversion van, completely decked out with furniture and a fridge—and tacky decorations.

I tell myself to stop picturing a van with wall-to-ceiling leopard-print carpeting, and focus. I'll never be any-where near that van unless I get close to Steve again. I have weird goals. I realize that. "So, um, what are you doing for work now?" I ask.

"Delivering the *Gazette*," Mike says. "On my bike."

"You?" I squeak, before I can stop myself.

"Yeah, me," he says. "Why is that so surprising?"

"You have to be up . . . really, really early," I say. "I always thought you were one of those, I don't know. Night owls. Staying up all night watching movies with Steve or whatever."

"I don't sleep much," Mike says. "I kind of don't like sleeping."

I stare at him. Who doesn't like sleeping?

"Whoa, here's my stop." He pulls the wire to let Kami-kaze Driver know he should think about pausing. "See you around."

"See you," I say as I watch Mike stand by the steps, ready to get off the bus. He has no butt to speak of. He has bony hips and then his jeans just sort of free-float until they hit his red flip-flops.

"Back of the white line," Kamikaze grumbles at him loudly.

Mike turns to me and rolls his eyes. "Help me," he mouths.

And we exchange smiles.

Then the Lindvillager screeches to a stop at the corner of Twelfth and Arizona, Mike nearly falls down, and then gets off the bus, and we're back on the road in under five seconds.

I just had the longest conversation with Mike Kyle that I, or perhaps anybody, has ever had. I learned that he's an insomniac with a paper route and an urge to destroy crops. He's really not so bad.

Sunny-side Down

After French class on Wednesday, Charlotte and I go to IHOP, even though I tell her it's pointless, that Steve and Jacqui are an item now.

"It's not pointless," she says. "You give up way too easy, Fleming."

"I do?" I ask. Because I thought I actually held on way too long.

"Yes," she says. "Make the guy see what he's missing already. Besides, I'm hungry."

Before we go inside IHOP, Charlotte and I pause in the parking lot of the hardware store next door so I can brush my hair. Charlotte insists on quickly braiding it into a thick French braid that, from what I can see in the hardware-store window, looks pretty good. I'm wearing low-cut faded jeans and a mint-green cap-sleeved T-shirt which fortunately doesn't have any coffee stains, thanks to my lovely Gas 'n Git apron. Charlotte pulls a tube of essential oil out of her purse and I put a few drops on my neck.

"I feel so essential," I tell her.

"Good," she says.

When we get to IHOP, I'm thrilled to see that Jacqui isn't working. We get seated in Steve's section. Everything seems to be going my way.

Charlotte taps her menu against the table as she gazes at Steve, who's walking toward us. "I'll stall him here as long as I can, don't worry. *Not* a problem at all. I can talk forever if I have to."

Just like my mom, I think. I hold my breath as Steve comes up to our table and stops. I let it out halfway and say, "Hey."

"Hey, Fleming. What's up?" Steve smiles. "How's French?"

"Finegood," I say, momentarily flustered and unable to choose a word. "I mean, *très bien*."

"Yes. Of course that's what you mean," Steve says. "I knew right away."

I feel my face turning red, contrasting with the cool mint T-shirt color. I want to ask him why he didn't take the class, like he was supposed to, but for some reason it would seem like whining, so I don't. "So, this is Charlotte. She's new here."

"Hardly," Charlotte tells him. "I feel like I've been here forever."

"Yeah. That's what we call the Lindville Effect. Right, Fleming?" Steve looks at me and smiles.

"Exactly," I say, feeling like the connection between us definitely isn't gone. It might be faint right now, like a bad cell phone connection, but it's still there.

"So, just to get the formalities out of the way, in case you guys are secret shoppers, taking notes on everything I do. My name is Steve and I'll be your server this afternoon."

I don't ever get tired of hearing him say that. I really don't.

"Did you get burned by a secret shopper recently or something?" I ask him.

"Oh, yeah. But I don't want to go into that right now." He glances over his shoulder toward the kitchen, as if he's being watched. I wonder if a secret shopper mentioned that he was too busy making out with a coworker to be a good server. Maybe he and Jacqui will be *forced* to break up. "So what can I get you?" he asks. "Or do you need a little more time with the menus?"

I need a little more time with the server, actually. But I don't want to be any more obvious than I'm already being. "I think I'm ready. Are you?" I ask Charlotte.

"I'm not sure. I was going to get French toast, you know, *vive la France* and all that. But now I'm thinking maybe just a two-egg combo thingy. Or three eggs. Yeah, that sounds good. Hey, go wild, make it a half dozen," she says.

"Are you serious?" Steve asks. He looks at Charlotte as if she's crazy. "I don't think you can order that."

"Sure I can. The three-egg combo plate, with three eggs on the side," Charlotte says.

"Three eggs on the side?" Steve repeats.

She looks up at Steve and smiles. "No, I guess just the two-egg thingy. Please."

"How would you like those two eggs?" Steve asks.

"Well, that's another thing. I have some egg questions," Charlotte says.

Steve raises his eyebrows.

"What does it mean, exactly, when it's sunny-side up? Is there a sunny-side down?" Charlotte asks.

"No. See, there's the sun. Which faces up," Steve says. "And then when you flip the egg over, it's called over easy."

"Hmm. I'll have to think about that. You go ahead, Fleming. I'll be ready in a second," Charlotte says.

While I order, I admire Steve's blue apron. It's not something you notice when it's on anyone else. But it's got this way of bringing out Steve's eyes, sort of the way my checkered-flag apron brings out the dark circles under my eyes at 6 a.m.

After I order, he turns to Charlotte. "And for you?" he asks.

"I'm not quite ready yet," she says.

Steve stands there. He glances at the tables around us to check on his other customers. He looks at me and smiles awkwardly.

"So. French. How is it, being in school when it's a hundred degrees?" he asks.

"Fine. The teacher's never there. I mean, we have subs," I say. Today's substitute looked like she had just come from playing golf, and was more concerned with her score card than with whether or not we could make any sense of the learn-French-by-video we were watching. "Really bad subs," I say.

"Huh," Steve says.

"Really bad," I repeat.

Steve just nods.

And I can't think of anything else to say. I fidget with my braid. The conversation is dead in the water. I nudge Charlotte's foot with mine. I need help.

She looks up at me, and then clears her throat. "So I want two eggs, sunny-side down," she tells Steve. "And if the cook says there isn't such a thing, just explain that I like saying that better than *over easy*. Okay? And I want pancakes and bacon."

"Sounds good. I'll be right back," he says. Then he leaves for the kitchen.

I watch him walk away, thinking: How did I blow it? Again? Why can't I think of anything to say? Why couldn't I have just asked him about movies he's seen lately, or the Camaro-cornstalk incident, or mention I saw Mike on the bus? Why does my brain atrophy like that?

"You know how you could really make him notice you?" Charlotte asks.

I shake my head. "Obviously not."

"Dine and dash." She raises her eyebrows. "Take off when the check comes. He'd have to run after you and tackle you then. And once that happened, well, it's all up to you what happens next." She grins. "Am I right?"

"Are you serious?" I ask her.

"Yes!" she says happily.

It's not the worst plan I've heard of, I think. But it's close. "I'd only do it if I could be sure he'd be the one who chased me. If Roger, that other waiter, ended up tackling me? That would be gross."

"Yeah, he'd probably break his glasses. I guess the whole plan is a little stupid and desperate." Charlotte shrugs. "I wouldn't mind doing the dine and dash, though. It might be exciting, and as we both know, we could use a little more excitement around here. I mean, this summer is off to a really slow start."

I nod. "I have to agree."

"Do you ever feel like doing something totally crazy? Just to shake things up, just to get someone's attention?"

Like talking to Mike Kyle on the bus? "Whose attention do you want?" I ask Charlotte.

"I don't even know. Someone's. Anyone's," Charlotte says. "The whole town's, maybe. It's so boring, like everyone's asleep."

"It's the heat," I say. "Or maybe the bad air."

"It might be smelly, but it's not carbon monoxide," Charlotte says. "There's actually no excuse."

"You could do something during the Rodeo Days," I suggest. "Be in the parade. Wear a really outrageous costume."

Charlotte thinks about it for a few minutes, then says, "I know. How about if I *don't* wear a costume? How about if I streak naked down the street?" she asks, just as Steve comes up to the table with our platters of eggs and pancakes.

Steve obviously overhears, because his hand wobbles as he tries to put our plates down. The sunny-side-down eggs that Charlotte ordered slither off the plate onto the table, nearly skidding into my lap. One of the yolks breaks and spreads slightly, but it's stopped by a hardened ridge of syrup on the table that holds it in, like a dam. All that's between me and Steve now is an egg moat.

"Of course, you guys are going to streak with me," Charlotte says. "I'm not doing it by myself."

Steve quickly grabs a wet dishrag from a nearby service cart. As he cleans the eggs off the table, he looks up at me, with a little smile that verges on being flirtatious. "Well, uh, what do you say, Fleming? Are we in?" he asks. I think he's adventurous enough that he just might.

"That depends," I say, looking right at him, wanting him to know I am serious about being seriously interested in him. As if he doesn't know that yet. "Can I wear my Rollerblades? Because I'd want to be moving pretty fast, I think, if I was streaking in a parade."

"You guys could both be on in-line skates. You could skate *together*. You know, like nude pairs skating, or whatever!" Charlotte says excitedly.

"Yeah, but, uh, I don't actually skate, and if I fell . . ." Steve blushes, as if he has just in fact imagined it, as if he's gotten a vivid mental picture of a naked me, on in-line skates, and a naked him. He picks up Charlotte's plate and drops the dirty dishrag onto it. "So I'll get you a new order of, uh, those eggs. Be right back." He shuffles off toward the kitchen, and Charlotte and I crack up laughing.

"I can't believe you said that to him!" I gasp between laughs. "God, that was so embarrassing."

"Hey, you're the one who brought up the Rollerblade part!" she shoots back.

"*Nude* pairs skating?" I can't stop laughing. "What is that?"

"Hey, you're the skater. You tell *me*," Charlotte says.

I sit back in the booth and smile. Steve might be seeing Jacqui, but for a second there he was thinking about streaking with me—and he didn't seem to mind.

Triple Ew

"Monsieur LeFleur is still under the weather," a new substitute informs us when we gather for our fifth French class.

Monsieur LeFleur must have something sort of serious, I think. He is supposed to be so dedicated to teaching that he broke up his marriage over doling out too much extra help on weekends. Well, that and the weeklong trips with the high-school French Club—which is 90 percent female—to Quebec every spring. If he can't drag himself out of bed for a simple summer session, then he must have a monster flu. Or something more serious.

It figures. Not only did Steve not take this class, now the teacher isn't even taking it.

"He doesn't have that flesh-eating bacteria, does he?" I ask today's substitute.

"What? No, of course not," the sub says. "What made you ask *that*?"

I shrug. "It seems like a thing that could make you miss a lot of classes, that's all."

"Yes. I mean, you might think he's seriously ill, but no, he's going to be fine," the sub says. "Just can't actually quite get out of bed yet. The vice principal told me he hasn't had a sick day in eight years, which sounds sort of sick in itself to me, know what I mean?" He smiles, and there's something green stuck between his front teeth. "But don't give up on him. Don't you *dare*. Not our Monsieur LeFleur."

"Okay. Sorry." I look over at Charlotte, and she shrugs.

"Now. He requested that we use today's class time to make a videotape," the substitute says. "He would like you all to introduce yourselves, so that when he returns, he'll already know you and you can jump right into the curriculum."

We go around the room, starting with me. I think the substitute is trying to give me extra attention because I seemed so distraught with my flesh-eating-disease comment.

"*Je m'appelle* . . . Fleming Farrell," I say, as quickly as I can, realizing that I've just made a horrible rhyme because I pronounced Farrell "Far-*elle*," as if it's French.

My face turns red as the substitute tells me to say a little about myself and why I'm taking this class.

What are the vital details that Monsieur LeFleur needs to know about me? What will impress him? "I'll be a senior at Edison next year, and I'm hoping to graduate early because I want to travel before I start college. And I'm taking this class because I just really enjoy French culture—French history, and French fashion, and French . . . toast." I smile, feeling like an idiot. Then I decide to go on, as if I'm doing an imitation of my mother and need to relate my entire life story. "So for this trip I want to do next spring, before college? I'm hoping maybe France, but definitely Quebec. I actually went to Quebec City and Montreal once, but I was too little to really remember. Except the crepes, I loved the crepes. So then I'm thinking that maybe in college I'll take a semester abroad, so I want to get a lot of practice speaking French before I do that. And then . . ." I notice everyone staring at me. Blankly. "So, I've heard that you're a really great teacher, so get well soon," I conclude. *Just call me Christie Farrell*, I should add.

The substitute turns to Charlotte next. I can't wait to hear her story so I can forget about mine.

"I'm Charlotte," she says. "I mean, *Jeu mappel* Charlotte Duncan. And I'm taking this class because I failed Intermediate Spanish and Intermediate Italian and I've got to pass

Intermediate Something. I mean, those are like the rules for graduating at Benjamin Franklin; you can't just take three Beginning classes, even though I personally think it makes a person more well-rounded than two years of only *one* language."

"Ahem." The substitute clears his throat. "Yes, well. Next?"

"I'm here to make up for failing French," the next person says. And the next and the next and the next.

I wonder, is Monsieur LeFleur avoiding our class because all of these people flunked the first time around?

After the introductions are complete, we get ready to watch our video lesson of the day. It's an ongoing story about some students, and we've been watching it the past three classes, but it seems to be a couple of levels above where we are—not to mention a couple of decades old. It involves racing around in small cars and rapid-fire conversations in outdoor cafes. I don't know what's going on until the end of each tape, when they stop to go over the vocabulary words.

"So do you want to do something Saturday before you go to work?" Charlotte leans over to ask me during the video. "Maybe you, me, and Ray could find Steve, and we could all hang out together. Or you, me, and Ray could go to breakfast at IHOP."

"I can't. I'm going to the rink with my dad on Saturday," I say. "Then my parents are going to some lunch thing, so I have to stay home." Finding Steve sounds a lot more interesting.

"Oh. Well, how about Sunday?" she asks.

"I have to help my mom while my dad's at an open house, and then I have to go to the hospital with her for childbirth class," I explain.

"*Ew.* Like, breathing and all that?" she asks.

I nod. "Tell me about it."

"You know what's really gross? Those *movies*—you know, of actual births?"

"What's really gross is that I'm her birth coach," I explain. "I'm going to *be* there when she gives actual birth."

"Triple *ew*," Charlotte says. "Hey, is that French? 'Cause I think that really sounded French."

The substitute walks in just as Charlotte and I are laughing. "Do I need to separate you two?" he comes over and whispers to us.

"No, we'll be quiet," I say.

"Sorry," Charlotte says. "I mean, ex-cue-say *moi*."

As soon as he walks away, Charlotte passes me a note with IHOP = STEVE GROPHER written on it.

As if I could forget that.

Absolute Hams

"He still has it." Dad's coach and choreographer, Ludmila, shakes her head as she watches him out on the ice.

I'm not sure what she's talking about. Does she mean he's had it? Or that he's got it? "Yes," I say, stupidly.

"Your father. It is so amazing. His agility, his strength." Ludmila kisses her fingers. "He might be twenty, not forty."

"He's thirty-nine, actually," I tell her.

She ignores my correction. "He is a young man when he takes the ice," she says.

Dad found Ludmila about six months ago through an ad in a skating magazine. She takes on students from about a two-hundred-mile radius. He only gets to see her once a week, so today is important for him. He ate three energy bars in the car on the drive here just so he would be ready. He has three hours of ice time with her this morning, and then he has to rush back for an open house, while Mom covers someone's Saturday shift and I once again hang out with Dorothy, Torvill, and Dean until I go to work at three.

"So he's doing that well?" I ask. "I mean, he looks polished to me, but he always did. And he's so critical of himself."

Ludmila shakes her head. "You cannot listen to him. He is crazy. He is insane."

"He is?" I ask. "I mean, I'd sort of suspected." My joke is lost on Ludmila.

"If he makes just one mistake, he does the entire program over," she goes on. "Entire! Entire thing! He is so *demanding*."

And she isn't even in debt to him. "Tell me about it," I say.

I was only being sarcastic, but Ludmila takes me literally and starts to tell me how my father has the strength of a bull and the grace of a large bird. I think she means a swan. "Very unique," she says. "One of a kind."

"So does he have a shot at making the masters tour?" I ask.

"Oh, yes. A shot," she says. "Yes, he does. He has very good shot. Only . . ."

"What?" I ask.

"Don't call us, we'll call you," Ludmila says.

I wait a minute, hoping she will explain this.

"That is how these tours work. They want Olympic gold, they want world champions. They call on the telephone, please join us. Your father . . ."

"No gold medal, no cereal box," I say.

She nods. "He needs to find a sponsor. To pay his way, to get him more lessons, more ice," she says. "Then it will be a pinch."

"A cinch?" I ask.

But she doesn't hear me. She is calling to my father, something about his takeoff for his combination triple jump.

I can't imagine how my father will find a sponsor in Lindville, but maybe he will. Could he skate with "Gabe's Auto World" stitched onto the back of his shirt?

I watch as he stops his program to work on his triple Axel with Ludmila. He's been doubling it today because he can't quite triple it, which makes sense to me because the Axel is the hardest jump there is. Ludmila shouts instructions to him. I can't understand half of what she says because of her accent.

Dad looks tired, like he'd rather be leafing through an interior design magazine or composing a new house-for-sale listing.

The rink smells like old, wet socks—sort of musty and

mothball-like. I don't miss skating at all, I think.

But then I remember skating at the town rink in Lindville one winter, when I was about eight. It was around Christmas, and there were a lot of people skating there, even though it's an outdoor rink and it was freezing cold. Dad and I hadn't skated there very often, because we usually skated here, at the arena.

First we were skating on our own, but then we started skating together. Everyone was watching us and looking sort of amazed. Dad and I did jumps at the same time—totally synchronized—and people started applauding. It wasn't even embarrassing, it was just fun. We improvised this program, on the spot. Dad told me what to do out of the corner of his mouth, and I did it. We totally ate it up. We were absolute hams. We posed for a picture. And after that, we did it occasionally, whenever we wanted to unwind and have fun.

It's something I can't even conceive of doing now. The last time I skated in public was such a disaster. It was like I could hear these imaginary commentators saying, "that'll be another point-four deduction," every time I fell or stepped out of a landing. When I finally finished my program, I skipped the so-called Kiss and Cry area, walked right past my dad, and went straight to "Kiss and Despair."

Come to think of it, I'm not sure if I've ever actually *left*.

Always
Tweedledee

"Monica?" a woman asks. "Please, can you help me?" She is lying on her back, unable to get up by herself.

"Me, too," another woman pleads. "Uh! I just can't—oof!" She struggles to roll over.

It's like being in a room full of turtles. Not that I've ever been around a turtle—never mind a roomful—but I'm guessing the Lamaze Lounge resembles a tank right about now.

Monica rushes over with a perky smile and gently helps them turn over so that they can climb up on their hands and knees. Childbirth class is so glamorous. We just learned that one of the birth coach's jobs is to remind the mother to pee before she goes into hard labor. "Repeat after me," Monica said. "Don't forget to urinate!"

Childbirth is one of the few adult things that I *can* wait for. Gladly.

"I guess your massage is being cut short today," Monica says to the two women. "Unless you want to be each other's partners until your significant others return?"

The women look at each other, consider it for two seconds, and then shake their heads.

"Now, this is why I'm glad you're here with me, Peggy," my mother says as I gently rub her back. I'm tracing little circles, as instructed.

"Why?" I ask.

"Don't you see what's going on? Their husbands went out to get a drink of water and they've been gone for at least fifteen minutes," she says. "And I'll bet you anything they're off in a bar somewhere having a beer." She sounds very bitter, instead of peaceful, the way she's supposed to feel during the massage session.

"Wait a second." My eyes widen. "Is that what Dad did? Is that why you asked me to help you this time?"

"No, of course not," she says.

"Oh." I sigh. That would have been interesting.

"No. But when you were being born in Boston, and I was in labor for sixteen hours, your father went off and had a glass or two of California merlot," Mom continues. "When he came back he had purple wine stains in the corners of his mouth. He tried to tell me it was grape juice from the cafeteria."

"Dad? Really?" I laugh.

"Your father is not like other men," she says with a smile. "However, he is still a man."

I pause for a minute, reflecting on this. "Hey, did you ever scream and yell at him when you were giving birth?" I ask.

"Constantly," she says. "When I had the twins? I told him to go back to the Ice Jubilee and get back into his Tweedledum costume and stay there." She laughs. "Which is so silly, because he was never Tweedledum. He was always Tweedledee."

"He was?" I ask. "I don't remember that."

"You were young. Dorothy's age. It was a traveling show that went bankrupt," Mom says. "Fortunately for us." She takes deep breaths in and out, in and out. "But you know what? Sometimes I wish we were still on the road."

"You do?" I ask.

"Sure. I mean, Lindville's nice and all, but it's not exactly unpredictable. You pretty much know what's going to happen every day."

"True," I agree. How very, very, very true.

"Especially when it comes to the weather," Mom says. "It's

sunny, it's hot, it's dry, it's windy. It doesn't rain enough. We don't get good *storms*. You know? I miss predicting storms. That intense, hyped-up feeling at the studio and around-the-clock coverage and telling people stuff that really *matters*." She glances over at the woman who critiqued her errant forecast. "Nothing exciting ever happens, so you stop thinking it's going to. And then something does happen, and you miss it. Completely."

I gaze at my mother with newfound respect. "I know what you mean." I can't believe she has thoughts like this. I thought I was the only one.

"I bet you'll be really glad when you graduate and go off to college," Mom says. "Then I can visit you. It'll be so much fun!"

While she's babbling about all the fun things we can do together, I get this picture of me leaving in a little over a year, standing by the minivan with all my duffel bags and some cardboard boxes with books, and a desk lamp and a clock and my posters. Torvill, Dean, Dorothy, and the new baby are all standing on the doorstep, happily waving good-bye to me as I head off to college. And in the picture, I am completely miserable and everyone else is smiling, and then they realize I'm not smiling and they rush over to hug me.

Maybe I don't want to leave my family and get out of

here. But how can I *stay* here? I'm not staying here. I'm *not*.

As I sit there massaging my mother's back, I switch gears and start thinking about my plan to sprint out of Edison High next spring—my pre-college road trip. How am I ever going to pull it off? How am I ever going to get out of my endless list of responsibilities? How will I pay back my parents, get enough credits to graduate, buy a car, and find someone— preferably Steve, but I can't picture him graduating early and I also can't picture my parents allowing me to go on a three- month road trip with a boy—to go with me?

"Peggy?" My mother shifts on her floor mat. "You're rub- bing really, really hard."

"Sorry!" I say. "I'll stop." I decide to stop trying to figure out my future, because it's obviously painful for both of us, and start thinking about something a little more amusing. Like Charlotte's idea to streak down the street during the rodeo parade. I picture Steve streaking naked.

Maybe not streaking completely naked, maybe wearing a little something. Like cowboy boots.

With spurs, of course. Definitely spurs.

The Crispest Crisp

At 6:55 a.m. the customers are all complaining to Denny, because gas prices have suddenly spiked fourteen cents. People are talking about politics and getting slightly irate. No one's paying at the pump because they want to come in and personally complain. Denny just keeps repeating, "It's not my fault."

I try to lighten the mood by offering free coffee samples. People glare at me. Then I mention how I fell down that morning trying to get away from the Doberman, and how the dog looked so pleased with himself when I wiped out and landed on my butt.

Denny starts laughing. So does the woman buying cigarettes, a soda, and chocolate cupcakes. I'm glad I can provide some comic relief. It's like some sort of strange cathartic release; gas prices are through the roof, but laugh at the clumsy girl and you'll feel better! We do what we can here at Gas 'n Git.

The truck driver with the minty-fresh breath comes in and is nice to me, and I almost ask him if he'll give me a ride so that I can get out of here. I don't really care where he's going. He could drop me at the next truck stop, and that would be all right.

"You have a nice day now," he says as he stuffs a dollar into the tip tank, and picks up a few wintergreen mints for the road. "Don't let this heat get to you. It'll pass."

I reach up to touch my forehead, which has sweaty bangs sticking to it. I hadn't realized how much the heat was affecting me, or at least my hair. "Thanks," I say, and I smile at him. "You, too."

I'm always saying "You, too" at the wrong moments, when the thing I'm responding to (like "have a nice day now") is already forgotten. I just told the nicest customer in the world that he would pass, too. But at least I made Denny happy because I said "U2."

After he leaves, I start wondering what's happened to World's Worst Coffee Breath, who is now five minutes past schedule. I can't believe I'm worrying about him.

"Hey, Kristi Yamaguchi. In all seriousness," Denny says when suddenly the store is empty of miffed customers.

"In all seriousness, don't call me Kristi," I say. "That's my mom's name. Spelled differently, but still."

"Okay, then. Miss Farrell. If you want, I can give you a ride to work some mornings," Denny offers.

"Thanks. I'll keep that in mind," I say. I can just picture my dad's expression as Denny roars into the driveway on his motorcycle at 5 a.m.

Then I notice Mike Kyle, of all people, walking into the store. He's wearing a baseball cap backward and his brown hair is sticking out from underneath. His T-shirt says, LIVING ON THE EDGE. He wears cutoff khaki shorts and red flip-flops.

"Hey," he says to me. "I didn't know you worked *this* early." He hands a credit card to Denny. "It's my dad's, he's outside," he explains. "Pump four."

"Okay," Denny says. "You know, we have pay at the pump."

"I know," Mike says.

He looks at me, as if I'm supposed to talk next. So I do.

"So. Did you just finish your paper route?" I ask.

"Nah, I finished it at five-thirty. Now my dad's driving me around to look for a new car."

"Cool. But why this early?" I ask.

"He says we have to scope the lots before the salespeople show up," Mike says. "So we can plan what we're going to offer." He rolls his eyes.

"But you're getting a car," I say, trying not to seethe outright with jealousy. Seething is very unattractive. Why I want to be attractive to Mike, I don't know. Maybe he'll mention to Steve that he saw me, and I wouldn't want to come off as a jealous seether. "Car shopping's a *good* thing," I say. I peer outside at Mike's father. The car at pump four is a teal minivan. Mr. Kyle must not be living on the edge, the way his son is.

"For *him*. He's getting a Corvette. He's trading in the Camaro *and* the van," Mike says as he signs the receipt. "Then he's getting me some cheap old beater."

I shrug. "It's a car. Right?"

"I guess," Mike admits with a shrug. He smiles at me. "Don't look a horse in the mouth when you get a gift and all that, right?"

"I definitely wouldn't look inside any horses' mouths," I say. "Really questionable dental hygiene."

Mike laughs, just as a familiar silver Lexus screeches to a stop in the No Parking zone. Speaking of dental hygiene.

"Now *there's* a nice ride," Mike says. "Well, gotta go, see you!"

After he walks out, Denny turns to me, just as World's Worst Coffee Breath is walking in. "You're not actually . . . friends with that guy. Are you?"

"I don't know," I say. "Why?"

"Let's just say . . . he's not the crispest crisp in the chip bucket." Denny swipes a credit card through the cash register reader.

"What's that supposed to mean? You're mixing your really bad British metaphors," I tell him.

"Just aspiring to be like your friend Mr. Western Wear," Denny says under his breath.

"Good morning!" World's Worst Coffee Breath greets me as he strides happily up to the counter.

"Hi. The usual?" I smile at him. I quickly pour him a giant Tanker-size cup from the new tank of High Octane Blend. "Did you know we have mint-flavored coffee?" I ask as I ring up his purchase. "Actually, I think it might be mint-chocolate. I'm not totally sure, but I could make some up for you."

"Oh, no, thanks," he says. "I hate flavored coffees. They just get in the way."

"You know, sir," Denny says, coming over to us. "We're having a special today. Buy one coffee, get a pack of spearmint gum for, uh, fifty cents." He holds up a handful of gum.

"That's a special?" Coffee Breath asks.

"Usually gum is sixty-five, so it's a deal," Denny says. "Definitely a deal."

"Hmm. Maybe next time. The special runs for how long?" Coffee Breath asks.

"Indefinitely," Denny says. "*In*definitely a deal is what I should have said, actually."

Coffee Breath laughs, and I turn to Denny and smile before making two lattes for the next customer.

After I finish that, and after Coffee Breath leaves, Denny and I both rush over to the door, racing each other. We fling it open and stand outside taking huge gulps of fresh air, before we realize this is a big mistake. You don't gulp air here in Lindville. You sip it.

Steve, What's So Funny?

A few days later, I go to meet Charlotte at her Shady Prairies job. She and Ray and I are going to the Lot in search of Steve. Ray doesn't know about the searching-for-Steve part.

I wait in the kitchen while Charlotte goes out to serve her last tray. She walks back into the kitchen with a trayful of untouched dishes of tan goop. "Everyone has to have their butterscotch pudding, except for when they all of a sudden decide they don't like pudding. Then they try to tell you how they've *never* liked butterscotch pudding, which is so ridiculous, because they ate it on Tuesday. But not according to them."

I shrug. "So what do you do?"

"I stand there and tell them they're not allowed to go batty on me, I don't care how old they are."

"How old are they?" I ask.

"Anywhere from sixty-five to a hundred," Charlotte says. "I have this one table, my favorite table, of old ladies who are ninety plus. They still dress up for dinner and they have like, drinks first, and then after dessert they go outside and smoke, even though this entire area is supposed to be a No Smoking zone. I love them."

"They sound fun. But you know what's weird?" I say. "Why don't they move to Phoenix or Miami, or somewhere else where everyone retires, somewhere that's a little more glamorous? You know what I mean?"

"They must like it here," Charlotte says as she scrapes uneaten butterscotch pudding into the garbage can. Clumps of it cling to the side of the trash bag.

"So is that how long it takes to like Lindville? Sixty-five *years*?" I joke.

Charlotte and I look at each other and start laughing.

"I don't think I can wait that long. I mean, I really don't," I say.

After Charlotte finishes serving all her tables, we go to find Ray, who's a dishwasher. He goes to Edison, like me, and is usually hanging out with Steve's crowd, so Charlotte and

I decided the four of us are meant to hang out this summer.

"This is Fleming," Charlotte introduces me.

"Yeah, I know," Ray says. "Hey." He runs a hand through his short black hair, and I check out his arms. They are definitely nice—why hadn't I ever noticed before? Ray takes off his dirty apron and tosses it into a plastic hamper. "So, we going to the Lot?" Ray puts his arms around Charlotte.

"Where else?" Charlotte says, snuggling up to him.

"I don't know. I was thinking maybe L.A. New York. Omaha," I say.

Charlotte laughs. "Yeah, okay, Fleming. Whatever you say."

An hour later, I'm at the Lot sitting on the tailgate of Ray's pickup with Charlotte, Ray, and Mike. Steve and Jacqui are a few cars away, leaning against someone's old convertible, inseparable once again.

This is so not how it was supposed to be.

There are clouds covering the sky, and whenever there are clouds at night, they trap the air here. It might be gorgeous and sunny and breezy all day, and you'd forget you were in the Penned Cattle Capital of the World. Then it gets cloudy, a few drops of rain spit from the sky, and suddenly the air sinks down over the town like a collapsing hot-air balloon.

But the smelly night is the least of my problems.

Mike has been telling Ray about his new car for about ten minutes. I haven't really been listening, though I did hear it was a yellow Geo Metro with 180,000 miles on it and a purple Princess sticker that he hasn't been able to pry off the bumper.

Charlotte and I were doing our French homework until we lost daylight. We tried to tell Mike and Ray that we were conjugating verbs and they started making jokes about conjugal visits and we haven't really wanted to talk to them since.

But now Mike gives up talking to Ray and turns to me. "So what kind of air freshener do you think I should get?" he asks.

"Air freshener?" I ask.

"For the car. The person who had it before was like a serious smoker," Mike says. "I've got to kill that smell."

I start to smile, glad that Mike and I at least have something in common. We both hate stink. But then, who doesn't? "Well, what are your options?"

"I'm trying to decide between new car and strawberry," Mike says.

"Hmm." I was thinking more along the lines of tropical

breeze. "I'd go for new car," I say. "For the irony factor."

Mike looks a little confused. "But I really like strawberry," he says.

"Well." I shrug. Strawberry seems kind of feminine, but whatever—I really don't care. "You could always get both," I tell him. "But then your car might *really* stink."

"Yeah," he says with a laugh. "Maybe I'll just leave the windows down for a while. It'll be easy with my new job, because it's going to be hot and I don't have A/C."

"What's your new job? Delivering pizza or something?" I ask. I've been down that road before—and crashed.

Mike's face falls. "Yeah. How did you guess?"

"Sorry. It was just the one job I really associate with driving. Which place are you working for?"

"Smiley's," he says.

I nod. "I worked for Bob's—last spring," I say.

"Really? Cool."

"Yeah. But I didn't last very long," I say.

"You hated it?" Mike says.

"Something like that." I smile, deciding not to tell him about the unglamorous crash I had. I might want to borrow his car someday or something.

What am I saying? The lack of pure oxygen must be

affecting my brain. Like I'd ever borrow Mike's car. Then again, I never thought I'd be sitting on a tailgate next to him, either.

I glance over at Steve. He's the one I'm supposed to be sitting next to. This is all wrong.

"So, uh, when do you start?" I ask Mike.

"Tomorrow," Mike says, sounding a little more proud now.

"So I won't see you on the bus anymore? You're leaving me to perish with Kamikaze Driver at the wheel?" I put my hand to my throat. "How could you?"

Mike laughs. "Sorry. Is that what you call him?"

"Among other things." I take a sip of my root beer. I glance over at Charlotte, who now has one leg thrown over Ray's. I check to see whether Steve and Jacqui have moved an inch away from each other yet. Nope.

I hate being in this type of situation. Where there are couples all around you hooking up, and you're so obviously not. When you don't know someone very well, and you're trying to make conversation and it's impossible. When you have to be home by 10:00.

As I'm staring at Steve, I notice Mike is kind of looking at me, observing my obsession. I don't want him telling Steve that I was staring, so I turn to him and blurt out, "You should have seen him today. Kamikaze. He was so obsessed with making every light. I swear he was counting them down out loud, as he went through each green or yellow light. There might have been some red ones in there—after a while I stopped looking because I didn't want to know."

"He's the kind of person who's going to be arrested, and then everyone will say, yeah, he seemed really weird," Mike says. "You know what I mean?"

"Yeah." I stare at Steve and Jacqui. They're entwined, like an exotic plant.

Why did she have to show up here this summer? Why did she have to ruin my plan? It wasn't much of a plan, but it was in development. Now it's dead.

"Hey, um, Peg?" Mike gently pushes his fingers against my thigh. I feel these strange shivers travel up my spine when he touches me. "Whoa. You've got really strong muscles," he says.

"It's, um, from skating," I say as goose bumps break out on my arms. "In-line."

"Fleming skates everywhere," Charlotte says.

Except on the ice, I think.

"She's amazingly good. Me, I can hardly make it around the block," Charlotte goes on, but I can't talk to her right now for some reason. I can't stop looking at Mike's hand, which looks strange just perched there on my thigh. What is he doing?

"You know what?" Mike says to me, giving my leg a little squeeze.

"What?" I say, sort of softly, because I feel really close to him all of a sudden.

"I'm *starving*," Mike says. "Let's grab Gropher and hit the Hamburger, okay?" He slides off the truck tailgate.

That wasn't exactly what I was expecting him to say.

Five minutes later, the four of us are sitting in the Happy Hamburger drive-thru—me and Mike in the front seats, Jacqui and Steve wedged into the backseat of the Geo, on top of each other. This is not the double date I had in mind. In fact, this is worse than the one I was on five minutes ago.

I order small fries and a lemonade. Jacqui and Steve split a concrete shake and a double hamburger and large fries, like they're incapable of ordering on their own. They have to share the ketchup and the mustard and the bun or they might self-destruct. I am probably jealous only because Steve and I never actually managed to have a meal together—our relationship wasn't deep enough for that. But we did share spilled ketchup, which is a lot more intense than people might realize.

Mike parks in the Happy Hamburger parking lot, which

seems kind of stupid when we could drive anywhere. Steve and Jacqui are eating and slurping their shake. It's a little more than I can take. I always thought the reason Steve and I didn't really go out was because he didn't want to go out with anyone long-term. But he seems okay with seeing Jacqui night after night, so why not me?

I glance over at Mike, who's staring at me for no reason. "So. Um. I think I need a refill," I say, shaking the ice in the bottom of my lemonade cup. This is my lame attempt to prolong the night. Why do I want to prolong agony, I wonder?

"No problem," he says with a nice smile. He reaches over and squeezes my leg again. Then he peels around the parking lot and we approach the speaker with a loud screech.

"I'll order," Steve says. "Pull up, Kyle, pull up!"

The car lurches forward as Mike holds on to the clutch a little too long, because he just got the car and isn't used to it yet. Then he starts doing it on purpose, inching forward, jerking and bucking the car.

"May I take your order?" a voice asks from the black speaker box.

"Can we get . . . can we get . . ." Steve stammers. He and Mike both start laughing so hard that neither of them can order.

"Hello?" the voice says.

"How about a new clutch?" Steve finally asks. "With fries?"

Mike peels away from the speaker and we fly past the drive-thru window, all of us laughing hysterically—except Jacqui.

"What's so funny?" Jacqui asks. "Steve, what's so funny?"

She's the kind of person who's never cracked up for no reason at a drive-thru before. I don't know what Steve sees in her.

I glance in the rearview mirror at Steve as I laugh and he suddenly leans forward and says, "I can't believe I did that, I can't believe I just did that, why did I just do that?" He smiles at me and for a second I feel like there's no one else in the car.

I smile back at him. At first I'm really flattered because he remembers, and because I think about him whispering it in my ear as he kissed me.

Then I'm mad because it was something he used to say to me in private, because it was our thing, and now he's saying it in front of his new girlfriend. I'm thinking, *I can't believe* he *just did that*.

Call Me Cinder-Peggy

"P. F., you are an hour late," my father says sternly when I get home. He looks at his watch. "Correction. An hour and twenty-five minutes late."

"Oh," I say. "Am I? I'm sorry—I didn't realize." However, I did realize that when we left the Lot, it was almost 11:00—making me an hour late. But I was just having such a good time, watching Steve and Jacqui split that last French fry.

"I worry about you!" my father says. "Do you know how many terrible things could happen to you on your way home at eleven-thirty at night on Rollerblades?"

I raise my eyebrows. If he feels that way, then why won't he let me drive? "I was perfectly safe. I was with friends." Of course, neither one of these statements is totally true. But

"I was with some boys who drive crazy and drive *me* crazy" wouldn't be the answer to give him right now.

"You were hanging out at that . . . *lot*, weren't you?" he says in a disapproving tone.

"Yes," I say. "Dad, it's where everyone hangs out."

"Yeah, well," he says. "That doesn't make it okay."

"You should be glad I don't hang out with the cemetery crowd," I tell him.

"There's a cemetery crowd? Which cemetery?" Dad asks.

"Eastman. There's the Lot crowd, and then there's the Plot crowd," I tell him.

"You live to worry me, don't you?" He closes the door behind me. "I really wish you hadn't told me that."

"Sorry," I say. "Just trying to keep you informed." I open the fridge and get out a carton of orange juice.

"You've got the early shift tomorrow," he says, eyeing the juice as if it's a dangerous stimulant. "Are you going to be up in time?"

"Dad, I'll be fine." I pour juice into a giant plastic cup with LINDVILLE SAVINGS & LOAN on the side—another of Mom's freebies, as she calls them. I hate the word *freebies*.

"Look, P. F., I'm begging you. Please don't be so late next time, okay?"

What about the fact that he and Mom are late every single

BETTER LATTE THAN NEVER 415

time they're supposed to come home and take over watching the kids? "Dad, it's summer, and I'm only taking one class, and nobody else has to be home by ten. I don't even get out of work until eleven on Saturday nights."

"Be home by eleven then," Dad says. "Fine. Eleven. But I need your help with something."

He needs my help? What could I do that I'm not already doing? "What." I don't say it as a question because I don't want to know the answer. I imagine more watching the kids, or maybe something new, like all the laundry instead of just some, or some new housecleaning or cooking assignments. Call me Cinder-Peggy. "Dad, I'm pretty much extended already."

"But this is something different—and fun. It's a skating thing."

I raise my eyebrows. Skating . . . different and fun? Since when?

He looks at the calendar on the refrigerator, nearly buried under Dean's drawings and Torvill's latest sticker attack. "I don't have much time to pull this together. It's coming up in about three weeks. So let me ask you something, and don't say no right away—just hear me out."

"It's about skating? Then no—right away," I say.

"P. F., come on." Dad laughs. "Cut me some slack here. Is

there any way at all you'd consider getting back into skating? Just for a onetime thing? Just to help me out?"

"Why, is it Take Your Daughter to Skate Day at the rink or something?" I ask.

Dad laughs. "Very funny. No. It would be you and me and . . . well, I don't know all the details yet. This is new to me, but someone wants me to perform and I just thought . . . P. F. and I could do this together."

Why on earth would he think that? I've told him so many times that I'm not interested in figure skating anymore.

"See, you and Mom have your childbirth class together and that's great, but I miss hanging out with you, too," he says. "And when the new baby comes, we're going to be even busier, so—I just wanted for us to do something together."

I really appreciate the sentiment, but there's no way I'm doing this, whatever it is. "Dad, there are a hundred reasons I can't help you with some skating thing," I say. "I don't have time to practice, for one. I'm working, remember? And watching the kids, and—"

"Okay, okay. So maybe you'd have to cut your Gas 'n Git hours a little to fit in some rehearsal time. And because you'd be doing that to help me, I'd forgive some of your debt because your paychecks wouldn't be as high. Whatever. We'd work it out."

I don't like the sound of this. He seems a little desperate. "Dad, come on. I told you. I don't want to skate in public, ever again—are you crazy?" Anyway, don't I do enough around here, without helping Dad's skating career, too?

"But you've *been* skating. Every day."

"That's completely different, Dad. And anyway, what is this *for?*"

He isn't giving out any specifics. "It's not for competition; it's strictly for entertainment. You and I would make up the program. You wouldn't have to do anything complicated—I just want it to be fun."

"Fun," I repeat.

"Yes, fun," he says.

We reach a stalemate where neither of us budges or says anything for a minute. I can't believe he's even asking me this. He knows I'm no good anymore.

Then he says, "Your spins were so nice," still pushing the idea. This is how he sells so many houses. He wears people down.

"You can have another protégé or whatever when Dorothy gets older," I tell him. Torvill and Dean have already tried skating and shown exactly zero interest in pursuing it. "Heck, don't even wait. Put her on skates now. Put *her* in your program."

Dad stares out the kitchen window at the street, as if he's considering it. He's juggling a silver Monopoly-size house in his hand, his reward for being a top agent one year. "I don't want Dorothy to skate with me. I want you to, P. F."

"Sorry," I say, "but no. And please don't ask me again. I mean it, Dad."

"Okay, but I think you'll be sorry," he says as he drops the little house onto the floor and it skids under the fridge.

Somehow I know that I won't be.

So Sorry, Fleming

"Monsieur LeFleur is feeling much better," the fifth substitute teacher of the summer tells us at our next class.

"So is he coming?" Charlotte asks.

"Mais non," the substitute says. "He was ready to return today, but there has been a death in the family."

There's a giant, collective sigh. It's like waiting for a rock concert to start, and then being told that the headliner's bus broke down on the highway. Monsieur LeFleur is kind of like that to us, at least by reputation. A rock star. Letting his fans down.

We had been making Monsieur LeFleur a giant, poster-size get-well card covered with French phrases. We now set that aside and begin our sympathy card. Nobody can agree on what to draw or say first.

Charlotte picks up a black marker and draws a smiley face with the smile upside down and a bunch of notches in the frown. It looks like a warning for poison. We can't stop laughing. I know it's wrong and disrespectful, but I can't.

"You know what? We need more info if we're going to do this right. So who died?" Rafael, one of my classmates, asks.

"Pardonnez moi?" the substitute asks. *"Répétez en fran-çais."* Only a few of our substitutes know French, and so far they've all been posers. Their knowledge expires after about five minutes—or five sentences, whichever comes first.

"Uh . . ." Rafael pauses. *"Mourir?"* he says. *"Famille?"*

"I still don't understand," the sub says. *"Je ne comprends pas."*

"In his family. Who *died*?" Rafael demands, sounding angry now. "I mean, what are we supposed to write?"

"Je ne sais pas." The sub shrugs. "Use your imagination. Be creative."

"What does that phrase mean again?" Charlotte asks me. *"Ne sais . . . ?"* She really should not be in Intermediate French, because this is one of the first things we learned in Beginning French, but somehow I sense it won't matter in this class.

"It means 'I don't know,' " I tell her. I write it down for her.

Charlotte starts writing. "On the loss of your *je ne sais pas*." She turns to me as she pushes the card across the table. "That has some French in it, so it counts," she tells me.

As the card gets passed around class, I open up my book and my dictionary and try to compose the perfect sympathy message. Monsieur LeFleur has been going through a terrible time lately. I want to tell him how bad I feel about all this.

The card is handed back to me last and there isn't any room left for me to write anything except, "So sorry, Fleming." In English.

When I walk out of the school, Mom is waiting in the minivan for me. Charlotte and I had planned to hit IHOP, but Mom insists I go bed shopping with her, Dean, Torvill, and Dorothy. This is because she knows she can't keep track of them *and* buy a bed at the same time.

"I had plans, Mom," I tell her as Charlotte and I stand beside the minivan.

"Sorry, Peggy." This seems to be the theme of the afternoon. "This is the only afternoon we can do this."

"There must be other afternoons," I say. "What about Dad? Why doesn't Dad go bed shopping?"

"Peggy, please. I'm really not in the mood."

Like I am? I look at Charlotte. "Sorry."

"Call me later," she says. "And don't worry, Steve isn't doing anything except spilling eggs on other people."

I laugh. "Yeah, you're right."

"Who's Steve?" my mother asks as I get into the minivan and pull on my seat belt.

"Just this guy from school we know," I tell her.

"Steve, Steve, Steve!" Torvill chants from the backseat.

"*Shh!*" I tell her. I don't know who would overhear us, seeing as how the windows are closed and the A/C is on, but it's a conditioned response.

"Do they make lambs there?" Dean asks from the backseat as we drive past a large sign for Majestic Lamb Company. On it, there's a picture of a small, very cute white lamb.

"No. They actually make lambs into lamb *chops* there," I say.

"Cool!" Dean says, kicking the back of my seat for emphasis.

"Peggy." Mom scolds me instead of him.

"Well, it's true," I say. "They process lambs."

"They're too young to hear about that now," Mom whispers as she makes a left. "What were you thinking? Come on,

Peggy, *try* to think of someone besides yourself."

This has to be an ironic comment. Doesn't it?

Ten minutes later, we are standing in Sleep City, in front of a maze of cribs and bunk beds. Mom is considering purchasing something called a Funky Bunk, which has a metal frame and ladder with bright orange and purple tiger-stripe patterns on it. Dorothy, Dean, and Torvill are playing with blocks over in the kids' play area. The strip mall we're in is known for its sub sandwich shop, and it's weird to look at beds and smell baking bread and melting cheese.

The salesman, who looks about two years older than me, has decided to give us "some moments to decide," because Mom wouldn't stop telling him what a hard time she's having sleeping through the night with her big belly and how she can't get comfortable and asking him for mattress recommendations.

I see him over at his desk, eating a sub from next door for lunch and eyeing us carefully, as if we're going to walk out with a crib while he's chewing his cold-cut special. Or maybe he's just worried that Mom's going to go over and start discussing water retention again.

Mom keeps wandering around, rubbing her giant

pregnant belly, describing things like a math logic problem with no solution. "Let's see. Dorothy could move in with Torvill, so then the baby could move into Dorothy's nursery. . . . Then Dean can move into that small room at the end of the hall—"

"Mom, that's a closet," I say.

"No, it isn't. We just use it as a closet. It's actually quite large," Mom says, sounding a little defensive.

"No, it isn't. It's not big enough for Dean. But look—he can have my room," I say. "I'll move up to the attic."

"What? No! Peggy, no." Mom shakes her head. "I will not have you living in the attic."

"The basement then," I say, though the second I suggest this I regret it, because the basement has a damp, forgotten-laundry smell that will seep into my clothes, my skin, my life. "No, the attic. And Mom, it won't be for long—I'll be leaving next year, anyway," I remind her.

Suddenly she starts bawling, right in the middle of Sleep City. Her face is pink and puffy and she sinks onto a rollaway bed with her head in her hands, and the bed screeches as it rolls under her weight.

I glance over at the salesman, who's staring at us, an onion slice hanging from his lip. He immediately looks away, embarrassed.

What's the matter? I want to say. *Haven't you ever seen a woman who's nine months pregnant break down before?*

"Mom, it'll be okay," I say, my throat tickling with emotion. I put my hand on her shoulder and she grips it tightly, making me worry about how hard she's going to squeeze me during her labor.

"I don't want you to leave," she manages to get out between crying gulps.

I feel like I'm about to start crying, too. This is bizarre because I don't cry in public, and I don't want to start now.

"I . . . what am I going to do without you?" my mother wonders out loud.

The way she says it, I can't tell if she's talking about missing me . . . or missing all my help.

I open her purse and hand her a tissue. Then I go and tell the salesman we'll take the Funky Bunk.

It's Only Lindville

It's Friday night, I've just finished making dinner for Dorothy, Torvill, and Dean, and am rushing to get ready to go out when my parents finally come home from the mall. Mom had a fit this morning and decided she finally needed actual and brand-new maternity clothes for her ninth month. Now I won't even have time to take a shower before Mike picks me up. I hate that.

I brush my hair, replace my spaghetti-sauce-stained white T-shirt with a black tank, pull on clean shorts, and quickly put on some mascara and lip gloss. I brush on some blush, too. Working at Gas 'n Git is not exactly helping to create a sun-drenched summer look.

I run downstairs and almost lose one of my black slides

and wipe out on the way. When I regain my balance at the bottom of the stairs, I see my father sitting in the living room, taking Western clothing out of familiar-looking red plastic bags and laying them on the sofa. There is country music on the stereo.

This isn't exactly a typical evening for Phil Farrell. What's going on? I wonder as I look at the gingham shirts, bandanas, jeans with a rope belt, and brown suede pants with fringe.

"Is that stuff from Western Wear Bonanza?" I ask, incredulous.

"Yes," Dad says. "Mr. Stinson wants me to evaluate them."

"Evaluate?" I ask. "Why would you want to?" My father's style is definitely not Western.

"I need a costume. They've asked me to put something together for the Rodeo Roundup Days. Mr. Stinson's on the board of directors, so he's outfitting me." Dad picks up a red gingham shirt and holds it against himself. "I know you won't skate with me, but could you help me figure something out? Am I a red gingham or a blue gingham kind of guy?"

"Um . . . *neither*? Dad, I don't understand." Or maybe I just don't *want* to understand. I'm getting this horrible sinking feeling. "You don't mean . . . skating at the rodeo. Do you?"

He nods.

I can't believe this. "*That's* where you wanted me to skate with you?" My father must not be getting enough sleep. He's going insane or something. Like I'd ever skate with him at a rodeo? In what universe?

He nods and then he loops a bolo tie around his neck and tries to shorten it. "They're trying to bring in different types of events this year, to attract a wider audience," Dad explains. "And if this goes well, there's a chance that Mr. Stinson and some others will sponsor me for my comeback. They very strongly hinted that they'd support me, if I helped them out with this."

I can't believe what I'm hearing. The plan is insane. "Excuse me. Dad? Ice skating? Where are they going to *do* this? It'll be ninety degrees—in the shade. We can barely keep ice frozen in the freezer in July."

"Listen, I'm with you, P. F. I told them it's not going to work, especially when we only have three weeks to prepare, but they begged me. They're converting the town rink—you know it's right next to the fairgrounds. They're closing it off and air-conditioning it. And they're bringing in a walk-in meat freezer expert from Majestic—they say he knows how to keep the surface frozen. If it's good enough for steak, it's good enough for me. *I* don't know."

"*Dad.* If it doesn't work . . . your reputation . . ."

"It's only Lindville," he says as he sets a black ten-gallon hat on his head. "And they're going to pay me. Quite a bit of money, actually."

"But Dad, you don't have to do this," I say. "You're *good*. You're an *artist*."

"P. F., I've worn smelly fur costumes and dressed as cartoon characters. I've played Tweedledee. Being in the Rodeo Roundup Days isn't *that* much of a stretch." He takes off the black hat and throws it onto the sofa with a flourish. "P. F., there comes a time when everyone has to—"

"Make sacrifices," I finish the sentence for him, then sigh. "Okay, but *this* one?" It's going to be so embarrassing. My father is talking about skating at the rodeo. And he's actually going to do it.

"Peggy, you know what they say. Every cloud has a silver lining." Dad yanks off the bolo tie and throws it on the coffee table, then walks out of the living room.

Even Lindville clouds? I wonder.

I pick up a suede vest and hold it up against me, inhaling its leather smell. I try to picture my father skating with Justin boots fashioned into skates. I try to picture the two of us out there, together. My mind goes blank.

A car honks outside, and I drop the vest as if it's radioactive.

"Be home by ten!" my father calls from the kitchen as I hurry out the door.

"Eleven!" I yell over my shoulder as the door closes.

"What's *your* favorite thing about the rodeo?" Mike asks me as he parks the Geo under a sign in front of the stadium that says RODEO FANS ONLY.

We're in the middle of what will soon be rodeo bedlam. Right now it's empty booths, banners announcing different events, and chained-off areas ready for petting zoos and carnival rides.

"The day it's over," I say as Steve, Jacqui, and I climb out of the car. *Especially this year*, I think as I notice the skating rink on the other end of the stadium, which looks like a construction zone with tarps and scaffolding. Ray and Charlotte are parking right beside us, in Ray's pickup—we all met up at the Lot about five minutes ago.

"What are they doing to the rink?" Steve asks, apparently following my gaze.

"Closing it off, because—" I start to explain, then stop. I don't want to tell everyone about this—I don't want anyone except Charlotte to know. "Actually I'm not really sure what they're doing," I say.

We head for the picnic tables already set up for the food concessions, with two pizzas that Mike brought from work. There must be about a hundred tables.

I don't know how I feel about this. I get to hang out with Steve, but only if I do it when Jacqui and Mike are there. It's like a very sorry logic equation on the SAT. The answer to "What do I like about this?" is "None of the above."

I wonder if Steve gets jealous seeing me with Mike. I hope he does. Not that there's anything between me and Mike, but if I can make Steve think there is . . . maybe he'll feel as terrible seeing us together as I do when I see Steve and Jacqui. Maybe he'll come to my rescue the way he did at that St. Patrick's Day party.

Somehow I doubt it, but isn't it worth a shot, at this point? Nothing else seems to be working, and we are constantly being thrown together on this awkward pseudo–double date.

"You know what I like?" Steve says. "I like seeing all the RVs and horse trailers and amusement rides pulling out of town. Because then we get the town back."

"Hmm. Do we *want* the town back?" I joke.

Steve starts to laugh, and I look at him and think, *You know, we could be having this much fun, like, all the time. If only you'd get rid of the girl with the plastic facial features and no brain.*

"Wouldn't we rather be *in* the trailers, leaving?" I ask Steve.

"Definitely. Stowaways." Steve grins at me. "But I don't know if we want to go cross-country with horses."

So he does remember what we talked about, our vague plan to pull a Jack Kerouac.

"You're riding across the country on horseback?" Jacqui asks, coming up beside Steve and taking his hand.

"No," Steve says, shaking his head.

"Then what?" she asks.

"Never mind," Steve says. "It's not important."

Yes, it is! I want to scream. *It's incredibly, vitally, excruciatingly important. And you are letting Jacqui get in the way of all of it.*

I walk over toward Charlotte.

"Does the parade wind up here, at the end?" she asks me. "And then everyone parades around the stadium over there?"

"Usually," I say. "It goes down Main Street and then— wait a second. You're not still planning to be in the parade, are you?"

"Of course I am," she says. "You're still thinking about it, too, aren't you?"

"No!" I glance ahead at Steve, remembering the streaking conversation at IHOP, and how embarrassed he got. "I mean, sure, I'm *thinking* about it," I lie loudly, hoping he'll hear me and be impressed. "But I'm not sure I'm going to do it," I tell Charlotte. One major humiliation in the family during Rodeo Roundup Days is enough.

"You're not?" Charlotte asks. "Not even if I can find a way for us to escape afterward?"

"We'd have to escape really, really far away," I say.

"What are you guys getting away from?" Mike asks, tuning into our conversation as he opens the top pizza box and tears off a slice. Suddenly everyone is looking at us; everyone is tuned in.

"We need to get away from a situation," Charlotte says. "Well, not now, but a few weeks from now. We'll need to be picked up and whisked away."

"Don't keep saying *we*. I'm not doing it," I tell Charlotte. I glance over at Steve. I'm not sure if he remembers Charlotte talking about streaking, that day at IHOP. He may have blocked it out.

"You're doing it, Fleming," Charlotte insists. "It's going to be the highlight of the rodeo."

"*What* is?" Mike asks. "What are you guys doing? Barrel racing or something?"

"Or something," I say.

"Whatever. You guys are weird," Ray says.

"Thank you," Charlotte says.

We all wander around, waiting for someone to pick a table for us to sit down at.

"My favorite part of the rodeo is the games," Steve says. "I could play those all day. I will, actually."

"I thought you quit gambling," Jacqui says.

"Hey, shooting at a metal duck is not gambling. Throwing a dart at a balloon is not gambling," Steve says.

"Yeah, they don't give you any money," Mike points out. "Just stuffed animals, and how many of those can you use?"

"You'd be surprised. Last year I donated about twenty to the hospital for kids," Steve says.

I am about to tell him how cool that is when Jacqui grabs Steve's arm with both her hands. "That's so incredible," she says. "Wow."

"Not really. They were pink and blue and they smelled funny," Steve says.

"Still," Jacqui insists, tugging at Steve the way Dorothy tugs at me when I'm on the phone and she wants attention.

Steve suddenly decides we should sit at the table that's right in the middle of all of them. He and Jacqui sit on one side, while Mike perches across from them. I sit down next to

Mike, scooting a little closer to him than may be necessary. When Steve sees me getting close to Mike, his jealousy will have to kick in, the way mine kicked in weeks ago when I saw him kissing Jacqui. Not that I'm going to kiss Mike. But we are spending time together—and that has to get to Steve eventually. Doesn't it? *Kick in, kick in, kick in*, I think, as if I'm Torvill. *Please.*

But nothing seems to get to Steve, because when he and Jacqui are together they create this disgusting force field of happiness that rebuffs any approaches. Especially mine.

I gaze across the table at Steve as I eat a slice of pizza and try to ignore the fact that Mike has slipped off his flip-flops and is trying to play footsie with me. Not that there's anything wrong with that. He's good-looking and he has nice feet. But still, this has to go down as one of the worst Friday nights in history.

I found out my father's going to embarrass me in public, and that Steve still wants to be with Jacqui and not me.

They've both got to be considered insane.

Protection

Denny taps a book of matches against the glass-top sales counter. It's been a slow Saturday night, so slow that we've run out of things to talk about and for some reason I feel compelled to confide in him about my dad's rodeo plan. After we have a good laugh about that, we start discussing our work history, the jobs we've loved, the jobs we've hated, the jobs we've lost.

"So, okay, can I ask you something?" I say. "Why aren't you working at a music store? Or a CD store? I mean, that seems more like where you'd want to work."

"You're a genius. You know that, right?" Denny snaps.

"Hey, forget I asked." I start to walk away.

Denny doesn't say anything for a few minutes, and I'm

kind of glad. Talk about a short fuse.

Then he walks over to me. "Remember how I said people end up here? Because of something that happened, because they have a story?"

I nod. "Sure."

"Okay. So, of course I used to work at a music store," Denny says. "I mean, come on. I worked at the stupid Disc Barn for like a year."

"In the mall?" I ask. I can't picture it. "You?"

"Yes, me," Denny says. "But I was too opinionated. I kept telling people they shouldn't buy stuff," Denny says, "and I couldn't stop, not even after the manager told me to. Like if someone was buying a really awful CD by a good band, or anything by a horrible band, or anything I didn't like. Which is a lot of things. Anyway, so about a year ago I got into this confrontation with this guy about which band was going to be considered more influential in like a hundred years."

"Let me guess. You said U2. And he said . . . ?"

"Velvet Underground. I was shelving discs in the U-V-W section. And I told him, I know Velvet Underground is really, really important—they're crucial—and I could see his point, but I said U2 is just as crucial, and then he said *Zooropa* was crap and called Bono a bleeding heart, just because he happens to be involved in the most important humanitarian causes on the planet—" Denny's voice gets strained so he stops himself, shaking his head. "Anyway, it turned into a huge fistfight. And he won, and I got fired." Denny points to his nose. "This used to be straight, okay?"

I start laughing. "Okay. Wow."

"But working here? How can I have an opinion on what kind of potato chips people want, or whether they should get Regular or Premium gas, or the Silver carwash or the Gold? I mean, I *really* don't care."

"Good point," I say.

"So then I can save my brain for my time off. And my writing." Denny opens his leather bag and starts to show me a notebook filled with lyrics and poetry. Of course, for all I know it could be copied U2 lyrics, or lists of Bono's favorite colors and foods and some of his best quotes, but I'm thinking it's original material and I'm about to tell Denny that I'm impressed, when we both hear tires squealing outside. We look up and see a car screeching out onto the highway.

Denny swears and takes off from behind the counter, and sprints out the door. He comes back a minute later, panting. "Another drive-off," he says, as if he has to explain. He picks up the phone and calls Jamie and then the police to report the theft. While he talks on the phone, I make a fresh tank of decaf for a couple on a date, who ordered and then went over to the circular beef jerky display to make out.

Denny slams down the telephone. "I *hate* drive-offs." He stares out the window for a few minutes. "And I hate Saturday nights," he says. "They're never what you think they're going to be."

"Really," I say in agreement as I deliver the decafs to the happy couple while Denny turns up the radio really loud and sits down behind the register, munching on a bag of fried pork rinds.

My father comes to pick me up from work at 11:15. He knocks on the locked door, and when I look out, I see he's wearing skin-tight workout pants and a sleeveless muscle T-shirt. He waves at me and smiles and then gulps from his sports drink. He looks like a runner who's just finished a marathon—especially with the giant brace over one knee.

"So there's my dad—I guess I won't need a ride after all," I tell Denny, grabbing my courier bag from under the counter. "But thanks."

"That's your dad?" Denny asks. "The guy who's going to skate at the rodeo?" He peers outside as he shuts down the last lights. "Interesting. He reminds me of a young Robin Cousins. No, wait. Toller Cranston maybe."

I stop with my hand on the door. "How do you know all

these skating names?" He's kind of freaking me out.

"My mom's obsessed. She keeps saying there ought to be a skating *channel*, okay?"

I laugh, say good night to Denny, and head outside.

"Sorry, P. F.," my father says. "I was down at the arena working on some choreography for my new long program and I lost track of time."

"That's okay," I say.

Dad pops open the car doors and we climb in. "I'm really glad that robber started hitting other towns," he says as he peers out the tinted window. "I'm also glad you don't have the graveyard shift."

"Dad, this place closes at eleven. There is no graveyard shift," I say.

"Still." He looks nervously around the station and at the dark shadows by the Dumpster. He nearly jumps as Denny roars out from beside the darkened store on his motorcycle. Denny pauses to nod to me, then peels out like someone in a fifties movie—Marlon Brando maybe, but with a crooked nose.

Dad locks all the doors. "I don't like the looks of this place at night."

"Dad, that was my coworker," I say. "Denny."

My father clears his throat. "Are you sure you don't want

to be our full-time baby-sitter for the summer instead?"

Like I'm not now? I think. "Yes, I'm sure," I say.

"Well. If anything . . . *untoward* ever happened at this place . . . you'd tell me, wouldn't you?" Dad asks as we pull out of the station.

"Of course," I say. "But don't worry, it's pretty tame."

"What about that thief? The criminal holding up gas stations. You have protection, right?"

The last time my father mentioned protection, he and Mom were giving me a sex talk. "You mean . . . a gun?"

"No! I mean security. They've told you, right—just give a thief all the money. Save yourself."

"Sure thing, Dad. We went over it in training," I tell him. Anyway, if anything happens, Denny's going to spring into action—he's promised me. "You know what? The biggest problem is this mean dog that runs after me every morning on my way to work."

"What? You're kidding. That's horrible," Dad says.

"You know what? If you'd let me drive again, we could buy a really cheap car, and I could use it just to get to work. I have this friend who got an old Geo Metro for practically nothing. Then you wouldn't have to pick me up, and I wouldn't have to skate past scary dogs."

"P. F., you haven't exactly proved you're responsible yet.

You still have some work to do on that front." Dad looks both ways and then peels out onto County Highway 87, barely missing a car coming toward us.

This is the man who's telling me about being responsible? "What are you talking about? That's all I'm doing—being responsible," I say.

"I wouldn't say that. I mean, you come home late at night, you won't skate with me, you don't offer to help your mother—"

"Offer? Dad, I get *asked* to help so much that I never get the *chance* to offer. And you're constantly late yourself—like tonight!" I point out.

"P. F., that's not the same thing, and you know it," he says.

I stare out the window. I really do not want to have this argument, not now. I want to pretend this is not happening. I'm not getting picked up from my gas-station coffee-shop job by my father, who's skating in a rodeo. This isn't my life. It can't be.

Free Ride

When I get on the Lindvillager after work four days later, it seems like a normal day, except that Denny was out sick and I had to work with Jamie instead, which was a little nerve-wracking. She kept insisting that I clean out all the machines and tubes so that the coffee would flow better and the "turbo dispense" function would work. And she kept insisting on making the coffee herself, which can't be a good thing for the customers.

I hand Kamikaze Driver his coffee and he pays me, giving me a dollar for a tip to make up for the fact he didn't tip me at all on Monday. Then I take a seat behind the elderly lady with the laundry bag who rides this bus every day I do.

When we stop at the railroad crossing because a train is

passing by, I hear Kamikaze swear. He hates not making it across before the train. They're long freight trains, and can take five minutes to go by. It messes up his entire life, it seems like, from his reaction.

Seconds later he gets up from his seat and turns around. I try not to make eye contact, but he has removed his sunglasses and is gazing right at me. Then he shuts off the motor and takes the keys. He walks right toward me.

I scrunch down in my seat, trying to avoid him. It's impossible. He puts his hand on the back of my seat. "The coffee is not good today. Not good at all." He tries to hand the cup back to me. "Taste it."

"What?" I say.

"Try this. It's undrinkable. It's lukewarm, it's as weak as a drink at a family wedding on a small budget," he says.

I stare up at him, thinking, I should not have let Jamie make the coffee. Jamie's Java Blend strikes again.

"Come on, taste it," he tells me.

"Are you crazy?" I ask. "I mean, no offense. But you've been sipping out of that cup. I'm not tasting it now," I say.

Kamikaze looks like he's about to explode. His beard is literally twitching. It may always twitch, but I've never been close enough to find out before.

"You know what?" he says, his slightly bloodshot blue

eyes unwavering. "Everyone in your generation is so freaked out about germs. When I was your age, I shared everything with everybody."

I get a really icky feeling when he mentions sharing. "Are you talking about free love?" I ask, not wanting to hear his answer. A man in his fifties who insists on wearing a peace button every day frightens me.

"I'm talking about living, about not being afraid of living," he says.

"What makes you think we're afraid of living?" I ask. "That's the stupidest thing I've ever heard. Just because I don't want to catch something—"

"What would you *catch*? I don't have anything," he says. "I'm as much of a healthy, red-blooded American as you are."

I decide to get back to the subject. "Look, if the coffee's that bad, then why would I even *want* to taste it?" I ask him.

He shakes his head. "Forget it. But next time you ride the bus, I want a free coffee," he says. "Tell your manager."

"Look, it was my manager who *made* that awful coffee. And you know, you don't exactly give us perfect rides every day," I point out. "Maybe *I* want a free ride."

"You wouldn't know what to do with a free ride if it hit you in the face," he says. Then he goes back up to the driver's seat, starts the bus, and we roar across the railroad tracks just as the bar lifts. The woman in front of me turns around and pats my arm in sympathy.

When we pull up in front of Edison High, Charlotte is waiting for me at the curb. "Don't get off—I'm getting on," she says when I start down the bus steps.

"What?" I ask.

"We're not going," Charlotte tells me. "I don't know how you say that in French, and I don't care."

Behind me, I hear Kamikaze Driver clearing his throat impatiently.

"But—wait. Why aren't we going?" I ask.

"Because it's a beautiful day, because we only have afternoons to ourselves this summer, and because our teacher hasn't shown up for three weeks," she says.

"But what if today is the day? What if Monsieur LeFleur is finally here—and we're not?" I ask.

"Please move out of the stairwell so that the bus can clear the stop," Kamikaze says. He sounds like he's reading off a bus driver training manual.

"Fleming, wake up. LeFleur's not coming! If by some slim chance it happens . . . then we'll just be *absent*," she says in her bad French accent. "We will bring Monsieur *le sick note* next time. *Oui?*"

We start laughing and Kamikaze Driver gets out of his seat. "You both need to get on the bus *now*, and sit down," he tells us. "People are waiting and I have a schedule to keep."

Charlotte drops her fare into the box. "Lighten up," she says. "This isn't a matter of life or death, is it?"

"How would you know?" Kamikaze says as he glares at her.

"So do you *ever* have a day off?" I ask him as he sits back down. He revs the accelerator and won't even make eye contact with me. Me, his personal coffee wench. Completely ignored. Charlotte and I shuffle to a seat halfway back and are flung together as the bus pulls back into traffic.

"So where are we going?" I ask.

"The mall," Charlotte says, popping her gum as she looks out the window. "If I'm going to do this streaking thing, I'll need a cowboy hat."

I glance over at the woman with the laundry bag, who raises her eyebrow.

I hope Charlotte isn't talking about going to Western Wear Bonanza. I've already been attacked once today. Then I remember how Mr. Stinson might sponsor my dad, how he's giving him all those clothes to skate in. "Um, Charlotte?" I say. "There's something I have to tell you."

And on the way to the mall, I explain about my father's

latest skating job. I expect her to laugh so hard that she falls off the seat, which isn't hard to do with Kamikaze at the wheel, but instead she's impressed and says she can't wait to see him skate.

Me? I can wait.

When we walk into the mall, the place is completely deserted. It almost looks closed, except for the seniors who are cruising around the walkway, getting their air-conditioned exercise.

"Man, talk about slow. I was hoping we'd *see* people here. People under seventy, I mean—I get enough geriatrics at work. You know, this is so lame. We've got to do something fun this weekend," Charlotte says.

"Like what?" I ask. We pass the two-screen Sunset Cinema and its popcorn smell fills the air for several yards.

"I don't know. That's the problem," Charlotte says. "The only thing I'm looking forward to is streaking at Rodeo Days."

"Well, the only thing *I'm* looking forward to is my mother's water breaking," I tell her.

Charlotte and I both start laughing.

"We're pathetic," I say.

"No, no, no." Charlotte stops to check out a pair of sandals on a spinner that juts out from a store into our path. "*We're* not pathetic. We're fine. We're good. We're fine*good* even," she teases me. "It's this place. It's just so hot and so *slow* here."

"It's like a bus stuck in traffic with broken air-condition-ing," I say as we continue walking. "That happened last week, on my way home from French class. And—"

"Fleming? You're telling *bus stories*," Charlotte interrupts. "Do you see what I'm talking about?"

We both start to laugh again. She's completely right.

"Why don't you and Ray go somewhere, on a trip?" I sug-gest. If I were with Steve, that's what I'd want to do.

"My mom would not let me do that," she says. "Not in a million years."

"But she'll let you streak?" I ask.

"She won't know about that until it's over," she says. "Any-way, I don't even know if I like Ray all that much—enough to spend a bunch of time in a car with him, I mean. He's sort of boring me. It's like all he ever wants to do is work out."

"Well, he has to keep the arms looking good," I reason as we pass the food court and arrive outside Western Wear Bonanza. "You know," I say before we go in, trying to talk her out of it, "they'll have you arrested if you do it. Lindville's a small town. They'll figure out who you are. You'll never live it down."

"So? Maybe that's a good thing," Charlotte says. "So I get

a rep. So what? Knowing my mom, we'll move soon enough, anyway."

"Don't say that! You're not stranding me here—you can't," I say.

"Okay, I'll tell her we're staying." Charlotte smiles. "Now, come on—let's find us some hats."

"Okay, but remember—if you see the owner, be nice," I say. "He's not fond of me."

Charlotte marches into Western Wear Bonanza, squeezing between two large circular racks of turquoise, orange, and red Western-style shirts with contrasting yokes, divided into L–XL and XXL–4X.

I know I shouldn't go in, that Mr. Stinson will go ballistic when he sees me. But if he's willing to outfit my dad for the rodeo, he can't have too many hard feelings toward me. Right? And what am I going to do, not shop for the rest of my Lindville life, just because I don't want to bump into Mr. Stinson? That's ridiculous.

It's terrible logic, but I go into the store, skulking as well as someone five foot eight can skulk. Charlotte's already at the counter, asking to try on the expensive hats behind the glass. I don't recognize the girl working, but I instantly feel sorry for her—not because of Charlotte, but because of her boss.

I stuff a cheap straw hat onto my head for camouflage and meander around the store, keeping an eye on Charlotte and an eye on the back office door. The rawhide chin strap tickles me and the strong smell of leather reminds me of trying to fit boots onto people's feet and how much I loathed it. I take the hat off and stack it on top of some others. Then I stare at the wall of Mr. Stinson's photographs of himself, posing with winning rodeo riders and bulls like Insane Zane.

"Got it!" Charlotte says, running over to me with a white cowboy hat. "It's *perfect*. Check it out." She tries it on with a giant smile on her face. "Isn't it great?"

"It looks good," I say, nodding. Her hair hits her shoulders in a wave. "You look like one of the girls in the saddle club— you could even be voted rodeo queen," I tease her, knowing that the real Lindville rodeo queens, including some girls from our high school, are accomplished riders, that they'd be miles away before I even figured out how to get onto a horse.

Charlotte turns back and forth, admiring herself in front of the mirror. "I prefer 'rodeo princess,' actually. Now if I could only ride a horse." She takes off the hat and hands it to me. "Can you hold on to this for a sec while I try some shirts on?"

"Uh, sure," I say, glancing around the store.

"Be right back." Charlotte grabs a few shirts and blouses

on her way into a dressing room, and I follow her, holding her new hat, which I put on. I stand in front of the three-way mirror to see how it looks on me.

Suddenly, behind me in one of the three mirrors, there's Mr. Stinson. His arms are crossed in front of his slightly round stomach.

I look in the mirror at him, not wanting to turn around. It feels like a showdown in an old Western movie.

"Precisely what are *you* doing here, Miss Farrell?" Mr. Stinson demands, lowering his tortoiseshell glasses to get a better look at me.

"Shopping?" I whimper.

He narrows his bushy eyebrows and they meet in a tangled-looking tuft above his nose, like a facial tumbleweed. "Shopping," he repeats.

"Yes," I say, gently taking the cowboy hat off of my head. "My friend wanted a hat."

"Your friend, is that right?" Mr. Stinson stares at the hat in my hand. "And where is this *friend*?"

"She's in the dressing room," I say meekly.

"Oh, really." Mr. Stinson seems to sort of laugh, as a strange-sounding snort escapes his nose. "This is all just a ruse for you to come in here, isn't it? Are you here to ask for your job back? Fed up with the petrol station? Are you that *daft*, then?"

"No, of course not," I say. "I still work at Gas 'n Git, and she's already bought this hat. And as soon as she tries on some shirts, we'll be out of here."

"Hmm. Yes, you will." Mr. Stinson starts refolding and stacking T-shirts. He doesn't move more than three feet away, as if he's afraid I'll shoplift.

"So," I say, trying to be friendly. "How's business?"

He turns to me and raises an eyebrow.

Wrong question. I decide to try again. "So, my father said you might sponsor him?" I ask.

"We'll see," Mr. Stinson says, the way a parent would.

"He was showing me all the clothes you sent over. That's really great. My dad won't let you down," I say. *Unlike me.* "I mean, he's an incredible skater, a great performer. He's a perfectionist. And he can definitely win over a crowd."

"Well." Mr. Stinson looks surprised that I'm talking so much. "That's very nice, but it all depends on his rodeo show."

"Whose rodeo show?" Charlotte asks, coming out of the dressing room. She's wearing a white satiny blouse with fringe around its yoke. It's not her usual style, but somehow she pulls it off and looks good in it.

Mr. Stinson turns, and his face lights up as he examines her. "That looks dead gorgeous on you," he says. "May I ask—is it for the rodeo? The parade, perhaps?" He smiles. He's really turning on his retail charm.

"Maybe pre-parade," Charlotte says, and I stifle a laugh.

"It comes in eight colors," Mr. Stinson says. "May I show you the royal blue? It would accent the hat quite nicely." He grabs the white hat from me, and runs off to fetch Charlotte more clothes.

Charlotte looks at me and holds up her hands. "I guess I'm going to look like a rodeo princess whether I want to or not."

I can't believe Mr. Stinson is being so nice to Charlotte. I thought he'd hate her, because she's friends with me. Maybe that means he's starting to forgive me. If he's considering sponsoring my dad, he must be.

Of course, it's only taken him seven months.

Aging Prematurely

It's Friday night and I'm on my way to meet Charlotte at Shady Prairies. Mom's upstairs giving the kids their baths, so I'm off the hook for the evening. I'm halfway out the door at 7:30, in my socks and holding my Rollerblades, when my father suddenly calls out, "P. F., got a second? I need a word with you."

His voice isn't very happy-sounding, so I shut the front door and go stand nervously in the doorway to the kitchen. I hope this isn't about me, in any way—not my visit to Western Wear Bonanza, or the fact I let the kids watch TV all morning instead of playing educational games with them, or about my skipping French. "What's up?"

"Well, it's time to tally up where you are," Dad says. He

jumps up and turns down the radio, which is tuned to classic rock, as usual. "Make sure your finances are in order and see where we are, loan-wise."

"Okay, but I'm kind of on my way out," I say. "Could we do this tomorrow?"

"Nope," Dad says.

I sink into a chair across from him and we go over my latest paycheck and what I've already paid him and Mom, and what I still owe them. I write him a check, while he launches into a lecture about financial responsibility, about how as soon as I pay them back, I need to start putting away money in a savings account so I can save up for a car of my own, if I'm serious about taking a trip. He whips out his calculator and starts calculating car-loan rates for me, the way he's always doing for clients and their mortgages. "The thing about amortization is . . ." he says.

I tune out and start daydreaming about the trip. I see myself in a convertible, cruising along that California highway by the Pacific Ocean, the one that's in all the TV commercials and movies. I go north from there and have to put up the top, because I'm in Oregon and it's raining. I head farther north to Seattle, where I stop for coffee, because coffee is very big there and because I'm tired from driving. I go north to

Vancouver, and there's a ferry leaving for Victoria, so there I am, on the deck, drinking my Seattle coffee, which has sort of gone cold—

But wait. I can't do all that by myself.

Before I take off in my convertible, I pick up Steve, who gets out of work from IHOP. I pull up in the parking lot and Jacqui is clinging to his apron and not wanting him to leave with me, so he takes off the apron and leaves her clutching it, drying her tears on it, as he tosses a beat-up old leather suitcase into the trunk and—

"P. F., are you listening?"

I clear my throat and sit up straighter in my chair. "Of course, Dad. Of course I am. And I appreciate all this advice, I really do. I should get going, though." I stand up, get my backpack, and grab my keys off the hook by the door.

Dad purses his lips and looks very disappointed in me. First I gave up skating; now I'm giving up liking math. "P. F., do me a favor," he says as he gets up from the kitchen table. "Take this a little more seriously. You've made a dent, but you still owe this family more than five hundred dollars." His voice is as cold as the outdoor ice rink in January.

"I know, Dad," I say. "That's why we have a payment plan."

"Which you're falling behind on," he says. "I'm expecting big things from you this summer, P. F. Good things. Please don't disappoint me."

He turns off the radio and leaves the kitchen, and a few seconds later I hear him put classical music on the CD player. He must be choosing music for his program again. He hasn't been happy with the last eight pieces he's tried to choreograph to. He keeps skipping from one track to another. He's not happy right now. When he's not happy, his skating suffers.

I can't picture classical music at the rodeo, where country and western is usually blaring from overhead speakers. Then again, I can't picture an ice rink, or a skating cowboy. Or maybe I just don't want to.

The sun is still out when I skate up in front of Shady Prairies. Charlotte's waiting for me in the lobby. "How was work?" I ask her.

"Easy," she says. "Except for the fact that everyone ordered liver and onions, and we ran out and I had to convince the second seating that chipped beef was just as good. Which nobody believed. And they were right. So a bunch of people started talking about how they need a new dining director here, and how there wasn't enough wheat bread at breakfast for toast."

"Mm-hmm," I say. "Very interesting." I take off my

Rollerblades and slip them into my backpack, then put on my black rubber flip-flops.

Charlotte starts laughing. "Sorry. I guess I just needed to vent. So, are you ready for an adventure?"

"That depends. What is it, and does it involve eating chipped beef? Whatever that is."

"*No.* We're going for a little ride," she whispers to me as we leave the lobby.

"In what?" I ask. "Is Ray coming? I mean, is he already here?"

"Forget Ray," she says. "We sort of broke up last night."

"You *did*? What happened?" I ask.

"It's not important. I mean, it was just a dumb fight, but the point is that we don't need Ray. We've got our own wheels."

"You got your Mom's car again? Wow, has it been a month already?" I ask.

"No, I actually don't have a car. But we are sort of renting one tonight," Charlotte whispers. "Free of charge. Come on."

I figure she's talking about someone lending her a car. I can't imagine that she's talked one of the retired Shady residents into lending her their Cadillac, but maybe she has. I've learned not to doubt Charlotte. She makes things happen. She insists on it.

We walk through an employee parking lot off to the side of the main building as the sun slowly sinks on the horizon. "See those carts over there?" she asks.

"The golf carts?" I look at the two small beige vehicles with the initials SP written in green script on the roof—as if they need to be identifiable by helicopter, like big-city buses.

"Yeah. But they're not used for golf. They're for carrying guests and visitors around, to show them the place. And for delivering packages and helping people with groceries and luggage and stuff." Charlotte rubs her hands together. "And tonight, one of them is going to carry *us* to the Lot."

"We're going to steal a golf cart?" I ask, feeling a little skeptical about this plan.

"Don't worry, we steal them all the time. Well, not steal exactly. Sometimes the guys from the grounds crew tool around on them, so we hitch rides and cruise around the property. Like before dinner starts, after we're all set up. They're really fun." She takes a key chain out of her pocket and shakes it in my face. "And I've got a key, so it's not technically stealing at all."

"How did you get that?" I ask.

"It's a long story. Don't worry about it."

"Won't we be sort of obvious?"

"We'll take the back roads," she says, popping her gum. "And it's nighttime. And if anyone asks how we got this, or what we're doing . . ."

I wait for her to finish the sentence. She doesn't.

"Then what?" I ask.

"I figured out how we're getting to the Lot. *You* figure out what to say if we get caught."

I think about this for a second. I really shouldn't do this. I know that. If the police are around tonight and we get caught, it might be decades before I get my license back from my parents. I could be carless for the rest of my life. And that's just the tip of the crimeberg.

Then again, it *is* Friday night, and what else are we going to do?

"Okay," I say. "But you're driving."

An hour later, we are bouncing down Twelfth Street in a golf cart. Its shocks are completely gone, and I think I have about three bugs in my teeth, not to mention one dead gnat in my right eye. I understand more than ever the purpose of windshields. Everyone's cruising tonight, so we pull out from a side street and fall into formation, safely sandwiched between a Jeep and an SUV.

"It's like being on a float!" Charlotte says, waving at

anyone and everyone, people passing us, people driving in the other direction.

It's my job to wave and also to study the crowd for cops. Everyone is staring at us and pointing. I didn't think we could get away with this. It's impossible.

But we are getting away with it. We made it here, and everyone's seen us. The police must be busy somewhere else. This is my first lucky break in a while, so I'm going to enjoy it. I see friends from Edison and wave at them. I see Steve and Jacqui parked in the Lot and wave to them. Steve waves back, his face lighting up when he sees us. He walks closer to the street to get a better look, while Jacqui just looks confused.

What's really bizarre is that I don't really care about them right now—about whether they're together, or whether Steve notices how much fun I'm having without him. I don't really care about anything right now. I feel like anything is possible tonight.

I see some people from our French class and we wave to them. "If Monsieur LeFleur could see us now . . . what would he think?" I ask Charlotte. "Well, who cares what he'd think? Because he doesn't exist!" I declare.

Mike and Ray pass us in Ray's pickup. Mike leans out of the passenger-side window and yells, "What are you guys doing? Where did you get that thing?"

"Charlotte! They'll fire you!" Ray screams across the seat at us.

"Who cares?" she calls back. Then she swears and says to me, "I forgot, I'm not *talking* to him."

We start laughing, and a few blocks later Charlotte suddenly takes a right turn, pulling into Dale's Fifties Drive-Up, where waiters and waitresses deliver the food to your car by skating on old-fashioned roller skates.

"Should we really do this?" I ask Charlotte. Now that we're out of the clump of cars, I feel even *more* conspicuous.

She pulls around to the darkest, most secluded parking place in the back, where people go to make out. Nobody's back here but us, which is a relief. "I'm buying," Charlotte offers, and she lifts the little red phone beside the cart to place our order, a fry basket and chocolate shakes.

"I figured we should stop," she says afterward. "I don't want to run out of gas, or battery power or whatever this thing runs on. Anyway, we made our point, didn't we?"

"Um . . . what was our point?" I ask.

"I don't know!" she says, laughing.

"Me neither, but it was a good one. People were freaking out," I say. "I'm surprised we didn't cause an accident, especially with my track record. It's amazing, actually." Then again, I wasn't driving, was I?

The waitress comes out to deliver our order a few minutes later. It's so dark where we're parked that she doesn't notice a clump of onion rings someone must have dropped earlier, and she trips and crashes to the pavement.

Somehow she manages to skillfully hold our tray in the air without spilling anything. It's as if this has happened to her before. She stands up and dusts herself off, brushing a large onion ring off her bare leg.

"Are you all right?" Charlotte and I call over to her.

"Fine—just give me a minute," she replies.

"Fleming, you should be the one who works here; it's so obvious," Charlotte says. "You skate a lot better than she does. You're fast—you'd get good tips."

"I know." I sigh. "That's what I told my parents. But they refused to let me wear the uniform."

"It *is* a bit short," Charlotte says as the waitress approaches in a modified fifties-style skirt that barely covers her rear end. She looks like she's my mother's age, so it seems extra risqué.

When she gets closer, she looks at us suspiciously as she tries to figure out where she can attach the tray. "Where did you get this thing?" she asks. "Are you supposed to be driving this around at night—on the streets?"

Charlotte turns to me and smiles. "Fleming?"

"Oh. Well, see, this is part of a new teen outreach program

at Shady Prairies," I say. "They're trying to sponsor a couple of teens every summer, and give them new opportunities. They chose me and Charlotte this summer."

The waitress looks me in the eye as she sets the tray on the hood of the cart. "And how does the cart fit in?"

"They think we should experience life slowly at first," I say. "You know, like the expression 'looking at the world through rose-colored glasses'? They want us to look at the world going like fifteen miles per hour. So that we can absorb it all, drink it all in. So we don't get ahead of ourselves and go too fast. This is, like, their whole point—to protect us from aging prematurely."

The waitress studies my face for a few seconds. My heart is beating so fast that it must show through my T-shirt, like something out of an old Bugs Bunny cartoon. Beside me, Charlotte has stopped, mid inserting straw into chocolate shake. The whole world is on pause while we wait for a not very coordinated roller skater to tell us our fate.

Then she nods. "You know my mother lives out there. I bet she'd like to get involved in the program. I'll have to mention it to her." She takes our money and skates back to the restaurant.

"Oh, God," Charlotte says.

"What?" I ask.

"That was so scary."

"I know," I say. "I thought for sure she was going to bust us."

"No—not that. I mean the way you just came up with that story," she says.

"I had a lot of time to think it up," I tell her. "We were going like ten miles an hour, remember?"

"So we could live more slowly," Charlotte says, paraphrasing me. "Oh, yeah. *That's* what we want to do."

I Am Sunshine

All weekend I sit around knowing that I've gotten away with something. My father's so wrapped up in selling houses and preparing for his rodeo performance that he doesn't even have time to notice that I look guilty. I like having this secret that nobody knows about, and my parents don't know why I'm in such a good mood or why I volunteer to baby-sit for two hours while they go grocery shopping. It's all because of the golf cart.

At work on Saturday night, I give random customers coupons for free specialty drinks and free muffins.

Charlotte drops by to visit me and drinks three vanilla lattes in an hour. When I introduce her to Denny, she says, "Did Fleming tell you what we did last night?"

"No," he says slowly, glancing at me. "Wait, don't tell me. Baby-sitting again?"

"No. We drove a golf cart through town," Charlotte says.

Denny laughs, and seems instantaneously smitten with her. "No, really?"

"Really," Charlotte says.

"Well, that's nothing compared to some of the stuff Fleming's done before," Denny says. "Like how she smashed the window at the mall by propelling Santa into it—did she tell you about that?"

They keep joking around about me and my bad job experiences. I laugh, too. It *is* funny. And I can see that Denny is really into Charlotte. After she leaves, I don't even tease him about it. Maybe she's into him, too. Maybe Ray is out of the picture for good, and Denny is now in the picture. Who knows? Ever since Friday night I feel like anything is possible.

My father comes to pick me up at 11:20, late as usual, but I don't point this out. Instead we talk about his new program on the way home. When we get there, I listen to the different musical numbers he's considering and tell him none of them will work, but not in a negative way. I run upstairs, get all my CDs, and stay up until 2:00 a.m. trying to create a medley using his music and mine, combining his favorites from the Rolling Stones, Aerosmith, and the Beatles with the Foo

Fighters, Lenny Kravitz, and Beck.

When he looks uneasy Sunday morning as I play the music for him, and tells me the rodeo organizers are pushing for something country—in fact insisting on it—I don't take it personally. I tell him we'll keep working on it and remind him that Elvis Stojko used nontraditional music and still scored 6.0s. Dad starts smiling and reminiscing about Elvis Stojko, for a second forgetting he's not shooting for a world championship here.

My name is not P. F. Farrell anymore.

My name is definitely not Peggy.

I am Sunshine.

Sunday afternoon, after Lamaze class—during which I am so kind and helpful that even Monica takes notice and tells the other birth coaches to watch *me*, of all people—Mom tells me in the elevator that we need to pick up party supplies for the twins' birthday on the way home, and then when we get home, that she and Dad are leaving for a friend's barbecue, so I'll need to watch the kids.

All this information doesn't even bother me; I just absorb it like a thirsty paper towel and keep walking in the direction of the minivan.

We stop at Party Party Party, and as we walk in, I wonder

whether Torvill started saying everything three times after a trip here. We have fifteen minutes to fill a cart with birthday decorations, and we're on a budget. I summon my math skills and pick out cups, plates, hats, balloons, and party favors. All of them match the twins' theme: Five.

Or, according to Torvill, "five, five, five."

"Peggy, you're good at this." My mother compliments me on the drive home. "You can buy all the party decorations from now on."

I think, *As if I wasn't going to be doing that, anyway*, but I don't say that. I just say, "Thanks." That's how good my mood is.

When Mom turns onto our street, she suddenly winces and reaches for her belly. "Oh. Wow. That was a strong one."

"A kick?" I ask.

She shakes her head. "A contraction."

"What? You're going into labor? But you're not ready. I'm not ready—"

"Relax, Peggy. It's nothing like that," she says as she pulls into the driveway. "I'm not in labor. However, I do think I should go inside and lie down for a while, because I'm feeling uncomfortable." She calmly puts the car in park.

"Maybe the baby doesn't like shopping," I say as I help Mom out of the car. Then I see a strange figure sitting on our front steps. It's wearing a black leather vest over a white T-shirt, and jeans, despite the fact that the afternoon heat is intolerable. What is *Denny* doing at my house?

"Wait a minute." Mom's eyes narrow as she spots him, too. "Who's that?"

"He's the guy I work with at Gas 'n Git," I tell her. "I have no idea what he's doing here, but that's who he is."

"Oh. Well, all right." I quickly introduce Denny to Mom, and then she goes inside to lie down. She's not feeling well enough to interrogate him.

"So what are you doing here?" I ask Denny as I get the shopping bags out of the car. "Why are you waiting outside?"

"Your dad said the kids were taking a nap, so." Denny shrugs. "Anyway, could you give this to Charlotte? I thought you'd see her before I do, so . . ." He hands me a brown paper bag.

"That depends. What is it?" I ask.

"I made her a mix," he says. "Of my favorite U2 songs. We were talking about it and she said she sort of liked them, but she didn't have any of their songs, so . . . you know. I would have made a few mixes but I can't afford more because I'm saving all my money for a trip to Ireland."

I am so jealous that for a second I can't speak. Everyone

has plans to get out of Lindville. "You're going to Ireland?" I ask. *"When?"*

"I don't know. Soon, though," he says.

I try not to hate him. "This feels heavier than just one CD." I shake the bag and hear rattling cases inside.

"Yeah. Well, it was going to be one ninety-minute CD," he says. Where his little mustache used to be, there's now a red strip of skin that looks like sunburn. "But then I couldn't fit them all on there, so . . . it's actually three and a half CDs worth of songs."

I don't say anything for a minute, because I'm thinking how Charlotte has three hundred minutes of U2 and how nice it would be to have someone that devoted to either me or to my band.

Thwarted

Inside Edison High the next day, everything is as usual. We have the golf player substitute again. "Unfortunately, Monsieur LeFleur has suffered a relapse in his health, due to the stress of attending the family funeral," the sub tells us.

"What? But the funeral was two weeks ago," I say. "And last week he wasn't here because of a family emergency."

"Yes. Well, I'm not sure exactly what's going on, but he won't be able to make it today. However, he wanted me to thank you all very much for your cards, and I have corrected homework to hand back to you, and a worksheet, as well as a CD of him teaching a class, which we can all listen to."

"Someone else's class?" I ask. "Like, we're getting a repeat?"

"Are we going to get credit for this course? Because I'm really starting to wonder here," Charlotte says.

"You will certainly get credit—if you can pass the exam at the end of the summer term," the substitute says. "It's an oral and written exam."

"How are we supposed to pass an exam when we never speak French in here?" another student asks. "There aren't enough subs that speak French, and we never practice. It's not fair."

"I'm sure Monsieur LeFleur will go easy on you. He's not expecting you to make a hole in one without a lesson from the pro, if you catch my drift," she says.

We don't. Or at least I don't want to. If I start having a rapport with golf pros, I'm not sure what that would mean about me, but it can't be good.

"As usual, he has prepared special materials for you." She walks around the classroom, her golf-shoe spikes clicking on the linoleum floor.

I stare at the worksheet she places on my desk. Monsieur LeFleur has made a list of vocabulary words for us, and we have to use them in French sentences. This is the list, which is titled Emotions:

Sad

Gloomy

Cheerless

Angry

Furious

Irate

Enraged

Depressed

Frustrated

Disturbed

Thwarted

Despondent

Hopeless

I'm not sure why the last word isn't *suicidal*, because it seems like the most natural progression. I go up to the front of the classroom, where the golfer is sitting at the desk filling out an attendance sheet, or her scorecard, perhaps. "Listen," I whisper to her. "Is Monsieur LeFleur dying? Does he have inoperable cancer or something?"

"What? No. That's absurd. Do you realize how absurd that is?" she asks me.

I nod. "Yes. But look at this list. The man is in trouble somehow."

"Well, he's not that sick," she says.

"Not *that* sick? Then how sick is he?" I ask.

"That's personal—but he's not dying. And I really have no idea. I'm sure it's just a sort of flu," she says.

I put my hands on my hips. "Then explain where he's been for the past three and a half weeks. The most dedicated teacher in Lindville. Missing."

She shrugs. "Look, I don't know; they don't tell me any more than you. All I know is, he has someone pick up the students' work and drop off his assignments. But I think you should go back to your seat now and get to work on that . . . worksheet."

I glare at her for a minute, then go back to my seat.

Charlotte taps my arm with her pen. "You were sort of harassing her up there. What happened?"

"I'm so mad about this class. I just—" I stare at the worksheet. "I really identify with this list right now."

"Me too," Charlotte says. "Except—what does *thwarted* mean?"

"You know. Me and Steve. Because of Jacqui," I explain. "Like that."

"So why didn't he just write *sucky*?" Charlotte asks.

"I don't think sucky is a word," I say. "But it should be." In French it could be *sucké*, and I could use it in several sentences, all relating to this summer.

We both focus on the list for a few minutes. Then Charlotte leans over and asks, "Hey, you want to go to IHOP after class?"

"Sure," I say. Then I remember: I have to take the kids to the park. Maybe this is a good thing. I'm not sure if I could take watching the "IHOPpers in Love" routine again. "Actually, I can't. But hold on—I have something for you." I dig the paper bag of CDs out of my bag and hand it to her. "These are for you. From Denny. His U2 favorites."

Charlotte peers into the bag. "Wow. This is so cool!"

"He'll probably quiz you sometime, so just be prepared, okay?" I ask.

Suddenly Monsieur LeFleur's voice booms out of the CD player on the sub's desk and she jumps up to turn down the volume. "Sorry, kids!" she says as a man's voice screams, *"Bonjour, mes amis!"*

Wild Streak

I finish loading the dishwasher as fast as I can on Tuesday night.

"Peggy, don't break the dishes," Mom says critically, as she sits at the kitchen table, watching me. "Just put them in."

"Mom, don't call me Peggy," I say. "All right?" I drop forks and spoons into the silverware basket.

"Well, *you're* touchy," Mom says, which is a funny comment coming from someone who's so cranky she swore at the stove earlier for burning the kids' mac and cheese.

"Ray and Charlotte are picking me up in two minutes," I say. They're back together again, so I have a ride tonight. I wash the saucepans and drop them into the drainer, while Mom goes into the living room to monitor Dean and Torvill, who are building a fort out of the sofa pillows.

"You're going out with Charlotte *again*?" my father asks as he holds Dorothy in the air above his head, preparing her for her career as either an air force pilot or a pairs skater doing a lift. "It's a Tuesday night."

"Dad, I'm not on a school schedule."

"I know. It's just that you work at the store tomorrow morning. You've got French. And I'm not exactly sure how I feel about you spending so much time with Charlotte."

"What do you mean by that?" I ask. "Don't you like her?"

"Sure. Of course. But she has quite a wild streak, doesn't she?" Dad says. "I could tell, when I met her outside French class that day. She just has that look. Or maybe it's an *attitude*."

"Wild streak? No, not really," I say, thinking, *Unless she really does streak.* "I mean, she's creative. She has a lot of creative energy." And creative ideas about driving nontraditional vehicles on town streets. But that hasn't gotten back to my parents yet, so I don't think it's going to.

"Translation: wild streak," my father says as he twirls Dorothy upside down. "P. F., I wasn't born yesterday, okay? I had friends like that. I was sort of like that."

I wipe my hands on the dishtowel. "You? Come on, Dad. Be serious."

My father glances at me with a wounded expression. "Why is that so hard to believe?"

"Because!" I peer out the window over the sink to see if Ray and Charlotte are here yet. "You've told me a thousand times how you got up at four to skate before school and how your schedule was so grueling and all that." And I can't exactly picture the male-figure-skating clique being known for its wildness.

"That doesn't mean I didn't occasionally do stupid things," my father says. "So. What do you two *do* exactly, when you go out?"

"Nothing, really. I mean, just hang out with people." I shrug.

"By people, I assume you mean . . . boys?" my father asks. "Anyone in particular I should know about?"

Fortunately, I see Ray's truck pull up outside just then, so I grab my Rollerblade bag just in case I need to skate home later. "I'll be home by eleven," I say.

"Be careful!" my father calls to me. "Don't do anything I wouldn't do."

Two hours later I am making out with Mike Kyle in a do-it-yourself car wash.

I don't know how this happened, but it did. We met up

with him at the Lot. Mike wouldn't stop talking about how cool I looked when he saw me skating across town the other day while he was out delivering pizzas in his Geo. He says I should audition for some kind of roller demolition derby they're supposed to be having at Rodeo Days this year.

"I think there's a roller-skating exhibition for kids, and a demolition derby for cars," I told him. "It's not combined."

"Oh. Well, have you seen *Rollerball*? You could do that. You'd pulverize the competition."

So he thinks of me as a bruiser, I thought. Not exactly the sort of girl anyone wants to go out with. It wasn't exactly shaping up to be a date night, which was fine, because I really didn't feel like yet another gruesome foursome evening, spent staring at Steve—and Jacqui.

I sat on the tailgate of Ray's truck while Mike tried on my Rollerblades. Everyone said they would be too small for him, but the skates fit Mike exactly. He'd never been on Rollerblades before, so I offered to help him out. We went to a corner of the Lot and he held on to my arm as he tried to steady himself. We kept laughing because whenever he got going too fast he'd sort of panic and I had to jog over and keep him from falling. There were all these pieces of broken glass he had to step over.

All of a sudden we heard shouting, and looked back

over toward the pickup. "They're just CDs!" Charlotte was screaming. "If you're so mad, then take me home!" She got in and slammed the door. Ray slammed the door, too, and they took off.

"My shoes were in that truck," Mike said, and we started laughing.

So I drove Mike's car, because he was still wearing my skates. I didn't tell him my parents keep my license in a locked box so I can't drive. I figured I wouldn't get pulled over on the way to the Cone Zone, for ice cream.

Afterward he wanted to take me home, and he was driving in his bare feet. It was sort of sexy, because he has really nice toes, which is a very weird thing to notice about a guy when you are hung up on that guy's best friend.

All of a sudden Mike pulled into the car wash. I knew this was a place people went to make out because it's on a side street, and because it's private since it has walls on two sides. But it didn't feel very private to me. There were other couples and cars in the next few bays, and people kept cruising by to see who was there.

Not sure what else to do, I got out of the car, and Mike did, too. I was joking around with the foaming brush and pretending to scrub the rust off Mike's car, which is practically all rust, when Mike just took my arms and sort of gently pushed me back a little toward the concrete wall. He was about my height in his bare feet, and his lips were soft and matched up with mine perfectly, like they were the matching half of a puzzle piece. I knew I was getting carried away, thinking things like this, and I just sort of gave in to it. There was cold water dripping from the rinse wand onto my feet and it was so cool and oasislike. I didn't even care that it smelled like wet metal and bad cleaning agents. Lindville seemed about a million miles away.

"So." Mike smoothes my cheek with his thumb, then kisses me again.

"Wait. Wait!" I push him away. "We shouldn't be doing this," I say. I stare at this yellow caution sign on the wall that shows a person falling down. WARNING: ICE MAY FORM ON WET SURFACES DURING COLD WEATHER.

"Why not?" He lifts a strand of hair off my forehead and starts kissing me again.

I should protest again, a little more forcefully, but I don't. Kissing Mike isn't like kissing Steve, but it's better than nothing. It feels good to be kissed, to have someone want to kiss me.

I shouldn't be doing this, though, because I still want Mike to be Steve. I've spent months obsessing about him. I can't just drop my Steve fantasy in a car wash because of someone's nice toes. Really, really nice toes. And lips.

"I—I should go," I say as I pull away. "I have this really strict curfew, so . . ."

"So we'll just start earlier tomorrow night," he says.

"Right. Exactly. That's exactly what I was thinking," I lie.

I'm jamming my feet into my Rollerblades and telling Mike how I'm going to skate home instead of catching a ride with him, when this single bright headlight shines right on me, like a police flashlight. Then I hear an engine cut off, and the light goes out.

My eyes adjust to the dark again and I see Denny sitting on his motorcycle. He flips up the visor of his helmet and glares at me, as if I've just set fire to a stack of U2 CDs. "What are you doing here?" he asks, making this not-so-sly head gesture toward Mike, who's standing by his car. "People only come here for one thing."

"In that case, what are you doing here? Unless your date fell off the back of your bike and you didn't notice?" I reply. "Or did you plan on washing your motorcycle?"

He leans back on his bike. "For your information, I was sort of looking around," he says. "I thought maybe Charlotte would be around here somewhere. You said you guys were planning to hang around at the Lot tonight, so when you weren't there, I thought I'd drive around and look. So, is she around?"

I shook my head. "She left."

"Where did she go?"

I shrug.

"Did you give her the CDs?" he asks.

"Yes," I say.

"Miss Talkative strikes again," Denny says in disgust, as if I'm deliberately withholding information. Which I am.

Mike pulls out of the car wash, giving me a little wave over his shoulder. He honks the horn a couple of times, then peels out.

"I can't believe you were here with *him*," Denny says disparagingly. "That's the guy who came into the store, talking about trading in his Camaro. Right?"

"Did you come here just to ruin my night?" I ask.

"Why? Was it really *special*?" Denny asks.

I glare at him. "At least I'm not driving around aimlessly looking for someone. You know, you could always go work at Shady Prairies so you can be close to her," I say. "Jamie would miss you at Gas 'n Git, but she'd get over it."

"Hey, you couldn't even hold a job before you came to Gas 'n Git," Denny scoffs as he starts up his motor again. "And at least I'M not making out with an IDIOT in a CAR WASH!" Denny flips down his visor, revs the engine, and then turns out onto the street. He pulls away from me, going faster and faster, until he has to stop for a red light about two blocks away, which sort of ruins his dramatic exit.

I sit down on the pavement to finish fastening my skates. It wasn't such a horrible thing being with Mike, no matter what Denny said. So he likes me. So . . . okay, good. Someone should.

Suddenly there's a loud sound approaching. I look up and see Denny circling back. He pulls up beside me. "So do you want a ride? Because it's not safe, skating after dark. By yourself."

"No, thanks," I say, getting to my feet.

"Come on." He scoots forward on his seat. "Fleming, come on. I'm not leaving here without you."

I consider my options. Neither one is all that great. "Do you have an extra helmet?" I ask.

He pulls one out of the black leather bag on the back of the bike. I put it on and climb on behind him. I'm trying to hang on by touching him as little as possible. I start to give him directions, but he reminds me he already knows where I live. I've never ridden on a motorcycle before. I like the way Denny leans the motorcycle down toward the street when he turns corners. It reminds me of the death spiral in pairs skating, where the woman's entire body skims just above the ice.

We're about four blocks from my house when I see the Doberman leap the fence and race toward us.

I'm convinced the dog has some sixth sense that screams "Rollerblade Girl" whenever I'm within leaping range. He sprints out toward the bike, but we blow past him, leaving him stunned and gazing forlornly after us.

Denny drops me off at the end of the block. He must know my parents wouldn't want me showing up on his motorcycle.

"That was the Doberman," I say as I hand him the helmet.

He nods. "I figured."

"So thanks a lot for the ride," I tell him. "And just so you know, Charlotte left tonight because she got into a fight with the guy she's been seeing. A fight over your CDs. Okay?"

"*Really?*" Denny smiles.

"See you tomorrow morning," I say.

"Yeah, okay. Be careful, Fleming."

"It's only a block."

"All right, don't be careful then," he says. He pushes off with his feet and takes off down the street.

When I walk into the house, my father's sitting at the kitchen table with a sketch pad. There are wavy lines all over the paper, and little figures shaped like animals—or people, I can't tell. "Hey, Dad."

"P. F. You scared me half to death," he says when I speak, catching him off guard.

If you only knew what I did tonight, I think. *You'd be really scared.* "What are you drawing?" I ask. "Your new long program?"

"Um, no," he says, covering the sketch pad with his right hand. "It's my short program. Very short. For the rodeo."

"I thought you were finished with that," I say.

He shakes his head. "I met with the rodeo people tonight. And Mr. Stinson. I did my program for them."

"Did they love it?" I ask.

"Not exactly. They told me I need to make some changes."

"Oh. Well, do you think it'll be okay?"

He chews his thumbnail. "Sure. Of course. It's going to be great." Then he puts his head on the table, doing a face plant on the sketch pad. "Who am I trying to kid? P. F., it's awful. It's going to be the worst program in the history of figure skating." He sits up, and I notice dark circles under his eyes. "I haven't told you this yet, but it has to have an *animal* theme. Sheep, cattle, horses—the things that draw people to the rodeo," he says. "P. F., I don't know a thing about handling livestock. How am I going to do this? Costumes are one thing, but since when do actual *animals* factor into figure skating? They want animals on the ice with me."

I stare at him. I don't want to say anything, but isn't this sort of his problem? He's the one who agreed to skate at a rodeo. I warned him not to.

"I can't even broach the subject with Ludmila. She'd have my head on a platter. I've called a couple of skating friends, and they all think I'm crazy to even attempt this. I still can't think of the right music. Tchaikovsky didn't write about bucking broncos much." He is still scowling as he starts laughing in despair. "Why did I say I'd do this? Am I insane?"

Yes, I think. But he has so much invested in this that I can't say that. "Is it too late to say you're not going to do it?" I ask.

He nods. "Way too late. They've already booked me for three shows a night, starting on the tenth—opening night. I've signed a contract. They've even advanced me some money."

"Oh. Three a night? Really?" That seems like a lot. "Okay. So we'll figure it out," I tell him. "You need a song with animals . . . is that what you said?"

"Yes, but not 'Old McDonald,'" he says. "Something sophisticated. Something I won't be embarrassed to skate to."

I decide not to point out that the entire fact he's skating with livestock is going to be embarrassing enough. "Hey, I'll ask Denny tomorrow," I say. "He knows a lot about music."

My father frowns. "Okay, but I don't want any heavy metal. Make a note of that."

"Don't worry, that's not what he likes."

I'm about to leave the room, when my father says, "So what did you and Charlotte do tonight?"

"Oh, um, not much," I say. "Nothing, really."

"Uh-huh. Well, you're only half an hour late, so that's an improvement, I guess." He taps his pencil against the table, then runs his hand through his thinning hair.

I quietly go upstairs to my room and close the door behind me. I stand at my dresser and look at myself in the mirror. My hair's slightly flattened from the motorcycle helmet, and my cheeks are extra pink. I can't believe my dad didn't notice that.

I also can't believe I was making out with Mike. What was I thinking? He's the wrong guy. And if he tells Steve about it, would that be a good thing or a bad thing?

I can't figure it out, but I stare at myself in the mirror, wondering what I'm up to.

No French Connection

"This is so easy. You really couldn't think of this yourself?" Denny says the next morning at Gas 'n Git after pressing me for more details on Charlotte, and Ray, and Charlotte's fight with Ray.

"No." I take a gulp of coffee. I cannot wake up this morning.

"He has to skate around a horse and some goats, right?"

"Sheep," I say, sipping.

"Whatever. Okay, are you ready? Here's the song. 'Who's Gonna Ride Your Wild Horses'! U2!" Denny says, as if it's a battle cry. "From *Achtung Baby*."

I try to think of the song. I'm not sure I know it. I'm not sure that I'm convinced. "Is that about horses?" I ask.

"No, but who cares?" Denny says. "That's one of my favorite songs in the entire world."

It's by U2, so doesn't that go without saying? I think.

"And it could work for skating, definitely," he goes on.

"Well, what about . . . a U2 medley or something?" I ask.

Denny looks deathly offended. "U2 doesn't *do* medleys."

"I know that!" I say, irritated and tired of this. "But see— figure skating? It kind of does."

"Hmm." Denny's face is turning a little splotchy. He looks like he's breaking out into a sweat. "If you could forget the animal theme . . ." He starts laughing nervously. "You could use 'Elevation,' that'd be good for skating. Or 'I Fall Down' from *October*—for all the jumps and stuff?" He continues to laugh nervously. "How about 'So Cruel,' you know, he could make it into this sort of statement about cruelty to animals. How about 'Even Better than the Real Thing' or 'With or Without You'? Or wait—he could forget the animals, do a lemon theme and use 'Lemon,' because that has that sort of clubby sound skaters go for." He's gone crazy. He's babbling. I wonder if I should slap him to stop him from reciting song names.

"A *lemon* theme?" I ask as the automatic door sensor rings. I turn and see Charlotte walking into the store. So that's why Denny is suddenly acting so weird.

Her face lights up and she hurries up to me. "I thought you were working today, but I couldn't remember—I took a chance and caught the bus. So Kamikaze says he wants a triple mocha today with extra whipped cream instead of his usual."

"Really?" I ask.

"No, I'm just kidding. *God*, can you imagine him and whipped cream and his beard?" She shudders and looks at Denny. "Hey. Thanks for the CDs."

Denny clears his throat and says, "Hey, no problem," then rushes off to pour himself a soda from the fountain. He stares at Charlotte while he's filling his cup with ice, and the crushed ice cascades onto the floor. He's just so suave.

While he cleans up, I tell Charlotte what happened the night before with Mike, after she and Ray left us in the Lot.

"You kissed Mike! Like, a lot," Charlotte concludes.

"Not that much."

"No, I can tell." She stares at me. "So how was it?"

"Weirdnice," I tell her, flustered by remembering very vividly how it felt. It wasn't like Steve. But was it worse? Or better? "I just don't think I'd want to go out with him. As anything long-term."

"Oh, is that all? Who cares about *that*?" Charlotte asks.

I laugh. "Denny actually showed up," I whisper to her,

"looking for you. Then he gave me a hard time about being with Mike. Then he gave me a ride home."

"I think he likes *you*, not me," she says.

I shake my head. "No. Really. You're the one. I didn't even get one CD," I tell her.

"Hmm. I'll have to think about this," she says. She looks over at Denny as he gets back behind the counter to ring up customers' sales.

I hurry over to a customer who's waiting for coffee. As I make her a latte, Charlotte comes behind the counter and says, "So you're coming to meet me at work tomorrow for the fireworks, right? We'll go see them together?"

"Sure," I say, "but what happened with Ray last night?"

"Forget Ray," she says in a low voice. "It's over. *Really* over this time."

I look over at Denny. Maybe there is hope for him.

Charlotte picks out a banana-nut muffin for breakfast, and I pour her a cup of coffee. She grabs a *Lindville Gazette*, takes her coffee, and sits at one of the tiny tables we have by the windows.

"Look at this!" she cries a minute later. She gets up from the table and comes over to me and Denny. "That robber guy is hitting the next town now. He held up a *grocery* store. Aren't you guys scared?" she asks.

Denny jiggles a key in the register. "Nah. Not really." He seems to have recovered a little from his first glimpse of Charlotte.

"God. Who wants to come to work thinking someone's going to stick a gun in their face? You guys are crazy to work here."

Denny giggles, and then must realize he sounds funny doing that, because he stops. He coughs, then says in a lower voice, "Yeah, it's just something you sort of deal with in this job. But it's a good place to work. We don't get harassed."

"Much," I add as I see Coffee Breath's car pull up in front. He's here for his second Tanker of the day.

"You guys are brave," Charlotte says. Then she goes back and sits at her table by the window.

"She has no idea," I say to Denny, but he's too busy staring at Charlotte. I know he wants to go sit with her and talk to her and ask about the CDs—and tell her about the songs he's writing. But he doesn't. He shows remarkable restraint. He doesn't even flirt with me to make her jealous. He's . . . mature or something.

Or else his Bono obsession doesn't leave room for anyone else in his heart. If Bono ever came in here, I don't want to think how Denny might act.

* * *

After I get out of work, Charlotte and I take the bus over to Edison for French class.

Kamikaze half grunts when I hand him his usual coffee with cream. He gives me back one of the dollars I hand him, as a tip, but he doesn't say a word.

"Good afternoon to you, too!" Charlotte says as she shows him her transfer.

He looks up at her, and then over at me. "Don't tell me. The mall again?"

"We're going to summer school," Charlotte says. "Okay? Not the mall. We've been to the mall *once* together. We're going to French class. *Parlez-vous français?*" she asks, and I notice that her accent is actually, amazingly, improving.

Kamikaze starts talking in French, and I don't understand a word he says. When he sees how confused we look, he says, "I drove a bus in Montreal for a while. Now sit down."

When we get to class, we find out Monsieur LeFleur now has car trouble.

"He's survived some sort of horribly disabling flu, he's lost a member of his family, and now he's going to let a busted starter keep him from teaching our class?" someone asks.

"He could call a cab. He could take the bus—like us," Charlotte says.

We all sit there at our desks, feeling small and pathetic.

He hates us. It's obvious. He's not even in town this summer. He's sitting on a beach in southern France, sipping wine and laughing as he thinks about us, the fools in his Edison High summer-school class.

"Today, Monsieur LeFleur thought you could absorb a little French culture and some of the language by watching an Academy Award–winning movie," the sub says. "It's called *The French Connection*. Has anyone seen it?"

Nobody has.

"Then you're . . ." The sub skims the note she received from Monsieur LeFleur, then glances at the back of the video box. "You're in for some nonstop action, featuring the best car-chase scene in movie history."

"Is it a French car?" Charlotte asks.

"Well, no. I don't think so," the sub says.

"Then what's the point? I mean, what's the connection to French?" Charlotte demands.

"This is *supposed* to be French class," I say angrily. "Why aren't we watching a French movie, at least? Doesn't anyone care that we're not learning anything?"

"Girls, relax. This movie features some French characters. It has subtitles and everything," the sub says. She taps me and then Charlotte lightly on the head as she walks past, as if we're small children, as if patting us on the head will solve anything. Duck, duck, cut it out.

The movie is rated R—the kind of movie they don't allow us to see in school. Parents would definitely protest this. Some students protest by actually getting up and walking out of class.

Charlotte falls asleep during the exciting chase scene, where Gene Hackman is driving underneath the elevated subway tracks, racing the train. I close my eyes and picture myself racing through the streets of New York. I drive as well as Gene Hackman and then I apprehend the evil French killer when he gets off the train. Only I catch him in French. I don't know how you shoot bullets *en français*, but that's what I do.

Then I stay in New York and get a very cool apartment.

When I open my eyes, I see that both the sub and Charlotte have dozed off in the afternoon heat.

Fireworks

It's the Fourth of July and it's almost dark. I am supposed to be meeting Charlotte right now, to go to the fireworks together.

Instead I'm at the town park's playground with Dorothy, Torvill, and Dean. Mom is doing a remote, a live broadcast from the big event, so she's perched at a table in the middle of the war memorial plaza. People keep stopping by to request songs and pick up free bumper stickers, and they all keep asking when she's due. I got tired of watching strangers touch her belly and listening to them predict whether she's having a girl or a boy.

Dad isn't here because he got some special session at the rink, because no one in their right mind wants to practice on a national holiday except Ludmila and Dad. He's supposedly going to meet me at the KLDV booth at 8:30, and then I get to find Charlotte in the huge crowd.

My parents make my life so complicated. They really do.

I told them I already had plans. But no. I'm pushing Torvill on a swing. I'm watching Dean climb on the jungle gym. I'm helping Dorothy create a sand sculpture. I'm trying really hard not to take how annoyed I am with my parents out on the kids, because it's not their fault our parents don't have a clue about how *not* to act on the Fourth of July.

"Just tell KLDV you can't do it!" I said to Mom when she came home this afternoon and informed me she had to work tonight.

"Just tell Ludmila you don't care if she doesn't celebrate July Fourth—you do!" I said to Dad.

"Peggy, honestly, we're only talking about one night here," my mother said. "Does one night really matter that much?"

In a word? Yes. Especially when it follows an afternoon, and a morning. But try telling my parents that. "I already promised Charlotte I'd go to the fireworks with her," I said. "I'm supposed to meet her at work."

"So call her and tell her to meet you at the park," my father said. "I'll be there by eight-thirty, I *promise*."

Yes, and that really means a lot these days.

"Dorothy shouldn't be out that late, should she?" I asked. "Shouldn't she be home?"

"It's just one night," my mother said. "Anyway, do you think she could actually sleep when fireworks are going off?"

They have an answer for everything. It's another gift of theirs.

At 8:25 I get the kids assembled and we circle back to the KLDV booth, but Dad's not there yet. So I take the kids with me to the place where I'm meeting Charlotte—at the top of the hill, near the statues of Lindville's founding fathers. As I crest the hill, I don't see Charlotte. I don't believe what I do see. It's Steve, leaning against one of the statues. And for the first time all summer, he is actually alone. Jacqui is nowhere to be seen.

So here it is, my moment. Me and Steve, alone. Except I'm not alone. Torvill and Dean are toddling along beside me, and I've got Dorothy on my shoulders.

I wave hello to Steve and walk over to him. I'm about to say something when the fireworks start going off. The first one makes a loud hissing noise, pops, and then nothing happens. No lights come out of it. It falls with a pathetic sigh, a complete dud.

Steve and I look at each other and start laughing. "Typical, right?" I ask him.

"Oh, yeah," he agrees. "So this is how Lindville celebrates July Fourth. Why am I not surprised?"

I laugh again, probably a little too hard, but I'm sorry—it's funny. There's a delay in the fireworks display, so they must be working on fixing something. "So have you seen Charlotte around here?" I ask Steve. "I'm supposed to be meeting her."

"Nope. Not yet," he says.

"Oh. Well, where's Jacqui?" I ask. I keep an eye on the twins as they chase each other, doing figure eights around the two statues.

"She had to work. Did Kyle have to work, too?" he says.

"Um, I guess so, yeah," I say. I haven't actually talked to Mike. And right now, I don't want to. "Hey, you know what? We actually got to watch a movie in French class the other day. Have you seen *The French Connec*—"

My sentence is interrupted as more fireworks are launched into the air. They explode with what seems like double force, as if they're trying to make up for the dud. There's a giant boom that nearly shakes the earth.

Torvill starts shrieking and crying, and runs away, heading straight for Mom and the KLDV booth. Dean chases after her, and then I have to leave Steve and bolt after both of them, which isn't easy with Dorothy on my shoulders. "I'll be right back!" I call to Steve. "Don't go anywhere, okay?"

He just waves as I hurry away. In the sky, bright red-white-and-blue stars flutter down. Dorothy holds out her hands and tries to catch them.

By the time we get to the booth and find Mom, Dad is there, too. "What happened?" he asks as he picks up Torvill and hugs her and tries to calm her down.

"That really loud one scared her," I say.

"Where were you? Why didn't you just wait here with your mother?"

"Um . . . because I have a life?" I say. Or at least, I'm trying to.

"What?" he asks.

"Nothing." I crouch down so that Dorothy can climb off of my shoulders. "Anyway, I'm late—I'm going to meet Charlotte. See you at home!" I rush off up the hill, eager to get back to Steve. We can still have our moment. This time, there won't be kids, there won't be Jacqui or Mike, there won't be . . .

Steve's not at the statue anymore.

"Sorry. Couldn't stall him long enough," Charlotte says, coming up to me. "He told me you were here but you had to run off after the kids. Sorry I'm late; it took me forever to get here."

"Traffic?"

"No. Slow vehicle," she says.

"Wait a second. I thought it was the car-of-the-month club night."

"Yeah. Well, Mom changed her mind. She said there are too many accidents on holidays."

"So, how did you get here?" I ask her.

"How do you think? The golf cart." She grins. "I mean, *le cart de golf*," she says.

I laugh. "I think you mean *la* cart," I correct her. "Wait— that's it. We'll travel *à la cart*."

"Oh, wow. That's so perfect." Charlotte and I both step back and look up at the fireworks lighting up the sky.

With each explosion of fireworks I scan the crowd, look-ing for Steve. Where did he go? How could he vanish so quickly? And why do I care, when he so clearly does not? I see faces bathed in red, white, and blue. But not his.

"Look—there's Mike," Charlotte says. She points across the lawn. Two figures are heading our way.

"And Ray's with him," I observe.

"I don't want to see Ray," Charlotte says. "I'm not really sure if that's how I want to spend my evening. You know?"

"Well, I don't want to see Mike," I say. "It's going to be weird. You know? And I just . . ." I get this really nervous, sick feeling in my stomach, like I shouldn't have kissed him the other night, because I'm still too hung up on Steve, but if I see him again I'll probably do the same thing.

Charlotte and I look at each other for a second.

"It *is* Independence Day," I say.

"My mom is picking me up at Shady Prairies later—she could give you a ride home. Do you need to go tell your parents you're leaving?"

"No, I said I'd meet them at home," I tell her.

"Then let's go!" she says. I follow Charlotte, and we race toward where she's parked the cart a few blocks away. We laugh as we dodge people, coolers, picnic baskets, dogs, kids. We leap into the golf cart, and Charlotte jams it into forward gear. We come out from underneath a clump of bushes like we're superheroes on a mission, except that we have bristly needles stuck in our hair and our vehicle only goes ten miles per hour.

As we go down an alley, trying to beat traffic and stay unseen, we nearly run into a man who is taking out the trash. He shakes his fist at us as we buzz on down the alley, doing our impression of an exciting getaway.

When we pull into Shady Prairies, Charlotte starts driving around the retirement-home property, giving me the grand tour.

"Shouldn't we just park?" I ask.

She doesn't respond. She heads up a sidewalk to the pool in the center courtyard, between all of the buildings. We hear a car honk a few times, and look at each other, panicked. "Security!" Charlotte whispers. She jerks the wheel to the right to turn around.

But she makes the turn too fast, and the pool deck is slick with evening dew. The cart suddenly tilts awkwardly to the right. "No!" Charlotte gasps as the cart tips all the way over onto its side, and we land sideways in lukewarm, chlorinated water.

I push myself out of the cart and swim to the surface. Actually I don't have to swim—I can just stand up. We careened into the very shallow end, and it's lucky we didn't hit our heads when we landed in the pool.

I grab my backpack from the submerged cart. Charlotte is already wading to the steps to climb out. She looks over at me and I don't know whether to laugh or cry. How did this happen? How did we end up here? We are so dead.

"We've got to get this thing out of here," she says, and we try to drag the cart out of the pool, but it's impossible.

"No, *we've* got to get out of here," I say, "before anyone sees us."

We run from the pool, shaking ourselves like wet dogs,

trying to dry a little before her mother comes to get us. The night is so hot that it shouldn't take long.

"All right, Fleming," Charlotte says as we sit on an unlighted bench out front. "Start thinking of a story for when someone asks. Because they're going to ask."

I nod, wringing out the bottom of my T-shirt. "A story. Sure."

She's
Uncomfortable

"I've only got a few minutes to do this," my father says when we sit down at his desk on Friday morning. He's home briefly, between final practice and a house closing, and my mother's upstairs, because she just started her maternity leave. My father jiggles the pencil cup on his desk. "So. Let's see what you've got."

I hand him a check. I'm glad he doesn't have much time. After what happened last night, I don't want to be around my parents too much. I might feel guilty, crack under the pressure, and tell them everything.

"Another hundred. Very good, P. F." He makes a note on the sheet of paper titled P. F.: Personal Loan, then looks up at me. "But I thought you were giving me one-fifty this week."

"I was. I meant to," I say.

"Okay. Tell me what happened." He looks me straight in the eye.

I panic for a few seconds. Is he talking about *everything*? "Well, I sort of forgot to budget—"

"P. F. The truth," he says.

I open my mouth, not even sure what I'm about to confess, when the phone on his desk rings, saving me. He answers it and then hands it to me.

"Fleming! Oh, my God. I have to talk to you," Charlotte says breathlessly.

"Oh . . . hey, Charlotte," I say. I glance across the desk at Dad. "Charlotte," I mouth to him. "Just be a minute."

He looks at his watch and then taps it to remind me he's in a hurry.

"Is this a good time?" Charlotte asks. "Can you talk?"

"No."

"Oh. Your dad's right there, huh? Well, someone from work just called with this incredible story—I've got to tell you."

"Mm-hmm," I say, afraid of what she'll say next.

"So at six-o'clock breakfast they opened the blinds in the dining room, and there was this really bright metal thing glinting in the sun, beaming right back into the dining room, hurting everyone's eyes. It was the cart. The sun was reflecting off it in the pool. So far everyone thinks it was some resident who wandered out of the Alzheimer's nursing-home division—we're cool. Talk to you later!" She hangs up, leaving me with a racing pulse and a lot of questions.

"Okay, bye, see you at class—and thanks!" I place the phone back into its holder.

"P. F. It's Friday," my father says. "You don't have class today."

"Oh." I slump a little in my chair, hoping this isn't the beginning of my unraveling.

"So, let's see, we subtract a hundred, and your remaining debt comes to four hundred. Wow, P. F. You're doing very—"

Suddenly my mother lets out a loud, hysterical shriek, and then shouts, "Come quick! Come quick!"

We both jump up and run for the stairs. The kids abandon their Lego sculpture in the living room and follow us. "Oh, no," my father says. "This is *not* the day to have the baby."

"What are you talking about?" I say. "*I'm* the one who has to—has to—" When I start thinking this is the actual delivery we're talking about, I can't talk. I can't breathe normally. I'm almost hyperventilating.

Mom is propped up on their bed watching TV. Her feet

are on a pillow, and she's sipping water from a bottle cradled in her arms.

"Look!" she says as we skid into the bedroom. "Isn't that where Charlotte works?"

A reporter is wrapping up a story from Shady Prairies. This is big because Lindville is never on TV, unless there's severe weather. It takes a tornado, or at least a gale-force wind, for them to send out a satellite truck.

There are dozens of senior citizens crowded around the pool. The reporter is saying that there has been a head count and that one person is missing from the complex. They seem to think the missing person and the flipped cart are connected.

"Gee, I hope nobody got hurt," Mom says as the kids climb onto the bed with her. "What if someone hit their head?"

"Did Charlotte tell you about that just now?" my father asks.

"No." I shake my head. "She hasn't gone to work yet—she works nights," I say. That, and the fact that she didn't have to tell me about it, because I was there.

"Hmm. Well, I've got to run, or I'm going to be late," my father says.

"Peggy, you're going to help me clean the house today,

right? While the kids nap?" my mother asks after my father kisses her good-bye and rushes down the stairs.

"I am?" I say. I thought maternity leave meant I was now off the hook—not more on it.

"Yes. I was hoping we could do some relaxation exercises, too. This heat is really making me uncomfortable," she says as she shifts position on the bed. "So what on earth do you think happened at Shady Prairies?"

Her. *She's* uncomfortable.

Love among the Pancakes

I'm restocking the napkin dispenser

Saturday night at work when Ray's truck pulls up outside at the pump. I stare out the window at the truck, wondering what Ray is up to tonight. I really hope he isn't going to come in and punch Denny for giving Charlotte some CDs. Denny's nose is already crooked, and we both know he's not the best fighter in town.

Ray gets out to pump the gas. The passenger-side door opens and Mike gets out. He peers at the gas station, and there I am, staring right out at him. He waves and then jogs toward me, looking happy to see me.

"So, Fleming. Where've you *been*?" Mike asks when he walks into the store. He's wearing his usual red flip-flops.

"Around," I say, feeling nervous.

"Around, huh? What have you been doing?" He comes up really close to me and when I look in his eyes, I start remembering the car wash.

Behind me, I hear Denny humming. I wish he'd turn up the radio so that he can't eavesdrop.

"Well, I've been busy. Really busy," I say as I fidget with my stupid apron. "My family . . . and the job . . . and the new baby coming . . . and . . . " I shrug. "You know."

"Yeah. I've been busy, too. You wouldn't believe how many people order pizza during a heat wave," Mike says. "It was *insane* on the Fourth. So do you have a break or something coming up?"

"Um . . ." I'm about to say no when for some reason I look right at Mike's mouth, and I remember how kissing him was sort of thrilling, the feel-good movie of the summer so far. Without another thought, I hang up my apron, ask Denny to cover for me for a couple of minutes, and Mike and I head out back. Denny glares at me the entire time it takes to walk past him. It's like having an extra father around.

"Is this okay with Ray?" I ask as we go out the back door.

"Sure. He's cool," Mike says.

I prop the door open with an empty container of 10W-30 motor oil, then turn to find Mike. In the dark, I stumble over some discarded cardboard boxes on the ground and Mike catches my arm. He puts his arm around my waist and pulls me close, right up against him.

"Careful," he says. "You're as bad as me trying to Rollerblade."

"That bad? Really?" I tease him.

"Hey, not all of us are born skaters, okay?" Mike smiles, and in the deserted area behind the store, I notice how white his teeth are. I haven't been back here except to toss trash bags into the Dumpster. It smells horrible. I try to close off my nose, to stop breathing, to stop absorbing the noxiousness.

"A born skater? Interesting," I say, glancing down at my feet.

His hands are on my hips and he pulls me toward him again and kisses me. His lips don't feel the same as they did that night in the car wash—they're dry, maybe a little sunburned or windburned. Then again, it's hard to kiss while I'm also holding my breath to avoid Dumpster smells.

"You know what's bizarre?" Mike pauses to look at me. He runs his fingers up and down my bare arms. "Gropher is, like, the biggest liar in the world. I mean, usually nothing he says is true."

"Oh, yeah?" I say. "Really?" I hadn't thought of him as a liar before.

"Are you serious? The dude has made up almost everything," Mike says.

"Like what?" I challenge him.

"Like all that stuff about gambling and being an addict and all. He's never lost big at gambling. He's played poker like *twice* in his life, and he sucked at it," Mike says. "I beat him. My father beat him."

"Really?" I ask. I can't believe it. Everyone at school thinks he's on his tenth step.

"That scar he says he got from jumping off a roof? Okay, he fell off his bike or something. Going down a hill and turning too fast. I mean, he's just . . . he takes stuff and he makes it sound like something else."

"Really?" I say again.

"He's supposed to be saving all that money from waiting tables for his road trip? Then explain how he owns like a thousand CDs and DVDs. You know what I mean?"

My heart starts to sink a little—no, a lot. Or maybe it just didn't have that far down to go.

Steve was supposed to take French, but he didn't. Maybe all his talk about getting out of Lindville is just that: talk. Because if you look at it one way, it does seem as if maybe he's working really hard toward being the IHOP manager here, instead of toward escaping town.

Mike moves closer to me and kisses my neck. "Anyway, that's beside the point. Because even though he lies? The really cool thing is, everything he said about you is true."

"About me?" I step back from Mike. "What about me is true?" I ask him, and at the same time I don't want to know.

Mike kisses my neck again. "He said you were a really good kisser. He said even though you weren't his type, he just felt like he had to kiss you again, after the first time."

I stare at him, this awful burning in my throat. "Oh, yeah? I'm not his *type*? When did he say that?"

"I don't know. Who cares? The point is, he was right," Mike says. He tries to kiss me again, and I shove him away, nearly knocking him against the Dumpster.

"What? It's a compliment," Mike says.

I go back inside, tossing the plastic oil container aside, and I close the door behind me, which locks it. Then I realize that anyone, even Mike, can walk into the front of the store as long as it's open, so it doesn't matter whether I close that door or not.

"I don't want to talk about it," I say before Denny can ask. Headlights flash against the windows and I glance out and see Mike and Ray driving away.

I take some bleach and cleanser and start scrubbing the sink, one of the chores Jamie left for me. I can't stop thinking about how I was so stupid, how this whole thing got so ridiculous. I kept thinking that Steve and I had this connection, because of the way we met and the things we talked about. I thought we were . . . soul mates or something. I figured he was only with Jacqui because they worked together and that kind of stuff happens when you work with someone. Or so I've heard. It isn't happening here at Gas 'n Git, which is fine by me.

Anyway, it turns out Steve never meant anything he said, that he's so shallow he believes in "types," and that he liked kissing me—enough to tell Mike about it—and that's it. He made out with me and then reported on it. Which I would have thought was really beneath him. But now I guess it's obvious that I don't know him at all.

Now I know two things I didn't want to: that Steve isn't interested in me, even though he likes making out with me, and that Mike probably only came after me because of what Steve said about my kissing . . . skill, or whatever you'd call it. I guess I can't be mad at Mike, though I am. I only went out with him because I wanted to get to Steve.

We're thwarted all around.

Denny walks over and puts a fruit drink on my counter. "With my compliments," he says. "That is, if you can drink anything after inhaling all those bleach fumes."

I laugh, and for a second forget how angry and upset and furious I feel.

"So the guy's a loser. You realize that."

"He's not the problem," I say. "There's this other guy—his best friend, Steve. I sort of used to . . . I don't know." I can't say I ever dated him, can I? "Anyway, he's going out with this other girl now. They both work at IHOP."

"Love among the pancakes," Denny says dryly. "How romantic."

"I have to leave work a little early tonight," I say. I flip open the phone book and look up *Taxi*.

"Okay, I'll tell people we're out of coffee. But be careful." Denny looks at me and I can tell he knows what I'm about to do. "Don't slip on any butter pats."

Back When I Was Delusional

Lindville Limousine drops me at IHOP precisely at 11:00 p.m. I'm not in a limousine, I'm in a green van, but the driver assures me that she can make my arrival look fancy if I want, not seeming to notice that I'm wearing a T-shirt and jeans, which is not even a good outfit for what I have planned. The driver keeps a red carpet in the back, she tells me, for just such occasions.

"Don't worry, this isn't prom night," I tell her. "Not even close."

"All righty. How long are you going to be?"

"I'm not sure," I say. "Five minutes?"

"Tell you what. I could use some coffee, so how about I turn off the meter and we meet back here in five?" she says.

"That would be great," I tell her. I get out of the cab and face the restaurant building. The parking lot is almost full.

I remember Steve telling me that he worked on Saturday nights because the restaurant is busy and he makes a lot in tips. That's one of the reasons I agreed to work at Gas 'n Git Saturday nights, back when I was living in fantasyland, back when I thought we'd go out this summer, back when I was delusional.

I walk into the restaurant with my head held high. The hostess station is vacant, so I decide to seat myself. I spot Steve heading for the kitchen, and I'm about to walk over to him when Jacqui rushes up in front of me.

"Oh, hi, Fleming. It's you," she says. "What are you doing here so late?"

"You're going to seat me in Steve's section," I say.

She stares at me. "What?"

"Just do it. Don't ask questions," I say. I pick up a menu from the stack on the hostess station and shove it into her hands. "Let's go."

Jacqui glances over her shoulder at me three times as she takes me to a booth, as if I'm dangerously unbalanced and need to be watched. She places the menu on the table and steps away slowly, guardedly. "Steve will be your server tonight," she says robotically. Then she turns and nearly sprints back to the hostess station, to help my cabdriver.

I don't open the menu, because I know it by heart and because I'm not planning on ordering.

I'm also not planning on sitting here in the future, wishing something would happen with Steve.

I look around as I wait for him to come out of the kitchen. Maybe Jacqui has told him that I'm sitting in his section and I'm acting crazy. Maybe he's already talked to Mike. Maybe he won't *ever* come out.

As I rehearse what I've planned to say, which is woeful and dramatic and unrealistic, I look around at the other tables. The customers seated at them are here for fun occasions, or at least occasions, or at the very least, pancakes. They're not here for the same reason I am. That much is for sure.

Suddenly there's a blue apron in my field of vision. "Hello, my name is Steve and . . ."

"And you're a complete and utter jerk," I say. I look up at Steve. He's dyed his blond hair sort of pink since the last time I saw him. What is up with that? Is he taking hair-dye lessons from the bleached-blond plastic girl?

"What?" he says.

The rest of my witty and devastating speech vanishes as I look at him. I stare at the menu for a second to reorient myself. "I talked to Mike tonight," I tell him.

"Oh, yeah? Well, cool," Steve says, looking flustered. "I mean, you guys are sort of like together now, so—"

"No, we're not!" I say, a little too loudly for the general IHOP diner. "We're not *together*."

"Um . . ." Steve bounces up and down on his toes a little. "Fleming? What's this all about? What's the deal?" I don't say anything, and he sits on the edge of the booth bench across from me and looks at me nervously.

"I guess . . ." I look down and realize that I'm tearing my napkin into shreds. "Look. I thought you were different. And I thought we . . . I thought you . . ." I stop for a minute. This isn't what I rehearsed. But I'm not going to blow it.

"I know we just made out a couple of times, but I always really liked you," I say. "I thought you liked me, too. A little, anyway. I thought we had this connection. I thought we were going places together, not as in go places, you know, achieve great things, but literally go, get out of town, see other states, cities." The Christie Farrell talking gene strikes at the most inopportune moments. "But now I find out you lied about everything, you never planned on taking French, you aren't buying a truck, or a van, you aren't going anywhere. You just liked making out with me. That's it? And you tell your friends they should go after me because I can kiss good? Kiss *well*, I mean. No, wait—not just good. Really, really *good*well?"

"What?" Steve just sits there, looking stunned.

"Well, don't I?" I ask.

I'm an idiot to ask this. I know that, but it still comes out.

"Sure. Yes," Steve says. He glances around the general area, and a man waves a coffee pitcher in the air, asking for more. "Um, I sort of have to—"

"You're such a hypocrite!" I cut him off, not done yet. "We totally hit it off, and you liked kissing me—but you can't go out with me because I'm not your *type*? Instead you want to go out with *her*?" I practically scream as I throw my arm out to point at Jacqui. "She's your type?"

A busboy is walking by with a tray full of dishes and he veers away at the last second, avoiding a crash.

That's when I realize that I don't know whether I'm sitting here begging and humiliating myself, or whether I'm finally standing up for myself and telling him what *I* want. And what's the difference, really?

"So did you want to order anything?" Steve asks. "I mean, maybe we could talk on my break. I'm not sure, because we're sort of busy tonight, but—"

"No. I can't stay. I don't want to talk. I just—I thought you were different," I say as I get to my feet. "I don't know why. But you're not. And I don't even know what I'm doing here." I start to run for the door.

"Hey! Are you skipping out on the check?" Jacqui yells after me.

Dine and dash, Charlotte told me once. But this isn't what she meant. I leap into the waiting cab and tell the driver my home address.

"Denny said you left work in a cab. Where have you been?" My mother and father are sitting outside on the front steps, with the door ajar so they can listen to the kids inside.

"What are you doing out here?" I ask, grateful that Denny didn't tell my father where I went. I can just imagine my dad running into IHOP in his skating gear, shaking his fist at me.

The Lindville Limousine driver pulls away with a friendly good-night wave. From the looks on my parents' faces, maybe I should whistle for the taxi to come back.

"I can't sleep. My back hurts and I'm too huge," my mother says. "And your father just got home from driving around, looking for you after you weren't at Gas 'n Git and you didn't show up here."

"So where were you?" my father asks.

"I can't explain right now," I say.

"Yes, you can, and you're going to," my father says. "P. F., what's going on? You're worrying us."

"It's nothing," I say.

"Nothing? Then how about answering our questions? You're spending money to take a cab. Why? Where did you go?"

"Look, I had a really bad night," I say. "I'm only half an hour late, and I don't want to talk about it."

My father stands up. "Maybe not, but you're going to."

I can't tell them that I had to go confront someone I've been obsessing over. "I had to take a cab," I say, "because you won't let me drive. Sometimes there are places I have to go that I don't want you to take me to. And I can't skate there, at night, and there's no buses at night, and I can't get a ride. So that's why. It's the first time I've done it, and it cost me twenty-one dollars, and I don't plan on doing it again, okay?"

My father's staring at me and blinking rapidly. I can tell that he's reached his personal boiling point—I've seen him like this before. "Fine," he says. "But we still want to know where you went in that cab. If you don't tell us, we'll call the cab company. It's not that hard."

"Fine. Go ahead," I say. "Call them. Whatever. I'm tired." I walk into the house and go upstairs to get ready for bed. While I'm brushing my teeth, I hear my mother and father in the hallway, talking. I can't hear what they're saying, but I know it's about me.

The Skating of the Lambs

My father's first performance is at 7:00 on the opening night of Rodeo Roundup Days. It costs four tickets to see him, which means Dad is worth more than the petting zoo but less than the Ferris wheel.

I look nervously around the bleachers as we sit down, to see if anyone I know is here. So far I recognize some kids from school, and several of my parents' friends. Mr. Stinson is rinkside, with a few other Lindville bigwigs.

I look around the non–regulation-size rink, which they didn't exactly finish closing off the way they were supposed to. There's a new roof to keep out the sun, and both ends and one side of the building are completed; but one side is only half done, covered with a chain-link fence and chicken wire, with random boards nailed to it. This goes with the decorating theme, because they've also nailed wooden boards against the rink's interior to make it look like a corral. Generators are whirring loudly, trying to keep the ice and the rink area cold.

There's a concession stand just outside the rink and a hawker yelling, "Get your frozen lemonade right here!" Torvill and Dean keep bugging me, then Mom, then me again, for frozen lemonade. Dorothy is sitting beside me patiently, waiting for the program to begin.

Dad told us not to come tonight; in fact he almost sounded like he was begging us not to. I seriously considered skipping this. For one thing, I don't want to run into either Mike or Steve at the rodeo. For another, I don't think Lindville's going to appreciate my dad's skating, and I feel a major embarrassment coming on. And for still another, it's very awkward to be here with my mother, to watch my father, when they're both still mad at me from Saturday night.

But I can't not be here. You don't want to miss any of Dad's performances. There's always something really incredible about each one of them—he'll throw in a difficult jump at the last second, when he's got the crowd on his side and things are clicking along. He'll draw them in, have them clapping to the music, and then afterward the ice will be littered with roses and stuffed animals. At least that's what used to happen, in all the videotapes I've seen of him competing. I don't know about tonight. The ice might be littered with something else, I think as I look at the three lambs and two horses standing on the ice, posed as part of the cowboy scene. Fortunately Dad doesn't have to skate with the animals—just around them.

My father is wearing a red-checked gingham shirt and pants that look like brown suede, only they're fake and made out of stretchy material that won't split when he jumps. The pants actually have real suede fringe running down the side seams. He's wearing a black ten-gallon hat, and black skates that match it. Mr. Stinson must be so proud, I think.

The temperature outside is still in the eighties. To help the ice stay frozen, they've dumped in tons and tons of cubed ice and tried to smooth it over, so my father has to skate on a melting and bumpy surface. It's impossible to skate well on soft ice. The performance is going to be a disaster—in more ways than one.

Dad has to round up the lambs as he skates around them and leaps over bales of hay, while two rodeo clowns with shoes on slide on the ice and fall down. The rodeo clowns look like some of the people Dad used to skate with in the ice shows. So much makeup, so little time. This is a step down, not just for my dad, but for the rodeo clowns, too. They're professionals.

They keep bulls from killing riders. They don't goof around on skating rinks. I hope they're getting paid overtime for this.

I don't know what the horses are for, but at least they'll go with the country music the rodeo guys insisted Dad use, after they said first our alternative-rock medley and then Denny's U2 mix was too rebellious for Rodeo Roundup Days. They ended up handing Dad a tape and saying he had to use the three songs on it. "So much for artistic interpretation," Dad said when he showed me the tape.

At exactly 7:00 there's an announcement from the audio booth. "Ladies and gentlemen, introducing the one . . . the only . . . Phil Farrell in 'Cowboy Bo Peep'!"

Torvill and Dean shriek with excitement and the audience applauds as the music begins: first, just a harmonica playing a sad cowboy ballad, as my father steps onto the ice and circles around. He stops to joke with the rodeo clowns and circles the rink while a horrible voice-over from a grizzled old cowhand goes on about "the life of a lonely cowboy."

Then the real music starts: It's a medley that kicks off with a high-energy Garth Brooks song called—appropriately—"Rodeo." The crowd loves it and Dad plays to them, smiling and clapping as he does tricky footwork and makes his way up and down the ice. Then he grabs a lasso from one of the rodeo clowns and tries to make rope circles as he skates, only he can't do it, and the clown chases him and shows him how to do it right. People laugh, but then settle into watching Dad as he tosses the lasso away and builds speed, skates forward, does a quick double Axel. He moves so quickly and gracefully, especially considering he has to skate around livestock. Dad jumps over a bale of hay and the crowd gasps, then applauds. He does a double toe loop and then a triple flip, and even the sheep look impressed.

Suddenly, outside the rink, there's a huge commotion. People are screaming, and there's the sound of thundering hooves. Everyone in the bleacher seats turns around to look out the open side of the rink. I see a giant black bull go rushing past, on the loose—completely out of control.

"Insane Zane's escaped!" a woman screams.

"He's gone crazy from the heat!" a man behind us yells.

The rodeo clowns bolt off the ice and sprint after Insane Zane. Cowboys ride past the rink, in hot pursuit, throwing ropes to try to lasso him. He's one of the meanest, toughest bulls, and it's a big challenge every year to see who can stay on him the longest. Apparently no one could stay on him—or with him—tonight.

When the noise subsides and we all turn back around, my father has stopped skating. He stares dejectedly at the horses and the sheep. He looks completely baffled, like he doesn't know how he ended up doing this or how to make sense of it. My heart really goes out to him—this isn't how his first performance should go, no matter how inane it is.

"He hates having his program interrupted," Mom says as Dad steps off the ice.

"I know," I say.

Mom turns to me. "I wasn't saying that for your benefit. I was explaining to the little ones."

"The little ones don't understand, so what's the point?" I say.

"Peggy, what is *with* you? Your attitude is terrible," Mom says.

How could it not be? I'm stuck at the rodeo with my family.

The crowd gasps and shouts as Insane Zane rushes past the rink again. Dean suddenly jumps out of his seat and scampers down the rows of bleachers.

"Dean, come back!" Mom yells. "Come back here right now!"

But Dean either doesn't hear her or doesn't care. He lands on the bottom bleacher and races for the exit.

I go after Dean before Mom can tell me to go after him. That would just really irritate me right now. I catch up with him just outside the door. Insane Zane is racing around the concession stand and knocks down both the frozen lemonade cart and the Boots for Sale booth. Dean darts toward the bull before I can grab his shirt. I run after Dean, even though people are shouting at us to get back. Above our heads, ropes are flying as the cowboys attempt to lasso the bull's horns.

Insane Zane stops racing and slowly trots toward us. He has a black coat, and seems about as long as a railroad car. He's taller than I am, wider than I am, and has long, sharp-looking horns and stuff dripping out of his quarter-size nostrils. With those he should definitely be able to smell our fear, and anything else about us.

I decide not to look at him—staring at him might be challenging him in some way. I decide not to breathe. Then maybe he'll think I'm already dead. I step in front of Dean to shield him, but he jumps out and does a high karate kick, yelling "Hi-ya!"

At the same exact moment, three separate ropes circle Insane Zane's head, stopping him in his tracks. He stands there, staring at us, looking bewildered but still mad.

"Cool!" Dean says as the cowboys tighten the ropes and rein in the bull. "I got him. Did you see how I got him?"

I just drop to my knees and hug Dean for all he's worth. I'm shaking all over, and I squeeze Dean's tiny shoulders until I stop.

"I'm going to be a cowboy," Dean says. "Peggy, let me go; I'm a cowboy." I release him and he runs around kicking the air and pretending to lasso things with an imaginary rope.

"Sure you are," I say. "Of course you are."

When we go back inside the rink, Mom wants to know what took us so long. Dad is smiling and playing to the crowd as he skates down the ice, doing some fancy footwork, snapping his fingers to the country beat.

What Boy?

We wait for Dad by the burgers, ribs, and pork-chop-on-a-stick stands for a quick snack after his eight-o'clock show. I desperately hope his second show went better than his first.

I've gone on two rides with Torvill and Dean, because Mom can't. She's letting the kids stay out late tonight, but she's the one who looks completely beat. Mom is sleepily eating a half slab of ribs, Torvill has corn on the cob, and Dean a grape Popsicle. Dorothy has fallen asleep in her stroller, which isn't like her at all. I stand at the end of the picnic table and keep looking around for Charlotte and Denny, who are supposed to meet me either here or over by the Scrambler ride.

"Peggy, have a seat—there's room," Mom says, patting the bench beside her.

"That's okay," I say. "I'm actually not going to be here much longer."

"What do you mean?"

"I'm meeting my friends. We're going to hang out here for a while," I say.

"But that's impossible. You can't go hang out late with your friends tonight."

"Why not?" I ask. "Mom, the rodeo's only here for ten days. It's the only time anything ever happens here. So can't you let me enjoy it?"

"That's not it. You never *mentioned* you were meeting Charlotte," Mom says.

"Well, I'm mentioning it now."

"What boy is it this time?" Mom asks. I start to shake my head, but she insists. "No, really, what boy?"

"There's no boy," I say.

"Do you expect me to believe that? After Saturday night?" Mom says.

Just then, Dad comes over to join us, carrying a dish of fried pickles and wearing clogs with his cowboy costume. As he gets closer, I see he's got makeup on, too.

Dean runs up and tells him how he took down the runaway bull, how he stopped Insane Zane. "That's nice," Dad says, distracted. "The second program went much better. This thing with the animals . . . it's a learning curve, I guess," he says as he crunches into a deep-fried pickle spear.

"Well, Peggy is now going out with her friends," Mom says in an angry tone, before I can tell him how well he skated, how he made something decent out of nothing.

"Yes, I am," I say, staring at her.

"Hey, Fleming." I turn around and Denny is standing behind me. He has this knack for coming to my rescue.

"Hey," I say, turning toward him. "Have you seen Charlotte?"

"Not yet, but I'm kind of early," Denny says. "Were we meeting by the food, or by the rides?"

"Here or at the Scrambler," I say. "Should we go over there now?"

Mom sets down her ribs and wipes her face and that's when I know she's getting serious. "You're not going anywhere with him."

"Mom, he's a friend," I say.

"I asked what boy and you said there's no boy," Mom says.

"My *friend*. Denny. The guy I work with," I say. "You and

Dad even met him at our house," I remind her.

"So. Does that mean I know anything about him?" she says.

She's picking a really bad time to all of a sudden get involved in my life again.

"Fleming, I'll meet you over there, then," Denny says. He takes off, and I know how he feels. No one wants to be around someone else's family fight.

"Why is he wearing sunglasses?" my father wonders. "It's almost dark. I don't trust him."

"That's not it—I don't trust *Peggy*," Mom says to him.

"It's Fleming, Mom," I say. "God, could you just try sometimes?"

"Could *I* try? Oh, that's good. That's really good." She rips open a second packet of hand wipes. "Fleming, then. I've been *trying* to keep you involved in this family. But it's like you don't even want to be involved."

My father sets his little container of fried pickles on the table. "Look, let's not make this bigger than it has to be. P. F., you can't hang out with your friends tonight and come home late again. You have class tomorrow. You work tomorrow. End of story."

"My French teacher has blown off every single class so far—we have subs who don't even speak French," I tell them.

"Of course, you wouldn't know that because you don't ask how my class is going. And work? I'll be fine for work. I always am. Have I missed a day yet? Have I missed *anything* yet?"

"Yes. You've missed the last, like, five family nights in a row, so—"

"I have family night every day!" I say, which makes more sense than it sounds like. "I'm the one who's home while you guys are out skating and forecasting and remoting and whatever else you do when you strand me at home without a car."

"You know what? I know what this is all about," Mom says. She shakes her head and says quietly, "You can't stand the fact that you don't get all the attention now. That you've got a brother and sisters, and you're mad at us about that. You've never adjusted to this, so you're taking it out on us by running around with these guys this summer—"

"I'm not running around with anyone!" I say, which isn't completely true, but it's close. "Look, I have adjusted, I am adjusting, I am adjusted. Do you want me to conjugate this for you in French? If I had an actual teacher, maybe I could, but no, my summer sucks. My entire summer is about paying you back, and making good on my promises, which I'm doing. Can't you see that?"

"P. F., your entire summer hasn't been about paying us back," Dad says.

"No, actually, my entire summer has been about helping you guys out," I say. "Peggy, can you do this, Peggy, can you do that? Except you usually don't ask. You just assume. You totally take me for granted. You just make plans for me without me knowing about them."

"That's—that's not true," my father stammers. "We always ask."

"We're a family," my mother says. "Family means thinking about other people besides yourself, family means—"

"Family! Does family mean that you guys can completely forget about *me*, about what I might want? I've given up so much time to help you guys out, and you don't even notice— you just cruise in when you want to, when KLDV doesn't need you, or some homeowner doesn't need you, or when the rink is closed because it's midnight. You expect me to take Lamaze class and figure out your skating program? And if you figure out your skating, and get your sponsors, you're going to *leave* for a few months on tour? Are you serious? Are you even thinking about anyone besides yourselves?"

"We *always* think about you," Mom says, looking stung, and Dad nods slowly in agreement, almost as if he doesn't know what I'm talking about.

"Right. You think about me when you're off deciding to have another child right before my senior year, and you think about me when you're off deciding to leave home and go on a skating tour during my senior year," I say angrily. "And you guys are always telling me how I have to learn to be more responsible—*me.*"

All of a sudden I notice Dorothy has woken up and is staring up at me with these big, watery blue eyes, blinking, not understanding, not recognizing this tone of voice, about to burst into tears.

I can't take it. I can't see Dorothy cry right now. She never cries, and if she starts, then I might, too.

I quickly walk away, leaving the food booths. I go past all of the games of skill, looking through tear-blurred eyes at furry white bears and pandas hanging from strings, and metal ducks being shot to a hollow *ting ting ting* sound. Steve is probably there, trying to win smelly stuffed animals for Jacqui, his *type*, but I don't want to know if he is. I don't want to see him—or anyone—right now. I can't believe my parents can just stand there and tell me how much they think of me, how considerate they are, how I'm the one who doesn't understand "family." They've got it all wrong. They're so different from how they used to be. The three of us used to be so close; we did everything together. Now it's the two of them—and I'm the nanny.

I pass the rodeo stadium. Inside, loudspeakers blare girls'

barrel-racing results, and the crowd screams in excitement as the bareback bronco riding begins. Everyone's shouting and applauding and having a great time. Everyone except me.

When I get to the Scrambler, Charlotte and Denny are standing in line, waiting with tickets for me, too. I fake a smile and Charlotte says, "I heard you and your parents got into it. Everything okay?"

"No," I say.

"*Ew.* I mean, triple *ew.*" She hands me a wide silver-toned belt buckle with the initials PFF on it. She shrugs. "They were engraving them and I thought it looked cool."

"A warning," Denny says to me. "She's really into this rodeo thing."

"Thanks. Just don't make me pose for the caricature guy," I say. "Or those old-fashioned saloon-girl portraits."

"Come on!" Charlotte's jaw drops. "You are no fun."

"Oh, God. How did I let you guys talk me into this?" Denny says as he climbs into the Scrambler cart and closes the gate behind him, and the three of us are squashed together. "Do you know what this is going to do to my rep?"

"You *have* a rep?" I ask.

"Yes, she's alive! Fleming's alive!" Charlotte puts her arm around me and hugs tight.

She and Denny are laughing and talking about the parade

tomorrow, but I don't really listen. The ride doesn't feel like it's been put together right, with metal scraping on metal as we revolve. I close my eyes so I don't have to look at the faces in the crowd watching us as we whip past, so I don't have to see if my parents came to find me or not.

Beaucoup Busted

Around 11:30 the next morning, Denny and I are watching the tiny black-and-white TV behind his register. We're taking a break because we've been mobbed with customers for the last five hours. When the Rodeo Roundup Days get into full swing, it's like this every day, all over town. Tourists wanting to buy everything. It keeps the town financially afloat for the rest of the year, but it's ten days of traffic jams and restocking soda. Jamie is even here to help, though she disappeared into her office about half an hour ago.

The lead story on the news is the rodeo parade that starts at noon. As I said, Lindville doesn't get onto TV often. We have to watch when it does.

"So," Denny says. "I haven't had time to ask yet. Did you and your parents talk when you got home last night?"

I've been so busy this morning that I've managed to sort of forget that my parents and I had a huge fight last night. I didn't see them after that. Denny dropped me off, a block from home, at about 10:30.

"Not really," I say. When I walked into the house last night, they were sitting in the living room, propped on opposite ends of the sofa, rubbing each other's feet. I looked at them, and then I went upstairs without saying anything. Later there was a knock on my door, but I didn't answer it. For all I know that could have been Dorothy, not my parents.

"No? Not at all?" Denny asks.

"No."

"Well, what was the fight *about*?"

"Nothing," I say.

Denny tosses his empty glass bottle into the recycling bin. "Fine. Be the most unloquacious coffee wench of the century, see if I care."

Jamie walks out from the office in the back. "What are you two doing? Just sitting here, watching TV?" She quickly checks all the coffee pumps. "We're running on empty here, and you're watching TV!"

"We were taking a break," Denny says.

Jamie starts to make coffee. "You get everything ready and *then* you take a break."

"Hey. I don't even work on that side, so don't yell at me," Denny says.

"I've got it," I say, rushing over to intervene before Jamie can ruin the brewing. I only have fifteen minutes left on my shift, and Kamikaze's coffee has to come out of this batch.

The phone rings and Denny answers it. "Gas 'n Git."

He holds the receiver away from his ear, and I hear a woman's hysterical voice. He slowly hands the phone to me. "Your mother. I think."

I grab the phone, wondering why Mom's calling here— she never does that. "Mom?"

"Peggy! I mean Fleming—*sorry*, Peg—I mean Fleming," Mom stammers. "I thought it was heat stroke, but then my water broke, and—it's time. My contractions are coming really close together and it doesn't make sense, the barometric pressure's over thirty, and I'm early, but . . . I'm on my way to the hospital . . . hurry and meet me there!"

"But Mom—can't you pick me up first?" I ask. "On the way?"

"No time! Baby coming fast . . . parade today . . . blocking streets off . . . now or never! Hurry, please!" She hangs up.

I feel panic grip me. I'm thinking in gasps; I'm not

breathing right: It's time. For me. To help. Deliver a baby. My new brother. Or sister. I grab the counter to steady myself, to keep from keeling over.

"I—I have to go," I tell Denny as I fling off my sandals, grab my skates, and start jamming my toes into them. "She's having the baby. I have to be there."

"You're skating to the hospital?" Denny says. "No. Come on, Michelle Kwan. I'll drive you."

"What's going on?" Jamie asks.

"Fleming's mom is having a baby," Denny begins. "Fleming has to get to the hospital, so I'm going to drive her."

"No," Jamie says. "You can't."

"Why not?" Denny asks. "This is an emergency."

"The store can't be open with just one employee," Jamie says. "Gas 'n Git regulation. It's not safe! I'm sorry, I really am. But I can't have you both leave."

"But this is an emergency," Denny says again.

"Look, this might sound harsh, but Fleming isn't the one about to have a baby," Jamie says as she starts arranging the Muffins of the Month into a neat circle.

I pull at Denny's sleeve and tug him away from her. "Don't push it—it's fine, I can get there myself. Anyway, you're meeting Charlotte here in like ten minutes for the parade—remember?" They wouldn't stop discussing the plan last night.

Denny's just glaring at Jamie. "She's so obsessed with those stupid muffins. I feel like pegging her with one."

"Well, don't. We'll get fired."

"So?"

"So I don't want to get fired!" I say. "This is the only job I've had that I've kept, and I have to keep it so I can get out of debt, because if I don't get out of debt I'll owe my parents forever and—"

"Fleming! *Breathe*," Denny says.

"So you don't have to take me, because I can go really fast on my skates. If the parade traffic's bad, I'll be able to pass all the cars. No problem," I tell him as I put on my helmet. "My mother has this crazy idea that I'm never around when she needs me, so I'm going to be there this time."

"It's okay, I get it. You have this need to skate to the rescue. Okay. Whatever," Denny says. "Good luck." He shakes his head.

"Let us know if it's a boy or a girl!" Jamie calls out cheerfully as she goes back into her office and closes the door.

I skate over to the exit. As I'm going out, a man is walking into the store. I hold the door for him and he mumbles a thank-you to me. He looks sort of familiar, but I can't place him. Is he someone I know from the bus? I can't really tell, because he has on a baseball cap and sunglasses. He's probably a tourist, I tell myself. He needs cold beverages, like everyone else. I could use one myself as the blistering hot midday air hits me like a wave.

The door is closing behind me when I hear the guy ask Denny for a couple of scratch tickets. *Wait*, I think. Now I'm sure I know him—his voice is familiar. He has a slight accent, but I can't quite place it. I turn around to look at him one more time. How do I know this guy?

As Denny leans over to pull out the scratch tickets, I see the man reaching in his pocket. Then he holds up a small gun and points it right at Denny.

Oh, my God! It's the c-store robber! I think, and now I really can't breathe at all. I've got to pull it together, I tell myself. I've got to do something.

My body is shaking with nerves but I go back inside as quietly as I can. I glide over to the coffee counter on my skates without making a sound. Jamie is nowhere in sight.

Denny holds up his hands, clutching lottery tickets in each. "So you're the famous robber. Hmm. Interesting."

"Give me all the money in the register," the man says.

I slip behind the counter and grab the first coffee tank pump, then the second. It's a good thing I just made fresh coffee.

"Yeah, okay. But you don't really want to shoot me, do

you?" Denny says as he puts the scratch tickets on the counter.

Denny! Just open the register and give him the money! I'm thinking. *We covered this in training!*

"How do you know I don't want to shoot?" the man says. He thrusts the gun toward Denny. "Do it. Now."

I flick the "turbo dispense" button and aim the two coffee tubes at the robber and start shooting coffee at him. My aim isn't good at first and I drench his shoes with coffee, and I hear him mutter, *"Qu'est-ce que c'est?"* Then I turn it on full blast and keep spraying, hitting his legs, his stomach, his throat, and he starts shrieking in pain, singed by Jamie's Java Blend.

Denny rushes around and tackles him to the floor, and I skate over to help. The robber swears in two languages as Denny pulls his arms around and I sit on his back to hold him down.

And now I know why he looks and sounds so familiar. So that's where he's been all summer.

"Monsieur *LeFleur*?" I say. "I was in your class this summer. The one you never showed up to teach because you were too sick and devastated?"

He doesn't say anything.

"Je m'appelle Mademoiselle Farrell," I say. *"Et vous êtes très beaucoup* . . . busted."

"Your accent is terrible," Monsieur LeFleur mutters through gritted teeth.

"Well, whose fault is *that*?" I ask.

Jamie rushes out from the back office carrying a set of handcuffs. "All right, everything's under control," she says.

Denny looks at me and rolls his eyes. "Yeah, thanks to you, Jamie," he says.

"What? I was calling nine-one-one," she says. "*Somebody* had to."

Then we drag LeFleur over to the wall of sodas and handcuff him to one of the fridge door handles.

I say good-bye again and take off skating for the hospital. I glance at the clock as I'm leaving. It's now just after noon, when I usually catch the bus. I skate in the breakdown lane, and I only get a few blocks before I get to the cars that are completely stopped, held up due to the parade roadblock.

I veer around a dead prairie dog. Then up ahead I see cars pulled over, blocking my way. I glide over and skate on the other side of the stopped cars. No one's moving except me.

I pass the Lindvillager, which is stopped in traffic, not moving at all, looking like a beached battleship.

Then all of a sudden I see this silver car's door opening, and I try to move out of the way, but it's too late. I slam into the door. I feel like I've been cut in half.

You're Kidding, Right?

The next thing I know I am coming to, and there is a cloud of terrible stale coffee air around my head. I'm enveloped in a coffee cloud, and there's no oxygen. I can't breathe. I don't want to breathe.

I open my eyes, and World's Worst Coffee Breath is looming over me. "Look! She's awake! She's going to be just fine, everybody!" He leans down and looks into my eyes. "Are you okay? Can you get up?" he asks cheerfully.

I wince and shake my head, my helmet scratching against the asphalt.

"Sure is a hot one today. Gee, I'm so sorry. What can I do?"

Stop breathing! Eat a Tic Tac! "I have to get to the hospital," I say.

"Really? You're that badly hurt?" Coffee Breath is starting to look very nervous.

"Yes," I say. "But mostly I need to meet my mother there; she's in labor; I have to help." I try to move, and my right side tells me not to.

I gaze up at the people standing over me like I'm a freak show. I can't believe it, but Kamikaze Driver is here. He's talking with Coffee Breath and gesturing wildly. What did he do, abandon his bus? Why isn't this traffic moving, anyway—is it me?

Then I remember—the parade is going on, and the highway is blocked until the parade finishes passing down Main Street.

I'm hoping Kamikaze won't give me mouth-to-mouth resuscitation, just to give me germs, just to share bacteria. I'm hoping Coffee Breath won't come close enough to even attempt mouth-to-mouth.

Above me, I hear the two of them saying things like "hospital" and "ambulance" and "parade traffic" and "never make it." My body feels cold and clammy, and at the same time the hot black asphalt feels like it's burning through my clothes. I wonder if I'm on my way out. I can't believe I ran into a car door, I can't believe I just did that. Did I really just do that?

Is *this* horrible air—car exhaust being blown on my face,

intense heat, feedlot smell—the last breath I'm going to take? That's not fair—none of this is. I'm supposed to be there to help my mother. Maybe she knows how to do everything, but I'm her rock, she said during our last childbirth class—I'm her stationary front. She needs me. Who else will remind her to pee?

"Can we get going?" I mumble from my prone position on the street.

Coffee Breath and Kamikaze gather me up gingerly. I think I scream a little when they lift me. They carefully put me in the backseat of the silver Lexus and try to prop me in the least painful position. I ask them to take off my helmet, but they refuse, saying we'd better wait until we get to the hospital. Then they both get into the front, and Coffee Breath starts to inch forward in traffic.

"What about . . . the bus?" I ask Kamikaze.

"I told everyone to get off and then I locked it up. Don't worry, nobody's going anywhere in this traffic," Kamikaze says.

"That's the problem!" Coffee Breath says, sounding very tense.

Kamikaze keeps giving him advice, telling him to pass cars, to drive in the wrong direction, against traffic, to drive on the shoulder. Coffee Breath stays in the right lane, hardly moving. They start arguing, louder and louder.

"You think you can do better? You think you can do better?" Coffee Breath asks. "Okay, let's see. Let's switch." He gets out of the car and starts to walk around the back.

Kamikaze slides over to the driver's seat and takes off without him. I hear Coffee Breath screaming behind us as we make an abrupt left and cut between two cars, and it's so tight that the driver's side mirror gets ripped off the car.

I'm not sure if I'm still conscious or not, but I think we're now driving down the wrong side of the street. We're flying, and horns are honking all around us. For a second it feels just like we're cruising on a weekend night because of all the noise.

I try to sit up a little more, and I see that we've reached the roadblock. A mime is standing on top of a sawhorse, walking across the top as if it's a balance beam, trying to amuse all the people in the cars that are backed up for miles.

I glance at Kamikaze. He doesn't look amused.

"There's only one way to get you to the hospital. And you know what it is," he says. I'm not sure if he's talking to me or to himself.

First he jumps out and tries to talk to the mime. The mime makes fun of him, imitates the way he walks.

Kamikaze gets back into the Lexus and nearly runs him

over. He pulls past the sawhorse and slyly enters the parade.

I haven't been in the Rodeo Roundup Days parade since fifth grade, when I appeared as a figure skater on the Lindville's Athletes of Tomorrow float. I probably looked better then than I do now. I'm getting blood on the leather upholstery from my cuts.

We weave around the edge of the marching bands, scoot past the square dancers dancing on a truck bed, pass some slowly parading llamas, who get spooked by us and start spitting. Kamikaze finds an open space and blows past some twirlers and jugglers. Then we get stuck, hung up behind a small herd of Longhorn cattle, completely stalled.

"Just one more block and we can cut through the alley to the hospital," Kamikaze tells me. "Just hang in there. What's your name?"

"Coffee Wench," I tell him.

"Pardon?"

"Peggy," I say, and my ribs hurt when I talk. "Fleming."

"Peggy Fleming?" he says, tapping his fingers on the steering wheel. "You're kidding, right?"

"Farrell," I add.

He looks confused and stares at me in the rearview mirror. "What's your name again?"

That's when I hear a motorcycle roar behind us.

"Well, holy cow, would you take a look at this!" Kami-kaze cries.

I try to look out the back window. I see Denny on a motorcycle, with a naked girl who's wearing blue-tinted sunglasses and a white cowboy hat. Her long red hair streams out behind her as they zip around us.

Then I black out again.

Web of Evil

"You're in shock, that's all it is, shock," a nurse says to me as I sit on a bed in the emergency room and she checks my vital signs. "You know what it is? You probably haven't eaten a thing today and you drank too much coffee—I know how you kids are."

She's right, but actually I think it was the fact that I was held at gunpoint and then nearly killed, rather than the lack of a balanced breakfast, that makes me keep passing out.

They X-ray my wrist and ribs and make sure nothing is broken, then bind and wrap everything tightly with tape, as if they're trying to hold my bones together just in case they decide to fall apart later. The patches of road burn on my knees, elbows, and palms get doused with antiseptic solution and wrapped in gauze bandages. When the nurse starts talking about whether I should have a tetanus shot, I decide I'd rather pass out again for a while than look at any needles.

The next thing I hear is my father's voice. "We're naming him Elvis," he's saying as he leans over my bed. "For Elvis Stojko. But his middle name's going to be Miles, in case he decides to go by that instead, like his big sister."

"What?" I murmur. I don't know if I'm dreaming this or it's really happening. With my dad and his names, you never know. Miles is my mom's maiden name. Isn't it? They must have given me some medication because I can't quite focus on Dad's mouth, on the words he's saying.

"First we were going with *Scott* because, as you know, we love Scott Hamilton. Then we were convinced we'd pick *Brian*—because of Orser and Boitano. But *then* we considered *Viktor*—for Petrenko—and of course *Alexei*—for Urmanov and Yagudin," my father says.

I don't understand what he's talking about. I don't know why he's speaking in Russian. Has he been studying that with Ludmila, too?

"He's a strong, healthy baby," my father says. "And your mother is doing great."

Unlike me, I think as I look down at the various bandages

wrapped around my chest and my legs. But actually, I don't feel all that bad.

"P. F., I'm sorry about our fight," my father says as he sits beside my bed. "I thought about what you said, and I'm going to put off my comeback for another year or so. Otherwise your senior year will consist of baby-sitting and little else, and your mother will go insane, and I've got to practice what I preach. Who knows? Maybe I'll never do it. It doesn't matter. The point is that I can't tell you to be fiscally responsible when I'm acting like I don't have five children who depend on me."

"You're still young," I say. "And Ludmila thinks you're . . . well, that you've still got it. That you have always had it. So just don't lose it."

"Right," my father says. "P. F., what are you talking about?"

"I don't know," I mumble. "It's Russian. You know Russian."

When the nurse comes to check on me, I tell her I'm okay and ask if I can go see my parents. She insists on having an aide wheel me down the hall to the elevator, even though I can walk, and we go upstairs to the fifth-floor birthing suite. I decide on the way that I have to confess everything.

I work my way up to it, though. I ask my parents about the new baby, and where Torvill, Dean, and Dorothy are.

"He's gorgeous, and they're at day care," my mother says.

I look at Elvis, but I can't hold him because my wrist is all wrapped up. I also have two jammed fingers, a couple of bruised ribs, but mostly it's lots and lots of road burn. Hence the mummy look, as my legs are covered in white gauze. My parents won't stop talking about how awful I look, how it must be so painful.

"Come on! Tell me!" I say. "How was the delivery? I mean, talk about pain."

"Five point six for technical merit. Five point nine for presentation," my father says. "Presentation includes your mom screaming at me and asking why I'm not Peggy. 'Where's Peggy, where's Peggy, I need Peggy I mean Fleming where is she!' " He imitates her.

Mom laughs. "I just can't believe—after all our preparations. It must have been one of the fastest deliveries in history." Her face is shiny and at the same time very pale, like she's gone through something incredible but exhausting.

"I'm sorry I missed it," I say. "Well, um, while we're all here, there are some things I have to tell you." I take a deep breath and my ribs hurt. "You're not going to like them, so here goes." I start explaining about borrowing the Shady Prairies golf cart. And how Charlotte and I drove it more than once, and how we also drove it into a pool, and how I went to

IHOP that night to confront Steve, and how I've been spending all this time stupidly pursuing him and in the meantime hanging out with his best friend.

While I talk, Mom won't stop crying. "It is sort of sad and pathetic, but it's not *that* bad," I tell her.

"No—that's not it!" She says she can't get over the fact that I got held up by a robber and skated into a car, and she keeps saying it's all her fault.

"It isn't your fault!" I tell her. And then I have to smile, because suddenly I'm remembering everything that's happened in the past few hours. I remember Denny and I busting Monsieur LeFleur; Kamikaze leaving Coffee Breath in the dust, then frightening majorettes into dropping batons, freaking out llamas into spitting, scaring square dancers who missed their do-si-dos; and then being passed by Denny on his motorcycle, with Charlotte, naked, riding in back of him.

"You know who came up to tell us you were here?" my father asks. "This bus driver with a really big beard. He drove you here, I guess, and you told him you had to meet Mom," my father says. "He's a very intense person. I've heard there are complaints about how he drove through the parade, but when everyone heard he was trying to save your life, and that you got hurt by stopping a robbery—"

"But Dad, that's not how I got hurt," I say.

"Yes, I know that, but *they* don't know that. It's one of those stories that got told wrong and it's taken off like wildfire. You're some kind of hero around Lindville now, and so is that bus driver. It's good publicity. Ride it for a while," my father says.

"Okay," I agree. "But I'm still sorry about the golf cart, you guys. And I'm sorry if I've had a bad attitude. It's just . . . staying here this summer, without a car . . . I feel so trapped sometimes. Like you know the way the air here gets at night after a hot day, and it just feels like the air's really bad and it's just sort of sitting on top of you? And smelling?"

My mother nods. "It's called inversion."

"Inversion, then. That's sort of my life right now," I say.

My father looks at me. "Is it that bad?"

"No. Well, sometimes," I admit. "I mean, there are all the changes we talked about. We used to have kind of exciting lives, you know? And now . . . I mean, I love Dean and Torvill and Dorothy, so much. But couldn't I love them in New York or L.A. or somewhere fun?"

"But this is our home now," my mother says slowly, as if I'm the baby. "We can't move."

"I know. I know that," I say.

"But you were right—what you said last night. We've been taking advantage of you," Mom says. "I'm going to quit asking you to do so much stuff around the house. You're just so capable that I kept adding on without realizing—you're sixteen. You have your own life. You shouldn't be home on Saturday nights—you should be on a date. I know *I* would have been."

Dad looks at her a little sharply, alarmed by this news.

I smile. "The thing is, I might not be able to actually get a date. Anytime soon."

"Who cares about dates?" my father says, looking a little happier now. "Friends, then. Maybe I don't like the Plot and the Lot and the whatever comes up next . . . the Cot . . . wait, forget I said that . . . anyway, I know you well enough to trust you. You might not be the best driver, okay. But we can work on that."

"Really? So does that mean I could maybe start driving again soon? Not right away—I know I still owe you money, so I'll pay that back first. But at the end of the summer, or when I turn seventeen, in November? I could buy an old car, or borrow one of yours once in a while?"

"Yes," my mother says. "Of course."

"You know, I thought of giving you back your license yesterday, actually," my father says. "Just in case you needed to drive Mom to the hospital. But I actually couldn't *find* your license. I don't know what I did with it. It's in my desk some-where, but things have been so hectic. . . ."

I smile. That fits in with everything else lately. I have my license back, but I don't have an actual license.

Which is okay, because I don't have an actual car.

Which is okay, because I can't really drive right now, because of my bandaged body.

"But P. F. About the golf cart," my father says. "You'll need to call Shady Prairies when we get home and tell them what you did. And let them decide what action to take."

"Right. I know," I say.

"And we're going to have more driving lessons, you and me. A lot more. Remember how intense I was about your skating a few years ago? Like that."

"Four hours a *day*?" I ask.

"Sure. In very, very short shifts. Lots of errands. Driving Elvis around until he falls asleep—things like that." He glances at my mother, who's rubbing Elvis's tiny fingers. "And once a week you can practice highway driving by taking me to the arena to skate. Maybe. If it's convenient for your mother."

"We'll see," she says. "Torvill and Dean will be in kinder-garten, so . . ." She lets out a deep sigh. Suddenly her eyes are brimming over with tears. She opens her mouth to talk, but she can't. Dad gives her a hug, being careful to leave enough room for Elvis between them.

I ask an aide to wheel me out of the room into the hallway to give them some privacy. She parks me just outside the door so they won't have to look far for me.

Charlotte and Denny come to the hospital at about 5:30, just as my dad is preparing to take me home. They heard about my accident when Coffee Breath showed up at Gas 'n Git, looking for a phone. Charlotte's called three times already to check on me and see when I'm being released. Denny doesn't come inside, but I can see him through the sliding glass doors, perched on his bike. He waves at me and blows me a kiss, like he's the one on parade now.

Charlotte rushes up to the admissions desk and is about to throw her arms around me when she notices my bandages. "Fleming! I can't believe you!" she says. "You saved Denny's life!"

"I did?" I ask.

"Yes! *And* you took out that idiot LeFleur."

"So what about you?" I say. "Did I see what I think I saw?" I'm talking nonsense again. I haven't been able to speak clearly all day.

"Charlotte? What did you do?" my father asks, turning around from filling out some insurance paperwork.

"Just rode a motorcycle, that's all," Charlotte says, smiling at him.

"So it *was* you I heard about," my father says. He turns to me. "Wild streak. Emphasis on *streak*. Okay? I told you, P. F." He starts laughing and Charlotte's face turns nearly as red as her hair.

When my father turns back to the desk, Charlotte says quietly, "So I saw Mike and Steve after the parade, and they both asked about you, and I told them about the robber thing and they were both *so* impressed and worried about you. So. Which one do you like?"

"I don't know," I say. I think about it for a couple of seconds. "Neither, I guess."

"Really?" she asks.

"Really."

"Oh. Well, okay. We'll find a new FEN for you, then."

"What's a FEN?" my father wants to know as he comes back toward us.

"You know, Fleming, you look sort of terrible," Charlotte says, deftly changing the subject. "Let me come over tonight and fix you up."

"How exactly are you going to get to our house?" my father asks her with a critical stare. "Do you need a ride, or were you just going to . . . hmm, I don't know. Jump-start a golf cart?"

"Denny will drive me, of course, Mr. Farrell." Charlotte smiles nervously.

"Good answer," my father says. "I think."

That night, while Charlotte's painting my toenails blue to match my taped wrist, we see Monsieur LeFleur on the 9:00 TV news. The theory is that he will plead not guilty by reason of temporary insanity. This doesn't make sense to me because his insanity—otherwise known as a stealing spree—lasted a few weeks, at least.

His written statement says that he devoted his whole life to teaching, lost his wife over it, and never made enough to live on. That's why he cracked. Extreme burnout. It could make anyone into an armed robber of convenience stores.

"Do you realize what this means?" Charlotte says. "They're going to *have* to pass us all now. With *A*s."

"Even if we didn't really learn that much?" I say.

"It's a public relations nightmare for the school," she says. "Their best teacher is a criminal. They'll do *anything* to get us to be quiet."

"But he was never there," I remind her. "We never had any contact with him."

"We didn't, but *you* did," Charlotte says. "He had a gun, Fleming."

"It wasn't a real gun. It turned out to be a toy," I say.

"So what? He was still dangerous. Very dangerous. He could have affected us somehow, drawn us into his web of evil," Charlotte says. "Without us even knowing it. He could have been controlling us with his homework assignments."

I start laughing. "Oh, yeah, definitely," I agree.

"And if he ever *had* shown up, he probably would have taken us hostage or something, and demanded a ransom." She laughs. "We'll point all this out if they try to give us *B*s. *And* we'll mention how he put your life at risk, and how you saved Denny's life."

"And how the subs were so bad that we want a refund!" I cry, pounding my fist on top of the coffee table. For a second I picture Kamikaze Driver demanding free coffee, and our "free ride" conversation. I'll have to find him and thank him for bringing me to the hospital. I still don't know his name, but I do know his route. "You know, all this stuff with Monsieur LeFleur is the most I've ever done just to get an *A*," I tell Charlotte.

"I've never *gotten* an *A* before," she admits, and we start laughing so hard that she paints the rug with blue nail polish.

Fortunately, it blends in with the stain from the last time Dean spilled grape juice.

Because I Really Like Pink

It's noon on Torvill and Dean's birthday, and I'm standing by the main entrance at Shady Prairies, waiting for my father to pick me up. I just got out of my brand-new job. Starting today, I'm teaching water exercise as part of my community service, to pay back Shady Prairies for stealing a golf cart and then flipping it into their pool. Until I go back to work at Gas 'n Git, where there's now a plaque on the wall naming me and Denny "Employees of the Month," I'll be here swimming with seniors. My hair now smells like chlorine, but other than that, it wasn't bad at all. I can definitely do this for two weeks, especially since Jamie insisted I take some time off.

Charlotte has to work the breakfast shift now instead

of dinner, because the people in Shady Prairies' personnel department know how much she hates mornings. She got it much worse than me, because they trusted her and she let them down. Also because she admitted that traveling "à la cart" was her idea, and that she was the one who drove. She also has to clean the pool and "maintain" the bathroom by the pool.

I hear a rumble of thunder above me and glance up at the sky. I see some dark clouds building in the west. It looks like we might get a storm later. I may not be Christie Farrell from KLDV, and I'm no link to Mother Nature, but I think I see something heading our way. I hope it doesn't ruin Torvill and Dean's birthday party.

I hear a car honk and am amazed to see my father pulling up. He's actually on time. This is . . . unheard of.

Later that afternoon I am walking across our backyard carrying a giant Gabe's Auto World cup of cold water for my mom. The thermometer says it is ninety-seven degrees, but it feels hotter. It's the sixth day in a row where it's been over ninety-five.

There are twenty five-year-olds and one three-year-old, Dorothy, sprinting back and forth across our lawn, chasing each other all over. Grass is flying up from their sneakers.

I tried to kick off the party with a quiet little game of pin the tail on the donkey. Then Dean pinned the tail on Torvill. She turned around and started chasing him, and suddenly it turned into a giant game of free-form tag, where everybody seems to be "it." Dean's wearing the cowboy hat I gave him for his birthday, only it keeps flying off his head. Torvill hid the little suede change purse I gave her in her room—which means she'll probably never find it again.

Mom is sitting in a chaise longue under an umbrella, with Elvis in a little sack snuggled against her chest. Dad is chasing the kids around with a pitcher of lemonade and making sure that they all get enough to drink, so they don't get dehydrated.

As I set the glass of ice water down next to my mom, I notice a car coming up the cul-de-sac. There's smoke coming out of it. The motor dies and the car coasts up to our house. I notice that it's a rusted yellow Geo Metro. *No*, I think. *It can't be.* Then the door opens and Mike gets out, cursing and kicking the car.

Of all the pizza places to call in Lindville, Mom had to call Smiley's? I really don't feel like seeing Mike right now. I have multiple bandages on my legs. I also have a party hat on my head and three colors of frosting smeared on my shirt. I don't know why it still matters what I look like to Mike, but it does. Not because it could get back to Steve, but because the last time I saw Mike didn't exactly go well. I owe him an apology, and I don't want to do it wearing a pointed pink hat with a 5 on it.

Mike lifts the hood and props it open, using the bottom of his T-shirt like a potholder. Steam billows out and nearly engulfs his head. He jumps back, coughing and wiping his face. Like Denny said, Mike's not the crispest crisp in the chip bucket, although he was almost pretty crispy there for a second.

He grabs his delivery sheet to check the address. Then he reaches into the backseat and pulls out a giant stack of pizzas. He doesn't seem to have noticed that it's me or my house yet as he trudges up the driveway in his flip-flops.

"Farrell residence? Christie Farrell?" Mike asks, standing cluelessly in front of me. He can't really see over the top of the stack of pizza boxes.

"Right," I say, sliding the party hat off my head. "Could you come set them down over here, on the picnic table?"

He clears his throat and follows me. When he sets down the pizzas and looks at me, his face is beaded with sweat. He opens his mouth to say something, then stops. Then he says, "Hey."

"Hi," I say.

He peers around me at Dorothy, who is now clinging to my leg. This is extremely awkward.

"So how are you?" I ask him.

"Hot." Mike mops his forehead with his sleeve. "And my car overheated."

"Sorry." I nod, feeling like a complete idiot. I don't know what to say to him, but it has to be something besides "sorry" and "how are you." We spent half the summer hanging out. We melded in a car wash once.

"So it's sixty-eight dollars," he says.

I stare at the wad of cash in my hands. My father had forgotten he needed to go get cash, so he spent the morning flattening dollar bills that had been stuffed into the "cloudy day" jar. "This should be eighty," I say as I hand the clump of ones to Mike.

"Oh. Yeah?" He finally smiles and runs his hands through his sweat-soaked hair and I look at his cheekbones and black T-shirt and for a second remember why I was attracted to him. "That's great."

"No problem. I mean, it's my parents, so . . . I mean, it's not like I have any money, so . . ." Dorothy tugs on my leg again, as if even she can tell I am blowing this. "So, Mike. Sorry about what happened that night. I shouldn't have yelled at you. I guess I just overreacted, but I didn't mean to take it out on you."

Mike dodges a couple of racing kids who nearly slam into his leg. "It's okay," he says. "I mean, I know you and Gropher . . . whatever. I actually don't know."

"Yeah. Me neither," I admit with a laugh. Mike's summary seems pretty accurate.

"Hey, do you think you could maybe give me a ride back to work?" he asks.

"I can't, but my dad could, right after the cake."

"Yeah, okay." Mike sighs and sits down at the picnic table. "It's too hot to work, anyway. "You got anything to drink?"

"Lem'nade," Dorothy says, and hands him an empty cup. She points to the folding table by the house.

"Thanks," Mike tells her with a nice smile. "I'll get some." He gets up. "Is it pink?"

Dorothy shakes her head.

"Oh. Because I really like pink," he says, disappointed. He turns to walk across the lawn.

As I watch him, I can't quite believe we almost sort of went out. Even though it might not count because I was using him to get to Steve and that makes me a very bad person. But I'll never do that again, not to anyone. And definitely not to impress Steve Gropher, or anyone else. For some reason, I really don't care about impressing anyone anymore.

Dorothy looks up at me. "P. F. okay? Need lem'nade?"

"No, I'm good," I tell her.

"Attention, everyone, attention!" Dad says, clapping his hands above his head. He blows a whistle to get the kids to stop racing around. "We've got pizza! Kids! Sit down, please!"

Dad helps gather Torvill and Dean, and the kids suddenly drop onto the lawn under a tree, desperate for shade. Another parent grabs several pizzas and brings them over to the group.

I seek shelter under the umbrella with Elvis and Mom, both of whom have fallen asleep. I crouch beside Mom's chair and gently rub Elvis's fuzzy head. I hold my hand out and feel warm drops of water spitting from the sky.

Mom is instantly awake. "Rain. Of course," she says, as rain taps on the canvas umbrella. "I felt it coming. It won't last long, though. Don't worry, Fleming," she tells me.

And she's right, because almost as soon as it's started, it stops.

"Peggy, I'm a cowboy!" Dean yells as he races past me carrying Torvill's new stick horse, pretending to gallop. His cowboy hat flies off his head and lands on the ground.

"*I'm* a cowboy!" Torvill cries, chasing him. "Give me back my horsey!"

I pick up Dean's hat just as Dad comes over to me. I set it on my head, and he smiles. "Hey, thanks for all your help today."

"No problem," I say, fixing the clasp on the stretchy ACE bandage around my wrist. When I went in for a follow-up appointment, the doctor removed the tape, because it's healing so quickly.

Dad points to it. "How's the wrist? Not bothering you, is it?"

"Not at all. It feels totally fine," I say. "In fact, I almost feel ready to get back to my old routine."

"You mean, going back to work at Gas 'n Git? Or what are you saying?"

"Any second now, it's all going to come together," I say.

Dad looks confused. "What?"

"Clouds, silver linings. Sacrifices. You know."

"P. F., you don't sound like yourself. Make sure you drink plenty of water, okay?" Dad shakes his head and walks away, convinced I'm dehydrated.

I just smile and go over to sit with Mike.

Do Not Adjust Your Sets

It's the final night of Rodeo Roundup Days. The heat has broken after a cold front came in the night before, bringing strong winds, occasional thunder and lightning, and heavy rain. The cooler temperature is good for keeping the ice frozen, but bad for the other events. The final bull-riding challenge was canceled because the arena's too muddy, the petting zoo has closed early, and the rides are all closed due to risk of lightning strikes. The wind is rattling the chain-link fence, and the boards sound as if they might fly off.

But the skating cowboy show must go on. So I'm standing here at the end of the rink, waiting with everyone else for the 7:00 show.

There's a strong gust of wind, and I smell a slightly manly lavender and oatmeal fragrance blowing through the air. It's familiar to me, but I can't quite place it. I turn to my right and see Mr. Stinson standing right next to me.

"He's quite good, your father," Mr. Stinson says. "I've been here almost every night, and he's quite consistent."

"Yes, he is. I told you he wouldn't let you down, didn't I?" I say.

"Yes. It's a shame he's decided not to go for that tour after all," Mr. Stinson says. "I'd have sponsored him for sure."

"Well, maybe another time," I say.

"Right. Or perhaps I'll sponsor a show here—I've been thinking about asking him to skate a special Christmas show." There's an awkward pause as we both think back to last Christmas. Then he steps a little closer to me. "It's ironic, don't you think?"

I turn toward him. "What is?" I ask. Or maybe I should ask, *What isn't?*

"Your encounter with the robber," Mr. Stinson says. "It's ironic that you would be the one to dispense justice, after your own checkered past." He makes me sound like a convicted felon, as if I were in a work-release program. Or maybe that's just how I feel. "But I suppose you have a right to evolve as much as the next person."

Evolve. Is that what I've been doing? "I'm not a bad seed, and I'm not evil. Is that what you're saying?" I ask him.

He almost smiles. "I suppose you simply needed to find the right employment. The right outlet for your talents. And lucky for you that you have. Selling petrol is a noble profession."

"I don't actually have anything to do with . . . petrol," I say. "I make the coffee. Sometimes tea. I'm good at picking up muffins with tongs."

"Ah. Well. No matter. It's a shame that ungrateful excuse for a French teacher got the best of you. French. What did we expect," he complains, shaking his head.

"*He's* not French," I say. "He only *taught* French. Anyway, it was a car door that really got me."

"Yes. Well, not to worry. You're young; you'll heal." He slaps me on the back, so hard that I can feel it in my ribs.

It hurts, but I'm not going to let it stop me tonight. And since Mr. Stinson apparently doesn't hate me anymore, I have a question. "Can I ask you something, Mr. Stinson?" I say.

"I suppose," he says, somewhat grudgingly.

"When you moved here to Lindville, however many years ago, why did you do it?" I ask. "I've always wondered. What made you stay?"

"I had an excellent business opportunity, a great chance

to invest in—oh, look." Mr. Stinson sighs as he unsnaps his heavy yellow rain slicker. For once, the weather actually suits his outfit. "I came to America because I wanted a cattle ranch, all right? That's why I came here to Lindville. That's why I'm still here."

I hate to state the obvious. "But you don't have a ranch," I say. The last I knew, Mr. Stinson lived in a large ranch *house*, in our general neighborhood. "Do you?"

"Yes, I know. I'm well *aware* of that." He pushed his glasses up on his nose, the frames mashing his bushy eyebrows. "However, I will someday. I'm not giving up yet. In the meantime I have my shop, and life is not too hard to take around here, now, is it?"

I don't say anything. A month ago, I would have said "Actually, *yes*, it is," without even hesitating. But now, I'm not so sure. Maybe I'm not going anywhere in a hurry, either.

At 6:59 there's a crackle over the loudspeaker. Then a voice says, "Attention, ladies and gentlemen. There has been a slight change in tonight's program. Do not adjust your sets."

I watch my father's face as he steps out of the warm-up room and peers at the hockey penalty box that's being used as an audio booth.

Denny looks out and waves at him. "I repeat, ladies and gentlemen, do not adjust your sets," Denny says in a deep voice. Then he smiles and starts playing the music that begins Dad's program.

"Excuse me," I say to Mr. Stinson. "Would you mind holding this for a second?" I take off my coat and hand it to him, then lean over to retie my laces and pick up Charlotte's hat.

When I straighten up, Mr. Stinson is staring at my outfit: a vintage pale green Western-style shirt I found at the thrift shop two days ago, a pair of boot-cut stretch jeans with a black belt, and my new silver PFF belt buckle. I pull the white hat over my hair, which is in two braids. Mr. Stinson looks down at my feet and for the first time realizes that I'm not wearing shoes.

"What on earth . . ." he mutters as I slip the rubber guards off my white figure skates. "Miss Farrell? What's the meaning of this?"

My father skates to center ice and suddenly his usual country music comes to an abrupt end. He looks over at Denny, confused. He stares at me as I open the side door and glide onto the ice. I skate toward him and stop with a flourish, spraying him with ice flakes. He looks like he's going to faint. I don't know who's more surprised at the fact I'm doing this, Dad or me.

"Ladies and gentlemen, presenting Phil and Fleming

Farrell in, uh, 'Cowboy' . . . 'Cowgirl' . . . oh, forget the title. Here they are, so start clapping, already!"

The audience applauds politely, looking confused as Charlotte drags a few small hay bales over to the sides of the rink. As arranged, the rodeo clowns gently lead the lambs and horses off the ice to make room for us. I asked for their help when I first came down to practice a few days ago.

"You won't need this," I say, taking the rope lariat from Dad and tossing it aside.

As the opening notes of U2's "Who's Gonna Ride Your Wild Horses" play over the loudspeaker, my dad says out of the corner of his mouth, "P. F.? Are you sure about this?"

"No," I admit.

"What are we going to do?" my father asks as we push off and start to circle the rink, to the sound of Bono's voice.

"We'll wing it," I say as we both turn and start skating backward. "Just like we used to."

The Summer That Changed Everything

How to Meet Boys

CATHERINE CLARK

For best friends Lucy and Mikayla, summer at the lake was supposed to be perfect. But when Jackson, the boy who broke
Lucy's heart, meets Mikayla and sparks fly, the girls wonder if
this summer to remember is one they'd rather forget.

More must-reads from
CATHERINE CLARK